Walking into
Spiderwebs

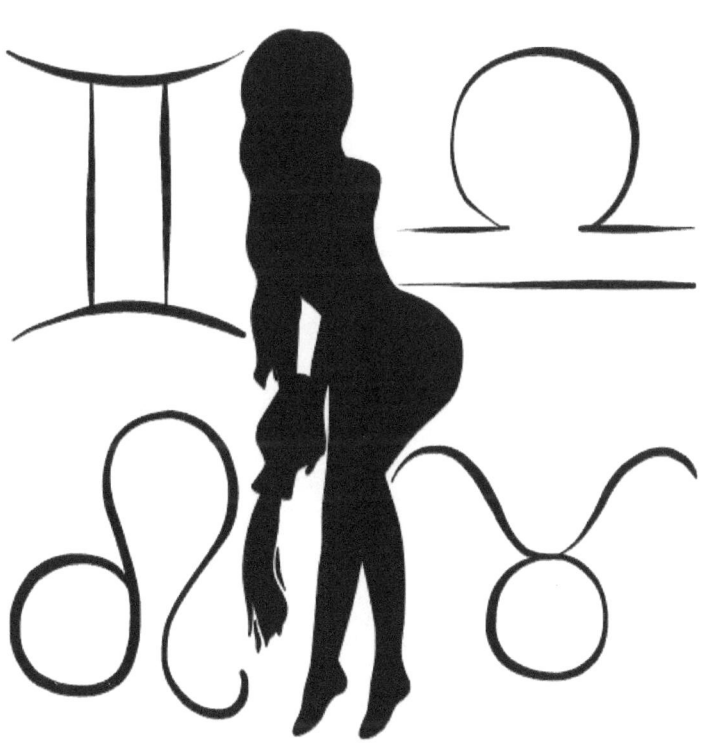

Walking into Spiderwebs

About a Girl: Book Two

William Michael Stephens

Severline Press

ISBN: 979-8-9864612-5-0 (hardcover)

ISBN: 979-8-9864612-4-3 (paperback)

ISBN: 979-8-9864612-3-6 (eBook)

www.severlinepress.com

Front cover image by Romariolen. Licensed at shutterstock.com

Back cover image by Pereslavtseva Katerina. Licensed at shutterstock.com

Background image by Vovan. Licensed at shutterstock.com

Cover, spine and interior elements licensed at canva.com

Part One astrological illustration by Salbine B. Licensed at canva.com

Part Two and Three astrological illustrations by Ennona_art. Licensed at canva.com

Cover design by William Michael Stephens

I would like to thank everyone that read my first book, About a Girl, for taking a chance on a new author. This endeavor is a labor of love and I appreciate all of my readers. I would like to dedicate this book to my students; however, because your interest in my work has motivated me to continue writing.
-Mr. Stephens

Contents

Part One

Chapter One

Birds of a feather

"Onion...Onion, hey, Onion!" I heard a familiar voice yell from across the hall. I looked up and saw Joe Anderson walking toward me. It was the first day of school my eighth-grade year and Joe was already being a jerk. He was the most popular guy at school. All of the girls wanted to be with him and all of the guys wanted to be him. He looked like a young Abercrombie and Fitch model. He had short, wavy brown hair and muscle definition that put all of the other boys at Fesler Junior High School to shame. He played football, basketball, and baseball. The rest of the time, he played most of the girls at school. He walked up to me with a smile as wide as the ocean and didn't say anything. He stared at my chest and I crossed my arms in front of me. "If you don't want me to look then you shouldn't wear shirts like that."

"Like what Joe? It's a t-shirt. It's a regular orange t-shirt."

"But, damn, Onion, it's tight, really tight, like your tits are gonna rip right through."

"You're so stupid, Joe, and my name's Hannah."

"I know what your name is, Onion." Joe's smile somehow grew even wider. His perfect white teeth glistened in the sun. I looked down at his polo shirt and noticed that his collar was popped up. *What a douche.*

"Why do you call me Onion?" *It doesn't make sense.*

"Because that's your name." *Oh my God, so stupid.*

"Was there a reason though? Did I say something? Did I do something? Did something happen last year that I'm not aware of?"

"Yeah, I don't know. It fits you though." *I don't know what that means. This is dumb.*

"I gotta go, Joe. I need to find Mel." *And I really don't want to talk to your dumb ass anymore.*

"Listen, Onion, we should hook up."

"Not this again."

"Yes, this again. You're the hottest girl at school and I'm obviously the hottest guy. It just makes sense."

"I don't think so Joe. You can't even call me by my real name."

"You don't like Onion?"

"That's not even the point."

"Wait, what were we talking about?" *Oh my God.*

"We were talking about how much of a jerk you are."

"No, we weren't." *Please God, do me a favor, kill Joe where he stands.*

"Yes, we were, because only a jerk wouldn't call a girl by her real name. Why would I want to be with anyone like that?"

"Because I'm the best-looking guy at school. That's right, since you're the hottest girl..."

"I'm not the hottest girl."

"No, we've run the numbers and you are definitely the hottest girl."

"Who are we?"

"Everyone." Ryan Snapp, Joe's best friend, walked up to us. Ryan was a shorter, even more annoying version of Joe. "Hey, Ryan, Hannah's the hottest girl at school, right?" *Well at least he said my name.*

"Yeah, Hannah...I wanna get on ya, get it? I wanna get Han ya," Ryan replied.

"The only one getting on Onion is me!" Joe said and pushed Ryan's chest.

"Okay, okay, can I have your left-overs?" *Gross.*

"No one is getting on me!" Joe looked at me cross-eyed.

"So now you want to play hard to get?"

"What's that supposed to mean?"

"I heard about all of the dudes you hooked up with last year."

"That's bullshit. What'd you hear?"

"We heard that you hooked up with a bunch of guys at the high school," Ryan said.

"What high school?"

"Don't play dumb, Santa Maria High School, duh," Joe said.

"I didn't hook up with anyone at Santa Maria High school."

"You're lying. I know you did."

"And how do you know if you weren't there? Do you have the pictures to prove it?"

"No, but..."

"Exactly Joe. It sounds like you'd believe anything."

"I'm not stupid." *Haven't convinced me.*

"Hey, man, let's go," Ryan said. "She's not going to admit to anything."

"Wait a second, I was just about to ask her out."

"Joe, you really didn't think about this did you?"

"What do you mean?"

"If I really am the hottest girl at school and I supposedly have been hooking up with high school guys then why would I want to settle for you?"

"Oh, shit, dude," Ryan said to Joe. "I think she has a point."

"Not even, I'd kick all of their asses." Joe pulled up his polo shirt revealing his stomach. "Look at those abs." Joe started counting his individual abdominal muscles. "Let's see here, one, two, three, four, five, six, and look at those, seven and eight. An eight pack of abs." He dropped his shirt. "What, not impressed?" Joe pulled his right sleave away from his arm and then flexed his bicep." Ryan looked on but didn't say anything.

"Okay, I get it, Joe, you're strong. Stop making a fool out of yourself," I said.

"I'm not making a fool out of myself, Onion. Every girl wants to be with me."

"I don't." Joe gave me a confused look. Ryan perked up and said, "What about me?"

"No, not you either. I don't date jerks. Both of you are the biggest jerks at school."

"Whatever, Onion, I'll find you later, you'll come to your senses."

"Bye Joe. Bye Ryan." Joe and Ryan walked away from me. I felt a sense of relief as I walked around to the side of the school and saw Melissa playing basketball by herself. I approached the court and dropped my backpack on the ground. Melissa ran up to me a gave me a big hug. "Hey, Mel, when did you get here?"

"I've been here for a while."

"I haven't even been here for five minutes and Joe already started hitting on me. Ryan too."

"Well, you are the prettiest girl at school."

"Awe, thanks, Mel, but I don't really think so. There's a lot of prettier girls than me. I think you're prettier than me."

"Thanks, Hannah, but that hasn't been true since..."

"What do you mean?"

"You...I don't know how to say this without sounding..."

"Mel, I don't understand…"

"…Your body…you've filled out, and well, I haven't."

"That doesn't mean you're not pretty."

"Yeah, thanks, but it's not the same. You could go to high school right now and no one would even question it."

"I guess that's true. I can't help it though."

"I know." Melissa dribbled the ball and then took a jump shot. "I remember you telling me when you got your period."

"Yeah, fourth grade. It was the worst year ever."

<hr/>

"Hannah, sweetie, what's wrong?"

"Ms. Wallace, I think that I started my period," I whispered as I stood at my teacher's desk.

"What was that dear?"

"I said, I think I started my period."

"Oh dear. Sweetie, I don't think so. You're only nine years old." I looked back at all of my classmates and hoped that no one knew what I was talking to her about.

"I think so. I need to call my mom."

"Maybe your stomach is just upset. Maybe it was something you ate."

"I didn't eat anything though."

"Well, that's the problem, let me get you some crackers." Ms. Wallace got up from her desk and walked over to a cabinet that contained all of her snacks. She was an older woman, slightly overweight, and had an interesting white patch of hair that flowed out from the top of her head. I felt my underwear getting wet as I stood impatiently at the desk. Ms. Wallace walked back over to me and handed me the crackers. "Okay, Hannah, go have a seat and finish your math worksheet."

"Can I go to the bathroom."

"You mean to say, may I please use the restroom?"

"Yes, may I please use the restroom?"

"Yes, you may, please take the pass." I put the crackers in my jacket pocket and walked slowly over to the classroom door and took the girls bathroom pass. I walked across the hall into the bathroom. I felt the blood move down my leg. I went into one of the stalls and shut the door tight, double checking the lock. I unbuttoned my pants and all I could see was red. I wasn't afraid though; I knew what was happening. My mom was a nurse and she talked to me about it the year before. I was embarrassed. I didn't know what to do. I couldn't stay in the bathroom forever. I grabbed a bunch of tissues and stuffed them inside of my underwear. I figured that I would be ok until I got home. I wiped the blood off of my leg and the outside of my underwear. I flushed all of the red tissue and then quickly washed my hands and went back to class. No one was paying any attention to me as I put the pass back next to the door. I walked to my desk and heard a loud gasp. I turned around and a boy named Jimmy was pointing at my butt. He turned to Ms. Wallace and yelled,

"HANNAH's BLEEDING!" The entire class stopped and focused their attention on me. I was so embarrassed that I couldn't talk. Ms. Wallace walked over to me and checked the back of my pants. She immediately grabbed my hand and led me outside.

"Hannah, are you okay?"

"Yeah, I told you I got my period."

"I'm sorry I didn't believe you, you're just so young." Tears filled my eyes as I attempted to not cry. "It's okay, Sweetie, go to the office and call your mom." I walked to the office and told the secretary that I needed to call my mom. She asked me why and I showed her the back of my pants.

"Oh my...what happened?" *This again?*

"I got my period." She looked around the office like she didn't know what to do. "Can I call my mom?"

"Yeah, wow, I'll call her for you. Should I call your house number?"

"No, she's at work. Call the hospital." She dialed for me, asked for my mom, and then handed the phone to me. "Mom?"

"Hannah? What's wrong?"

"I started my period."

"My little girl's all grown up."

"Mom! I need you to pick me up."

"Okay, I'll call your dad, he can..."

"No! Please, don't tell him!"

"Hannah, I'm at work." *I know you're at work.*

"It's not a big deal. I'm going to hang up now. Your dad will pick you up."

"Wait, don't hang up!" As soon as I finished my plea, I heard the sound of silence; the sound of disappointment. I handed the phone back to the secretary.

"Your mom hung up on you?"

"She's gonna call my dad to pick me up."

"Okay, have a seat over there." She pointed to one of the chairs next to the door to the school. "Oh, wait, maybe not...Just stand next to the door." *This is so embarrassing.*

"Okay." I walked over to the door and stared out of the window and waited for my dad to pick me up. It must have been about a half an hour later when I saw him walking up to the school. "My dad's here, can I go?"

"He has to sign you out first." *Okay, sheesh.* My dad opened the door and then hugged me. He walked over to the front desk and signed me out.

"Let's go, Hannah," my dad said as he turned around. I pushed open the door to the school and ran towards my dad's truck. *How am I going to be able to show my face here tomorrow? I don't think I can. I can't ever come back here. No more school for me.* "Slow down, slow down...I want to put some newspaper down on the seat before you get in." *Oh no. SO embarrassing.* My dad laughed. Tears filled my eyes and I looked down at the ground in front of me. "Hannah, I'm kidding. It was a joke."

"That's just mean."

"I didn't mean anything by it. Look, Hannah, sometimes in life you either laugh or you cry." *What do you mean?* "Get in the truck, Hannah, I'm sorry, it was a stupid thing to say." My dad opened the passenger door of the truck and I got inside. He shut the door and walked around to get in on the other side. He pulled his keys out of his pocket and then started the truck. He looked over at me. "Are you not going to talk to me ever again?"

"I told mom I didn't want you to know."

"To be honest with you, I didn't want to know."

"What do you mean?" My dad turned his head and then started driving us home.

"Your mom got her period when she was ten. Did she tell you that?"

"Yeah."

"I knew that it was going to happen eventually, but this is just too soon." *Yes, it is.*

"What am I going to do? I can't go back to school tomorrow."

"You're going back to school tomorrow."

"But I can't. You don't know how embarrassing it was. They were all pointing at me. They're all going to make fun of me tomorrow."

"You can't care about what other people think about you."

"I don't but this is different."

"Talk to your mom about how she dealt."

"That was a long time ago. It's different now."

"I don't think it's that different." *How would he even know? He doesn't know.*

"You're just trying to make me feel better."

"Is it working?"

"No, and I don't want to go back to school."

"You don't have to go back to school." *Oh, thank God.* "Today." *Hey!* "Hannah, you have to go to school. What do you think you're going to do? Stay home all day and watch TV?"

"Yes. Anything but school."

"You're going to school tomorrow so it's best that you just accept it." *I hate you.* I didn't respond. I crossed my arms and pouted my lips. I was hoping I could get him to feel sorry for me so I could get my way. He didn't even look over at me though. "Your mom should be getting home around four, but I have to go into work early today so I need you to watch your brother." My dad worked at Frito-Lay in Nipomo, mostly nights. I wasn't sure what he did there exactly, but he brought home chips all the time. When my dad was at work, my mom was asleep. When my mom was at work, my dad was asleep.

"I don't want to babysit Michael, dad, he acts like a baby."

"You don't have a choice." My dad pulled into our driveway and before the truck even stopped rolling, I jumped out and started running for the front door. "Hannah, shit! Wait for the truck. God damn it!" I got to the front door and pulled on the doorknob, but it was locked. *I should have my own key.* My dad walked up behind me. "Hannah, don't ever jump out of a moving..."

"Dad, it wasn't even moving."

"Never again. It's not safe. Promise me."

"Okay, fine, I promise."

"Promise what?"

"I promise that I won't jump out of a moving car."

"Good. Hannah, I swear you're gonna give me a heart attack." I smiled.

"It's good that mom's a nurse then." My dad opened the front door.

"Yes, I suppose it is," my dad said while shaking his head. "Your mom's feminine hygiene products are under our bathroom sink."

"Thanks." I started walking to their bathroom.

"Do you know how...Never mind."

"I think I got it, dad." *What was he gonna do anyway? Help? Gross.*

"Okay, well, I'm going to head into work. If you need anything call your mom. And keep your eye on Michael when he gets home."

"Okay, dad, bye," I said as I looked back at him.

"My precocious little girl." *Precocious?*

"What does that mean?"

"Before your time." *Before my time?*

"Okay, dad, have fun at work."

"Sure." My dad dangled his keys in his hand, waited a few seconds, and then headed out the front door. I continued down the hallway into my parent's room and then into their bathroom. I opened the cabinet below the sink and saw all kinds of stuff. There were three bottles of Olay body wash, Irish Spring bar soap, which my dad used. I thought it smelled awful. There was toilet paper, four packages of hydrogen peroxide, in the brown bottles, a ten pack of unopened toothbrushes, and an industrial size can of my dad's shaving cream. My dad had one of the thickest beards ever. It was dark brown and reddish, but if it were white, he could pass for Santa Clause. I looked to the right side of the cabinet and saw my mom's Always Maxi pads. It read: Extra heavy overnight. *This is not good.* Underneath that box was the Tampax tampons box. *I think I'll skip those for now...* My mom taught me about how to use tampons, but I was grossed out when she told me so I didn't really pay attention. I took out one of the pads and looked at it very carefully. *This thing is huge!* I pulled down my pants and saw a lot of bloody tissues. The blood on my legs had also dried. *So gross. I need to take a shower.* I took off my clothes and left them on the bathroom floor and then flushed the tissues. I got in the shower and washed all of the blood off of me. As soon as I was clean, I stepped out of the shower and grabbed one of the towels hanging on the door. I tried to be careful not to get any blood on the towel, but my attempts were in vain. I quickly grabbed the pad and put in between my legs. *This is the worst. What do I do now?* I dropped the blood-streaked towel on the floor and then waddled my way to my room. I grabbed a fresh pair of underwear and gingerly slid them on over the pad, which protruded out from both sides. *Well, this is not going to work. Oh well. Better than nothing for now.* I grabbed a pair of jeans and a shirt from my dresser and finished getting dressed. *I wonder if I look any different?* I walked into the bathroom that my brother and I shared and stared at myself in the mirror. *Still super skinny. Hmmm.* I walked back into the hallway and tried to adjust the giant pad between my legs. *What time is it? I need mom.* I went back into my room and checked my alarm clock. It was almost two. *Two hours.* I turned on the radio and sat on the floor against my bed. *Michael will be home at three. Such a pain.* Michael was in the first grade. The school bus stop was right down the street from our house so my parents weren't too concerned with him walking home from there. When I was in the first grade, riding the bus wasn't even an option for me. My mom always picked me up from school. That changed last year though when she started working all the time at the hospital. My dad was usually home in the afternoons, but his work schedule was weird so Michael and

I both started riding the bus. I looked over at my nightstand and stretched as far as I could to get ahold of my book, 'Holes,' which I got from the school library. I read the book until I was interrupted by a knock on the door. *It's three; must be Michael.* I got up from the floor and walked to the front door. *I must look like a duck!* I unlocked and opened the door.

"WHERE WERE YOU!?" My brother screamed.

"I had to come home early."

"Why?"

"Don't worry about it, Michael!"

"You're in trouble! I'm gonna tell mom! Where's dad?

"He's at work and mom already knows."

"What? I don't believe you."

"That's fine, Michael, go play your Nintendo."

"I will, but not because you told me to." *Such a pain.* My brother walked down the hallway and dropped his backpack on the floor in front of his room. I went over to the refrigerator to get something to eat. Michael would usually play Nintendo as long as he could, at least until someone forced him to stop. *At least he'll leave me alone.* I was in the middle of making myself a peanut butter and jelly sandwich when he came running into the kitchen.

"Hannah, there's blood all over the floor in mom's bathroom." *Oh no. I forgot to clean it up.*

"Michael, why were you even in there!?"

"It's closer."

"No, it isn't, Michael."

"What happened?"

"Nothing happened. Go play your game."

"I'm gonna tell mom!"

"Michael! She knows. I already told you."

"She knows what?" *Oh my God.* I decided to stop arguing with him and walked into my parent's bathroom. I cleaned everything up and then started a wash and threw my bloody jeans and the towel in. I walked into the living room, sat down on the couch, and turned on the tv. Michael sat down next to me. *Oh no.* "Where did that blood come from?"

"Michael, please go play your game."

"I don't want to." *That's a first.*

"Michael!"

"Blood, blood, blood, blood, blood, where did the blood come from? Blood, blood, blood..."

"IT CAME FROM ME, ALL RIGHT! Leave me alone." My brother's face turned a shade of grey. He didn't say anything at first. After a few seconds he said,

"Are you okay? You're gonna be okay, right? Hannah?"

"Yes, Michael, I'm fine."

"I don't see any cuts on you. Where did you hurt yourself?" Michael began pawing at me.

"I didn't hurt myself, Michael, leave me alone." I pushed him off of me.

"I don't get it."

"You don't have to get it, Michael! GO PLAY YOUR GAME!"

"Fine." *Finally.* My brother sat up and cheerfully skipped to his room. *Oh, my sandwich!* I walked back into the kitchen and finished making my sandwich. I decided to make it extra sloppy and caked on the peanut butter and jelly. When I pressed the two pieces of bread together, gobs of jelly dripped onto the plate. I ate my sandwich slowly and methodically enjoyed every last bit in my momentary peace. I licked the jelly off of the plate and put it in the sink. I sat back down on the couch and did some channel-surfing to pass the time while I waited for my mom to get home.

"Hannah?" My mom said after she opened the front door.

"Yeah, mom, I'm in here." She walked into the living room and sat down next to me. A strange smile radiated from her face.

"So, you're a woman now?" *A woman? What?*

"Mom, oh my God, I'm nine!"

"I know." She laughed. "I'm kidding." She put her hand on my cheek. "But things are going to be different now."

"Mom, can I ask you a question?"

"Of course."

"You got your period when you were ten, right?"

"That's right."

"What did all of the kids in your class say?"

"Oh, sweetie, they didn't know. I was in the shower one day and..."

"MOM! Everyone in my class knows! I bled through my pants. Everyone saw. I can't go back to school."

"It's not the worst thing in the world. It could have been something else." My mom laughed.

"Mom, that's not funny."

"Honey, getting your period is a natural thing. Your friends will understand that."

"No, they won't. They don't know about this stuff."

"I should talk to your teacher. Maybe I could talk to your class about it."

"Do you think that will help?"

"Yes, I do. They need to start doing sex education sooner." *Oh no.*

"Mom, your pads are too big for me."

"Right...I'll, well, you know what, let's just go to Walgreens right now. MICHAEL!" My brother came running out of his room.

"Mom! Hannah got blood all over your bathroom." *Great, thanks Michael.*

"Michael, we're going to Walgreens, and we need to have a talk," my mom said. We made our way out to my mom's car. I got inside and put on my seatbelt. My mom started driving and then told my brother just about everything she had told me the year before. I sunk deep into the seat and slouched down hoping that I would disappear.

"My mom bought me some small pads and tampons at Walgreens. My brother didn't say anything else that day. I think he was trying to avoid me. And the worst part was when my mom wanted to show me how to use a tampon!"

"Oh gross, how would that work?" Melissa asked and then took another jump shot.

"I don't know. I didn't want to find out. My mom was really open about all of that stuff, but I was nine. I told her I would just use pads."

"So, you don't use tampons?"

"Yeah, I started using them last year, and thank God my mom didn't ask to assist. I guess she thought I was old enough."

"You were twelve?"

"Yeah."

"Did it hurt when you put it in? Did you bleed?" I laughed. "What's so funny?" Melissa held the basketball against her right hip.

"It's just that I was already bleeding, and, no It didn't hurt."

"Hannah, I have to tell you something. I want to tell you something."

"What do you want to tell me?"

"You have to promise not to tell anyone."

"Who am I going to tell? You're like my only friend; my only real friend."

"You have to promise."

"Okay, I promise."

"I haven't gotten my period yet," Melissa whispered.

"So, what's the big deal?"

"I just thought, maybe, you would think less of me because I, maybe, wasn't as mature as you."

"Mel..."

"Which is why I didn't tell you last year."

"Mel, that doesn't matter to me." *Why would she think I care about her period?* "You'll get your period...probably this year. Don't worry about it."

"Thanks, Hannah, you're a really good friend." Melissa dropped the ball and then gave me a hug.

"You're a really good friend too." I let go of Melissa and picked up the basketball and walked to the free-throw line. I shot the ball and it was perfect.

"Nice shot! Are you going to play this year?"

"Maybe. I don't know."

"You should, you're really good."

"I'll play if you do."

"Deal. So, you never told me what happened the day after you got your period." I laughed and took another jump shot.

❧❧❧❧❧ ❧❧❧❧❧

"Mom, I told you I don't want to go to school! They all made fun of me yesterday. No one wanted to sit with me at lunch. Jimmy said that I was going to bleed on him. Ms. Wallace didn't do anything about it."

"You're going to school and I'm going with you." My mom usually made my brother and I ride the bus so that she could get to work on time. I knew it was serious if she was willing to be late for work. We got to school earlier than usual. It was about seven-thirty. My mom wanted time to talk to Ms. Wallace before everyone got there. My mom and I walked my brother to his class and then walked to mine.

"Ms. Wallace?" My mom asked. Ms. Wallace was writing on the blackboard as we approached.

"Yes, oh hi Hannah, you're here early. Is this your mom?"

"Yes, I'm Hannah's mom. Hannah tells me that's she's being harassed about her period."

"Kids can be mean."

"What kind of a response is that? What are you going to do about it?"

"There's not much I can do. The district won't allow us to teach about...that kind of thing until fifth grade for girls and sixth grade for boys."

"What!? How does that make any sense?"

"If you're not going to say something, then I will. I'll teach your class if you're not going to." *Wow, mom. Wait...*

"I'm afraid I can't allow you to do that. You'll need to talk to the principal."

"Okay, I'll do that, this is ridiculous. Hannah, stay here. I'm gonna go see your principal."

"Okay, mom." My mom left the classroom. I sat down at my desk and put my head down on my arms. Ms. Wallace went back to writing on the blackboard. I could hear the screeching of the chalk as she wrote.

"Hannah," Ms. Wallace said. "I know this is hard for you, but it will get better. You just have to ignore them." *Yeah, right.* I didn't say anything. Without even realizing how much time had passed the bell rang for class to start. *Oh, no, where's my mom?* I slowly lifted my head off of my arms and saw everyone streaming into the classroom and taking their seats. Jimmy; however, made a beeline straight for me. I looked over at Ms. Wallace who was distracted at her desk. *Like she's going to do anything anyway.*

"Hannah, do you know what day it is today?" Jimmy said with a wicked smirk on his face.

"Thursday."

"No, it's Sunday...Sunday bloody Sunday." *Oh my God. How did he even come up with that?*

"Shut up, Jimmy, just leave me alone." Jimmy started laughing and then tapped a boy named Mark on the shoulder and then chanted,

"Sunday bloody Sunday." He said the line over and over again until Mark joined in and they both started chanting. I put my head back down and felt tears fill my eyes. I felt trapped. I felt helpless. I felt totally alone. I heard Ms. Wallace say,

"Boys, leave her alone. Take your seats." They didn't stop though. They just kept chanting over and over and over again. I felt a warmth in my chest and then a sense of calm. I got up from my seat and wrapped my hands around Jimmy's neck knocking him to the floor. I got on top of him and strangled his neck as hard as I could. I watched him turn red as the last few of my tears dripped on his face. All of my classmates quickly gathered around displacing desks. I heard one of them yell, 'Ms. Wallace, Ms. Wallace, Hannah's killing Jimmy.' Ms. Wallace ran over from her desk and tried to pry me off of Jimmy but I held tight. At that very moment I heard my mom's voice.

"Hannah, let him go." I unsheathed my hands from Jimmy's throat and smiled as I could almost see my fingerprints in the white indentations lining his neck. I stood over him for a second to bask in his misery; to fully enjoy his embarrassment. It felt good. Before I knew it, I was in the principal's office.

"Ms. O'Connor, we can't condone violence of any kind no matter what."

"Hannah was just defending herself."

"She needs to learn to defend herself with words."

"Look, Mr. Akin, Hannah's not violent."

"Well, you could have fooled me."

"This is the first time this has ever happened. Like I said, she got her period and they were all giving her a hard time. What did you expect her to do, nothing, like your teachers?"

"Okay, Ms. O'Connor that isn't...and I expect all of my students to not physically attack their peers." *Am I in trouble or not?*

"Self-defense is not the same thing as an unprovoked attack, Mr. Akin."

"We're not getting anywhere here. Hannah," Mr. Akin scowled at me, "Are you sorry for what you did?" *No. I'm not sorry. I'm happy about it.*

"No, Mr. Akin, he deserved it."

"You see, Ms. O'Connor, this will not do."

"He was chanting 'Sunday bloody Sunday' at me and even got Mark Breen to join in," I said.

"I agree with Hannah, Mr. Akin, he did deserve it," my mom said. *Thanks, Mom.*

"Be that as it may, that is not the way things are handled at this school or in this district. Therefore, I don't have any choice but to suspend Hannah for three days, starting with today.

"Three days!? A three-day suspension for Hannah defending herself? That's rich." *What's rich?*

"I'm sorry, but that's our policy. When Hannah returns on Tuesday, she'll be in Ms. Reed's class."

"You're changing her class too?"

"Yes, I feel it's for the best. I do not want another incident."

"Don't you feel like, I don't know, like you're persecuting the victim here?" My mom inquired.

"You do realize that I'm going to have to have a conversation with Jimmy's parents here shortly and I'm sure they're going to be wondering why Hannah is still at this school. She's lucky it's just a suspension. If this ever happens again, I'm going to have to move for expulsion."

"That's a little harsh don't you think?" My mom asked.

"That's up to her, Ms. O'Connor. Hannah, I expect better from you when you return. Can I get your word that your behavior will improve?"

"Yes, Mr. Akin," I said.

"Okay, then, good day. I have to get ready for the next meeting I don't want to have."

"Come on, Hannah, let's go," my mom said as she pulled on my arm. We walked out of the front of the school and got into the car. My mom started driving us home and didn't say anything for a while and then,

"Hannah, I understand why you did it, but there are always consequences for every decision. Suspended for three days...Shit! Hannah, this can't happen again."

"I know, I'm sorry." *I'm really not though.*

"It's okay, it's not your fault. Maybe I should try to get you into another school. I think Tunnell is a K-8 school. Maybe it would be better for you to be around older kids."

"I don't know, mom, maybe."

"On second thought...Let's just see how your new teacher works out."

"Okay, mom. Are you going to tell dad what happened?"

"Yes, I have to." *Great.* Don't worry, he'll probably like having his little girl home."

"He'll be asleep. He won't even know I'm there." I laughed.

"Yeah, your dad works hard. We both do."

"I know, mom, I know."

⚜ ⚜

"That's the bell." Melissa said and held the basketball. "Another slow, painful year at Fesler." I laughed.

"I'm more of a glass half-full type of person I guess."

"What do you mean?"

"I think this year will go by fast. I'm looking forward to high school."

"Yeah, like I already said, that's where you belong." Melissa and I started walking towards the center of the school.

"What! You mean I don't belong here?"

"You know what I mean." Melissa briefly glanced down at her chest and then back at me.

"I know, I'm kidding."

"What's your first class?"

"I don't remember. Let me check." I reached into my pants pocket and pulled out my schedule.

"Math. Damn. Let me see your schedule." Melissa handed her schedule to me and I compared them side by side. "It looks like the only class we have together this year is P.E."

"That totally sucks."

"It's better than nothing."

"Yeah, I guess, but we had three classes together last year. How do they even do these schedules? It doesn't make any sense."

"I don't know, but here's my class. I'll see you after." I gave Melissa a hug and then let her go.

"Okay, see you later." I walked inside of my math class and my eyes rolled around in the back of my head when I saw that Joe and Ryan were both in my class. Joe walked over to me with an especially aggravatingly cocky demeanor.

"Hey, Onion, have you thought about what I said?"

"No Joe, I haven't, I was catching up with Mel." Ryan walked up to us and interjected.

"...That girl with zero tits?"

"Why do you have to be such an asshole, Ryan?"

"Yeah, Ryan," Joe added.

"What are you talking about? The truth is the truth." Ryan rubbed his hand over the desk in front of him. "Flat as a desk." Joe and Ryan both started laughing and I walked away from them to the other side of the classroom. Joe followed me and grabbed my arm.

"What do you want, Joe?"

"I want you. I thought I said that already."

"Well, I don't want you. You're a dick and your friend is an asshole. Why don't you date each other?"

"I'm not a fucking faggot," Joe said quietly. I could tell that he was angry, but he was apparently smart enough to not get kicked out of class the first day of school.

"You guys are perfect for each other, though," I said and laughed.

"Fuck you, Hannah," Joe whispered.

"Ha-ha, you wish, but thanks for saying my name."

"Listen, Onion..."

"There's the bell, sorry Joe." I smiled and pushed my hair behind my back and sat down. Joe sat down in the desk next to me.

"You're a fucking cock tease, Onion," Joe said while glancing over at me. I smiled but didn't look at him. I looked toward the front of the classroom and whispered,

"My name's Hannah, asshole."

Chapter Two

Gemini girl

"Hannah, oh my God! I have to talk to you!" Melissa frantically said. It was Friday at lunch and the end of the second week of school.

"What's wrong Mel? What happened?"

"I heard some guys talking about you in my English class."

"What do you mean talking about me?"

"It's not good."

"What's not good?"

"They were talking about how they heard that you sucked two guys off at the same time in the park this summer."

"I did what!? I didn't do anything this summer."

"Yeah, I know."

"I went to Disneyland with my family, but that's about it. Why would someone even make something like that up?"

"I don't know, maybe they're jealous or something."

"And it's two guys...at the same time?"

"Yeah..." Melissa looked at me and we both started laughing.

"That's just stupid. If people are going to lie, they should at least make it believable." *I wonder if Joe and Ryan have something to do with this?*

"Do you think anyone is going to believe it?"

"No, I mean, I hope not. Why would anyone believe something so stupid?"

"Because they're stupid."

"Yeah, but I'd like to believe there are more smart people than stupid people at this school."

"I wish I could be more like you, Hannah. I love that about you. You're so optimistic."

"Thanks, Mel, it's just the way I am."

"Hannah...never mind, it's nothing."

"Ummm, okay, well, thanks for telling me. Maybe we can squash this and find out who started it."

"I don't know, Hannah, it's not like anyone is going to admit to it."

"You're probably right, but the truth has a way of coming out."

"Does it? What are you going to do?"

"The first thing I'm going to do is confront those jerks Joe and Ryan."

"Do you think that's a good idea?"

"Yes. They either started the rumor or they know who did. Mel, I know you. I know that you don't like all the drama, but there are times like these where you have to fight for what's right."

"I guess so, but it just seems like..."

"Mel, I need you to do me a favor. Find out where those guys in your English class heard the rumor."

"I don't know them. I don't even know their names."

"Mel, I need your help."

"Okay, you know I'd do anything for you."

"I know, you're my best friend, I'd do anything for you too.

It was seventh grade on the first day of school at Fesler. I didn't have any friends so I sat down alone on one of the benches outside of the office. I was watching people stumble by when a girl walked up to me without hesitation.

"Hi, what's your name?"

"Hannah, what's yours?"

"Melissa, but you can call me Mel." Melissa had long, wavy brown hair and seemed to be taller than me, but I couldn't really tell because I was sitting down. She was very pretty but in a strange, almost masculine way. She had a defined jawline and brown eyes much like my own. She was wearing blue capri pants and a white shirt with red flowers embroidered on it.

"Hi, Mel, I really like your shirt."

"Thanks, my mom bought it for me. So, why are you sitting here all alone? Where are your friends?" *Wow, rude much?*

"I don't have any friends."

"I don't believe you. You're so pretty."

"Pretty people automatically have friends?" Melissa looked at me for a second and cocked her head to the side like a dog when someone says something familiar to it.

"Well, yeah."

"The past couple of years have been bad, and, I don't know, I just avoided everyone..."

"So...what happened?" *I just met you, sheesh!*

"I don't really want to talk about it right now."

"Oh, I'm sorry, I shouldn't have..."

"No, it's okay, it just sucked that's all." Melissa sat down next to me.

"Well, Hannah, do you think we could be friends?"

"Yeah, we can be friends."

"Awesome." Melissa grabbed my hand and stood up. "Come on, let's do some people watching." *I'm pretty sure I was just doing that.* Melissa and I walked around the school and down each hallway.

"Hey, look over there," Melissa said. "There's Joe Anderson and Molly Mikenna." I smiled and then laughed.

"Okay, am I supposed to be impressed?"

"Joe was the most popular guy at Fesler and Molly, well, she's a pretty big slut, so I guess that's why he's with her."

"Yeah, but I don't know why I should...wait, do you like him?"

"Me?" Melissa started laughing uncontrollably. *I'm confused, did I say something funny?* "Joe isn't exactly my type, if you know what I mean." *No, I have no idea what you mean.* "I'm friends with Molly. Come on, I'll introduce you." Molly pulled on my hand once again.

"Mel, didn't you just say she was a slut?"

"Yeah."

"And you're friends with her?"

"Yeah, more like acquaintances. I don't really know if she's a slut, but she does look slutty...right?" *Not really.*

"I don't know." We walked up to Joe and Molly. They were making out in the middle of the hallway in front of a classroom.

"Hey, slut," Melissa said. *Why would she say it to her face?* Molly stopped kissing Joe and turned toward us.

"Hey, whore," Molly responded. They both stared at each other angrily and then laughed. *Some kind of inside joke, I guess.*

"What do you want Mel? Hey, who's your friend?" Joe inquired.

"This is Hannah," Melissa said.

"Hi Hannah," Joe said and smiled.

"Hi," I said and then looked over at Molly. *She does not look happy.*

"What school did you go to last year?" Molly asked.

"Adam."

"Why are you even at this school?" *What's that supposed to mean?*

"Molly, don't be a bitch, she doesn't have any friends here," Melissa said. *Oh, wow, thanks, Mel!* At that very moment as if by divine intervention, Jimmy approached our group. *Are you kidding me?*

"Hi Hannah, can I ummm, talk to you for a minute?" Jimmy nervously said. *You put me through hell and now you want to talk?* Everyone stared at Jimmy like he was a foreign invader. Jimmy was shorter than me which I found amusing. *The tables have turned.* He was wearing a full black ADIDAS track suit with the shoes to match.

"What's with the track suit, bro? You're trying way too hard," Joe said and wrapped his hand around Molly's waist.

"Yeah, are you going to run a marathon today or what?" Molly added. Joe, Molly, and Melissa all laughed, but I didn't. I felt sorry for him. I was angry with him, but I didn't think that it was right that he was being laughed at for his choice of clothing. I was conflicted. I didn't want to join in the laughter at Jimmy's expense, but I wasn't enthusiastic about defending him either.

"Jimmy, just go away," I said. *That's as nice as I can be right now.*

"I wanted to apologize for..." Before Jimmy could finish his sentence, I interjected.

"Jimmy! GO AWAY!"

"Yeah, Jimmy, don't you have a track meet to get to?" Joe said. "Run along poser." Jimmy looked completely defeated. He looked down and then slowly walked away without saying a word. *I feel bad for him even though I shouldn't.*

"That's right loser, walk away," Molly added. *Laying it on a little thick, don't you think?*

"Hannah, who was that guy?" Melissa asked.

"Nobody. He went to my school."

"Why was he trying to apologize to you?" Melissa probed.

"It was this thing. It's not a big deal. I'll tell you later," I said. *I hope that's the end of that.*

"You never said why you're going to this school," Molly said. *I know I didn't.*

"Molly!" Melissa said.

"It's okay, Mel. I live really close to Fesler so my parents made sure that I went to this school. I didn't have a choice."

"Satisfied, Molly?" Melissa said and smiled. Molly smiled back. Her smile turned into a disingenuous smirk.

"Yeah, it's cool," Molly said and then looked at me up and down and then again.

"Like what you see?"

"I do," Joe blurted out seemingly without thinking.

"Shut up, Joe," Molly instructed.

"Molly, I said to be nice," Melissa said.

"I just don't get how she doesn't have any friends," Molly added while pointing at me.

"I'll be your friend," Joe said.

"JOE, I told you to shut up," Molly said.

"It sounds like someone is jealous," Joe said and stepped away from Molly.

"Jealous of what? This bleach-blond, Barbie-doll looking bimbo?" Molly pointed at me again.

"Yeah," Joe confidently said.

"Whatever!" Molly exclaimed and then stormed off in the opposite direction.

"What a bitch," Joe said.

"I'm gonna go talk to her," Melissa said. "Hannah, let's meet back here at lunch, okay?"

"Okay," I said and watched her walk away. I turned back to Joe. He had a smile on his face. *Oh, no, this is not good.*

"You have a boyfriend, Hannah?" *Just say yes.*

"No, but I'm not looking either."

"But what if he is looking for you?"

"He is free to look all he wants, but that's all he is going to get to do."

"That's cold, Hannah, so cold." *I've been here for like ten minutes. Come on...*

"I don't want to cause any problems. You should go make up with Molly."

"Molly's all right, but I don't know." *He is cute.*

"How long have you been together?"

"Like..." Joe started counting on his fingers as if he wasn't sure. "...Five...Six months."

"Yeah, you should go check on her." Joe had a perplexed look on his face but before he could say anything else, the bell rang. "See ya, Joe."

"Hannah, wait..."

"I've got to get to class. Bye." I turned away from Joe and took my schedule out of my pocket. My first class was English. *Cool, I like English. It's better than math.* I walked to class and then took a seat in the front row. *This shouldn't be so bad. Molly looked like she wanted to kill me. I hope Mel was able to calm her down. Where's the teacher?*

Hmmm. I opened my backpack and took out my new 'Seventeen' magazine, which my mom bought me. I read the headline on the cover: How to be a guy magnet. *I wonder if there's an article on how to do the opposite.* Another article read: Do you play mind games? Take the quiz. *Do I play mind games? How about everyone else?* The bottom of the page caught my attention though. It read: Astrology. Are your sun signs a match. *Astrology...I think I heard my mom talking about this.* I turned to the page in the magazine and looked for my birthday. *January 21ˢᵗ...Hmmm. Aquarius...*

"Good morning, ladies and gentlemen, I'm your teacher, Mr. Cantu." *Damn, I was about to start reading.* "Please take out a piece of paper and write your name on it. I want you to write a paragraph about the most important person in your life. "You have five minutes...and go." *The most important person in my life...Everyone always says that I take after my dad, even my mom says that, so I guess, my dad.* I put my magazine away and took a piece of paper and pencil out of my backpack. "Four minutes and then we're presenting." *Presenting? That was not a minute.* I frantically started writing my name. *Mr. Cantu...Good thing he's not a math teacher. He Cantu even count.* I laughed, but not loud enough to attract any attention. *Five minutes. Yeah, right.* "Two minutes." *What happened to three? Is this a joke? Okay, focus, Hannah...My dad is a great guy. He works really hard and takes care of our family. He can sing, dance, and act, which is called a triple threat. He's understanding and helpful and he loves me more than my pain-in-the-butt little brother.* "That's your time, please put your writing utensils down." *Why doesn't he just say pencil. He is kind of old...and bald.* I smiled but held in my laughter. I raised my hand as Mr. Cantu walked in front of the class, but he didn't see me.

"Mr. Cantu," I said quietly.

"Yes, let me see here." Mr. Cantu turned around and then looked down at his clipboard. *Does he have our pictures from sixth grade?* "Hannah O'Connor?"

"Yes. Ummm, Mr. Cantu, that wasn't five minutes; maybe like two." The class murmured and some of my classmates laughed.

"Yes, well, thank you for volunteering, Hannah, you get to present first." *You say that like it's a privilege.*

"Fine." I stood up from my seat and started reading my paragraph. "The most important person in my life is my dad..." *Wow, my handwriting is terrible...Maybe if I didn't have to write so fast.* I finished reading and everyone clapped.

"Your dad sounds like a wonderful man; I look forward to meeting him at back-to-school night."

"He works nights, so he probably won't be able to come."

"Well that surely is a shame; please have a seat, Hannah." I sat down and then listened to everyone else read their paragraphs. I wasn't really paying attention though. *The best part about going first is not having to pay attention afterwards. I wonder what Mel's doing...*

Melissa asked me to stay over at her house that Friday night and I said yes because I really didn't have anything better to do. My normal Friday night consisted of my family going to Blockbuster, renting a new movie, and then having Michael harass me the whole time. I don't think that I ever watched a movie all the way to the end, even if Michael wasn't being a total pest. I asked my mom if I could stay the night at Melissa's and she said yes, but only on the condition that she meet her mom first. After school on Friday, my mom got off of work early and picked Melissa and I up from school. I had already packed a change of clothes in my backpack. Melissa gave my mom directions to her house, which wasn't too far from mine.

"Okay, this is it," Melissa said. My mom stopped the car and Melissa and I quickly jumped out.

"Hannah, wait! Let me get my purse," my mom said. We ran to Melissa's front door and my mom followed slowly behind. Melissa opened the door and walked toward her kitchen. Her mom was doing the dishes.

"Hey, mom, this is Hannah, and her mom," Melissa said.

"Hi," I said.

"Nice to meet you, I'm Hannah's mom, Anastasia, but you can call me Stacy," my mom said.

"Nice to meet you too," Melissa's mom replied. She grabbed a towel off of the counter to wipe her hands and then walked toward us. "So, Hannah, Mel hasn't stopped talking about you this entire week." *Really?*

"MOM!" Melissa frantically said.

"Oh, I'm sorry, I didn't embarrass you, did I?" Melissa's mom asked.

"NO, but you did now! Can we just go to my room?"

"Yes, I'm going to talk with Hannah's mom for a minute, but you girls can go ahead."

"They're at that age," my mom said.

"Yes, they are. Remember when we were their age?"

"Don't even get me started." My mom and Melissa's mom laughed. Melissa pulled on my hand and led me down her hallway and into her room. It felt very feminine. She had a twin bed which was adorned in pink blankets and a pink comforter. She even had pink throw pillows and a pink teddy bear stuffed between them.

"So, Mel, you like pink?"

"How'd you guess?" I pointed to her bed.

"Because, pink…" Melissa laughed.

"It's my favorite color so that's how I decorate. What's your favorite color?"

"I don't know, I think maybe orange."

"That's a good color…I thought that maybe your favorite color was brown or green, you know, because of your eyes."

"I don't really like my eyes."

"Why…what!? You have beautiful eyes like the ocean after a storm." *Yeah, I don't know…*

"Heh. Are you gonna start writing poetry now?"

"Yes, and you are my muse, Hannah, my inspiration!"

"Haha. Anyway, I'm thinking about getting blue contacts."

"They have those?"

"Yeah, let me show you." I opened up my backpack and pulled out my 'Seventeen' magazine and turned to one of the back pages and pointed to the advertisement for the contacts. Melissa and I walked over and sat on the edge of her bed.

"Those are so cool, but I still think brown suits you."

"Maybe, I don't know, but I think that blue eyes go better with blond hair."

"Maybe, but you'd be beautiful no matter what your eye color."

"Ummm, thanks…wait until you meet my brother, Michael. He is so spastic you'll think that I was adopted. Except for my dad. I look a lot like my dad, except like a girl, you know?"

"Yeah, maybe I can stay over at your house next week."

"I'll ask, but my brother is a real pain in the butt."

"It's okay, I'll deal."

"You're so lucky that you don't have any siblings. It must be nice to have peace and quiet."

"I get lonely sometimes."

"I would trade places with you any day of the week. My brother seriously bugs."

"I think it would be nice to have a little sister, maybe not a brother." We both laughed. My mom knocked on the door which Melissa had left ajar and let herself in.

"Hey, Hannah, I'm going to go. Melissa's mom has my information. If you need anything, just call."

"Okay, mom, I'll be fine. I'll call you tomorrow."

"Okay, bye Melissa, you girls have fun."

"Okay!" My mom left and shut the door behind her. "So, what do you wanna do?" Melissa asked while looking around her room. *I wonder what her astrology sign thing is.*

"Hold on." I turned the page in my magazine until I got to the section on astrology. "Mel, when's your birthday?"

"June fifth."

"That makes you a Gemini..."

"What's that?"

"Astrology."

"Oh, cool, what does it say?"

"Let's see...Aquarius and Gemini friendship: one of the strongest pairings in the zodiac. Aquarius and Gemini are both hungry for adventure, so they will never be bored when they're in the same room. They will always come up with plenty of new, fun ideas on how to spend their time together." *That's so cool.* Melissa and I looked at one another and then laughed.

"Wow, that's awesome!"

"It's amazing how accurate it is. I'm gonna ask my mom to buy me an astrology book." *Maybe she has one.* "I think she's into this."

"Yeah, me too. It sounds super interesting! You want to play a game?"

"Sure, what do you want to play? Life? Monopoly? I'll kick your butt at Monopoly. I've been known to make my brother cry." Melissa laughed.

"Maybe later. I was thinking truth or dare?"

"I've never played that before."

"It's easy. You just say truth or dare and the other person has to pick. If they pick truth then you can ask them anything you want and they HAVE to tell you the truth."

"What about dare?"

"Then they have to do something you say. It's usually something risky, so truth is the safer option." *Is it really?*

"Ummm, okay..."

"I'll go first. Truth or dare?"

"Truth."

"Have you ever kissed anyone before?"

"Like a boy?"

"...Yeah."

"No, but this one boy tried to kiss me last year, but I just pushed him off of me."

"You didn't want to kiss him?"

"No. I mean, it was weird. He was shorter than me. It didn't feel right."

"Hannah, you're taller than all the boys, except for Joe. I think Joe's a little taller than you. And then there's the eighth graders and I think some of them are taller than you."

"And it was at school. At recess. I was minding my own business when a face came out of nowhere. I didn't even know him. He was in a different class."

"Stranger danger!"

"Yeah. So, what about you?"

"That's not how you play. You have to say truth or dare."

"Oh, sorry. Truth or dare?"

"Truth."

"Have you ever kissed a boy?"

"You can't repeat questions. Them's the rules." *Is she making this stuff up as we go along? Hmmm...*

"Okay...why did you really talk to me on the first day of school?"

"That's an easy one. You're the prettiest girl I've seen, like prettier than in the magazines. And, well, you looked lonely...like the way I feel sometimes. I just had to talk to you. I didn't have any other option. I was drawn to you. *Okay, this is beginning to get a little weird.* "Truth or dare?"

"Ummm, let me go with dare." *That seems like the safer choice.*

"I dare you to kiss me." *Yeah, not safe...Should have gone with truth again.* I felt a little sick to my stomach like that time I walked in on my parent's having sex, but worse.

"Ummm, I ummm..."

"You can't say no. The rules are that you can't take back what you choose." *All of these rules...*

"But, Mel, I'm not..."

"...Neither am I. It's just a kiss, you know, for practice." *For practice? Practice for what? My first real kiss...With a girl, with Mel? I'm not a lesbian. I don't think I am anyway.* As my thoughts raced through my head, Melissa stared at me and smiled. She moved closer to me and wrapped her hand around my shoulder. *This is weird. Oh well.* Melissa pressed her lips into mine and I shut my eyes. I felt her tongue move slowly past my lips and into my mouth. *This isn't so bad.* She moved her hand from my shoulder to my head and pressed her lips into mine even harder. She let go of my head and then pulled back away from me. "See, it's just a kiss. It's not a big deal."

"I guess not, but it was nice. You're a good kisser, Mel."

"Thanks, you're a good kisser too. Let's go see what my mom is cooking for dinner. That kiss made me hungry."

"Okay, yeah, I guess I am getting hungry." *What just happened right now?* Melissa opened her bedroom door and I followed her into the kitchen where her mom was cooking.

"What's for dinner, mom?" Melissa asked.

"I'm making spaghetti with garlic bread." *That sounds really good.* "Your dad will be home soon. Can you girls make up the table?"

"Yeah. Hannah, grab those plates and I'll get the silverware." Melissa pointed below one of the cabinets where the plates were stacked. I put the plates out on the table and then Melissa set the silverware next to each plate.

"Thanks, girls. You can watch TV if you want until dad gets home."

"Cool," Melissa said. "Hannah, have you seen that show, The Real World?"

"No, what's it about?"

"Life...I guess. People dealing with problems. You wanna watch?"

"Sure." Melissa and I sat down on her couch and she turned on the TV and then changed the channel to MTV. "It's on MTV?"

"Yeah, I thought that was weird too, but...Oh no, they're playing music."

"You don't like music?" I asked and gave Melissa a disconcerted look.

"I do, I mean...who doesn't like music? But I just don't like watching music videos." *Interesting. That garlic bread smells awesome.*

"I like music videos."

"Well, if you like music videos then I like music videos." *Okay.* MTV seemed to be playing a mix of videos. It wasn't genre specific. The first thing that we watched was a Madonna video for her song 'Vogue.' I looked over at Melissa and she was totally enthralled.

"You like Madonna?"

"Yeah, I really like Madonna. She's so cool," Melissa said without looking at me and then said, "What, you don't like Madonna?"

"She's all right, but I'm not really into pop music. I like rock music." Melissa turned to me and put the remote to the TV on her lap.

"Rock music? Like what?"

"Nirvana, Hole, that kind of thing. It just seems more real than pop music, like more...authentic."

"Huh, I never thought about it before." Melissa looked back at the screen and picked up the remote even though she had no intention of changing the channel. Billy Ray Cyrus' 'Achy Breaky Heart,' came on next, and then Deee-Lites' 'Groove Is in the Heart.' *Is there a theme going on here?* The next song was Wilson Phillips' 'Hold On.' I was beginning to lose interest in what MTV thought was good music. *They're just all so, I don't know, like, cookie-cutter. Where did I hear that from?* Nirvana's 'Smells Like Teen Spirit' came on next and I immediately perked up and smiled. I turned to Melissa and pushed her shoulder.

"Now this is music," I said and got up from the couch and started dancing and pretending like I could play the guitar. I looked down at Melissa. She was smiling and watching me make a fool out of myself. I transitioned from guitar player to singer during the chorus and softly sang along. Melissa started laughing. "Hey, what's so funny?" Melissa motioned with her eyes to look behind me. I turned around and saw a slightly overweight man with dirty clothes wearing a belt of tools. He looked very tired, but also had a slight smirk on his face.

"Dad, this is my friend, Hannah," Melissa said.

"Hi, Hannah, so you're the one staying over...all right, well, you girls keep it down tonight. I have to go to work early."

"Okay dad, we'll be quiet." Melissa's dad shook his head and then disappeared down the hallway.

"Mel, dinner's ready." Melissa's mom said.

"Okay, mom." Melissa turned off the TV. *Hey! The song wasn't even over yet. What a bummer.* Melissa and I sat down at the table and then her dad joined us a couple of minutes later. Her mom brought the food over and we all served ourselves.

"This is really good," I said after eating a forkful of spaghetti.

"Thanks, Hannah, it's nice to have some appreciation around here."

"And here we go. So, I don't appreciate you? I don't work twelve hours every day, six days a week to support this family," Melissa's dad said. "What do you do, Mary? Wash the dishes, make an occasional dinner? Maybe if you got a job, I wouldn't have to bust my ass every day." I looked over at Melissa who was looking down at her plate.

"Mel, take your food to your bedroom, your dad and I need to have a talk."

"That's right, Mel, do what your mom tells you, that's what we all do around here."

"Hannah, let's go," Melissa said. We took our plates and walked down the hall into her bedroom. Melissa shut the door behind us and then locked it.

"I'm so sorry, Hannah, I'm so embarrassed."

"Embarrassed about what?"

"My parents...I hate them so much. They're always fighting.

"It's okay, my parents fight too."

"Really, about what?"

"I don't know, probably the same stuff your parents fight about."

"Thanks for staying over, Hannah. I'm really happy you're here."

"Me too, Mel, I'm glad we're friends." Mel put her plate down on her dresser and I did the same. She turned around and hugged me.

"Hey, Mel, I'm still hungry, so I'm gonna finish my food, okay?" Melissa pulled back away from me and smiled.

"Yep, you should definitely finish your food. You're looking extra skinny tonight."

"Me! Seriously, Mel, you're skinnier than me!" We looked at each other for a few seconds and then started laughing. We grabbed our plates and sat down on the edge of Melissa's bed thigh to thigh. We finished eating and then placed our plates back down on the dresser. "Shouldn't we take the plates back to the kitchen?"

"No, my mom will come and get them later."

"Does this happen a lot, Mel?"

"Yeah, but it's okay. I don't want to hear them argue anyway."

"Yeah, so what do you want to do now?"

"You want to continue our game?" *Truth or dare? I'm gonna take a pass this time.*

"Maybe some other time. Why don't we read my new magazine together?"

"You mean the one with the astrology?"

"Yeah, I haven't had a chance to read it yet."

"Sure, I guess so."

"It'll be fun, I promise." I opened my backpack and pulled out my copy of 'Seventeen.' I lay stomach-down on Melissa's bed and she lay down next to me. I started turning the pages slowly from the beginning of the magazine and quickly realized that the only thing we were looking at was advertisements. I turned the pages until I got to the section on astrology. Melissa and I both started reading as she slowly leaned her head into me and rested it on my shoulder.

❦❦❦❦❦ ❦❦❦❦❦

"Okay, Mel, I'm gonna go find Joe and Ryan, you go find those guys in your English class. We'll meet back here in ten minutes," I said. *We'll have this figured out before the end of lunch.*

"Okay, but don't do anything I wouldn't do." *What does that mean?*

"I'll be fine. I can handle myself."

"I know, Hannah, I know, but you don't want to make it worse than it already is."

"How is that possible?"

"I don't know."

"Mel, are you on my side or not?"

"Yours, always."

"Mel, is there something you're not telling me?"

"...Shit." Melissa's face turned red and she looked down and away from me.

"Mel, what is going on?"

"...I...I don't know if it's her...but..." Melissa slowly looked back up at me.

"But what? Who are you talking about?"

"I didn't tell you because I didn't think it mattered."

"What didn't matter? Oh my God, Mel, seriously?"

"Because I knew that you didn't like him."

"MEL!"

"Joe broke up with Molly."

"Okay, so what does that have to do with anything?"

"Joe told Molly that he broke up with her for you."

"What!? That's just stupid."

"Molly was pissed...but not at Joe, at you."

"This is so dumb. This has nothing to do with me."

"I tried to tell her, but she wasn't listening to me. I told her that you weren't interested in Joe, but she said you had to have done something to..."

"That...fucking bitch!"

"Hannah, she's my friend. She's just hurting right now. We don't even know if it was her that started the rumor."

"You're defending her!? I thought we were closer than that, Mel..."

"We are, but I've been friends with Molly for a long time."

"Mel, it's either her or me."

"Hannah, please don't make me choose." Melissa started crying and then wiped the tears away from her face. *Okay, sheesh. I need to deescalate this.* I walked up to her and gave her a hug.

"I'm sorry, Mel, I shouldn't have said that."

"I don't want to lose you."

"You're not going to lose me." I pulled back away from her, looked into her eyes, and held her shoulders. "But if Molly did start that rumor, she's gonna pay."

"I know, I get it, but what are you gonna do?"

"That's easy, I'm just going to ask her."

"She's not at school today." *Well that just about figures.* "I could call her tonight and ask her. She wouldn't lie to me."

"So, you think she would lie to me?"

"Yeah, probably. I wouldn't say she was the most honest person I know."

"Okay, fine, but call me as soon as you get off the phone with her."

"Okay. Shit, Joe and Ryan are right behind you." *Wonderful.*

"Hannah, I've been looking all over for you," Joe said as he wrapped his arm around my shoulder."

"Get off of me Joe," I said. "Why did you break up with Molly?"

"Because I want to be with you."

"More like in you," Ryan quipped. "Am I right or am I right?" Ryan put his hand up in the air waiting for affirmation, but received a round of disappointed stares.

"You are so immature, Ryan, grow up...and I mean that literally too," Melissa said.

"Shut up, Mel...vin!" Ryan laughed randomly and pointed at Melissa's chest. "You might as well be a dude with tits that small."

"SHUT UP, RYAN!" We all seemed to say in unison and Joe smacked him on the side of his head.

"Owe, shit, that hurt, it was just a joke," Ryan pleaded. I tried to hold back a smile. *Good, it's what you deserve. What a creep.* I turned to Joe. He was wearing his football jersey. *Oh yeah, they have a game after school. Hmmm, he does look kind of hot.*

"Joe, did you hear the rumor going around about me?"

"Which one? There are so many I can't even keep track." Joe didn't laugh. Ryan started to laugh, but then caught himself. Melissa looked down at the ground and shook her head with disapproval.

"Seriously?"

"No. What rumor? The high school guys? I was just giving you shit." *No, not the high school guys.* "Anyway, I'm thinking about seeing a movie tomorrow and want to know if you'll go with me."

"You should get back together with your girlfriend," I insisted.

"Who? Molly?" *I don't think Joe's dumb, but he sure does play dumb a lot.* I crossed my arms and stared at him. "Look, Hannah, I thought I already explained this...I'm a ten and you're a ten and Molly's what, Ryan, a seven...eight, maybe on a good day?"

"Yeah, I'd say a solid seven," Ryan answered but didn't elaborate. *So stupid.*

"So, we all have a rank? We're just all numbers then?" I asked and then uncrossed my arms.

"Hey, babe, I didn't make the rules, but I'm definitely happy with them. *Yes, I'm sure you are.*

"Come on Mel, we have to go." I grabbed Melissa's hand and we started walking in the other direction towards the basketball courts.

"Oh, come on Hannah, don't be like that," Joe said. "Well, I hate to see you go, but I love to watch you leave." *Very original, Joe.* I walked with Melissa out to the basketball courts and then stopped.

"Maybe it's not Molly. Maybe it's just some random asshole...I still want you to call her though to make sure."

"Yeah, I'll call her tonight."

"Call me right after...promise...." Melissa smiled and rolled her eyes at me.

"I promise to call you tonight after I call Molly."

"Thanks."

"You wanna shoot some hoops?"

"I guess, but I think we only have a few minutes of lunch left." Melissa picked up a stray basketball.

"Would you rather walk back and talk to Joe?"

"Nope."

"Okay, cool, your ball."

Chapter Three

Altruism

"**M**el, what the hell!?" I said as I walked up to Melissa. She was playing basketball as usual before school started. "Why didn't you call me this weekend? Did you call Molly?"

"Nice to see you too, Hannah, wanna play?"

"MEL!" Melissa held the ball close to her body.

"She didn't start the rumor..."

"Is that what she told you?"

"Yes, that's what she told me."

"Why didn't you call me?"

"My mom wouldn't let me use the phone after I got off the phone with her." *Yeah right, Mel.* "She said that I'm on the phone too much."

"Is she at school today?"

"I don't know. I think so, but I haven't seen her this morning, why?"

"I'm gonna ask her myself. I don't trust her."

"Hannah, please let it go. People aren't even going to care in a week."

"What if someone was spreading rumors about you slutting yourself around town?"

"I think that would be an improvement for me." Melissa laughed.

"It's not funny, Melissa..."

"Melissa...wow, you must be serious."

"That bitch probably started the rumor about the high school guys too."

"I'm gonna go find her right now!"

"Hannah, calm down. Joe even said he was making that up."

"I don't think he was. And he didn't say that."

"Are you coming with me or what?"

"No, Hannah, I'm not." *Some friend you turned out to be.*

"Fine, I'll see you later." I turned my back to Melissa and walked around campus until I spotted Molly hanging out in front of the girl's locker room with two girls that I didn't know. *They must be seventh graders. What is she up to?*

"Molly," I said as I approached her group. "Can I talk to you for a minute."

"What do you want, Hannah? Why don't you go and steal someone else's boyfriend." *What a bitch.*

"I didn't steal your boyfriend. I can't help it if he likes me. I don't like him."

"Now you think you're too good for Joe?"

"No, I don't think I'm too good for anyone."

"Yes, you do. Look at you. You're a God damn Barbie doll." Molly's friends both started laughing. *Don't get mad. Just ask her the question.* "Walking around shaking your ass like you own the school." *What is she talking about? I can't help how I walk.*

"I don't want any problems with you, Molly, but I do want to know one thing..."

"What would that be? I'm not sure that I know any Ken dolls. You are looking for Ken, right?" The three girls laughed.

"Did you start those rumors about me?"

"What rumors?" *She's going to make me say it. Great.*

"The high school guys. Giving blow jobs in the park." Molly let out a sinister laugh followed by her underlings.

"Answer the question."

"I didn't start any rumors about you. If I had something to say to you, I'd say it to your face." *Yeah, that's probably true. She is pretty nasty. Wait...*

"What about when Joe broke up with you? You obviously know he broke up with you because of me."

"What's your point?"

"You never said anything to me. You just complained to Mel."

"...Mel." *I shouldn't have said that. Damn it!*

"So, that's talking behind my back. You just lied to me," I insisted.

"I didn't lie to you. Look, bitch, Joe can have your skanky ass for all I care."

"Did you start the rumors!?" *I know this bitch is lying to me. She better tell the truth!*

"NO!" Molly yelled.

"I'm going to give you one last chance to confess."

"Or what?" *I'm not getting anywhere with this.* Molly smiled. *She must think I'm not going to do anything. Wrong!* I clinched my right fist and then punched Molly as hard as I could in her mouth. She fell backwards and lost her balance on the way to the ground. She looked up at me and her face was paralyzed like she had seen a ghost. She brushed her fingers over her chin where blood was dripping from her mouth. "Oh my God, Oh My God." Molly started to panic and put one of her fingers in her mouth and pulled down her bottom lip and pressed into her teeth. "You...you...you knocked one of my teeth loose." *Good.* I looked down at my fist and stared longingly at the two plastic rings that most likely did the job. I had forgotten that I was even wearing rings. Molly started crying. I felt bad, but I didn't feel bad for her. I was afraid of what was going to happen to me. *Are they going to kick me out of school? Oh, shit, not this again. My parents are going to kill me.* I looked at each one of Molly's three friends who all seemed like they were in shock. Their eyes were wide. They didn't say anything. They didn't even move. I looked back down at Molly.

"That's what you get when you fuck with me." Molly's friends gasped like they had never heard the word 'fuck' before.

"Hannah..." Molly sobbed. "I didn't say anything about you. I promise." *I don't believe you.* I looked around and much to my curiosity, no one seemed to know what happened. No one ran over and yelled 'fight!' like normal. No teachers. No administrators. It was like it didn't happen. And so I acted like it didn't happen and walked to my first period class and took my seat. About twenty minutes into class, the principal, Ms. Gonzalez, came in the room. *I guess it did happen.*

"Hannah, get your stuff and come with me," she said. I heard some 'ooohs' and 'ahhhs' from the class. They knew I was in trouble. I knew I was in trouble. The principal never came into the classes unless somebody did something wrong, and I had done something wrong. *It was the right thing to do. I don't care what happens.* I followed Ms. Gonzalez to the office. "Hannah, sit down."

"Okay." I sat down on a padded blue chair across from her desk and then she sat down.

"You know, Molly Mikenna had to go to an emergency dentist." *I'm happy about that, but I can't show it.*

"I'm sorry, Ms. Gonzalez, but she was spreading rumors about me and I had to do something about it."

"You're supposed to tell an adult and we would do something about it." *Yeah right.* "You're lucky you didn't knock her tooth out." *I am?* "It looked like they would be able to save it." *That's too bad.* "She'll be all right."

"I don't know what you want me to say..."

"...You should at least say you regret the choice that you made." *I don't regret the choice I made.*

"I regret the choice I made, Ms. Gonzalez, I should have used my words."

"You should have told one of your teachers."

"Yeah, that too."

"Well, I already called your parents to pick you up. You'll be suspended for five days pending the expulsion review." *Expulsion!? Last time I was only suspended.*

"What do you mean, like, expelled from school?"

"Yes, this district has a zero-tolerance policy for violence and according to your records, this isn't the first time you've attacked another student." *Jimmy.*

"He deserved it. Does it say what happened in my records?"

"No, it doesn't." *Really?*

"Well, he..."

"It doesn't matter what he did," Ms. Gonzalez quickly interrupted.

"It does matter though, and Molly deserved what she got too."

"Hannah, I'm going to try to tell you this one more time: There is no place for violence at this school, in this district, or in this city for that matter."

"Okay, I get it." I shifted uncomfortably in my chair and crossed my legs in front of me.

"Hannah, you're a beautiful girl, you shouldn't be attacking other students."

"It was just a fight."

"Hannah, a fight is when two people engage in physical combat. Molly didn't fight back." *No, she didn't. Strange actually. Her bark is definitely worse than her bite.* I laughed.

"Is something funny?"

"It's something my mom always says. It's nothing."

"Is your mom going to be okay with this?"

"No, my parents are going to kill me."

"Hannah, let me ask you a question: What do you want to do with your life?"

"Like for a job?"

"Sure..."

"I guess I want to be a nurse like my mom."

"That's good. That means that you'll have to go to college and nursing school after." *I know, thank you.* I rolled my eyes. "Do you think that you'll be able to accomplish all of that if you keep getting into trouble?" *Maybe.*

"No, Ms. Gonzalez, probably not."

"Exactly. We're gonna wait for one of your parents to pick you up and then..." Someone knocked on the door and then poked her head inside of the office.

"Hannah's dad's here." *My dad, really? Oh no.*

"Send him in," Ms. Gonzalez replied. My dad walked in a few seconds later and stared at me with intense anger.

"Mr. O'Connor?"

"Yes."

"Have a seat, please." My dad sat down on the chair next to mine. I looked down at his hand, which was shaking. He grabbed the arm of the chair and squeezed it until the shaking stopped. *Well, that's not good...*

"Hannah is going to be suspended for five days for unsolicited battery of another student. *Unsolicited? What does that mean? It sounds like she's saying that Molly didn't deserve the beating I gave her.* I wanted to say something in my defense but I didn't. I was afraid my dad would use my throat for his stress relief. "She knocked one of the student's front teeth loose, but we think she'll be fine." My dad listened closely while Ms. Gonzalez continued. "The other party may choose to press charges or file a lawsuit. In which case, we will have no choice but to cooperate." *Lawsuit. Shit, like they're gonna sue my parents!?* "After Hannah's five-day suspension, the district will either move to expel Hannah from the district..." My dad looked over at me crossly and I saw his left eyelid begin to twitch. *This is really not good.* I uncrossed my legs and looked down onto my lap. "...Or, they will move to suspend the expulsion."

"What does that mean, to suspend the expulsion?" My dad inquired under his breath.

"It means that Hannah will be able to stay at this school but will have to sign a strict behavior contract. If she were to get into any trouble again, she would be expelled immediately."

"Is there anything we can do to make sure she gets that chance?"

"No, Mr. O'Connor, it's up to the district. It's out of my hands as well."

"That's just perfect. Hannah! Your mother and I do not need this right now!" My dad raised his voice while turning to me. I kept my eyes on my lap. He turned back to Ms. Gonzalez. "When are they going to make a decision?"

"Next Monday, following the five-day suspension, counting to-day, they'll make a decision. Hannah will be eligible to return to school next Tuesday if they decide to suspend the expulsion."

"What are we going to do until then? Can we get the work she'll miss?"

"Yes, of course, her teachers will have packets available for you to pick up tomorrow."

"Okay, I'll pick her work up tomorrow morning."

"We'll have it here for you in the office."

"Thanks." My dad stood up from his chair and shook Ms. Gonzalez's hand. "Hannah, let's go."

"Hannah, remember what we talked about..."

"Yes, Ms. Gonzalez." My dad and I walked outside of the school and towards the front parking lot.

"Get in the truck, Hannah," My dad said harshly. I got inside of the truck and buckled my seatbelt. I fully expected my dad to yell at me as soon as we got inside of the truck, but he didn't. *He must be really mad. Not saying anything at all is really bad.* When we were about halfway home, I decided to break the silence.

"Dad..." He didn't respond. He looked straight forward and grimaced as if her were in pain. "Dad..." Nothing. "Dad..." Nothing. "DAD!"

"What! Hannah, what!" My dad finally responded with ferocity, but still kept his gaze on the road.

"I'm really sorry."

"What happened?"

"There's this girl, Molly Mikenna, and she was spreading rumors about me doing stuff with guys in the park."

"What kind of stuff?"

"Like, sexual stuff."

"All right, I don't even want to know. Why would she do that?"

"I don't know."

"You don't know?"

"It might be because her boyfriend broke up with her because he thought he could get with me."

"Thought?"

"Yes, dad, I turned him down."

"Well, at least there's something..." My dad trailed off. "...I have to get some sleep...before I go back to work. I'll be gone before your mom gets home. You'll have to tell her everything you told me. We can figure this out tomorrow." Tuesday was my dad's only day off and I could tell from the exhaustion in his voice that he was not happy that he would have to spend that time trying to clean up my mess. My dad pulled into our driveway. We got out of the truck and then went inside the house. My dad made a beeline straight for his bedroom to go to sleep. I sat down on the couch and picked up my brother's Gameboy. *I think I'll play Tetris for a while. Why not? I've got nothing else to do.* I played Tetris for almost an hour when I felt my eyelids getting heavy. I closed my eyes intermittently until it was game over for me on my game of Tetris. *Damn it. I was doing so well...* I turned off the Gameboy and then folded myself up sideways on the couch, moved a pillow under my head and then closed my eyes.

I woke up to the phone ringing. *Is someone going to get that?* "Dad? Okay, fine, I'll get it." I got up from the couch and answered the phone on the other side of the room. "Hello?"

"Hannah?"

"Yeah, Mel?" *How long did I sleep?* I looked over at the clock in the kitchen and it read: 3:35.

"Yes, it's me. What happened, Hannah? You punched Molly? What were you thinking?"

"I was thinking she deserved it. You really should stop defending her, she's not a good person."

"You knocked her tooth loose...This is serious."

"Yeah, I got suspended for five days and they might expel me." Melissa didn't immediately answer and I heard her breathe out with an extended sigh.

"So, what happens then? Are you going to have to go to a different school?"

"I may have to go to a different city..."

"What!? No, that can't happen. What the fuck did I do?" *That didn't sound right.*

"What do you mean, what did you do?"

"Hannah, I have to tell you something..."

"Then tell me."

"This is all my fault..."

"What's all your fault? Mel, you're not making any sense right now."

"I made up the rumors about you. I lied about everything. I didn't overhear anything. I lied to you. I'm so sorry, Hannah," Melissa said quickly.

"WHAT!? WHY?" *No way...I don't believe it.* My heart felt like it was descending deep into the oblivion and on its way out of my body.

"I love you, Hannah." *What!? Love? There's something very wrong with you.*

"What are you talking about? Answer the question!"

"I did it for you, ummm, I did it for us."

"I don't understand what you're..."

"I'm in love with you Hannah. It was selfish. I know that now. And Molly...she didn't deserve that. I made a mistake. I thought..."

"...I still don't understand..."

"You remember last Halloween?"

"Yeah."

"That's when I knew for sure..."

❦❦❦❦❦❦   ❦❦❦❦❦

"Hi, Mel, you look so cute! Come in." I invited Melissa to spend the night at my house on Halloween and my parents said yes. The only condition was that I had to take my brother trick-or-treating.

"Hannah, you look absolutely stunning," Melissa said as I shut the door behind us.

"Thanks, Mel." I was wearing a long pink dress that my mom bought me. It was based on Sleeping Beauty, which was one of my mom's favorite movies.

"Who are you?"

"Princess Aurora."

"Ummm, yeah, I don't know..."

"Sleeping beauty...The Disney movie."

"Ahhh, okay. I love it, especially the color."

"Yeah, I thought you would like it." I smiled and we both laughed. "Who are you?" Melissa was wearing a neon green top with sequins that reflected the light and oversized matching pants.

"Vanilla Ice."

"Okay, I can see that." We laughed again. "You're much cuter than him though."

"Thanks, Hannah, you're gonna make me blush." My mom came into the room and then walked into the kitchen.

"Hi, Mel, I like your costume."

"Thanks. It's Vanilla Ice."

"Vanilla ice cream?" Melissa and I laughed.

"No, mom, he's a rapper." My mom grabbed the candy bowl and walked over to us.

"Wrapper, like this?" She held up a miniature Snickers bar and smiled.

"MOM! Rap music!"

"I know, I'm just being funny." She placed the candy bowl down on the living room table and then walked into the hallway. "Michael, hurry up! Your sister's waiting."

"Your mom is cool."

"I suppose she has her moments." My brother came running out of his room like a bat out of hell and jumped on my back. "Michael! Get off of me!" I said and wiggled free from his grasp. "MOM!"

"Michael, stay off your sister," my mom said as she came back into the living room.

"Nice costume, Michael," Melissa said.

"I'm Spiderman!"

"Yes, you are, aren't you," Melissa added.

"Okay, girls, I want you to be safe out there. Take Michael around the block and be back home by nine."

"Do we really have to do this?" I quipped. "Why can't we just stay here and pass out candy?"

"Michael wants to go and you did too when you were his age." *I guess that's true.*

"Okay, fine, Mel let's go."

"It's okay, it'll be fun!" Melissa said. *I remember when I use to care. I'm just too old for this stuff.*

"Michael, mind your sister."

"Okay, mom, I will." He jumped up and down like he had already eaten all of the candy that he was going to get.

"Calm down, Michael, sheesh," I said. I opened the front door and Melissa, Michael, and I headed down the street. Everyone in town seemed to be out trick-or-treating. *Lots of superhero costumes. Girls dressed as prostitutes...*

"Hey, Mel, is it just me...I'm feeling a little over-dressed." Melissa laughed.

"Yeah, it's not just you. Sluts are always in, especially on Halloween."

"Michael, we're gonna wait here on the sidewalk. Go get your candy." My brother didn't say anything and ran to the house in front of us almost before I finished saying 'candy.'

"Did someone say candy? I'll take some of that candy," a voice called out from behind Melissa and I.

"Who's that?" I turned around and saw two older boys. They looked like they were sixteen or seventeen.

"I'm Craig and this is my friend Tim."

"We don't actually have any candy, we're out here..." I said but was quickly interrupted by Craig.

"No, I wasn't talking about actual candy...if you know what I mean..." Craig and Tim started laughing in a cringy sort of way.

"Oh gross," Melissa said. "We're only twelve..."

"I wasn't talking to you little boy," Craig asserted.

"Don't talk to her like that!" I said and crossed my arms.

"And what will you do for me in return, princess?"

"I'll call the cops, pedo!"

"Yeah, we'll call the cops!" Melissa reiterated.

"The cops. Yeah, I'm sure they'll get right on that. And where's your phone?" I looked at Melissa and she looked back at me with raised eyebrows. "Yeah, that's what I thought."

"Just leave us alone," I said. "We're too young for you."

"If there's grass on the field...then play through." *If there's grass on the field?* "I think that's how it goes," Craig said and looked over at Tim. "Tim?"

"Yeah, that sounds about right," Tim answered.

"There is grass on the field, right?" I didn't understand his question at first, but it finally came to me as Craig stared at my crotch. *Oh gross!*

"You're perverted! And you're pedos!" Melissa exclaimed.

"Yeah, go away pedos!" I added.

"Okay, I'm tired of this shit," Craig said and grabbed my arm forcefully. Melissa turned around and with the full force of her voice started screaming.

"RAPE! RAPE! SOMEBODY HELP! RAPE!" Craig dropped my arm and ran in the other direction down the street.

"Shit, wait for me," Tim yelled and followed his friend into the darkness. *Wow, Mel! Awesome.*

"That's right, run away you pedo bastards!" I turned to Melissa. "Thanks, Mel, I owe you one."

"I knew that would work. Friggin cowards." An older woman approached us.

"Are you girls all right?"

"Yeah, just some pedo jerks," I said.

"I don't know what's happening in the world. This used to be a safe city. You used to be able to walk down the street without getting harassed, but now...I just don't know anymore," she said. "Do you want me to call the police?"

"No, it's fine," I said, "They're probably half-way to Canada by now." We all laughed.

"Okay, take care, girls, be safe." The older woman walked back into her house.

"It's nice that there are still people that care," I said.

"Yeah, it is. She was nice," Melissa added.

"Come on, we need to find my brother." Melissa and I walked down the street and eventually caught up to my brother, who had seemed to make a new friend. "Michael, who's your new friend?"

"It's Batman, and I'm Spiderman!"

"Sorry...Spiderman. I didn't mean to expose your secret identity." Melissa and I laughed. "Come on...err, Spiderman, we need to keep going."

"Can Batman come?"

"I guess. Batman, are you alone out here?"

" "
...

"Batman doesn't talk," my brother said. *Batman definitely talks. Weird kid.*

"Okay...Let's go." My brother and his friend walked in front of Melissa and I and we made the rounds at every house around the block that my mom had outlined. We got back to my house well before nine and my mom was at the front door still handing out candy. "Hi, mom."

"Did you guys have fun?" My brother jumped in front of me and opened his pillowcase.

"Look at all the candy I got!"

"I don't want you eating all of that at once. Remember what happened last year," my mom said. Last Halloween my brother did indeed try to eat his entire bounty that night and ended up vomiting all over himself at two in the morning.

"I won't, mom. Can Batman spend the night?" *Oh, that's just great. Please say no.*

"I don't see why not." *Oh, come on!* "I'll need to call Batman's mom."

"Batman doesn't have a mom," my brother insisted.

"Batman has a mom," my mom retorted. "And if he doesn't have a mom, he can't stay over."

"I have a mom," my brother's friend added and gave my mom his number. *So much for not talking.*

"Mom," I said. "Can you make sure that they leave us alone tonight? Michael bugs."

"I do not bug," my brother said.

"You are a bug," I added.

"Michael, leave the girls alone tonight. Stay in your room and play your Nintendo."

"Okay," my brother said and led his friend down the hallway and into his room.

"I hope it wasn't too much trouble for you girls to take Michael out."

"Well..." Melissa started to say but I cut her off by looking at her sternly and shaking my head. I then mouthed the word 'don't' to her. "It was fine, there were just a lot of weird people."

"Yeah," I said. "Really strange people out tonight."

"It is Halloween," my mom said.

"Yeah," Melissa agreed.

"We're gonna go to my room," I said.

"Okay, don't stay up too late."

"We won't, I'm actually pretty tired. Come on, Mel." Melissa and I walked to my room and I shut the door behind us.

"Why didn't you want to tell your mom about those creepy guys?" Melissa inquired as I walked over to my mirror.

"I didn't want her to worry. It wasn't that big of a deal."

"What do you mean? I'm pretty sure that Craig guy was about to abduct you."

"Not even, Mel, you scared the hell out of him and his stupid friend. Besides, I would have kicked him in the balls." Melissa laughed.

"I believe it." I looked back at Melissa.

"Can you help me with my dress?" I turned back to the mirror.

"...The zipper?"

"...Yeah..." Melissa walked up behind me and looked into the mirror. She put her hands on my shoulders and gave me a light massage.

"That feels good."

"Mirror, mirror, on the wall, who's the fairest of them all?" Melissa asked, almost singing.

"Shut up, Mel," I said in jest. "Are you going to get my zipper or what?"

"Yeah, sorry." Melissa started to unzip my dress and slowly moved her hand ever so slightly down my back as the zipper met its end. I turned around and faced Melissa and dropped my dress on the floor.

"You have a beautiful body."

"Thanks, Mel." Melissa stood in front of me and alternated her gaze upon my bra and then my panties and then back to my bra. *This is a little awkward.* "Ummm, Mel?"

"...Yeah."

"Can I get over to my closet, please?" I smiled and Melissa smiled back.

"Yes, I mean, sorry." She moved to her right just enough for me to slip by. I walked over to my closet and slipped on an oversized Pink Floyd t-shirt I got from my dad for Christmas. "Nice shirt."

"Thanks, it's a little big for me, but I like it. The only thing I don't like is how small my boobs look in it." Melissa gave me a somewhat dumbfounded look.

"At least you have something..."

"Yeah, but my mom has big boobs. I guess I just thought it would happen faster. I don't know..."

"You and me both." Melissa and I both smiled and then laughed.

"Are you going to get changed?"

"Yeah, can I use your bathroom?"

"Sure, but..."

"I'm not as...I don't know...free as you are...I'm shy."

"It's not a big deal to me I guess."

"I wish I had your confidence." Melissa grabbed some clothes out of her bag and then opened my door and went to the bathroom. I sat on the edge of my bed and waited for her to come back. Five minutes later, she came back in my room, shut the door, and then sat down next to me. She leaned her head on my shoulder.

"I like your pajamas."

"Yeah, thanks, my mom got them for me...Hannah?"

"Yeah..."

"What do you wanna do?"

"I don't know. I am getting kind of sleepy."

"You want to go to sleep?"

"Yeah, I think I do. Here; get underneath the covers and I'll get the light." I got up from my bed and walked to the other side of the room to hit the light switch. Melissa got under the covers and then I snuggled up next to her.

"Hannah..."

"Melissa..."

"Haha. I have a question for you."

"I turned to face her. Don't you mean truth or dare?"

"Okay, yeah, truth or dare?"

"Truth."

"This is gonna sound really weird, but...Do you masturbate? *Wow. That's random.* "I'm sorry, was that too weird?"

"No, that's not weird. I did not expect it, but...yeah, so yeah, I have before..."

"How do you do it?" *Ummm.*

"This one time, I was in the bathroom brushing my teeth. I have one of those electric toothbrushes. My mom takes dental hygiene very seriously. I think she may be giving up on my brother though. Anyway, I don't know what gave me the idea, but I put the end of the toothbrush over my panties and, I don't know, it just felt good, so..."

"So, what...what'd you do?"

"I took all of my clothes off and lay down on the floor, and well, held the end of the toothbrush over my, well you know, and held it there until I had an orgasm."

"You had an orgasm?"

"I think so."

"Wow, Hannah, can you show me how to do it?"

"Maybe, but it's not hard, well, the toothbrush is hard, but it does all the work. I call it the magic rod." Melissa and I both quietly laughed. "What about you?"

"Yeah, but I've only used my fingers. I'm not as advanced as you."

"I wouldn't say that. Hey, Mel, do you think that sex hurts. I mean having a dick inside of you. It sounds like it would hurt."

"Yeah, it probably hurts...like really bad."

"Yeah, I still want to do it anyway...to see what it feels like."

"...Yeah, me too."

"I just have to find the right guy."

"...Yeah."

"You really think you're ready?"

"Yeah, I think so. I've talked to my mom about it and it doesn't seem like a big deal."

"That's good. I mean, it's good that you can talk to your mom about this stuff. I could never talk to my mom...about...she would kill me if she even knew I was thinking about it."

"You should try. You might be surprised."

"Yeah, thanks, Hannah, I'm so glad I met you." I yawned loudly.

"Me too, Mel, me too...time for sleep." Melissa wrapped her arm around my shoulder and I kissed her on top of her head.

"Good night, Hannah."

"Good night..."

❦ ❦

"I'm gay, Hannah, and...I'm in love with you...And you don't have to say anything. It's something that I've been dealing with for, I don't know, forever."

"But, Mel, I'm not gay."

"How do you know for sure though?" *Because I'm not gay.* "I think I'd know something that important."

"Maybe you'll change your mind."

"I don't think it works that way, Mel...So, all this time you were trying to get with me?"

"I guess so...I don't know. I thought you felt the same way and all the guys like you...and when I found out about Joe...I don't know, I just freaked out. I felt you slipping away from me. I didn't want to lose you."

"But why would you?"

"I figured that if everyone thought you were a slut, guys wouldn't like you and I could have you for myself."

"Mel, I don't even know what to say. It's just crazy."

"I know it was stupid, but I didn't think all of this would happen. I didn't think that you would react the way you did. I thought you would let it go..."

"Then you don't know me as well as I thought you did. I mean, seriously, Mel, how did you see this working out?"

"In my mind, which is apparently a pretty fucked up place, you would denounce all boys for being stupid and immature and we would be happy together..."

"As some lesbian couple walking around campus?"

"I hate that word, lesbian."

"Whatever you call it, it's just not normal...Not in Santa Maria at least."

"I know it's not, but I thought you would be more open...are more open than most people."

"I am, but I just don't feel the same way as you..."

"...I know...I know that now."

"I've got to go, Mel, I have to figure out what I'm going to do with this. I need to apologize to Molly, for one. *Shit, what is wrong with me? I didn't even have any proof and I just hit her...*

"Do you think we can still be friends?"

"I don't know, Mel, this is a lot to deal with..."

"I'll tell Molly that it was my fault. Whatever happens to me, happens." Melissa quietly sobbed. I waited for a few seconds.

"...Mel, I...I have to go." I hung up the phone and then sat on the couch and cried like I had never cried before. My dad came into the room and I attempted to dry my tears with my hand before he questioned me.

"Hannah, I'm going to work...what's wrong?"

"Dad..." I continued to cry. "It's so much...it's too much to take...I can't believe..."

"Slow down, what are you trying to say?" I calmed down enough to get a coherent sentence out.

"It's a long story. I'll tell you later. I don't want to make you late for work."

"Okay, are you sure?"

"Yeah."

"Okay, your mom will be home soon..."

"I know, dad, but I could use some time to think."

"...Okay, if you say you're okay..." *I'm not okay...At all.*

"I'm fine dad, you should go to work."

"Okay, I'll talk to you tomorrow."

"Bye, dad."

"Bye." My dad left for work and I went to my bedroom and sat down on the edge of my bed. I looked to my left where Melissa always sat next to me. *I feel so...I don't know...Empty. So depressed. My best friend!? My only real friend. This is so fucked! I don't know what to do!* 'ahh' I yelled as I fell back on my bed and stared at the ceiling.

Chapter Four

Reputation

I woke up the next day after eight. I didn't get out of bed until my mom left for work. I talked with her the night prior about what had happened between Molly and I at school and about the suspension and the possibility of expulsion. I assured her that I had overreacted and that I was going to apologize to Molly when I got back. She didn't press me further. I guessed that she had a long day at work or she wanted to wait until my dad was with her before proceeding with the lecture. I didn't mention Melissa or her role in what happened. I was still trying to figure that out myself. I went into the bathroom and took off my clothes. I stared at myself in the mirror for what must have been five minutes. I analyzed every inch of my body and every strand of hair on my head. I breathed in deeply and then out. *A blessing and a curse.* I got in the shower and stood still in the water for a moment. I looked down at my bony fingers and made a fist. *I really shouldn't be fighting. How am I going to apologize to Molly? Should I forgive Mel? I don't think I can trust either one of them. I should stop thinking. The water is going to get cold.* I decided to put Molly and Melissa out of my mind and finished my shower with hot water to spare. I stepped out of the shower and wrapped a towel around my hair and then another around my body. I went into my bedroom and started getting dressed like I was going to school, but then stopped and laughed when I buttoned my jeans. *Duh, Hannah!* I took my jeans off and then slipped on some boy shorts and a white t-shirt. *That's more like it. What am I going to do today? Mel...I can't believe Mel is gay. And she's gay for me. That doesn't sound right. Hmmm, I guess I should have known. It just doesn't seem real. How did I not see it?*

❧❧❧❧❧ ❧❧❧❧❧

Melissa and I had become very close friends by the time that Christmas vacation rolled around, marking the half-way point of seventh grade for us. It was the beginning of January and the week-end before we had to go back to school. I invited Melissa to stay over at my house once again, which had become a tradition. I was either spending the night at Melissa's house or she was spending the night at my house. It seemed like we spent every weekend together, in addition to every day at school. It was the first weekend since November that I had her stay over at my house though. We had to 'take a break for the holidays,' according to my parents. I opened the door for Melissa and she immediately gave me a hug. "It's good to see you too, Mel," I said while still holding the doorknob. "Were you going to let me shut the door?" I laughed.

"Oh, sorry," Mel said, "I just missed you." Melissa unhooked herself from me and I shut the door.

"I missed you too, Mel. Hey, I want to show you something."

"Oh, do you? Sounds exciting."

"Come on." I walked down the hallway to my room and Melissa followed closely behind. I shut the door behind us and walked over to my dresser. "Guess what I got for Christmas?"

"You got me for Christmas!" Melissa laughed.

"No, silly, I got an astrology book! It was from 'Santa.'" I held up my fingers in air quotes. "Also known as my parents...It's weird, I think my brother still believes in Santa Claus and my parents expect me to play along. Oh well, anyway..." Melissa laughed again.

"That's funny, Hannah. I don't have that problem. We don't celebrate Christmas."

"Really, why?"

"We're Jewish."

"What's that?"

"It's a religion...Well, it's actually more than that, but, yeah, we celebrate Hanukkah."

"Wait! That almost sounds like my name!"

"Yeah, it does, doesn't it?"

"That's crazy, Mel, your religion has my name in it."

"It's Judaism, but yeah, sure, I like it."

"How come you never told me that you weren't Christian?"

"I don't know. I guess I thought it didn't matter..."

"...It doesn't, so I guess you were right." Melissa and I both laughed. I sat down on the edge of my bed after grabbing my new astrology book. Melissa sat down next to me. "Can I see your book?"

"Yeah, I started reading it, but I haven't made it to me yet, or you, I mean, Aquarius and Gemini." I handed her the book and she started turning the pages. "It starts with Aries for some reason. I still haven't figured out why. I will though. I'm not sure I know any Aries people. I read about them though. Apparently, they're babies..." I continued talking about the things that I had already read, but soon realized that Melissa wasn't paying attention to me. She was reading. I looked down at the page she was so focused on: Aquarius and Gemini relationship compatibility. "Hey what are you reading?" Melissa turned the book in my direction.

"This is a love match that was made in the stars."

"Cool, so just like friends, it's the same."

"Yeah...Just like friends."

"Are you going to start looking for an Aquarius boy now..." I laughed.

"...I, my parents, want me to find a nice Jewish boy, when I'm older."

"So, a nice Jewish Aquarius boy then? I'm sure they must exist, right?"

"Hannah..." Melissa said and put her hand on my leg. She looked into my eyes, but didn't say anything. "...It's nothing...I, ummm, I don't think there are even any Jewish boys at Fesler."

"Yeah...I wouldn't know, can't help you there." I laughed but Melissa didn't. She sulked into herself and closed the book. She handed it back to me and looked as if she were about to cry. "Mel, what's wrong? I didn't mean anything by it. I'm sure there's someone that's..."

"...It's okay, Hannah, I don't think...I think I should just concentrate on school."

"Yeah, you're right, me too. We're too young to be thinking about boys right now anyway."

"Really!?"

"Well, I did kinda sound like my parents right now...I do kinda want a boyfriend."

"You do?"

"Yeah, it would be nice to have someone, you know, to care about, to love, that kind of thing."

"Hannah...you already have me. I care about you. I love you."

"I love you too, Mel, but I don't know, it's just not the same."

"It's not?"

"No, I mean, I don't think so."

"But you don't know for sure."

"Mel, I think I get it..."

"What do you mean?"

"If I get a boyfriend, you don't have to worry, we'll still be friends forever."

"...Really?"

"Of course, we'll be friends no matter what happens. I'll never let a boy come between us."

"You promise?"

"I promise." Melissa hugged me and leaned her head against my shoulder.

Melissa had been giving me clues for a year about her feelings for me and I found a way to ignore them. *I should have never kissed her. That was it. That changed everything. She said it was practice. Yeah, Hannah, practice for what? How naïve could you be? I feel so stupid. Wait a damn minute!* I sat down on my bed and looked around my room curiously darting my eyes around my window. *It's not like I led her on. Right? Oh my God, why is this even a thing?* I lay back on my bed and put my feet up on my bed frame. I heard a faint knock on my door and then my dad let himself into my room. "Hannah?"

"Yes, dad."

"I'm going to go pick up your school work. I'll be back in 30 minutes."

"All right...thanks, dad. I'm sorry..."

"We'll talk about it when your mom gets home."

"Okay..." My dad shut my door behind him. I heard him get into his truck and then drive away. *Wow, I forgot all about my school work. What should I do now? I know!* I got up from my bed and grabbed my astrology book off of my dresser. I walked out into the living room and sat down on the couch. *What did I miss?* I turned to the section on Gemini and I flipped through the pages until I found a section called 'The negative characteristics of people born under Gemini.' *Did I not read this before?* One line immediately struck me: 'Geminis have a universal and natural ability to deceive others.' *Wait, what?* And: 'Geminis often live by their wits: lying, cheating, and swindling.' *That's not good. Did I just ignore this before? I think I've seen enough. Where did I leave off anyway?* I turned the pages forward past Leo and Virgo and found my overly elaborate book-mark with a blue tassel and various stickers comfortably resting on Libra. *Libra...all right, all I've got is time.* I pulled my feet up on the couch and placed one of the many throw pillows behind my back while holding the book open. I read through the overall description of Libra before moving on to the section on relationship compatibility. My eyes moved quickly to what actually mattered to me. *Libra Male and Aquarius female. That's me! This combination of the zodiac creates one of the most perfect unions. This perfection is created just by these two being together...Hmmm, really. Interesting. Do I know any Libra guys?* I continued reading. *There is an immediate and undeniable connection between these two air signs. The Aquarius female is creative and intelligent; whereas the Libra male is thoughtful and wise. The relationship between these two is automatic, creating a naturally nurturing, long-lasting relationship.* I closed the book and then looked out across the living room. *Am I creative and intelligent? I'm pretty smart but I don't know about creative...I wonder if I've met a libra guy before and didn't even know it. I wonder what Joe's sign is...He couldn't be a Libra...He's not thoughtful or wise.* I laughed. *Ha! I should look up to see if it says who the biggest asshole is...I should just look for Joe's picture.* I smiled and then laughed at the absurdity of seeing Joe's picture in an astrology book. *Joe, hmmm, I wonder...I'm curious now.* I opened the book and continued reading the section on Scorpio. About half way through Scorpio, I heard my dad's truck pull into the driveway. My dad walked through the front door and looked to be in a good mood. *Well, it is his day off.* He shut the door and then looked over at me. I closed my astrology book once again.

"I got your work."

"Okay, thanks, dad." My dad set the books and worksheets on the coffee table. *Worksheets? So dumb.*

"I've got good news."

"Really? Good for me or good for you?"

"It's good for all of us. It looks like the school board is leaning toward keeping you in school...the suspend the suspension, no, expulsion thing."

"That's good," I said unenthusiastically. *I don't even know if I want to go back to that school.*

"Your principal told me that they were moving to a restorative justice model of discipline."

"What does that mean?"

"I think it means suspending kids is costing them money." My dad let out a light chuckle. "No, I'm sure that's the reason."

"Dad! What does that mean for me?" I pleaded. My dad laughed.

"Well, my dear girl, you may have to see a therapist."

"What!? I'm not crazy." *Mel could use a therapist...*

"If that's what it takes for you to go back to school, yes, you better believe that's what you're going to do."

"Great." My dad continued laughing.

"We'll talk about it more when your mom gets home."

"Fine, I'm gonna finish my astrology book."

"I remember when your mom bought that for you." My dad walked to the kitchen and pulled a beer out of the refrigerator. "I mean Santa." He looked over at me with a guilty smile on his face.

"Dad, give me a break. It's not like I'm Michael."

"I know, I know, you're all grown up." My dad sat down on the couch right next to me. "It all happens so fast."

"What happens so fast?"

"Life." He put his beer down on the coffee table. "It was like you were a kid one minute and now you're not."

"Dad, I'm still a kid..."

"...You know what I mean."

"No, I really don't."

"Pretty soon you'll have boys knocking down the door." *Pretty soon, huh?* "And then you'll be driving."

"You're gonna buy me a car?" My dad laughed and then caught himself."

"Wait, I think I said that backwards. Driver's license first and then a boyfriend, maybe." *Maybe...*

"You didn't answer the question..." I widened my eyes and pouted my lips.

"Don't give me that puppy dog look...We'll talk about a car when the time comes, a few years from now."

"I think it's closer to three than a few."

"A few is three."

"A few sounds like more than three."

"No, a couple is two which makes a few three."

"Really, now? Are you sure?"

"Yes."

"You're funny, dad."

"I am? I wasn't trying to be funny..." I laughed.

"See, that's funny."

"Anyway," My dad pointed to my astrology book and then picked up his beer. "I thought you'd be done reading that by now."

"Yeah, I don't know. I'm gonna finish today though."

"Don't forget about your school work." *Right...*

"Dad, do you know any Libras?"

"...Bob's a Libra, I think."

"Bob?"

"You know him. He's Jessica's dad. My best friend from Visalia. You remember Jessica...right?"

"Yeah, but it's been a couple of years..."

"Yeah, it has. I need to find some time to visit..."

"That would be fun."

"Yeah, if I could only afford to take time off work...And your mom works all the time too." *Buzzkill.*

"Do you miss your friend?"

"Yeah, Bob, he's a good guy. We had some good times at Redwood."

"So...make some plans to go see him. Visalia's not that far away, right?"

"Right, but, it's complicated, Hannah. You'll find out soon enough that the older you get the more convoluted it gets."

"Convoluted?"

"...Messed up. I guess that's the easiest way to define it."

"So, life is messed up?"

"Yeah, well, no, it doesn't have to be, but it can be."

"Okay, dad. Your explanation is a little convoluted." My dad laughed.

"Yeah, I guess it is. Like I said before, it gets more and more complicated the older you get."

"...Yeah, it sounds like it."

"What were we talking about, anyway?"

"Bob, Jessica..."

"Right, but what brought them up?"

"I asked you if you knew any Libras."

"Oh, right, yeah, I think his birthday's sometime in October. Libra, right?" My dad pointed at my book again.

"Depends."

"On what?"

"It changes on October twenty-third."

"Yeah, I think his birthday is October twelfth."

"You think, huh? And you call him your best friend?"

"It's October twelfth, I'm sure."

"Okay, then, he's a Libra."

"See, I know what I'm talking about. To tell you the truth, anything I do know about astrology is thanks to your mother."

"Mom's a Pisces and you're a Capricorn..."

"That's right." I opened my astrology book to the section on Pisces to check her compatibility with my dad."

"What does it say?"

"It says that you and mom are a harmonious pairing, but that's all you get because I don't want to ruin it for myself. I haven't read this far yet. Pisces is the last chapter."

"So, what's the deal with Libras?"

"My book says that my perfect match is Libra. I don't think I know any Libras though."

"Aquarius and Libra...I don't know, you should ask your mom."

"You know my sign!"

"Of course, I do. You doubted your dearest father?"

"A little bit, yeah, but I'm impressed. I didn't think you'd be into this."

"Again, thank your mother."

"I will. I'll talk to her later about it. I'm gonna go to my room to finish reading my book."

"That's a good idea, Hannah, go finish your book." I got up from the couch and started walking towards my room and before I even got to the hallway, I heard the TV turn on. I looked back at my dad and smiled.

"Let me guess, the Dodgers are playing?"

"The Dodgers are always playing, but today I get to watch them play."

"Okay, dad, enjoy your game."

"Thanks, enjoy your book," my dad said without taking his eyes off the screen. *Boys and their sports.* I turned around and walked to my room, shut the door behind me, found a comfortable spot on my bed, and continued reading my book.

I read my astrology book for the rest of the morning and only took a break to make myself a sandwich for lunch. My dad was still watching baseball. I took my freshly made turkey sandwich to my room and then continued reading. In the early afternoon, I finished reading and decided to take a nap. I was woken by my mom a couple of hours later. "Wake up sleepy head," my mom insisted.

"...All right...hmmm."

"Come out in the living room, your father and I want to talk to you." *And, here we go...*

"Just give me a minute." I rubbed the sleep out of my eyes and then walked to the bathroom. I looked in the mirror and made a slew of ridiculous faces. *I look terrible!* I walked out into the living room where my mom and dad were waiting for me.

"Have a seat, Hannah," my mom said. I sat down opposite of my parents. "Your dad told me that the school wants you to see a therapist."

"Yeah, but I don't think I..."

"...I think it's a good idea." *Great.* "You take after your dad...with your anger issues." *I'm not angry.*

"Mom, seriously, it's not like I'm going around starting fights with people. I was defending myself...My reputation." I looked over at my dad and he gave me a wink but then shrugged his shoulders.

"You need to stay out of trouble," my mom added.

"Dad..." I pleaded. "...It wasn't my fault." I was fully expecting my dad to have my back, but after he looked at my mom, he seemed to change his mind.

"Listen to your mother, Hannah."

"What am I supposed to do, let people talk shit?"

"Hannah!" My mom screeched. *Wait. Mel. Molly...*

"I have to tell you something," I asserted.

"Go on," my mom said.

"...I screwed up. The girl I punched, Molly, she wasn't spreading rumors about me."

"Then why did you hit her?" My mom inquired.

"I thought she was, but then Mel told me it was her...and that she made the whole thing up."

"What!? Your friend, Mel...The one that's always here? That Mel?" My mom added. My dad sat quietly with a confused look on his face.

"Yeah, listen, mom, it's complicated...Ummm, can I talk to you alone?" I looked at my dad. He immediately looked at my mom.

"Patrick, give us a minute..."

"...Okay, I think I have something to do in the garage anyway." My dad got up and walked down the hallway. I looked back at my mom.

"Do you think that a girl can, ummm, like another girl, like that, you know, or love, yeah, if that makes sense..."

"Where is this coming from?"

"Like if a girl has feelings for another girl...Do you think that's normal?"

"Well, yes, I think it's normal, but I don't understand..."

"Mel told me that she loved me...In that way."

"Did she? Hannah, is there a reason that she would feel that way? Did you ever give her a reason..."

"We kissed one time...It wasn't a big deal."

"Maybe to you it wasn't, but maybe to her it was..."

"...Yeah, I'm not gay."

"And you think she is?"

"I don't know. She told me she was so I guess I believe her."

"Well, in my experience, when people tell you who they are you should believe them."

"Yeah, when I look back over this past year, it should have been more obvious to me."

"What do you mean?"

"She was always extra touchy, feely...I didn't think about it at the time."

"Wait a minute. Didn't you just tell me that Mel made up the rumors?"

"Yeah, that's what she told me."

"That doesn't make any sense."

"I know. I think Mel is the one that needs a therapist, not me!"

"Maybe...I don't want Mel staying over here again..."

"After what she did, I don't think I can be friends with her anymore, anyway."

"It's probably for the best..."

"Yeah, but it makes me sad...She was my best friend." *My only friend.*

"You'll make new friends, especially in high school." *High school, yeah, I guess so.*

"Mom, did you ever have a crush on a girl?"

"No...not that I can think of." *Why did she hesitate? Hmmm. I wonder...*

"So, if I, say, had a crush on a girl, you would be okay with that."

"I guess so," my mom said unconvincingly. She looked away for a moment and then back at me. "...I do want grandkids someday so..."

"Yeah, mom, I get it, but what if I were in love with a girl?"

"Well...I...you can't choose who you love. I would have to be okay with it, but you said you weren't..."

"...Gay, mom, gay." I laughed.

"That's funny to you?"

"Yeah, because I'm not gay."

"So, grandkids are still on the table?" *On the table?*

"I don't know yet. I know I like boys. I don't know if I want kids though."

"Hannah, I have an important question to ask you...Have you?" *Uh, oh, the birds and the bees again.*

"No, mom, seriously!? I haven't had sex."

"Okay, I just had to ask."

"And you asked me last year too...I don't even have a boyfriend."

"Just promise me...You can always talk to me about this stuff."

"I promise." *Yeah, right, seems like a trap!*

"Good, I don't want to be one of those moms. I want you to feel like you can always come to me and talk about anything...even sex. No judgement." *Hmmm.*

"Okay, mom, so when did you lose your virginity?" My mom blushed. She did not seem to be prepared for that question."

"...I was sixteen."

"Was it with dad?"

"No, it wasn't with your father."

"Really!? Who was it with? Did it hurt? Did it not hurt? How many times did you do it?" My mom's eyes widened.

"I...I'll tell you when you're older."

"MOM! But you just told me..."

"I know but you're still so young." *I am not!*

"I'm going to be fourteen! How old should I be?"

"I'll tell you what, we can have that conversation when you start high school."

"What difference does it make?"

"It makes a difference to me."

"How so?"

"Maybe...I just want to pretend that you're still our little girl." *Oh my God.*

"Mom, look at me." I looked down at my not exactly inconsequential breasts and then back at my mom. "I'm not a little girl anymore."

"Physically, yes, but mentally, I don't think..."

"...That doesn't even make sense," I quickly interjected.

"You're too young, no matter what..."

"I'm not too young. I can handle it."

"I don't know..."

"I do." The stalemate was broken by the ringing of the phone. "I'll get it," I said. "Mom, don't tell dad."

"Don't tell dad what?"

"Don't tell him anything!" I walked over to the kitchen and picked up the phone.

"Hannah?"

"Yeah." I looked back at my mom. "It's Mel, I need to take this." My mom nodded her head. "Hold on." I took the phone into my room and then shut the door behind me.

"Hey, Mel, I was going to call you later...I'm sorry about the way I ended our call yesterday." *I'm really not sorry. Why did I just say that?*

"It's okay, Hannah, I layered it on pretty thick."

"Yeah. I can't argue with that." We both laughed. *Don't forget what she did...*

"Hannah...I miss you." *This isn't going to work.*

"Mel, I don't know what you want me to say. I already told you I don't feel that way."

"You don't have to say anything...I just, I don't know...Can we maybe just...go back to the way things were?" *That's not even possible.*

"Mel, you..."

"I promise you I didn't tell anyone what I told you...I made it up."

"I know, I believe you, but how did you even come up with such an elaborate...Giving blowjobs in the park. Come on, Mel, seriously? I've never...in my life...gross!"

"I'm sorry, Hannah, I don't know what to say. I'm stupid. I don't deserve your forgiveness. I just couldn't imagine you with anyone else, especially a guy."

"Mel, you're not stupid..." *Psycho much, but not stupid.*

"...Hannah, I told Molly the truth."

"What did she say?"

"She was pissed. She said...She said that she doesn't want to talk to me ever again." I could hear Melissa's voice growing weaker as she began to cry. *I shouldn't be talking to you right now either.*

"It's okay, you just need to give her some time. I need to apologize to her...If they let me come back to school."

"You want her number?"

"No, I need to do it in person. I owe her that much."

"Yeah..."

"I should find out Friday if they're gonna let me come back, I think."

"I really need you right now, Hannah." *Don't.* "I was wondering if maybe I could stay over at your house this weekend." *Ummm, no.* "We'll celebrate you coming back to school." *Shit, I need to tell her.*

"My mom won't let you stay over anymore..."

"...What!? Why!?"

"I told her everything."

"What do you mean everything?"

"Everything."

"You told her that I'm gay!?"

"Yeah..."

"What the fuck, Hannah!? You're the only person that I've told. Oh my God, oh my God, oh my God...FUCK!" *Damn, what's the big deal?* "Hannah, fuck, I haven't even told my own parents yet.

"It's not like my mom is going to tell anyone. She doesn't talk to your parents."

"You don't understand. My parents are super, ultra, like stupid conservative."

"Okay..."

"They'll kill me."

"You should tell them. You shouldn't keep it a secret."

"Fuck, I know, but I'm scared."

"I'll tell my mom to not tell anyone and then you can just tell your parents when you're ready."

"Hannah, I don't deserve your help, but I really need your help...Will you help me?" *Just say no.*

"What do you need me to do?" *I'm gonna regret this...*

"When I decide to tell them...will you be there with me...just for support. I don't think I can do it alone. I really need you." *Yeah, I'm really going to regret this.*

"Of course, Mel, I'll be there for you."

"I love you, Hannah...Like, you know, as a friend." *Right...*

"So, when do you think you're gonna tell your parents?"

"I don't know yet. I guess when the time is right, even though there is no right time. Shit, I don't know. I guess sooner is better. I don't want to wait for the holidays. That would be bad. Maybe I should just wait until high school. No, I can't wait!" *Mel is on another level of crazy.* "Maybe before basketball starts. After basketball? Maybe this is a bad idea."

"No, it's not a bad idea. Your parents should know, and once they do, they'll deal with it. They love you and that won't change because of this."

"Thanks, Hannah, you're so positive. I love that about you. I wish I could be more like you."

"You're a lot like me. You just don't give yourself enough credit."

"I don't think you'd make up some stupid shit about me for some stupid shit reason."

"Well, no, but other than that..." I laughed and then Melissa followed.

"I don't know what I'd do without you."

"You'll find a nice girl and live happily ever after."

"Ahhh, you really think so?"

"Of course!" *That wouldn't be the worst thing in the world. Maybe I could help her...Or...I should just stay out of it. I don't know.*

"Thanks, Hannah, I know it's the Disney version of things...well, the gay Disney version of things, but I feel better now."

"I'm glad. Hey, I've got to go. I can smell my mom's cooking and I'm getting hungry. And then I've got homework..."

"All right, call me later, okay?"

"Okay, bye, Mel."

"Bye, Hannah." I hung up the phone and then opened my bedroom door. I walked down the hall into the kitchen where my mom was making what smelled like lasagna.

"Lasagna?" I asked.

"Yep," my mom responded. "Your dad's favorite."

"Is he still in the garage?"

"I think so."

"Good...I told Mel that I told you that she was gay. She freaked out because I'm the only person that she told. She hasn't even told her parents."

"Okay..." My mom focused on making the layers of lasagna perfect.

"Don't tell anyone that Mel's gay, mom."

"Okay." *She's not even paying attention.*

"Mom, I'm serious, don't tell anyone!" My mom stopped making dinner and looked over at me.

"Who am I going to tell?" *Yeah, that's what I said.*

"I don't know. I just promised her that I would tell you not to say anything."

"I won't say anything, Hannah, but like I said before, I still don't want her staying over at night."

"She's not going to do anything."

"I just don't think it's appropriate."

"Not appropriate?"

"I wouldn't allow a boy to sleep over."

"That's different."

"Is it?"

"Yeah, Mel doesn't have a dick!"

"Hannah! End of discussion."

"That's not fair."

"Life's not fair."

"No, you're not fair."

"Wait a minute. Mel caused all kinds of drama and now you're defending her?"

"I understand why she did it."

"You do? Well, it's safe to say that I don't understand your generation at all. It wasn't even thirty minutes ago that you said you weren't going to be friends with her and now a total one-eighty."

"I don't know...I don't even know if we're going to be friends again...at least not like we were before. But, mom, Mel needs help."

"That reminds me..." My mom turned away from me and continued making dinner. "...I need to find you a therapist tomorrow before you to go back to school."

"I don't need a therapist."

"Maybe not, but you have to go to school...Dinner will be ready in an hour." My mom put the lasagna in the oven and then walked over to the couch and sat down. I sat down across from her and crossed my legs and folded my arms in front of me. My mom picked up the remote and turned on the TV. "What do you want to watch?"

"Not the news." My mom turned the channel to the news and I rolled my eyes. *She did that on purpose!* "Mom, what if I had a boyfriend?"

"Do you have a boyfriend?"

"No, but what if I did?"

"You don't need a boyfriend right now."

"What if I do need a boyfriend right now?"

"Hannah! Stop it!"

"Stop what? At that moment my dad came back into the house and walked into the kitchen.

"Something smells great," my dad said.

"Patrick, your daughter thinks she needs a boyfriend right now," my mom quickly and sarcastically proclaimed.

"Hannah, you're too young for a boyfriend," my dad responded.

"I am not too..." My dad interrupted me.

"...Yes, you are, and that's about the end of it. Haven't we had this conversation before? Anyway, I can't wait to eat, I'm starving." My dad sat down next to my mom and put his arm around her. They both smiled at me awkwardly and I quickly got up from the couch.

"I'm gonna go to my room."

"Can you go find your brother before dinner? He's playing with his friend outside somewhere," my mom said.

"Yeah, I'll get him before dinner." *Stupid parents. Stupid Michael. They don't even care what he does...* I walked into my room and shut the door. I sat down on the edge of my bed and stared over at my astrology book. *I am not too young...*

Chapter Five

Therapy

"Dad, I already told mom that I don't need to see a therapist."

"You're lucky that the school even agreed to have you back, so you're going to do what they say and see the flippin' therapist!"

"Whatever," I said and looked down at my lap. It was Monday morning and my dad was driving me to my therapy appointment. My mom called around to a lot of different people until she found one with an opening. The school had called Friday morning and told my parents that I was going to be allowed back at school with the condition that I see a therapist before I return. I already figured that was going to happen but I still wasn't happy about it. *What are we even going to talk about?* The therapist's office wasn't too far away from my house so we we're there before I knew it.

"This is it," my dad said as he stopped the truck.

"Are you coming in with me?"

"No, this is all you..."

"...But, I..."

"You're all grown up now, right?" My dad laughed. *Shit, I know he's being sarcastic but he does have a point...*

"Fine, I'm going." I got out of my dad's truck and shut the door."

"I'll be back in an hour," my dad said and drove away. I walked up to the door and read the sign: *Scott Kelley LMFT. Licensed Marriage and Family Therapist. What the hell?* I opened the door and saw an overweight Hispanic woman behind the reception desk filing her nails.

"Hi, how can I help you?"

"I have an appointment."

"What's your name?"

"Hannah O'Connor..."

"...Yes, Hannah, please have a seat, Scott will be with you in just a moment. *Scott? Super-professional. Did this guy even go to school for this? Whatever.* I sat down in one of the four chairs in the reception area. The chairs had blue fabric and were quite dilapidated. *So gross.* There was a stack of magazines on the table between the chairs. I noticed a 'Seventeen' magazine on the top and grabbed it. It was an old issue, but my eyes immediately moved to one of the subtitles. *How to help a friend in trouble. Awesome, maybe this was worth it after all.* I turned the pages until I got to the article and just as I started reading, I heard my name called.

"Hannah?" *Shit.*

"Can I take this magazine in with me?"

"No, sweetie, you don't need the magazine." *Actually, I think I do, but, yeah, damn, sweetie?* I put the magazine back on the table and followed the middle-aged man back into his office. He was wearing thick black-rimmed glasses and had a quite pronounced, receding hairline. His voice and the way he walked were both very feminine. *I wonder if he's gay...* He sat down behind his desk and I sat down opposite of him. "My name is Scott Kelley, but you can call me Scott. Hannah, tell me about yourself...Who is Hannah?"

"Ummm, I'm thirteen, I'm in the eighth grade...I like to play basketball...I don't know..."

"That's good, but I want to know who you are, not what you are..." *Huh, what's with this guy?*

"I don't understand."

"Do you consider yourself a good person?"

"I guess so."

"Can you explain why?"

"I don't know. I care about people...Like a lot...Sometimes more than I care about myself."

"Interesting..." Scott grabbed a pen and wrote down some notes on a tablet in front of him. *What are you writing? What's so interesting?*

"Hannah, I want you to be honest with me. Have you ever had suicidal thoughts?"

"What!? No!" I insisted. *Yes.*

"Hannah..."

"Okay, I used to, but not anymore. I'm okay now," I said. "And it's not like I was gonna do anything..."

"Do you want to talk about it?"

"Not really."

"I think it will help if you talk about it." *Hmmm, maybe it will. I never told anyone about this before. How did he know?*

"Okay...It was in the sixth grade..."

"Ms. Buchanan, Josh keeps snapping my bra," I said. I waited for everyone to leave the classroom at lunch before I approached my teacher. A kid named Josh Story had been harassing me since the beginning of the school year. It was the middle of October and I was growing tired of him.

"Hannah, he probably just likes you," my teacher said.

"I don't like him at all." Josh thought he was the most popular boy in our class, but I hated even looking at his face. He was a bully. He pushed the other boys around and snapped my bra whenever he had the chance, which was way too often because he sat right behind me. I'm sure he would have harassed other girls, but I think I was the only girl in our class that wore a bra. I was the only girl in our class that needed to wear a bra.

"Just tell him that. He'll leave you alone."

"I don't think he will, though. Can you move his seat somewhere else?"

"No, Hannah, I don't think that's a good idea."

"Why?"

"Because he has problems with a lot of the boys in this class. I have them all separated."

"So, I just have to deal with him all year?"

"I'm afraid so, it's what's best for the class." *You are a terrible teacher.*

"You're not going to do anything about it?"

"There's nothing I can do."

"At least tell him to stop."

"Okay, I'll talk to him before class starts."

"Thank you." *Why does this have to be so difficult?*

"You're welcome, Hannah, now go to lunch."

"Okay, but I'm really not hungry." I walked out of the classroom and into the cafeteria. I grabbed a lunch tray and the lunch lady plopped down the science experiment that they passed for food one scoop at a time. I sat down at the end of one of the benches alone and poked at the solidified gruel with my plastic spork. I looked up and saw Josh sitting with a bunch of people. They weren't really his friends but they were afraid of him. He wasn't that much bigger than any of the other boys but he was much more aggressive. He was irritatingly aggressive. I was jealous of him though. It at least seemed like they were having a good time. I was alone. I was always alone. I felt like an alien the way everyone avoided me. I was taller than everyone in my class, including the boys. I was almost as tall as my teacher. I had boobs. They were small boobs, but they were there, and I had to wear a bra. All the other girls were girls and I was somewhere in between a girl and a woman. It was my own personal hell...My own personal purgatory. No one understood what I was going through and worst of all no one cared. I forced some of the gruel into my mouth and down my throat, but left most of it behind as the bell rang for class to start. I waited for a minute to walk back to class. I wanted to give Ms. Buchanan time to talk to Josh. When I did finally walk back to class, I saw Josh sitting at his desk and shaking his pencil in the air. *What an idiot!* I walked right up to my teacher.

"Did you talk to Josh?"

"Yes, Hannah, he said he'll leave you alone."

"Okay, good." I walked back to my desk and sat down without acknowledging Josh's existence.

"You're a rat," Josh whispered into the back of my head. I didn't respond. "I said, you're a rat, Hannah. I'm gonna make your life miserable now." *Great. Tell me how anything's changed.* "I'm gonna snap that bra so much, it's going to put a hole in your back." *Your funeral.* I once again did not respond to Josh's harassment.

"Okay, guys, open up your math workbooks to page 109 and..." My teacher said and I felt Josh grab a thick handful of my shirt and bra, pulled back and then let go. It snapped into my back and a sharp pain radiated throughout my body. I immediately turned around.

"FUCKING STOP!" I screamed. Josh looked horrified. The class went silent. Ms. Buchanan walked over to me.

"Hannah, what did you just say?"

"Josh snapped my bra again," I said without hesitation.

"I did not, she's lying," Josh quickly added. *Oh, you've got to be kidding me.* I heard whispers and slight laughter from some of my classmates.

"Hannah, go to the office!"

"What, why me? What about Josh?"

"You're not allowed to use that kind of language in this class."

"Yeah, Hannah!" Josh said.

"Shut up, Josh!"

"Hannah, just go to the office, we'll talk about this later." I got up from my desk, grabbed my backpack while shaking my head, walked out of the classroom with murmurs surrounding me, and slowly dragged myself to the office.

※※※※ ※※※※

"You felt like you didn't have any control over your situation," Scott said.

"That's because I didn't."

"That made you want to end your life?"

"No, not really..."

"It's because you felt alone."

"I was alone. I didn't have anyone to talk to."

"There must have been someone. Your parents?"

"Yeah, but it's not the same. They don't understand."

"I understand your feelings, Hannah, but you're not alone. And now you have me to talk to...And all you really need is one person." *Mel...*

"Thanks, Scott, but you're like older than my parents...no offense." Scott laughed.

"None taken. You know Hannah, age is just a number. Even older people can offer their ear."

"I guess so."

"What happened afterwards?" Scott asked and readied his pen.

※※※※ ※※※※

"Mr. Akin," I said, "Josh has been snapping my bra all year and Ms. Buchanan won't do anything about it."

"Hannah, I was hoping I wouldn't see you back in my office." *Yeah, me too.*

"Mr. Akin, I'm sorry but I was just fed up with him."

"Well, Hannah, at least you used your words this time, even if those words were profane."

"Yes, sir."

"Hannah, you know we don't allow that kind of language at this school."

"I know, Mr. Akin."

"Hannah, I know that you're not going to like this, but I'm going to recommend changing your class. I'll call your parents and..."

"Again!?"

"Yes, Hannah, we have to maintain a positive learning environment for everyone."

"Why is it always my fault?" I felt the tears filling my eyes and tears gradually began to roll down my cheeks.

"It's not always your fault."

"Then why does no one else get in trouble? Nothing happened to Jimmy and now nothing is happening to Josh. If it's not my fault then why am I the only one that gets in trouble?"

"It's hard to explain. You're too young to understand." *Of course I am.*

"I'm not too young!" I pleaded but Mr. Akin was focused on some papers he had shuffled around on his desk.

"I think I'll put you in Mr. Esteban's class. He's only at twenty-seven students. I think it'll be a good fit." *Whatever.*

⁂

"My parents didn't care. They were glad that I didn't get suspended again."

"Why did you get suspended?" Scott asked.

"I strangled Jimmy for making fun of me." Scott wrote some more notes on his tablet.

"What are you writing?"

"I'm just taking notes on what you're telling me." *Yeah, right. It's probably more like how I'm crazy and need medication.*

"Can I go back to school or not?"

"I'm not sure what you mean. I don't make that decision."

"You don't?" *Then why am I here?*

"As far as I know you've already been approved to go back to school."

"But I have to be here?"

"Yes, but I don't report to your school."

"I don't understand."

"Tell me more about Jimmy."

"There's not much to say."

"It must have been pretty serious to strangle someone."

"Okay, well, it's embarrassing, but..."

"It's okay, this is a safe place." *Safe place? As opposed to what? A not safe place?*

"I got my period in class and Jimmy, well, he made up a song about me. He called it Sunday Bloody Sunday, I think. Something snapped inside of me and I wanted to choke the life out of him."

"I'm sorry that happened to you, Hannah."

"Yeah, me too. That was when it all started. People ignored me. I would say 'hi' to people and they would say 'hi' back and that kind of thing, but I could tell that they didn't want to be anywhere near me."

"I'm really sorry to hear that, Hannah, it must have been hard on you."

"It was. After the Josh thing happened, I think I just stopped caring, or something. I started in Mr. Esteban's class the next day and it was okay, I guess."

"It was just okay? You didn't have the opportunity to make any new friends?"

"No. Everyone just left me alone, which was better than it was before..."

"You didn't try to make friends?"

"No. I was sad. I felt alone, but I didn't know what to do about it."

"You could have talked to someone."

"I was afraid they wouldn't like me. I already felt different than everyone else. Out of place. I didn't want to make it worse. That's when I started having those thoughts..."

"Suicidal thoughts?"

"Yeah, I think so. I mean, I didn't have a plan or anything...I just, I don't know, didn't want to be alive. Like I thought the world would be better off without me." Tears filled my eyes.

"Hannah, you're not the only one that ever felt that way." *I'm not?*

"A lot of people have these thoughts?"

"They do?"

"Yes, and you know what helps?"

"What?"

"Talking with someone about it." *I knew he was going to say that.*

"Yeah, I guess, I do feel a little better..."

"Hannah, at the beginning of our session..." Scott looked down at his notes. "You said that you were okay now."

"Yeah, I am okay, I don't think about that stuff anymore."

"What changed?" *Mel...Shit.*

"I don't know...I grew up...And I made a friend."

"Really, what's her name?"

"Melissa, but she goes by Mel. She was my best friend."

"Was?"

"Yeah, she's the reason that I'm here right now."

"What happened?"

"She lied to me about some rumors. I punched her friend. Here we are." Scott continued writing. "We're okay now though. I forgave her. I think I understand why she did it."

"Why is that?"

"She said she's in love with me. She said she's gay." Scott stopped writing and looked up at me.

"Hannah, are you gay?" *What the hell? Again?*

"No."

"Does she know that?"

"Yes, I told her. She's okay."

"Is she?" *I don't know.*

"Yeah."

"Are you sure?"

"No...Scott, she needs help. She wants to tell her parents that she's gay but she's scared."

"Yes, coming out to your parents can be a traumatizing experience." *It sounds like he's speaking from his own experience...*

"She wants me to be there when she does it."

"That's a really big step. Do you think you're ready for that?"

"I don't know."

"It's something that you should really think carefully about?"

"Really? I thought I was just doing my friend a favor."

"Hannah, I don't know this for sure, but it seems like Mel still has feelings for you."

"But...She said that she wanted things to just go back to the way they were."

"That could be a coping mechanism."

"What?"

"She could be telling you what you want to hear." *Shit. She did lie to me before...*

"Oh my God, I'm so naïve."

"No, I think you're trying to be a good friend. She's probably very confused right now."

"Yeah..."

"Well, Hannah, we've come to the end of our session."

"Okay, so, what happens now?"

"We'll call your school and let them know you attended today." *Hey! I thought you said...Oh, whatever...*

"So, do I have to come back?"

"That's up to you and your parents."

"Okay. Thanks, Scott, you know, for listening."

"Thanks for being so open, Hannah, it was a pleasure."

"Scott, do you think you could talk to Mel?"

"Sure, if she wants to."

"I'll ask her. I think she...Scott, can I ask you a personal question?"

"Shoot."

"Are you...gay?"

"Yes, Hannah, I am."

"I knew it! I really think you could help Mel."

"Maybe. It all depends on if she's willing to be open and honest."

"I think that Mel and I have a lot in common so I'm sure you'll be able to help her."

"All right, Hannah, stay out of trouble."

"Of course!" I said and walked out of Scott's office and over to the receptionist. "Hi, can I use your phone? Wait, never mind, my dad should be on his way." I looked at the chairs in the reception area. *Nah, I'm good.* I walked outside and stood on the sidewalk and waited patiently for my dad to pick me up.

The following Monday morning, I walked right up to Molly before school started. "Molly, I need to talk to you...alone." I looked at both of her friends and they looked back at me with fear in their eyes. They looked down and cowered. They started backing away when Molly reached out both of her hands and stopped them.

"I can't believe they even let you back," Molly said quietly, with a sort of sadness in her voice. She seemed like a different person than the one that I knew. Physically, she seemed fine, other than a split bottom lip where I hit her. Mentally, though, she seemed shaken. Her bold, brazen personality was gone.

"I'm sorry, Molly, I shouldn't have hit you. It was really shitty of me. I thought that..."

"...I know, Mel told me," Molly interjected. "I still don't get why she was talking shit about you in the first place."

"Mel has some issues she has to work out."

"What are you talking about?"

"It's not my place to say. Ask her. I'm sure she'll tell you if you ask."

"I don't want to talk to her ever again."

"I understand how you feel, but Mel really needs us right now."

"Wait..." Molly gave me a confused look and then shared it with her younger friends, both of whom looked to be perfectly content not saying anything at all. "Are you still going to be friends with her?"

"I don't know. She needs help."

"I don't think she deserves anything."

"I just wanted to apologize to you..."

"You already did."

"Yeah...I need to talk to Mel. Have you seen her?"

"She hasn't been to school since..."

"You said that you talked to her though..."

"She called me the other day, but, yeah..."

"Now I'm really worried about her." Molly shook her head disapprovingly as if I had said something that bothered her. "She made a mistake, Molly, I made a mistake too..." Molly didn't respond. "People deserve a second chance."

"I don't think so, Hannah." Molly said and turned around. She made a motion with her hand and her friends followed behind her. *Well, that went better than I expected. What am I gonna do now? Where's Mel?* I turned around and walked back to the office. I walked inside and looked at the clock on the wall. It read 7:45.

"Ummm, hi, can I use the phone?" I asked the secretary behind the front desk.

"Do you want to call your parents?"

"Ummm," *She won't let me use the phone if I say no.* "Yeah, ummm, I forgot one of my books at home."

"Okay, here you go." The secretary handed me the phone and I dialed Melissa's number. Her mom answered.

"Hello?"

"Hi, Is Mel there?" The secretary gave me a funny look but directed her attention back to some paperwork she had in front of her.

"Is this Hannah?"

"Yeah."

"Oh hi, sweetie."

"Ummm, hi."

"Mel's not feeling well."

"Yeah, I'm calling from school and wondered why she wasn't here."

"She's been sick for a few days now. I hope we're not having an early flu season this year. That wouldn't be good. We haven't even got our flu shots yet." *Oh my God...Please stop talking.* "It came out of nowhere too. One day she's fine, the next day she's sick and..."

"...Can you have her call me tonight?" I quickly interrupted.

"Yes, of course, I'll tell her you called."

"Okay, tell her I hope she feels better."

"Okay, Hannah, bye now."

"Bye." Melissa's mom hung up the phone. I handed the phone back to the secretary and the funny look she had given me before returned.

"Is your book on its way?" She asked sarcastically.

"Ummm, no, I mean, I forgot I already...I have my book after all."

"I see," the secretary said with a lowered tone and then went back to work.

"Anyway," I said and then walked out of the office. I sat down on the bench and waited for the bell to ring for class to start. A sense of sadness came over me but didn't last very long as Joe and Ryan approached me. They hadn't even said a word and I was already irritated. "What do you want, Joe?"

"You. I want you, Onion," Joe said and Ryan laughed.

"No, what do you want right now?"

"...Same answer," Joe said and flashed his perfect smile. *I'm really not in the mood for this right now.*

"Joe, why don't you just go away? Leave me alone..."

"Careful, man, she might pull a Molly on you," Ryan said to Joe and they both laughed. *Real original...pull a Molly...* Joe sat down next to me and looked up at Ryan.

"Hey, man, give us a minute," Joe said.

"A minute for what?" Ryan said and looked perplexed.

"I want to talk to Hannah alone, dumb ass," Joe said and I smiled.

"Whatever, I'll see you later then," Ryan said and then walked away.

"I hate him so much," I said.

"He's my friend, but he is pretty stupid," Joe added.

"Then why are you friends?"

"I don't know...football, I guess." Joe scratched his head like he was thinking about what to add to that list, but didn't say anything. "So, you kicked Molly's ass, huh?"

"I punched her once."

"Why'd you do it?"

"It's a really long story."

"I get it." *No, you don't.* "She's a bitch, and she probably ran her mouth...She got what she deserved."

"No, she didn't!" I raised my voice. "She didn't do anything wrong. I made a mistake."

"I don't get it."

"And you never will," I said and smiled.

"Onion, what are you talking about?"

"How many times have I told you not to call me Onion? You're such a jerk."

"It's not a bad thing...okay, I'll tell you..."

"Tell me what? You were born into a long line of jerks and you just can't help yourself?"

"No...Why I call you Onion?" *Oh, this should be good.*

"I'm listening." *I bet that it's somehow a metaphor for my vagina. Stupid boys...*

"You're the prettiest...Most beautiful girl..." *Yep, I can see where this is going...* "...And you have a really nice body and..." *Just get to it then...* "...And you are also really smart...And athletic. I always watch you when you play basketball." *Sweet or creepy? Hmmm.* "So, it's everything...You're like an onion, you have multiple layers..." *Interesting...Not bad, Joe.* "...And at first, you can't see the layers, but as you peel them back you realize that they go on forever...That's you." Joe pointed at me and smiled brilliantly. *That's really thoughtful...Like really smart.* I swooned. A strange feeling came over me. *What is happening right now?* Joe put his hand on my thigh and lightly squeezed. I didn't stop him. I smiled.

"So how long did it take you to come up with all of that?"

"A really long time..." I found the honesty of his answer endearing. All of the pretense was gone. He was being truthful.

"...I believe you."

"It's true. I practiced in the mirror." *Okay, that's a little too much information, but it's kind of cute.* "It's just like football. Coach says you practice the play until you can't get it wrong. That's what I did."

"Yeah, you did." *Impressive.*

"Joe...I have to give you credit. I didn't expect..." *He's smart...since when?* "Why do you act so stupid all the time when you're not stupid?"

"...I don't know."

"And now Ryan makes even less sense."

"Yeah. I just guess that being smart, or, showing people you're smart doesn't win any popularity contests."

"You want to be popular?"

"Yeah, who doesn't."

"Me. I don't care. I'm going to be me and I don't care if anyone likes it."

"That's exactly what I'm talking about...Onion!"

"Okay, I get it." I smiled. The bell rang for first period but Joe didn't move. His hand was still on my leg.

"Hannah, I want you to be my girlfriend." I felt myself blush and a feeling of euphoria came over me.

"Okay," I said without thinking.

"Is that a yes?" Joe asked and was seemingly shocked.

"Yes, even though you didn't really ask me a question." Joe smiled.

"No, I guess I didn't. Let me walk you to class." Joe and I stood up and started walking to my first period class. He wrapped his arm around my waist and I put my hand inside of his back pocket and gently palmed his butt. *It's as hard as a rock! Wow...* Joe smiled as he attempted to make eye contact with every single person at school. He seemed to want to make sure that everyone knew that we were together. When we got to my classroom, he pulled me closely and quickly kissed me directly on my lips and then stepped back. My heart skipped a beat. I momentarily felt breathless. "I'll see you later," Joe said.

"Bye," I replied and turned around to walk in the classroom. Before I could cross the threshold of the door, I felt a light pinch on my butt and turned around. Joe kissed me again, but this time held it for a few seconds. He let me go and smiled. "Joe, you're gonna be late."

"Totally worth it." Joe walked away and I took my seat in the classroom. I smiled as I opened my backpack and pulled out my notebook. *What just happened?*

I practically ran out of my class when the lunch bell rang. I wanted to see Joe. I had been thinking about him every minute that I was in class. When I found him in the middle of the school, I ran up to him and hugged him from behind. "I missed you," I said.

"Oh, hey, Onion," Joe responded and turned around to hug me back. Ryan had a dumbfounded look on his face as usual.

"What, aren't you happy to see me?"

"Yes, I'm always happy to see you," Joe said.

"Me too," Ryan added.

"SHUT UP, RYAN!" Joe and I said simultaneously and we both laughed. Ryan shook his head.

"That's fucked up," Ryan said.

"You can't talk to her like that anymore. She's my girlfriend now," Joe said and wrapped his arm around me. I smiled and stared down Ryan, daring him to say anything derogatory. *This feels good.* I saw Molly through the crowd. We made eye contact, but she quickly looked at Joe who was showcasing his million-dollar smile. Molly didn't look happy, but she didn't look mad either. It was almost as if she was indifferent. *I feel like such a hypocrite. All this time I've thought Joe was a jerk... That I'd never be with him...And now... Molly doesn't seem to care, but what is Mel going to think? Shit...Mel. Oh my God. I haven't even thought about her all day. What is going on with me?* "Onion," Joe said, "are you okay?"

"Yeah, what do you mean?"

"You just don't seem like you were here right now."

"I was just thinking..."

"About what?"

"What I'm going to tell Mel?"

"Huh?"

"You think that Mel cares who you date?" Ryan said.

"I don't know."

"Why would she care?" Joe asked. *Shit, I need to stop talking.* "Why do you care what she thinks?"

"She's my best friend." *Is that even true? I'm so confused.*

"Then what are you worried about?" Ryan forcefully said. Joe looked at him sternly, but then looked at me as if he wanted to hear the answer.

"I'm not. I just don't want her to feel like I'm not going to hang out with her anymore."

"It's not like we need to be together all the time," Joe said, "right?" *I guess so...*

"Yeah, I'm just overthinking it."

"Let's go get some food."

"All right." Joe put his hand on my hip and slowly moved it over to my butt. We walked stride for stride to the cafeteria while Ryan followed behind.

After dinner that night, I decided to call Melissa again to tell her about Joe. I didn't want her to find out about it from anyone else. I dialed her number and put the phone to my ear and sat on the edge of my bed. *I really hope she's not mad.*

"Hello?"

"Mel?"

"Yeah, Hannah, it's me."

"Are you feeling better?"

"Yeah, I guess so. I just feel terrible. Everyone hates me now."

"I don't hate you."

"Honestly, that makes me feel worse."

"What do you mean by that?"

"...You should hate me. If it were the other way around..."

"...I was mad, you know, but it's all right now."

"I don't deserve your...you're such a good person."

"So are you, Mel, you just made a mistake..."

"Do you think that we could hang out at school tomorrow? I mean, if you want to..." *I have to tell her about Joe.*

"Mel, you're not going to be happy about this, but, yeah, ummm, Joe and I are a thing now."

"...Oh, wow, ummm...I'm happy for you, Hannah." *No way is that true.*

"Mel, I know you're not happy about it..."

"Yeah, I guess that's just what people say..."

"People should just be honest though...Don't you think? I think it's for the best."

"So...Joe's been trying to get with you for a long time? Why now?"

"Well, he is cute."

"That's always been true, but you didn't answer the question...Why now?" *She got me there. It's a really good question...My dad...Maybe.*

"Joe was really sweet. He asked me to be his girlfriend. I've never seen that side of him. I liked it...And he's cute...And it might have a teensy bit to do with my dad."

"Your dad? That's...Wait, that's weird, Hannah!" I laughed. "What's so funny?"

"He told me that I'm too young to have a boyfriend. I disagreed."

"Maybe he's right..."

"What!?" Melissa laughed.

"You know...Too young for a boyfriend, but the perfect age for a girlfriend."

"Mel!"

"I'm kidding, Hannah...Haha."

"That's pretty good. You had me going there."

"I hope everything works out with Joe, seriously." *Hmmm.*

"What does that mean?"

"Joe's a player, Hannah, he's been with a lot of girls."

"I know, Mel, but I have to at least give him a chance, right? Maybe he'll turn over a new leaf..."

"Turn over a leaf?"

"You know, change for the better."

"I hope so...Now that I think about it, if he were going to change, it would be for you."

"Thanks, Mel, that means a lot...Mel, I want you to know that...I'll always be there for you."

"So, you still wanna be friends?" *She still needs my help.*

"Yes, of course...I almost forgot to tell you about the therapist I saw..."

"Oh, yeah, how was it? Did they psychoanalyze your childhood?" Melissa laughed. *Wait...Did he? Maybe. Is that what happened?*

"No, Scott mostly just listened to me."

"Wow, you're on a first name basis?"

"He was really nice. And he's gay..."

"Why does that matter? How do you even know?"

"He told me."

"He just told you?"

"Well, I asked him. It seemed like he was and I thought maybe he could help you so..."

"Hannah, you didn't tell him about me, did you?" *Uh oh...Maybe I should lie...*

"Well..."

"Hannah!?"

"Yes, I told him, but only because I thought he could help you."

"I can't believe that you told another person and after I told you not to."

"Mel, I want to help you."

"Why do you think I need help?" *Because you do.*

"I think you should talk to him. I can give you his number..."

"I don't want to talk to some stranger about my life, Hannah, shit!"

"He really helped me."

"I don't want to talk about it anymore, Hannah, just drop it."

"...I won't mention it again..."

"Good. Hey, I gotta go...I hear my mom calling me." *I don't hear anything.*

"Okay, I'll see you at school tomorrow."

"If I go. I don't know if..."

"Mel, you need to come to school. You'll get behind on your work."

"Don't worry about me, Hannah, I'll figure it out." *That doesn't sound good.*

"Mel, I'm sorry, I shouldn't have said anything...to anyone."

"It's fine." *Yeah, it's not fine.*

"Mel, I promise you I won't..."

"I said it's fine, Hannah, I gotta go." Melissa hung up the phone. *What else can I do?* I put the phone down on my bed. *I should call Joe. I wonder if I should tell my parents about him...No, probably not.*

Chapter Six

Ascendants

"Onion, we've been together for like two months, when are you gonna let me hit that?" Joe asked as we walked around campus at lunch while holding hands. He let go of my hand, grabbed my butt and then slid his fingers between my legs.

"Stop it, Joe, people are watching."

"Let them watch," Joe said and then laughed.

"Why do you have to be so...Vulgar?"

"Shit, I thought you were gonna say something about me being a jerk."

"Yeah, that too."

"I've never waited this long for anyone." *Wait...What?* "We've only made out and my balls are seriously getting blue." *That's funny.*

"What's wrong, Joe? Did you get tackled by your nuts again?" *Haha.*

"What!? No! Hannah, this isn't a joke." *I guess not. Well, shit...*

"It's not like we can just do it here at school..."

"Why not? I have before." *Ummm, no, you didn't just say that. How did I not know this?*

"...With who? When? WHERE?"

"Bathroom. Specifically, the girl's bathroom," Joe said and smiled.

"At lunch?"

"Before school, at lunch, after school, you know, whenever."

"No, I obviously don't know."

"It's not a big deal." *It's a big deal to me. That is so gross.*

"You had sex with Molly...In the bathroom...Here at school?"

"Yeah, all the time." *I don't believe...Well, it is Joe. Oh my God!*

"Shit, Joe, how many times have you had sex?"

"I don't know...A lot." *Gross.*

"Did you use protection?"

"Sometimes." *Even more gross.* "My pullout game is strong though." *This is my boyfriend?*

"How many girls?"

"Five, including Molly."

"Wait, do they all go to this school?" Joe smiled.

"Maybe." *Maybe...Maybe Mel was right.*

"So, you want me to be number six?"

"Yeah, but like I said, if it wasn't you..."

"We wouldn't even be talking about this..."

"Right. You're the hottest girl at school. You're worth the wait, but come on...Two months? This is getting ridiculous."

"I'm a virgin, Joe..."

"Another thing I really like about you." *Great.*

"What I mean is that I'm not gonna have sex with you at school. And in the bathroom? You can't be serious..."

"Okay, Onion, what do you suggest then?" Joe asked and looked quite perturbed. *I'm going to have to do it eventually.*

"Maybe we could sneak out...My dad works nights. I think I could get away with it."

"Hmmm, maybe, but I think my parents would catch me. My mom's always waking up at night. She's got that sleep apnea thing going on."

"...That sucks."

"Yeah, anyway...Shit! I just thought of something."

"Oh yeah, what?"

"Summer Braithwaite is having a Halloween party at her house."

"Oh yeah, I know Summer."

"Yeah, the dyke girl."

"Don't be an asshole, Joe."

"What? She's gay as fuck."

"Who cares if she's gay?"

"I don't. I'm just stating a fact."

"Well, it sounds like you're being mean."

"I'm not being mean, Onion, shit, what is wrong with you today? Are you on your period?" *Fucking asshole! I am on my period...But that's not why...Shit!* I was getting angry and wanted Joe to know it without making a scene so I simply crossed my arms and then looked away from him. "Anyway, she invited me to go." *That doesn't even make sense.*

"No offense, but why would she invite you? It's not exactly like you have anything in common."

"I don't know. We we're in math class and..."

"Who are we?"

"Shit, Hannah, are you going to let me finish my sentence?"

"Maybe." I laughed. "Go ahead."

"Shit. Like I was saying...We were standing around in math class..." I shrugged my shoulders waiting for Joe to be more specific. "I was talking to Ryan and Mel..."

"You were talking to Mel?"

"Onion! Shit!"

"Sorry, I just didn't think that..."

"...We're in the same class...What do you care anyway? I thought you were friends with her..."

"I am, I mean, it's complicated."

"...I was talking to Ryan about football and Mel was just standing there listening to us. Anyway, Summer walked up to Mel and asked her to come to her party. Since Ryan and I were standing there, she invited us too." *Summer invited Mel? I think everyone knows that Summer is gay, but Mel hasn't told anyone...But me...That I know of. Interesting. Very interesting.* "I didn't really care at the time, but now, I think we can use it to our advantage."

"Nice, Joe, real nice."

"It is...Wait, are you being sarcastic?"

"What gave it away?"

"You know, Onion, you can be a real bitch sometimes." I uncrossed my arms and smiled.

"I guess we're perfect for each other then."

"What does that mean?"

"And all this time I thought you were smart." *Dumb...Smart...Back to dumb.*

"...I'm not a bitch!" Joe yelled at me and I boisterously laughed in his face and started walking away. Joe grabbed my arm. "What's so funny?"

"Nothing, just drop it...And let go of my arm."

"Fine."

"I think we should go to the party."

"Really?" Joe smiled.

"I'll have to ask my parents and I don't know what they'll say. They'll probably want to talk to Summer's parents...Do you know if her parents are going to be there?"

"I have no idea. I hope not."

"If her parents aren't going to be there then I doubt they'll let me go."

"How are we supposed to fuck if her parents are there?" *We're not, Joe.*

"Is that all you ever think about?"

"Yes." *At least he's honest about it.*

"I don't know what else to tell you...I'll ask my parents tonight and see what they say."

"Fine. We have to do something about this though or..."

"Or what, Joe, you're gonna break up with me?"

"Well, I don't want to, but..." *What a jerk.* The bell rang and Joe attempted to give me a hug, but I pushed him away from me.

"I'll call you later."

"Onion, are you mad at me?" I looked into his troubled grey eyes. *Dense, much?*

"No, not at all...I'll call you tonight."

"Don't forget."

"I won't. You'll be the first person I call after I talk to my parents."

"Okay. Do you want me to walk you to class?"

"No, I'm good."

"Are you sure?"

"Bye, Joe," I said and smiled.

"Bye." Joe and I walked in separate directions to our classes. *Do I even want to go to that party? I do but I don't...At the same time. Oh well. I wonder if my parents are gonna be cool. Yeah, no. Should I have sex with Joe? I guess it could be worse...Even though I don't know how. Hmmm.*

I waited until after dinner that night to ask my parents about going to the Halloween party. I knew that my dad would say no before I even finished my sentence so I figured I would work on my mom first. She was starting the dishes when I walked up beside her and said in my softest, most child-like voice I could produce, "Hey, mom, do you think it would be all right to go to my friend's Halloween party next week?" She looked at me surprised like I was crazy to even ask.

"You're too young to go to parties."

"I'm too young to go to a Halloween party?"

"I know what goes on at those parties."

"What goes on at those parties?"

"Sex, drugs, and alcohol."

"It's not that kind of party," I insisted. *Maybe it is.*

"Sure, Hannah, and how do you know that?"

"Mom, it's Summer Braithwaite's party. I don't think..."

"Braithwaite? As in Dr. Braithwaite?"

"I don't know. Why?"

"Dr. Braithwaite is my boss."

"Is that a good thing or a bad thing?" *It must be a good thing...*

"Patrick!" My mom turned away from me and yelled. *Maybe not a good thing.* My dad walked into the kitchen.

"What's up?" My dad asked nonchalantly.

"Your daughter wants to go to a Halloween party next week."

"No," my dad said without thinking.

"Dad, that's always your answer," I said. "Don't you at least want to hear..."

"No," he reiterated.

"Patrick, I think we should let her go," my mom said. *Where did that come from?* I smiled.

"Yeah, dad, mom says it's okay."

"She's too young to go to parties."

"Yeah, that's what I said too, but then I thought about it. I was her age when I went to my first party," my mom said.

"That was a different time," my dad countered.

"Was it really that different, Patrick?"

"Yeah, there are all kinds of crazy..." My dad said and then paused. "...She could get raped, you know, anything could...I'm not going to let that happen."

"Dad, I'm not going to get raped at a Halloween party, sheesh..."

"Patrick, I think you're overreacting..."

"I am not! I watch the news."

"Yeah, you do watch a lot of news," my mom said and laughed.

"Seriously, Stacy, it's not safe out there. It's my job to protect this family and that's what I'm going to do." My mom put her hand on my dad's shoulder.

"My knight in shining armor." My mom smiled and I laughed.

"Okay, make fun of a man that wants to protect his family," my dad said.

"Oh, don't be like that, Patrick. I find it endearing that you are the man that you are, but you, we, need to have some flexibility." My mom wrapped her arms around my dad and whispered something into his ear. *What is she telling him? It's probably something gross.* My dad smiled and then looked at me.

"Hannah, who's going to take your brother trick-or-treating this year?" My dad asked.

"Michael can take himself trick-or-treating. He has friends," I reasoned. "He's not a baby anymore."

"Patrick, I'm going to call Dr. Braithwaite later and if he's going to be chaperoning the party, I say we let her go."

"I don't know..."

"Dr. Braithwaite is a good guy. I didn't even know he had a daughter, but I'm sure that he's a good father too," my mom said.

"...Okay, call him and get the details. If he's going to be there then she can go," my dad reluctantly said. *Nice work, mom.*

"Awesome, thanks, dad," I said enthusiastically and gave him a hug.

"Don't thank me just yet...your mom needs to..."

"I know, I know." *I've been standing here the entire time...* "Can I call Mel?"

"Mel? Is she going to be at the party?" My mom asked.

"Yeah...Mom, trust me, she's not thinking about me like that anymore." *Oh shit...*

"What does that mean?" My dad asked and then turned to my mom.

"Mel's gay," my mom answered.

"MOM!" *I told you not to say anything!*

"What do you mean Mel's gay? She's just a kid. How does she even know what she is? That doesn't make any sense," my dad reasoned. *I just had to open my big, stupid mouth...*

"Well, she seemed to have a crush on Hannah..."

"MOM! SERIOUSLY?"

"What is happening with these kids?" My dad inquired while shaking his head.

"Nothing is happening," I said.

"At least she can't get you pregnant," my dad said and laughed.

"That's not funny, dad."

"Yes, it is. It's a relief, actually."

"It doesn't matter. She doesn't like me like that anymore."

"How do you know that? My mom asked. *Dammit.* My dad looked on with curious eyes as they both waited for an answer.

"...I think she's into Summer now. *Why do I keep talking?*

"Summer...So, is Summer gay?" My mom asked. *Too late now...*

"Yes, mom, Summer's gay...But I shouldn't have said anything. It's not my business." *Shit.* "Please don't say anything to anyone...Especially her parents. *I am in such deep shit.*

"Do all of these kids think that they're gay now? What is going to happen to us as a species if everyone thinks they're gay? Christ!" My dad barked and then walked away from us.

"What's wrong with him? I didn't know dad was homophobic." My mom laughed.

"That's not exactly the right word...Your dad's not afraid of them, per se, he just doesn't think homosexuality exists. He thinks it's a mental disorder."

"Hmmm, what do you think?"

"I think it's complicated...Go call your friend, Hannah, I need to finish the dishes." I got the phone off of the counter and walked down the hallway into my room. I shut the door and dialed Melissa's number. The phone rang a few times before Melissa's mom picked up the phone.

"Hello?"

"Hi, is Mel there?" I asked with enthusiasm.

"Hi, Hannah, yeah, just a minute..." Melissa's mom said. "It's Hannah, Mel, make it quick."

"Hey," Melissa said, "what's up?"

"I just called to see how you were doing. We haven't really talked much lately."

"Yeah, you're always with Joe now."

"Yeah, I know, I'm sorry Mel, I never wanted it to be like this."

"I knew it would be like this. That's what boys do."

"So, are you okay? I mean, well, I don't want it to sound like you're not okay, or you weren't okay..."

"I'm fine, Hannah, I'm over it." *Over what? Me?*

"...So, are you going to Summer's Halloween party?"

"Yeah, how did you know about that?"

"It's a small school, Mel," I said and then laughed.

"Yeah, I guess so...I guess a lot of people are going to be there huh?" Melissa tentatively asked.

"Yeah, Joe wants me to go with him."

"...Are you going to go?"

"I don't know yet. My mom wants to call Summer's parents to make sure they're going to be there. It's so lame."

"Yeah, they're going to be there."

"How do you know?"

"Summer told me."

"So, are you guys best friends now?"

"I think she likes me, you know, like I liked you."

"That's awesome! Wait, do you like her like that?"

"...Maybe, I don't know." *Okay, Mel, how many lesbian girls are there?*

"I think you should go for it. Summer's cute."

"She's all right...She's not exactly my type, though." *Yeah, she is! She's exactly your type.*

"What's your type then?" *That was a stupid question...*

"Do I have to say it?" Mel asked and sounded defeated.

"No, I get it..." *Your type is someone who's not gay. Makes total sense.* I laughed but then quickly caught myself. *Oh, shit.*

"What's so funny, Hannah?"

"Oh, nothing...I just think you should give her a chance."

"And that's funny?" *Great, Hannah, dig yourself out of this one...What should I say?"*

"...I just think it's ironic..."

"What's ironic?"

"That you're struggling with being gay and Summer is gay...everyone knows that..."

"I'm not struggling with being gay," Melissa whispered. "I'm struggling with telling other people."

"Yeah, that's what I meant. Summer doesn't seem to care who knows she's gay."

"Yeah, that's true. She even told her parents...And they support her."

"That's really good, Mel."

"But my parents would kill me, literally."

"I think Summer would be good for you. You'd make a cute couple."

"Hannah, you just don't understand. I love you for being so accepting of other people, but most people aren't like you. I know you've heard what people say about her. I don't think I could deal with that scrutiny."

"That's why she would be so good for you. She doesn't care what anyone thinks and neither should you."

"It's not that easy, Hannah, you just don't know what it's like and you never will."

"Okay, that's probably true, but I know Summer does."

"Yeah, she does...Maybe I could...Maybe I should give her a chance."

"You should."

"I know we don't really talk much anymore, but maybe we could hang out sometime."

"Yeah, of course, Mel, I miss you."

"I miss you too, Hannah...So, how are you? I forgot to even ask. How's Joe?" I laughed.

"Joe's still an asshole." Mel laughed.

"I know he's easy on the eyes, Hannah, but you're so much better than him in every way."

"I know, but he has a sweet side sometimes too...and besides, who else am I supposed to be with?" *Can I get through one conversation without putting my foot in my mouth?*

"...I don't know. You're just such a nice person and you're so positive and optimistic...the exact opposite of Joe."

"Opposites attract, right?"

"Maybe, but Joe is a different species of human so I don't think that counts." Melissa and I both laughed.

"He's pressuring me to have sex."

"Are you going to do it?"

"I don't know. I'm going to have to do it eventually, right?"

"I don't know, Hannah, do you even want to have sex with Joe?"

"Not really." Mel laughed. "I do want to know what it feels like to have sex, but Joe, yeah, I'm not so sure...At least he has experience, right?"

"That's true. Molly told me stories."

"Oh yeah, like what?"

"Just like stuff like how aggressive he was and oh yeah, she told me one time they were in the bathroom and she was on her period...And he wanted to do it anyway...So there was blood everywhere."

"Gross."

"Yeah..."

"And they never got caught? It's almost unbelievable."

"I guess the principal and the teachers just assume it would never happen...And nobody thinks about it."

"Yeah, wow, I wonder if anyone else is using the bathrooms for...Recreational purposes?" Melissa and I laughed again.

"I don't know of anyone else, but yeah, they most likely do. It's not like they would want to share that information. Not everyone is like Joe."

"Yeah, what a dick."

"Speaking of his dick. If you do have sex with him, make sure he wears a condom. You don't know where that dirty dick has been."

"That's good advice, Mel."

"Better advice would be to not do it at all, but I'm not stupid either. I know you, Hannah, and when you have your mind made up..."

"That's true. No one tells me what to do...So, he wants to do it at the party."

"At Summer's house? That's a really bad idea. You'll get caught."

"I know, which means it's not going to happen. Joe can continue complaining about his balls being blue." Melissa let out a riotous laugh.

"...That's so funny. He used to say the same shit to Molly all the time. He's so predictable."

"Sometimes he can be really smart...But sometimes I think I'm with the dumbest person alive. It's really weird." Melissa laughed.

"It's been good catching up, Hannah, but I gotta go eat something."

"Okay, yeah, so if I don't get a chance to talk to you at school, I guess I'll see you at the party."

"Yeah, I'll be there early, around seven, to help Summer. It's supposed to start around eight, though."

"Okay, I'll see you there...Oh wait, what are you dressing up as?"

"A sexy pirate."

"Nice. My parents wouldn't even let me out of the house like that."

"Mine either, which is why I'm getting dressed at Summer's house."

"That's smart."

"What are you going as?"

"I haven't decided yet, but I've got the week to figure it out...It sounds like it's going to be a lot of fun."

"Yup, but, hey, I really have to go."

"Okay, Mel, I'll talk to you later."

"Bye, Hannah."

"Bye." I hung up the phone and then headed back out to the kitchen to share the good news with my mom. "Summer's parents are going to be home for the Halloween party."

"Are they now?"

"Yeah, Mel just told me."

"I'm not saying that I don't believe you, but I'm going to call anyway."

"Okay...So, when are you going to call?"

"Hannah, I'll call after I finish the dishes, now leave me alone."

"Sorry, I didn't mean to sound pushy, I just want to call Mel back." My mom didn't say anything. "I'll be in my room." *Still nothing.* I turned around and walked back to my room and saw that I had left the phone on my bed. *How is she going to call without the phone?* I took the phone back to the kitchen and then went back to my room. I sat on my bed and then opened my backpack. *Maybe I should do my homework...* Before I had the chance to further contemplate my academic choices, my brother barged into my room.

"Hannnnnnnahhhh!"

"Ugh, what do you want, Michael?"

"Nothing." *Well, that sounds about right.*

"Then go away, I need to do my homework."

"I'm already done with my homework."

"That's great, Michael, but I'm not."

"Are you taking me trick-or-treating this year?"

"No, I'm going to a party."

"But we always go trick-or-treating together."

"Not this year...Actually, Michael, you're old enough to go alone, you know, with your friends."

"I'm too old for that stuff anyway."

"No, you're not."

"Yes, Michael, I am. I'm not going with you."

"I'm gonna tell mom."

"She already knows."

"She does?"

"Yes."

"I'm gonna tell mom anyway."

"Knock yourself out."

"What?"

"Go for it."

"Mooooooooooom!" My brother yelled as he stormed out of my room. I got up from my bed and shut the door. I took my binder out of my backpack and started doing my math homework. *Why is this even a thing?* About thirty minutes later my mom walked into my room.

"I called Dr. Braithwaite and he said that he and his wife are going to be chaperoning the party."

"So..."

"So, you can go to the party." *Yes!* I smiled as wide as I could without opening my mouth. *Don't be too obvious.* "You know, Michael's pretty upset that you're not going to take him trick-or-treating."

"I know, mom, but he needs to grow up sometime, right?"

"Yeah, he's just so immature. I worry about him."

"He'll be fine," I assured her. *I think.* "Can we go look at costumes this weekend?"

"Yeah, I'll take you to get a costume...On second thought, you could just wear that pink dress from last year..." *Ugh, no.*

"Mom, I need a new costume, and that dress is way too...it's just too much."

"Too much what? You liked it last year." *Too much dress!*

"I don't know. I just want something more grown up."

"Oh, I see...I think I understand."

"Wait, you do?"

"Yes, I was your age once too, remember?" I smiled.

"No, I actually don't."

"Okay, smart ass, what I mean is that you want something that shows off a little more skin." *Oh shit, she does get it!* "But, there's a fine line..."

"...I know mom," I interjected.

"Because your dad won't let you out of this house if it's too revealing."

"I get it. No prostitute costumes..."

"They sell prostitute costumes?"

"Maybe...I wouldn't know."

"Okay, Hannah, don't you have homework to do?"

"Yeah, I should...Wait, can I call Mel really quick?"

"Yeah, but make it fast."

"I will, mom, and...Thanks." My mom smiled and I grabbed the phone off of the counter and went to my room. After shutting the door, I dialed Joe's number. He answered after the first ring.

"Hello?"

"Hey, it's me."

"Oh hey, Onion, what's up?"

"I can go to the party."

"Oh, thank God, I've been thinking about tapping that ass for as long as I can remember." *Which isn't very long...*

"You're not going anywhere near my ass!"

"You know what I mean...My dick, your pussy...You know."

"Summer's parents are going to be home."

"Shit. God damn shit!" I laughed.

"It's not funny. We'll figure it out. There has to be a way. They have a big-ass house. I'm sure we could get lost in there somewhere."

"How do you know how big her house is?"

"I heard that she had a big house." *Right...*

"You heard that she had a big house?"

"Yeah."

"From whom?"

"Fuck, Hannah, what's with the twenty questions?"

"I was just wondering...you seem to have first-hand knowledge."

"What's that supposed to mean? Summer's a fucking dyke..."

"Don't talk about her like that! You're such an asshole, Joe."

"Anyway...I don't think she would fuck me if I wanted to, which I don't, by the way."

"Anyway..." I said, mocking Joe. "...I don't think it's going to happen, Joe, you know, fucking."

"Shit...Fuck that. It's happening, Onion!"

"Do you even have a condom?"

"Yeah."

"Where'd you get it?"

"From my dad."

"Why does your dad have condoms?"

"I don't fucking know!" *He's so full of shit.*

"Well, I gotta go, Joe, I'll see you at school tomorrow."

"We just got on the phone and now you have to go? I'm not done talking to you about..."

"...My mom wants me off the phone, sorry, Joe," I interrupted him and then hung up the phone. *I wonder if he ever thinks about anything else. How does he even pass his classes? I need to think about my Halloween costume...*

Chapter Seven

Halloween

W e pulled up to Summer's house just before eight-thirty. It was dark outside, but her house was lit up like it was a Halloween carnival. *This is crazy. Joe was right... This house is huge.* I admired all of the orange lights, pumpkins, and over-sized skeletons as we came to a stop at the end of the sprawling driveway. *This is the kind of house where they give out the full-size candy bars.* My mom stopped the car behind a line of other cars. "It must be nice to be rich," I said as I looked over at my mom who had a somewhat sad look on her face.

"Dr. Braithwaite is one of the only doctors in town. They have to pay him well." My mom started to open the door and I immediately grabbed her arm.

"What are you doing?"

"I'm going to go talk to Tom and his wife, I think her name is Autumn." *Autumn and Summer. Heh. Wait...*

"Mom, please! That's so embarrassing. It's fine." My mom didn't say anything for a minute, but then shut the door. "Thank you, oh my god! You scared me there." She smiled and then sighed.

"I remember what it was like..." My mom said and then stared off into the distance as if she were reminiscing about something.

"Well...I'm gonna go to the party, mom, I'll call you when I need a ride." I opened the door and then stepped gingerly onto the driveway in my costume slippers.

"...Okay, have a good time, and go easy on the candy tonight..."

"Ummm, yeah..."

"You'll thank me when you're older..."

"I get it, mom, thanks." *Don't get fat...*

"And this goes without saying," *And yet, you're going to say it...* "No drinking and no drugs."

"Mom, I know, and Summer's parents are here. It's not like they're gonna let a bunch of teenagers get drunk and destroy their house."

"I know...But, still. I wouldn't be a very good mom if I didn't say something. We've talked about this before. Girls get drunk and guys..."

"MOM!"

"Okay, okay, I'll let you go. Have fun, but not too much fun..." *What does that even mean?*

"Okay, bye, mom." I shut the door and then made my way to Summer's front door. I passed by her three-car garage. Each individual door was painted a dark burgundy red and was ornately adorned with black fixtures. My mom drove by and I waved good-bye. I stopped at a little gate that led to the front of the house. I looked up at the second and then the third floor. *It's like a castle.*

"Hannah, is that you?" Startled, I looked back down and Summer was standing in front of me on the other side of the gate.

"Yeah, hi Summer, thanks for the invite, you look awesome." Summer was dressed as a Marine. She already had really short hair, but even that was hidden underneath her white hat with a black brim. "It looks like a real uniform."

"Thanks, Hannah, you look as sexy as ever...Princess Jasmine, is it?"

"Yeah." I looked down at my bare stomach. "This is the most skin my mom was willing to pay for." We both laughed.

"The black wig kind of threw me off."

"Yeah, it's different, but I kind of like it."

"Yeah, it's cool...So, you wanna come in? A bunch of people are already here."

"Yeah. Is Mel here?"

"Yeah, she was the first one here." Summer opened the gate and then gestured her hand toward the front door.

"You have a really nice house, Summer."

"Thanks. You know, Joe said the same thing."

"Joe's here?"

"Yeah..." *Of course...* "...He was asking about when you were going to get here. That's why I came outside...kinda spooky."

"Yeah, it really is. So, your parents are here, right?"

"Yeah, but they'll leave us alone."

"Okay, that's cool." Summer opened her front door and let me inside. Salt-N-Peppa's 'Shoop' was playing in the background. *Cool!* Summer shut the door behind us.

"Come on, Hannah, everyone is out back." I followed Summer through her living room and into her kitchen. Mrs. Braithwaite was sitting down at the edge of the kitchen island. "Mom, this is Hannah."

"You're beautiful," her mom said to me.

"Thanks, Mrs. Braithwaite."

"Call me Autumn, dear."

"Okay, mom, we're gonna go outside now." Summer's mom poured herself a glass of wine. I waved at her as Summer grabbed my free hand and pulled me toward her back door.

"Your mom seems cool," I said.

"Yeah, she's cool. A little too cool." *Huh?*

"What do you mean?"

"She's a raging alcoholic," Summer whispered. "Maybe not raging...More like a drink-till-you-pass-out kind of alcoholic.

"That's not good. She seems so nice."

"That's why she's so nice."

"What about your dad?"

"My dad? I've never seen him drink...He's always at work. Actually, I hardly ever see him." *That's kind of sad, Summer.*

"By the way, where is your dad?"

"I think he's in his office upstairs, why?"

"No reason, just wondering..."

"Anyway, wait till you see Joe and Ryan's 'costumes.' Summer motioned her hands into air quotes and I laughed.

"Are they bad?"

"No, just stupid." *That sounds right.* Summer reached for the door knob and then opened the door. I followed her outside and was immediately struck by the overwhelming size of her backyard. *Oh my God! Her back yard is the size of our entire school!* I counted about twenty people from our class standing around a beautiful, sparkling pool. "Everyone's by the fire pit," Summer said and we walked over to a central fire pit surrounded by giant rocks and tall, manicured hedges. It was cold that night and as we approached the fire, I could feel the warmth engulf me. Joe, Ryan, Melissa, and another girl from our class named Randi were standing around the fire seemingly trying to stay warm. I walked up to Joe and laughed.

"You're dressed as a football player? Joe, you are a football player...You're supposed to dress up as something you're not," I said with a hint of cynicism.

"Onion? What's with the wig?" Joe responded.

"It's part of my costume...Princess Jasmine...duh," I said.

"I don't like you with black hair," Joe said in a serious tone.

"That's not the point, Joe, God..." I said.

"I think she looks as beautiful as ever," Melissa said.

"Thanks, Mel, so do you. You look hot," I said.

"Yes, she does," Summer said as she wrapped her hand around Melissa's hip.

"Gayeeee," Ryan quipped. *Oh, shut up!*

"That's right, Ryan, what of it?" Summer said.

"It's just wrong," Ryan answered.

"Yeah, seriously, how does that even work? It doesn't make sense," Joe added.

"You're too dumb to understand," Summer said. "No offense, Hannah; I know that..."

"No worries," I said. "You're right..." *Joe reminds me of my dad right now...that's not good. Homophobic...or whatever my mom says he is. Why am I even with him?* I looked at Joe with complete and utter disdain and hoped he would realize the error of his ways.

"Whatever, Onion, you know that shit doesn't make sense. What are they going to do rub their pussies together?" Joe asked and I immediately slapped him across his face. Ryan started laughing, and much to my surprise, Joe smiled. *There's definitely something wrong with him. But if that's true, and it is, then something is wrong with me because I'm with his stupid ass!*

"...It's okay, Hannah, I don't care what he says. I don't care what anyone says. Mel and I are together and it doesn't matter what anyone thinks about it." *Wow, that's awesome!*

"I'm really happy for you guys," I said.

"Thanks, Hannah," Summer responded.

"Yeah, thanks, Hannah, you're a really good friend," Melissa added. I smiled and then looked over at Randi. Randi was the shortest out of all of us and almost seemed like she was trying to hide in the shadows. She was dressed in a Tinker Bell costume and looked especially cold.

"Randi, I really like your costume," I said. Randi looked up at me quickly.

"...Ummm, thanks, Hannah," Randi said and then looked back down.

"Are you and Ryan a thing?" I asked.

"Oh, ummm, no, we're just hanging out, I guess..." Randi answered with haste.

"...Yeah, she's my girl," Ryan said.

"What? That's not true, you never even asked me out," Randi said, gaining some authority. We all laughed.

"Whatever, dude," Ryan said, defeated. Joe slapped the back of his head.

"Ask her right now, dip shit," Joe said. "Get on your hands and knees and beg her to be your girlfriend...right now. I want to see that shit." *What an asshole...*

"Ryan, you don't have to do that," I said.

"Yes, he does, Onion, he needs to man up or shut up," Joe asserted. *He does have a point...*

"All right...Ryan, I can't help you," I said. Ryan looked at me and then at everyone else. He had a look of terror on his face. I smiled but I held back the laughter that so desperately wanted to come out of me. Ryan took a deep breath and then got down on one knee in front of Randi.

"This is so embarrassing, but..." Ryan started to say but was interrupted by Summer's dad.

"Summer! Summer! Oh, there you are. What's going on out here? What are you doing down there?" Summer's dad asked and pointed to Ryan.

"Oh, nothing," Ryan said. And then under his breath after getting to his feet, "so embarrassing..."

"Anyway...Summer, I just got called into work. It's okay if your friends stay, but just keep it down. If you need anything..."

"We'll be fine dad," Summer said. "Mom's still here."

"Yeah...She is, okay, I have to go, I'll see you tomorrow. Bye kids." Summer's dad waved at us, turned around, and walked back into the house.

"Now the party can get started," Summer said. "My mom should be passed out drunk in an hour." *Does this happen often? Did she know that her dad wouldn't be here? Probably...*

"Yes!" Joe belted out triumphantly. *You're not getting any, Joe.*

"We just have to wait for my mom to go to 'sleep.'" Summer said while doing her air quotes thing again. "...And then we can move this party inside."

"Good, cause I'm starting to freeze my nuts off out here," Joe said. I smiled.

"That's okay, Joe, you won't need those tonight anyway," I said and then laughed.

"Wait, what?" Joe said, genuinely confused. We all laughed.

"Ryan, weren't you about to do something?" I asked.

"Thanks, Hannah," Ryan said and then looked around uncomfortably. "Fine, fuck it." Ryan got down on one knee in front of Randi and then quickly said, "Randi, will you go out with me?"

"Yeah, okay," Randi said. Ryan stood up and then gave Randi a hug.

"Awe, how cute," I said in an exaggerated voice.

"Fuck all of you," Ryan said and we laughed.

After some time and irreverent conversation, Summer decided to go into her house to check on her mom. Melissa went with her and left me alone with Joe, Ryan, and Randi. *I'm happy for her. She finally has someone that understands her.* I was sad though because that someone wasn't me. Ryan put his arm around Randi, who was starting to shiver in her almost non-existent outfit. I felt bad for Randi as I looked at the nefarious grin on Ryan's face. *She's so shy and he's such a douche.* I wasn't sure why I cared so much, but I did care. *She can do so much better...I can do so much better than...*Joe started to wrap his arm around me and I pulled away.

"...The fuck is wrong with you, Onion? It's cold. I was trying to be nice," Joe insisted.

"You don't even know the meaning of the word," I quickly answered back. Ryan and Randi stared at us in astonishment. The fire started going out and simmered down to light crackles and pops highlighted by diminished orange hues.

"I don't know what your problem is. I was just trying to keep you warm. The fire's almost out." *Yes, it is.*

"I can keep myself warm, thank you very much."

"What's your problem, Onion?"

"That's my problem. You're my problem!" I said, raising my voice.

"What are you talking about?"

"You can't even call me by my name."

"I thought that you were cool with it. I told you why I call you Onion."

"I'm not cool with it. Not anymore."

"Fine...HANNAH," Joe emphasized. "I'll call you by your name. Is that okay, HANNAH!?"

"Not if you're going to be sarcastic about it."

"So, I can't win, is that it?"

"Pretty much..."

"You can be a real bitch sometimes; you know that right?"

"Thank you."

"Fuck!" Joe said under his breath and then Summer and Melissa rejoined us.

"Is everything okay?" Summer asked. I looked down and saw Summer and Melissa holding hands. *What am I feeling right now? Am I Jealous?*

"Everything's good," I said. "Joe's just being Joe." Joe rolled his eyes and shook his head, but didn't say anything. "What's the matter, Joe, cat got your tongue?" *Ugh, I sound just like my mom.* Joe didn't say anything though, and looked around the group as if he didn't hear the question. *Hmmm, maybe he's learning after all...*

"My mom's asleep upstairs...She actually made it to bed on her own! She usually crashes on the couch...Anyway, let's move the party inside. You guys go ahead, I'm going to tell everyone else." I walked through Summer's back door and Joe pushed passed me and rushed toward the kitchen. Randi and Ryan followed me after Joe. I rounded the corner of the living room and watched as Joe rummaged through the cabinets.

"What are you doing, Joe?" I asked and then laughed.

"Looking for some alcohol, what do you think? Joe quickly replied.

"Shit, I'll help," Ryan said.

"You guys don't need to drink," Randi said quietly.

"Yeah, seriously, you're really going to get all drunk and stupid at..." I started to say.

"...I know her mom was drinking wine, but..." Joe interrupted me while opening some of the lower cabinets. "...I can't find anything. Shit. Ryan, did you find anything?"

"Nope."

"Shit, this party is whack," Joe said. *No, Joe, you're whack.* Joe stood up and looked around and then behind me. Summer came into the kitchen with Melissa still holding hands. Everyone else seemed to make themselves at home in the living room. "Yo, Summer, where's the alcohol?"

"My parents have wine and, I think, vodka in the basement."

"Oh shit, can we have some?" Joe asked. His eyes got really big like a dog waiting to fetch a tennis ball. I looked solemnly at Melissa and she looked at Summer and smiled. Summer squinted her eyes at joe and didn't say anything for a few seconds.

"Yeah, sure, it should be fine," Summer said. *This is not going to be good.* "My mom keeps it all in a cabinet next to the pool table." Summer pointed toward a door on the other side of the room. "It's downstairs and to the right. Get a couple of bottles and bring it back upstairs..." Summer paused once again and Joe started walking toward the door. "We can play spin-the-bottle and maybe..." Summer looked at Melissa longingly.

"...I'm on it. Ryan, let's go," Joe said and then disappeared with Ryan through the door to the basement.

"Summer, do you think it's a good idea to have people drinking? Especially Joe and Ryan..." I reasoned. I looked at Summer and then at Melissa. I looked at Randi and she was looking at the floor. No one said anything. "Really!? Summer...Aren't you worried that they'll break your parent's stuff or, I don't know, pee all over your house?" Everyone laughed. "I was being serious..."

"You worry too much, Hannah," Melissa said.

"Yeah, it'll be fine," Summer added.

"Randi, what do you think?" I asked. Randi slowly raised her head but avoided making eye contact with anyone directly. "Randi?"

"...I don't think we should," Randi said and then quickly looked back down as if she were anticipating severe backlash."

"It's okay, Randi, I'm not going to drink, so you'll have me," I said. Randi looked at me for a second and smiled slightly.

"Maybe I should just go home...I should call my parents," Randi said.

"You don't have to go home, Randi," Summer said. "It's okay if you don't drink."

"Yeah, Randi, you should stay, it'll be fine. You'll still have fun," Melissa insisted.

"...I don't know, you guys; I don't think any of us should be drinking. My parents would kill me if they knew..." Randi said.

"I think Randi's right," I said. "This is a bad idea."

"Hannah, please don't make a big deal out of this," Melissa said. *It is a big deal. I don't want to screw this up for her though.*

"I'm not...I mean, I'm not going to drink, but I guess, if other people want to drink, I'm not going to say anything."

"Thanks, Hannah," Melissa said and then smiled at Summer. Randi walked over to me.

"It might just be us, but that's cool," I said.

"Yeah, but what if Ryan...?" Randi asked and then hesitated.

"...Then I'll kick his ass," I said. Randi smiled while Summer and Melissa laughed.

"We got the hook up!" I heard Joe yell from the living room. *That's just great.* We walked out of the kitchen and saw Joe and Ryan both with a bottle of vodka in each hand. "This is the good shit!" Joe and Ryan put the bottles down on the coffee table in the middle of the room. I walked up to Joe while shaking my head.

"How do you even know what the good stuff is anyway?" I inquired.

"It's got a goose on it." Joe pointed at one of the bottles. "That means it's expensive."

"You're an idiot, Joe!"

"Why are you being such a bitch tonight? Do you have a clog in your tampon, or what?" Ryan laughed.

"I'm not even on my period," I said. *Wait...I could have used that...*

"That's a good thing..." Joe said and smiled. *No, just no.* "Hey, Summer, get some cups, or we could just pass the bottles around."

"No, we have cups, hold on," Summer said and walked back to the kitchen. Joe apparently couldn't wait though and picked up one of the bottles off the table and unscrewed the cap. He turned the bottle up in the air and started to drink.

"That was super smooth," Joe said and then started coughing. "Good shit." Joe passed the bottle to Ryan and he started drinking but then stopped abruptly.

"That shit is nasty. My throats on fire. Shit," Ryan whimpered. Joe laughed and took the bottle back.

"Don't be a bitch," Joe said. *I don't wanna be here.*

"I'm not...being...a bitch...my throat," Ryan said. I couldn't help but smile at Ryan's discomfort.

"That's what you get," I said. The words seemed to slip out of my mouth.

"It's your turn, Hannah. We'll see if you're talking shit then," Ryan asserted. Joe looked at me and then leaned the bottle in my direction. Summer came back from the kitchen with some cups in her hand.

"Guys, what the hell!? I told you I had cups!" Summer pleaded.

"I'm not going to drink, Joe, I said and put my hands on my hips as if to telegraph that I was standing my ground. I also heard my mom's voice in my head which was oddly reassuring.

"Yeah, I'm not drinking either," Randi added.

"Are you serious?" Joe asked. "That is so lame..."

"You're the one that's lame, Joe...I think I should go," I said and looked toward the kitchen.

"Yeah, me too," Randi said.

"Oh, come on you guys," Summer said. "Don't go. It's way too early to..."

"...No, let them go if they want to go," Melissa interjected.

"What!?" Joe and Ryan gasped. *Mel doesn't even care...*

"I'm gonna call my mom for a ride," I said and looked over at Randi who was nervously looking down at the floor. "I'm sure she could give you a ride home too if you want..."

"Ummm, yeah, thanks, Hannah," Randi muttered. I walked over to the phone and dialed my number. Joe hovered over me and stared at me with scornful intensity. I broke eye contact with him as soon as my mom picked up the phone.

"Mom, can you pick me up..."

"You want to come home?"

"Yeah."

"I feel like I just dropped you off. You don't want to stay a while?"

"No...I just want to come home...Oh, can you give Randi a ride home?"

"Who's Randi?"

"She's a friend."

"Oh, Randi's a girl?"

"Yes, mom...She wants to go home too."

"Is something wrong?"

"Nothing's wrong..."

"...Okay, I'll be there soon."

"Okay, bye." I hung up the phone and saw that Joe was still glaring at me. Everyone was glaring at me. "What's everyone staring at?" I pointedly asked.

"You fucking suck," Joe said and then walked away.

"I suck? Really? I suck because I don't want to be stupid and get drunk and stupid...and I know I just said that...I don't care though..." I was beginning to feel very anxious. There wasn't much of a reaction from anyone. "We're still in middle school. This is stupid." I pleaded with my unresponsive audience to no avail and then simply felt defeated. "I'll show myself out. Randi, are you coming? Randi..."

"No, Hannah, I think...I changed my mind. I'm going to stay."

"Fucking right!" Ryan exclaimed. *Oh, no, Randi...Well, It's just me then...*

"It's not too late, Hannah, you can call your mom back," Summer said. Melissa didn't say anything, but I could tell that she was indifferent to the prospect of me staying.

"It's okay. I need to go. This doesn't feel right. At least for me. You guys have fun." I walked toward the front door. No one followed me. I opened the door and then closed it softly behind me. I walked down the driveway and waited on the street for my mom to pick me up. About ten minutes later, I saw the dimly lit, square headlights of my mom's car creep up on me. I got inside of the car and my mom immediately started questioning me.

"Okay, Hannah, what's wrong?"

"Nothing. Can we just go? Please."

"Not until you tell me what's going on." *I can't tell her the truth....She would flip out...She'd probably go break up the party. Oh my God, so embarrassing. Maybe I should tell her...*I put my seat belt on and then looked over at my mom. *Maybe...It's...They shouldn't be drinking. Something bad could happen...I should tell her.* I slowly started to open my mouth.

"Well, I'm waiting..."

"...Mel and I had a fight." *Oh, awesome.*

"What happened?"

"I don't really want to talk about it." *I'm going to Hell. I'm definitely going to Hell.* I looked away from my mom and towards my feet. I was embarrassed about lying and even more embarrassed about the possibility of being embarrassed by my mom doing something about the party.

"Okay, let's go home. Maybe you'll want to talk to me about it later."

"...Yeah, maybe." My mom started driving us home.

"Mom?"

"Yeah."

"...Something's wrong...Well, maybe not wrong, but something's changed about Mel. She just seems so different lately."

"How so?"

"I don't know. Since..." *Shut up, Hannah!*

"Since..."

"I don't know, mom..."

"Well, people change. That's life."

"I guess so."

"You may have all new friends next year. *What?* I remember when I was your age..." *And here we go...* I rolled my eyes and then gazed outside of the passenger side window. "...Come to think of it, I don't remember any of my friends before high school. I remember all of my friends from high school. I'm still friends with a lot of them today." *Does this car go any faster?* "I'm going to ask your dad if he remembers anyone from before high school. That's weird now that I think about it. I should probably remember at least one person, don't you think? Anyway, what was I saying?"

"MOM!"

"Okay, okay, I get it. The point is that this problem that you're having with Mel...It seems like a big deal now, but you may not even remember it when you're my age."

"Yeah..."

"Everything will work itself out."

"I hope so."

"And if it doesn't, that's okay too." *I have a bad feeling that it won't.* "You feel better now?"

"Ummm, yeah, thanks." *No.* The rest of the drive home, my mom and I sat in relative silence, which was only interrupted by the subdued roar of the tires on the pavement. When we got home, my mom shut off the car and turned to me.

"Hannah, I've got to work early. I'm tired. Can you make sure that your brother gets to bed. He'd probably eat candy and play video games all night if he could." My mom laughed.

"Yeah, mom."

"You're a good girl, Hannah, I love you."

"...I love you too, mom." *Great. Now I feel even worse.* I unbuckled my seatbelt and stepped out of the car. I followed my mom into the house and saw my brother sitting on the floor, surrounded by candy, playing his Nintendo.

"Mom, that was spot on!" We both laughed and my brother glanced over at us and frowned, but that didn't stop him from continuing with his game.

"I'm gonna get ready for bed. Don't let him stay up too late, Hannah."

"I won't." My mom walked down the hall and into her room. I sat down on the couch and watched my brother play his game. I reached down and grabbed a couple of Starbursts off of the stack.

"Hey, those are mine!" My brother barked. I laughed.

"Sue me, Michael, you've got enough candy for your whole class!"

"Yeah, and it's mine!"

"Okay, stop crying. Play your game."

"Hmmm." My brother made a noise and then turned back to his game. I opened the first Starburst and put it in my mouth. *Damn! I forgot I hate the yellow ones! So sour.* I leaned back into the cushions and then pulled off my princess Jasmine Wig and set it down next to me. *That was a horrible Halloween. I hope Mel's okay. Oh shit, Joe! I forgot about Joe. I need to break up with his stupid ass. I should break up with him at school in front of everyone. No, that's mean. I should just call him tomorrow. I don't know...*

"Okay, Michael, you've got thirty minutes and then you're going to bed."

"Come on, Hannah, it's Halloween."

"I know what day it is. Mom said you need to go to bed."

"I didn't hear her say anything."

"She told me to tell you...Do you want me to go ask her again?"

"...No."

"All right, I'm gonna go take a shower. When I'm done, so are you...Okay?"

"Okay..." My brother responded and then made an audible groan. I walked to my room, got some fresh clothes, and then went into the bathroom. I stared at myself in the mirror before shedding my costume. *Did I do the right thing? If I did, then why do I feel so bad?* I stripped off my Princess Jasmine garb and then turned on the shower and let it run until steam filled the room. I stepped inside and embraced the warmth as my scattered mind was finally able to rest.

Chapter Eight

Despair

"**H**annah?"

"Yeah, it's me. Who's this?" I answered the phone and glanced over at the clock to see what time it was. The clock read 8:15. It was the morning after the Halloween party and I had just woken up. I held the phone up to my ear with my shoulder and poured milk over my bowl of Lucky Charms.

"It's Summer."

"Oh, hi, Summer...What happened last night?" I put the milk away and then went to grab a spoon from the dish rack.

"...That's why I called...Have you talked to Mel?" *I just woke up, why in the world would I have talked to anyone? It's only eight in the morning...*

"No, why? What's up?"

"Everyone was drinking and I don't even remember who suggested it, but we all ended up playing seven minutes in heaven. Randi and Ryan were the first to go into the closet. Oh my God, I don't even remember why they went in first, but that doesn't matter..." Summer said at a quickened pace, almost as if she was forgetting to breathe.

"Wait, slow down, Summer, take a breath," I said. I could sense that there was something wrong and dumped my cereal in the sink. I walked back into my room and shut the door. "What does this have to do with Mel?"

"After Ryan came out of the closet with Randi, he said it was my turn...so that meant me and Mel."

"Okay..." *I wasted my Lucky Charms for this...*

"Like I said, I had been drinking, everyone was drinking..." *I know, Summer, duh, that's why I left, remember?* "I shut the door and starting kissing Mel. And then I kissed her neck."

"Are you sure you want to be telling me this?"

"I took her bra off and then pulled her puffy pirate shirt off over her head. I kissed her chest...I got on my knees..."

"Summer! Really!?"

"...Ummm, sorry. I was drunk...I think I was drunk..."

"No, I mean, why are you telling me all this? It doesn't really, I don't know, seem like my business."

"Because...Okay, I'll just, well, I pulled her tights down and just as I got them around her ankles...Ryan opened the door and pointed at us and laughed. Joe laughed. Everyone laughed. Everyone was laughing and pointing. Ryan and Joe both said shit about us being gay. Mel was almost completely naked." Summer's delivery became panicked. "She...I...Was still on my knees. She pulled up her tights and grabbed her shirt off of the floor. She ran out of the house crying...I picked up her bra and watched Ryan and Joe laugh uncontrollably. I was furious with them, but it wasn't just them, it was everyone. I didn't care about them though...Mel. I was worried about Mel. I ran after her, but she was gone. I yelled after her. I yelled again and again and again. Nothing. She didn't say anything. Hannah, I don't know what to do. It's not like I can call her. She told me about her parents. I don't want her to get into trouble. I'm worried about her though."

"I'm sure that she's fine. She probably just walked home." *I hope that's what happened. I should have stayed...*

"You think so? That's pretty far, Hannah."

"Yeah, what else would she have done?"

"I don't know. I'm just worried. Hannah, why would she just run out like that? I know it was embarrassing, but..."

"I don't think she was ready to come out yet."

"But I don't get it...Everyone knew that we were together."

"Yeah, I'm not sure, Summer. You just have to give her some time. I'll call her right now to see how she is."

"So, you think she's home?"

"I do. I'll call you back if I get ahold of her."

"Hannah, there's something else..."

"What's up?"

"Joe hooked up with Jade last night."

"JADE!? That skanky bitch! Wait, you know what, she can have him, I'm done." *Damn, girl, you should have started with that.* "...What do you mean hooked up? No...Don't answer that, I don't care, it's over...Thanks for telling me."

"Yeah, I figured you would want to know even if..."

"Even if what?"

"Well, I thought for a minute that I shouldn't say anything because I thought that you already knew. Like I was being like a broken record or something. You know...That's just Joe being Joe." *Fuck.*

"No, I didn't know. Has he cheated on me before? Summer!?"

"...I don't know...I mean, I would guess that the answer to that question is yes, but I'm not sure."

"Has he ever hooked up with Jade before last night?" *I didn't even see her at the party...I guess she came after I left. I don't know, maybe she was there the whole time.*

"...I don't know."

"Summer, who invited Jade to your party?"

"...It was Joe. I'm sorry, Hannah, I thought you knew."

"And you thought that I was okay being Joe's main side piece?"

"I don't know what to say..."

"You don't have to say anything, Summer...It's not your fault. It's my fault. I just have to break up with his stupid ass." *I'm so glad I didn't have sex with him...*

"Yeah, so how are you gonna do it?"

"At school in front of everyone...tomorrow morning."

"Damn, Hannah, that's savage!"

"It's exactly what he deserves."

"Yeah, it is, but he is the most popular guy at school. That might not be the best idea, I mean, for you."

"Summer, I don't care what anyone thinks about me. I think that's something that we have in common."

"I think you're right about that," Summer said and laughed.

"I'm gonna call Mel now. I'll call you back."

"All right, talk to you soon."

"Bye." I hung up the phone and then paced back and forth in my room. I couldn't decide exactly what I wanted to do first. I wanted to call Joe and break up with him right then. I wanted it to be over. I also wanted him to suffer. *How dare he think that he can treat me this way! Mel, oh my God, I'm being so selfish. I want Joe to feel exactly like he made Mel feel. That's what has to happen.* I dialed Mel's number but no one answered. I hung up. *Oh no...* I dialed again. I let it ring a number of times. No one picked up. *What if she didn't make it home? What if she's lying in a ditch somewhere? What if she were raped?*

My mind raced and my heart sank. *This is all my fault.* I dialed her number again. No one answered. *What happened to her answering machine? What is going on?* I sat down on the edge of my bed and then put the phone down beside me. *Maybe I should wake my dad up? No...Wait for my mom to get home...That's too late. That's it!* I got up from my bed and then got dressed. I marched into my brother's room. "Michael...Michael..." I said, but my brother was completely unfazed and fast asleep in his candy-induced coma. *Great. I guess I'm not going to be able to ask him.* I walked outside of my house and picked up my brother's bike from the ground and started riding to Melissa's house.

I didn't like riding bikes. I didn't have a bike of my own even though my dad made sure that I learned how to ride when I was a kid 'just in case.' He was always thinking about possibilities and what could happen. *Why would I ride a bike when I could drive or be driven in a car?* It never made sense to me why someone would choose the slower, less-safe option. I was riding a bike though. I didn't want to but I had to so it turned out that my dad was right. I got to Melissa's house before I knew it and jumped off of the bike and ran to the front door. I rang the doorbell and knocked almost simultaneously. I waited for a few seconds but didn't hear anything. I knocked again and then hit the doorbell twice in quick succession. I waited again. I walked around to the front of the house and noticed that there weren't any cars in the driveway. *That's strange. Maybe they're at church. It is Sunday. Do they even go to church? I don't think Mel would be caught dead at church. Maybe her parent's made her go...She's never talked about it though.* I tried looking through the front window on the other side of the garage but the blinds were pulled tight and blocked my view. Out of desperation, I walked back to the front door and knocked again. I listened very carefully for any sound that would suggest that someone was home but I didn't hear anything. I felt defeated and helpless but I knew that I was wasting my time. I got back on my brother's bike and rode back home.

When I got home, I immediately grabbed the phone and went to my room. I shut the door behind me and dialed Summer's number. The phone rang once and Summer picked up. "Summer?"

"Yeah, Hannah, what happened? Did you get ahold of Mel?"

"No. No one answered the phone so I rode my brother's bike over to her house."

"You rode your brother's bike?"

"Yeah."

"Wow, I'm impressed."

"It's not a big deal."

"I think it's cool that you would do that. You're a good friend." *Mel's missing and it's all my fault. Yeah, great friend...*

"Anyway, there was no one home. We still don't know if Mel's all right and now her parents aren't even home. I don't know what to do."

"Yeah, I'm getting really worried." Summer sighed.

"Maybe we should, I don't know, call the police or something and file a missing persons report," I reasoned.

"Doesn't someone have to be missing for like at least twenty-four hours?"

"I don't know, but we have to do something!"

"I know, Hannah, but I'm not sure that...Oh hold on, I've got someone on the other line," Summer said and then put me on hold.

"Okay..."

"...Hey, Hannah, it's Mel on the other line!" *Oh, thank God.*

"So, what happened? Is she okay?"

"I think she's okay, but I'm gonna find out what happened right now. I'll call you back."

"Wait! Can't you do that thing where we can all be on the same call at the same time?"

"...I don't know how to do that...sorry, Hannah."

"It's okay, I'm just glad that Mel's okay. Call me back."

"Okay, bye."

"Bye," I said and ended the call. I put the phone down on my bed and then shook my head in disbelief. *What happened?* I walked around my room, pacing back and forth, waiting for Summer to call me back. A few minutes passed. *Is she going to call me back or what?* I opened my bedroom door and started heading down the hallway towards the kitchen when the phone rang. I ran back to my room and quickly answered the phone. "Hello?"

"Hi, it's me."

"So, what happened?" I asked and Summer paused.

"...Mel's in the hospital."

"WHAT!? Why? What happened?"

"I don't know if she wants me to tell you this, but..."

"SUMMER!"

"...Mel tried to commit suicide last night..." I couldn't believe what I was hearing and didn't have any words to express the sadness that I was feeling. I didn't say anything and Summer eventually continued. "...She told me that she didn't want to be alive anymore." *This is all my fault.* "Last night Mel ran all the way home and when she got there her parents interrogated her about what happened. She didn't want to say anything to them for obvious reasons. She wasn't ready to come out to her parents, but they pushed her and pushed her until she just couldn't hold it in any longer."

"So, she came out to her parents last night?"

"Yeah, and they were pissed. They yelled at her and denied that she could even be gay...that she was young and stupid and that she would get over it." *I promised her that I would be there for her when she came out to her parents. I wasn't there...* "She took a bunch of her mom's pain pills and then locked herself in her room."

"Oh my God! She's okay though, right?"

"Yeah, she's at the hospital though."

"The hospital? What hospital?" *Oh no, my mom...*

"Are you okay, Hannah? We only have one hospital..."

"...Ummm, yeah, I know, it's just that my mom works there and, this is not good."

"What do you mean?"

"She's going to ask questions about what happened last night. I know my mom."

"Well, what's the worst that can happen?"

"I don't know..."

"Well, hey, I'm gonna have my mom drive me to the hospital right now." *If she's awake...That's not nice.* "Do you want us to pick you up?" *Ummm, no, I don't really want to deal with my mom right now.*

"Ummm, I don't know..."

"I know Mel would want you to be there." *I don't think that's true...*

"Did she say that?"

"Well, no, but you're her best friend..."

"...Okay, I'll go." Summer asked for my address and I reluctantly gave it to her. She told me that they would be at my house in twenty minutes. I didn't know what I was going to say to Mel. *I should have been there for her. I should never have left the party.* I sat down on the edge of my bed and stared at the phone lying still in my lifeless hand. I grew impatient and went outside to wait for Summer.

Twenty minutes later, a silver Mercedes SUV pulled up to the curb in front of my house. The passenger window rolled down. It was Summer. "Hannah! Hi!" Summer waved frantically and then motioned for me to come over to her. *This is not a good idea.* "Are you coming or what?" I stood at the top of my driveway and took a deep breath. *I should just turn around and run back inside.* "Hannah!?"

"Yeah," I said and slowly walked toward the car. I opened the back door and got inside.

"What's your deal, Hannah? We don't have all day!"

"We don't?" Summer turned and looked at me.

"Are you being sarcastic?"

"No."

"Someone's in a bad mood..." *Wow, how is she not taking this seriously?*

"I'm not in a bad mood, I'm just worried about Mel."

"So am I, but she's fine." *She's not fine if she tried to kill herself. Oh my God!* Summer turned back around.

"Ummm, mom, were you going to go or were we just going to sit here and grow roots," Summer argued.

"I was just watching you two...It reminded me of when I was your age," Summer's mom responded and then started driving. She looked back at me through the rearview mirror. "How are you doing, Hannah?"

"I'm doing okay, Mrs. Braithwaite."

"Please call me Autumn, the whole 'Mrs.' thing makes me sound old." *You are old...*

"Okay, Autumn."

"Hannah, I want to talk to you about last night..." *That's funny.* I didn't say anything. I didn't know what to say.

"...I should have been...I know I shouldn't have been drinking. Maybe if I was...Mel wouldn't have..."

"Mom, it's not like you were going to do anything anyway," Summer said cutting her off. *This is really awkward.*

"It's not your fault, Autumn, it was Joe and Ryan," I said hoping to break the tension.

"Yeah, exactly," Summer quickly added. An uncomfortable silence followed.

"...I know that your mom works at the hospital and Summer tells me that you left early..." *What are you trying to say? Just say it!* Summer's mom trailed off and then sighed. "...You didn't tell your mom that I was passed out did you?" She continued to look at me through the rearview mirror. "...Because if she told Tom...I don't even want to think about it...Look, Hannah..." Her voice grew more stern with a seriousness that I didn't expect. *Scary, much?* "You didn't say anything did you? It would just cause unnecessary problems..."

"...No, I didn't say anything."

"Oh, thank God," Summer's mom whispered. "Well, what did you tell her then?" I panicked. I was not expecting a follow-up question.

"Ummm, I told her that...I got in a fight with Joe and had to leave the party." *I am such a liar and a terrible liar at that. What is wrong with me?*

"That's pretty good," Summer said. "And, it kind of did happen, right? You didn't even lie." *Yeah, except I didn't say that.*

"It's okay, girls, everything's going to be fine."

"Thanks, mom."

"For what, dear?"

"For saying the obvious part out loud," Summer said.

"You don't have to be such a bitch," her mom responded. *If I talked to my mom like that, I'd catch a serious beating. Wow.*

"...I know," Summer said and then they both laughed. *This is a seriously fucked up family. Maybe I could jump out of the car and escape at the next light.* As I was contemplating my imminent liberation, I looked out the window and realized that we were already at the hospital. *Hmmm, great. Oh well.* Summer's mom parked the car about as far away from the entrance as she could.

"All right, girls, I'm going to wait in the car." *Of course you are.* "Take as long as you need. I'll be here." Summer and I both opened our doors without saying anything and then closed them behind us. Summer grabbed my hand.

"It's going to be okay, Hannah, relax."

"I know, it's just that..." *Everything about this is wrong.* "It's nothing, let's go." Summer and I walked, still holding hands, towards the entrance to the hospital. *I really hope my mom is busy doing...anything.* I wasn't that lucky though because as soon as Summer and I stepped into the hospital, I saw my mom at the reception desk. I dropped Summer's hand and hoped that my mom wouldn't notice me.

"What's wrong?" Summer said and gave me a funny look.

"It's my mom. She's right over there." Summer started to turn around but I grabbed her shoulder. "Don't look."

"What else am I supposed to do?"

"I don't know, shit, never mind, she saw me."

"Hannah, get over here!" My mom insisted.

"Hey, I'm gonna go find Mel," Summer said.

"Okay, I'll catch up with you," I said and then turned towards my mom. Summer walked away from me and down the hall in the opposite direction. *I am so dead.* I slowly walked over to the reception desk. "I know you're probably wondering what I'm doing here..."

"I'm not. I know why you're here. Your friend, Mel." *Shit, she knows! This is not good. What am I supposed to say?*

"I wanted to see if she was all right, you know?" My mom crossed her arms and stared at me as if she expected me to confess something.

"What happened last night? Don't lie to me either," my mom said very quietly, which scared me more than when she yelled. I stood silent. I didn't have a good lie ready. My mom walked very close to me and uncrossed her arms. "We had to pump Mel's stomach." *What does that mean?* "She could have died." *I know.* "And you still don't want to talk?" *No.* "Who are you covering for?" *Everyone.* "Did Summer have something to do with this?" *You don't want to know the truth.* "Dr. Braithwaite is in Surgery right now, but when he gets out…"

"Mom! Stop!" I understood the implications. *Dr. Braithwaite left the party. He left his drunk wife with us. He's my mom's boss. Oh my God…*

"Hannah, you are going to tell me what happened so help me God!" I searched my mind for a plausible lie. *Maybe it was an accident. I could say…What am I thinking? You don't accidentally try to kill yourself. I've got nothing.* "One way or the other, I'm going to find out what happened." *Maybe it's better if I just tell her. Maybe…*

"…Mom, can I go see Mel now?"

"Her parents are with her. They're not saying much either…"

"What did they say?"

"They said it was an accident." *Hmmm. Wait…* "But swallowing a handful of hydrocodone is not an accident." *Yeah…* "Hannah, why did Mel try to kill herself?"

"MOM!"

"Does this have to do with her sexuality?"

"MOM, seriously!"

"That answers that question." *Wait a minute. How does she do that?* "I'm going to take you home now."

"What!? No, I have to see Mel first."

"No, you don't," my mom said and walked behind the reception desk. "You wait right here. I'm going to get my purse from the back."

"You can't just leave work, right?"

"To take you home, yes, I can. Wait here." *Yeah right, not gonna happen.* My mom walked down a short hallway and then opened a door. Before she walked in, she gave me one last stern look. I immediately turned around and walked down the hall that Summer went down. *Where am I even going? How am I supposed to find her?* I cautiously checked each room as I walked down the hall. I looked left and then right. I repeated this seemingly futile process over and over again. *I'm starting to look like a creeper. Where is she?* Most of the people that I saw were old and dying. *Why is Mel even here? This is my fault…* I was about to give up my search and return to my mom's scornful embrace when I heard what I knew to be Melissa's dad's booming, authoritarian voice.

"You weren't raised this way, Melissa, I am so disappointed in you," Melissa's dad said. I stood outside of the room.

"And what about my grandkids?" Melissa's mom added. *They are so terrible. I need to stop them.*

"Grandkids?" Melissa's dad inquired accusingly. "What about Hell? This girl is going to Hell. This is against God's will..." *Okay, I've had enough.* I walked into the room and saw Melissa lying in bed with tubes coming out of her arm. She looked exhausted. To her right were both of her parents and to her left was Summer.

"JUST STOP!" I yelled. "Leave her alone. She's your daughter. What's wrong with you?" Summer gave me an affirmative glance and then reached for Melissa's hand. Melissa's parents stared at me in shock, but as soon as Summer's hand touched Melissa's, her dad lunged across Melissa's body and knocked Summer's hand away.

"Don't touch her," Melissa's dad barked. He seemed to quickly realize the mistake he made and backed away. He looked at Melissa's mom who returned a look of horror.

"Now you're assaulting minors?" I quipped. "I think you should go." Melissa's dad stared at me with disdain.

"Let's give them some time," Melissa's dad said. He walked right by me without saying another word and then out of the room. Her mom followed without making eye contact with me. *I can't believe so much has changed so quickly. I thought that her parents were good people.* I walked over to Melissa and held her left hand. Summer held her right hand. I started tapping on her hand trying to find the right words. *Why did you try to kill yourself? Who cares what your parents think? I love you, Mel, it's going to be all right.* I looked into Melissa's eyes and I saw something that I had not seen before. I saw someone that had given up hope.

"It's going to be okay," Summer said. Melissa's eyes slowly turned to Summer. Melissa didn't smile. She was like a different person. *Oh my God. What's wrong, Mel?*

"...No, it's not," Melissa said coldly. The tone and delivery of those words gave me chills. I felt the goosebumps rise on my arms and the hair stand up on the back of my neck. "They say I'm bi-polar...They say I've got mental health issues...They want to send me to another school...A private school...Where they can...keep an eye on me."

"We're not going to let that happen, Mel, there's nothing wrong with you," I said. "Summer and I will fight for you, right Summer?" Summer nodded her head in agreement.

"Of course," Summer said and then added, "my parents have a really good lawyer."

"There's nothing anyone can do," Melissa said abruptly. "I'm the property of my parents." Summer and I uneasily stared at each other not saying a word. We knew that Melissa was right. "But one thing is for sure..." Melissa paused and then looked toward the door. "...They aren't going to get away with any of it," Melissa whispered. *What does that mean?*

"Mel, when are they going to let you out of here?" I said. Melissa looked at me as if she were confused by the question.

"I don't know, Hannah, maybe never."

"They can't keep you here forever," Summer said.

"...They can always keep me somewhere forever."

"Your parents have to be reasonable, I mean, right?" I asked. Melissa shook her head and then once again fixed her eyes on the doorway behind us. I turned my head to look and saw my mom standing there looking like the warden at a prison. *Oh shit.*

"Let's go, Hannah," my mom said. "...And you're grounded." Melissa squeezed my hand.

"I'll always love you, Hannah." *That sounds way too final.* I smiled.

"I love you too, Mel...Ummm, I'll see you at school..."

"I don't know, Hannah, I don't know." *I have to do something. I have to say something to someone. Someone has to be able to help...*

"Hannah, let's go!" My mom instructed. "Do I have to call your dad?"

"Shit," I whispered.

"It's okay, I'm gonna stay with her," Summer said. I smiled and then let go of Melissa's hand.

"I'll see you soon, okay?" Melissa solemnly looked down. "Mel?"

"...I hope so," Mel said. *I feel like crying.* I turned around and walked around my mom. My mom followed me down the hall. We walked into the waiting room where Melissa's parents were standing by the reception desk. They didn't say anything to me at first, but I couldn't leave without saying something.

"You can't control her life," I said.

"You need to stay away from her," Melissa's dad quickly responded.

"Hannah, don't say another word," my mom said and grabbed my arm. She practically dragged me out of the hospital.

"Mom, stop, you're hurting my arm."

"Good."

"No, it's not good, it's child abuse."

"If you want to act like a child then I'm going to treat you like a child." *Seriously?*

"How is supporting my friend acting like a child?" My mom let go of my arm.

"There are some things you just don't understand."

"About what?"

"Life."

"What about life?"

"That it's not fair and that you have to deal with it."

"But mom, Mel's parents are terrible people, they want to..."

"That's not for you to decide." *Yes, it is!*

"You don't understand..."

"Then help me understand. What happened at that party?" My mom and I stopped walking when we got to the back of the car. "Hannah, you are going to tell me what happened!" *No, I'm not.*

" "
...

"...Fine, get in the car."

Chapter Nine

Angst

T he next day, my mom took me to school. My dad was working overtime and he wasn't home. We didn't say a word to one another during our short ride together. She was mad at me for not telling her what happened at the Halloween party and I was mad at her for making me leave Melissa's side. When we pulled up to the front of the school, my mom slowly turned her head and looked in my direction but didn't make eye contact with me. "Your dad will pick you up after school. Remember, you're grounded. No phone when you get home." I didn't say anything and she finally looked me in the eyes. "Hannah, did you hear what I said?" *Yes, duh, I'm sitting right here...* "Hannah, where's your head at?" *...On my shoulders.*

"I've just got a lot on my mind." *Mel...Shit, Joe...Jade. I need to break up with Joe.* My mom continued to stare me down. "Yes, mom, I got it, no phone." My mom looked away from me and I got out of the car. I made my way into the middle of the school and looked for Summer. *I need to know what happened after I left.* I couldn't find Summer anywhere. I stood in place and turned my head constantly. I began to panic. *I have to find her. Where is she?* My panic turned to anger as I saw Joe approaching. *Oh yeah, Joe. Hmmm, what is he smiling about? I should just punch him right in the face. That's right! Right in his smug, stupid face! No, calm down Hannah. He's not worth it.* Joe walked right up to me and tried to give me a hug. I pushed him away with both hands as hard as I could.

"Babe, what's wrong?" Joe asked as he regained his composure. "Aren't you glad to see me?"

"No, I'm not glad to see you, Joe...By the way, where's your little girlfriend?"

"Yeah, are you feeling all right?" Joe looked more confused than ever. "I'm looking at her, you, right now."

"No, I meant Jade."

"Jade...Jade?

"Yes, I didn't stutter." *What an idiot.*

"Jade's not my girlfriend, you are."

"Was, Joe, try was your girlfriend."

"Wait, are you breaking up with me?" I nodded. "Over Jade? I know Summer told you that we hooked up, but that was it...I swear. It's not like I had sex with her or anything." *Oh, fuck you, Joe.* "Come on, Hannah, you know you're my number one girl." Joe reached for my hand and I slapped his arm away from me.

"You don't get to touch me anymore."

"This is your fault; you know that right?" *My fault!? My fault!?* I felt myself getting very angry and looked down at my thick plastic rings on my right hand as I made a fist. *Calm down. He's not worth it...He's not worth it. Don't.* "If you hadn't left the party..."

"SHUT UP! Just shut up, Joe. You're a stupid... WHORE!" The people around us stopped moving and I could feel a thousand eyes staring at the drama that was unfolding. *Good, stop and listen. Everyone needs to know that Joe's a piece of shit.*

"That's right everyone, I'm breaking up with Joe." I heard some oooohs and aaaahs from our audience. "Joe cheated on me with Jade and now it's over."

"It's not over, though. You're my girl. She doesn't matter." I looked over Joe's shoulder and saw Jade walking toward us. I started laughing and then held a smile."

"What's so funny?"

"Look behind you."

"Oh shit, Jade." I tapped Joe on the shoulder and he turned around to face me. He looked concerned, but his ego seemed to prevent him from taking any action.

"You're pretty dumb, you know. We all go to the same school." Jade stood between us and crossed her arms. She didn't look happy with either one of us. There was an awkward moment of silence that lasted longer than I was willing to tolerate.

"No worries, Jade, you can have him." I heard light whispering as I walked away from the crowd. I briefly listened to Jade scorn Joe for being Joe, but soon lost interest and started to make my way over to the basketball courts.

"Onion! Get back here," Joe yelled, but I didn't turn around. *Too bad, Joe.* As I approached the basketball courts, I saw Summer alone. She was holding a basketball in the middle of a court, but wasn't playing.

"Summer, hey, Summer, what happened yesterday?"

"Hey, Hannah. I've got good news, I guess."

"Oh yeah?"

"Mel's parents are going to let her finish the school year here."

"That's fantastic news, Summer, what do you mean by you guess?"

"They're gonna move after..."

"What? Where?"

"I don't know. I wanted to be with her in high school, you know...It's supposed to be the best time of our lives and, well, I'm just depressed."

"Maybe they'll change their mind. Anything's possible, right?"

"I don't know, Hannah, I was only eavesdropping, but I think I heard them pretty clear. They think that Santa Maria is the problem..."

"Santa Maria? That doesn't even make sense."

"I think that what they meant by Santa Maria was Summer Braithwaite."

"Oh, yeah, well I suppose you can add me to that list too."

"I don't know what to do, Hannah. Every day...I'm supposed to pretend to be happy...To pretend like everything is fine. And then at the end of the year I'm just supposed to move on and let her go?"

"Maybe we could, I don't know, kidnap her and pretend to be..."

"...Kidnap, Hannah, really?" Summer interrupted.

"Yeah, we could pretend to be someone else and ask for a ransom."

"Okay..."

"Then we could use the money to buy a house and then you guys could live in it."

"Wow, so you have this all planned out?"

"...No, but I'm just trying to help," I reasoned.

"I appreciate that, Hannah, I really do, but I don't think it works like that."

"Well, we have like more than six months to figure this out, right?"

"Right...hey, that's the bell, we should probably go to class."

"Yeah...Oh hey, I forgot to tell you, I broke up with Joe."

"Really!? What'd he say?"

"Nothing really. Jade showed up." Summer laughed.

"Then I just walked away."

"I don't think that's ever happened to Joe."

"It has now. He messed around with the wrong girl."

"Yes, he did."

The Friday before Thanksgiving vacation, normally a time of the year which was universally celebrated by the student body, was for me, a time of anxiety and depression. It had been three weeks since I saw Melissa in the hospital and she still hadn't come back to school. Summer and I spent every day together when we weren't in class. I got my phone privileges back after two weeks. I called Melissa every day and Summer did the same. It became painfully obvious that Melissa's parents had changed their number. It was hard to concentrate on anything. My grades started to slip. I was losing myself to the unknown. I focused only on the negative. The only feeling I had was a feeling of pervasive helplessness. At lunch, I met up with Summer almost every day. "I am feeling especially sad today," I said.

"Yeah, me too. I don't understand. I could have sworn that Mel's parents said she would get to come back to school. Maybe I was hearing things. Maybe I was hearing what I wanted to hear. Maybe they just changed their mind..." Summer trailed off.

"Maybe they lied."

"Yeah, but why? It doesn't make any sense."

"Maybe they just wanted her to believe that life was going to go back to normal so she wouldn't, you know..."

"Yeah..."

"Hey, I can't keep doing this," I said in a very quiet and timid voice, holding back my tears. "I'm going to go to her house right now...Will you come with me?" Summer's eyes widened.

"You mean right now, like ditch school right now?"

"Yes. If you don't want to..."

"No, I do, but how do we get out of here without getting caught?"

"There's no one watching the far side of the field behind the basketball courts. All we have to do is go pretend to play basketball and wait for an opening."

"An opening?"

"Yeah, the teachers aren't really paying attention anyway, but if we were to, say, chase after an errant ball, no one would think anything of it, and then we could jump the fence. Easy peasy."

"Hmmm, okay, I'm in." Summer and I walked to the basketball courts. I grabbed a ball off of the ground and then we went to the court that was the furthest away from everyone. We took turns taking shots like we were playing twenty-one, but we both kept very close attention to the supervision, or the lack thereof that the teachers were providing. It only took about ten minutes for the basketball courts to be free from adult intervention. I threw the ball as hard as I could at the backboard and it ricocheted violently and rolled backward, away from the courts and into the fence next to the street. We made our move and ran after the ball. Summer reached down and picked up the ball. We both turned around to see if anyone was paying attention. They weren't. I jumped over the fence, which was no more than waist high, and Summer followed. We ran and hid behind a tree and looked back through the fence.

"I think we're in the clear," I said.

"My heart is pounding," Summer responded.

"Are you worried about getting caught?"

"I don't know. I don't think my parents would even care if they did find out."

"I would get grounded again," I said confidently. "But, it's worth it. I have to know what's going on with Mel."

"You're a really good friend, Hannah."

"I'm just doing what I think is right."

"I can see why Mel always talked about you." *I don't think...I wonder if she knows...*

"What did she say?"

"You mean besides the fact that she was in love with you...

"Yeah, I mean..." I felt myself blushing.

"It's okay, I'm not jealous. I know that you're not, you know..."

"Yeah. We should go. We should get back as soon as we can. If I'm not here when my dad is supposed to pick me up, that'll probably be the end of my life."

"All right, lead the way." We walked along Chapel Street and then cut through Armstrong Park. Melissa only lived a few blocks away on Mill Street. I figured it would take about twenty minutes to get there. *I wonder when she knew.* I turned towards Summer as we walked stride for stride.

"I was just thinking...and you don't have to answer this if you don't want to, but when did you know?" Summer smiled and then looked confused.

"Know what?"

"You know..."

"Nope, I have no idea, Hannah, are you all right?"

"Yeah, I'm okay. *What is wrong with me?* "When did you know that you were, you know, gay? Sorry...Don't answer that."

"No, it's okay. I think I've always known. When I was little, my friends...like my old friends. I mean, they're not my friends anymore. They played with dolls and I liked playing with cars and

Transformers. You know, stuff like that. Later on, when they would watch the boys play sports and gossip, I would want to be the one playing."

"Well, wait, I like to play sports, and I'm not, and I didn't want to play with dolls either."

"Yeah. It's more than that though. I'm just not attracted to boys."

"Does that mean you're attracted to me?"

"Yes."

"Wow, that was fast. You wanna jump my bones, Summer?" Summer and I both laughed obnoxiously as we made our way through the neighborhood.

"Wait, was that a question or a comment?"

"Comment."

"Ahhh, you're no fun." *I wonder...I'm doing a lot of wondering lately. I wonder why I don't know this already.*

"Hey, Summer, what's your birthday?"

"September thirtieth." *A Libra. Of Course. How did I not know that.* "Why?"

"Because..."

"Oh, never mind, Mel told me about how you're all into astrology."

"Did she?" *Was there any time that she wasn't talking about me?*

"Yeah."

"What do you think?"

"About astrology? I don't know. From what I've read, it all seems pretty vague...like it could apply to anyone, really."

"No, it's so much more than that. I'll have to school you on it sometime."

"School me on it, huh? So, should I refer to you as Ms. Hannah?"

"Yeah, that has a nice ring to it."

"I was kidding."

"Ummm, yeah, me too." We both laughed. We continued onto Mill Street and I looked up at the ominous grey clouds that shrouded the sky. "I hope it doesn't rain."

"It will. We always have rain in November."

"No, I mean right now. That would suck."

"It's just water, Hannah."

"That's one way of looking at it...another is trying to hide being soaking wet from my dad."

"Oh, yeah, I guess that would be a problem. My dad wouldn't even notice...not like he's ever picked me up from school or anything..."

"I'm sorry, Summer."

"No, it's okay, I have a pretty great life because of him, but...it would be nice if he acknowledged me every now and then."

"I have the exact opposite problem. My parents are always in my business."

"It means that they care about you."

"...Summer, your parents care about you. They have to. Maybe they just have a hard time showing it."

"Yeah, I guess, thanks Hannah."

"Hey, we're almost there."

"Yeah...So, what should we say?"

"I don't know. I haven't thought that far ahead."

"I don't think her parents are going to let us talk to her."

"I'll just push them out of the way," I said. "I can be very forward when I have to be."

"That's a good thing. I think we're going to need it." We approached Melissa's front yard and we were immediately met with a large 'For Sale' sign. My heart sank. I looked at Summer. We didn't have any words. We looked toward her front door.

"No, no, no, this is not happening," I said as I ran to the door. I rang the doorbell. There was no response. I rang it again. Nothing. I then frantically began knocking on the door and then on an adjacent window. I looked through the window. There was nothing inside of Melissa's house that I could see. I looked back at Summer. "They're gone," I solemnly said.

Summer and I walked back the same way we came without saying much of anything. I didn't know what to say. I was in shock. We got back to school right before the beginning of seventh period, but didn't attempt to sneak back on campus. We found the same tree next to the fence that we used as cover before and decided to wait.

When the bell rang, we casually hopped the fence and walked right through the middle of campus and blended in with everyone else moving to the front of the school. "Hey, Summer," I said.

"Yeah."

"We have to find Mel."

"Where do we even start, Hannah?" Summer sounded defeated. There was no sense of optimism or hope in her voice. *Does she even care?*

"I'm not going to give up. This isn't right."

"I know, but..."

"But nothing!" I snapped. "We're going to find her."

"Okay, Hannah, call me later and we'll figure something out."

"All right, I'll call you around seven," I said as Summer moved in close to me and gave me a hug.

"I see my mom," Summer responded as she stepped away from me. "I'll talk to you later."

"Bye, Summer."

"Bye." Summer walked toward her mom's car and I looked up and down the street for my dad's truck. I spotted my dad seemingly a mile away and made my way over to him. I opened the door and pulled myself up into the truck."

"Hi sweetie, did you have a good day," my dad said with enthusiasm.

"No, not really...dad, can I ask you a question?"

"Of course. What's on your mind?" My dad started the truck and then waited for traffic to clear.

"I think Mel's family moved."

"That's not exactly a question," my dad chuckled.

"...I know, ummm." *What am I trying to say?* "Do you think it's okay for, I don't know, for like a family to move without..." *This isn't working.* "Dad, I know Mel didn't want to move and her parents just made the decision for her, you know."

"People move for all sorts of reasons...and Mel is a minor. So, unfortunately, that's the way it is."

"So, she doesn't have any rights then? Is that what you're saying?"

"According to the law, yes, that's what I'm saying. Sorry, that's the truth."

"It's just not fair." I sulked down into my seat and watched all of the cars buzz by.

"What do you want for dinner?" My dad asked empathetically.

"Nothing, I'm not hungry."

"Hannah, I know it's hard for you to understand because you're so young." *And here we go...* "Your friends will always change throughout your life. That's just the way things are. Nothing lasts forever. People come and people go." *That makes me feel much better, thank you.* "Except for family. I'm not going anywhere." My dad let out one of his big belly laughs that I found more obnoxious than endearing. I stayed silent. I didn't have the energy to argue with anyone, let alone my dad; that was always a losing battle anyway. Traffic finally broke and my dad pulled out onto the road and drove us home.

My dad made the decision that year, with my mom's blessing, to host Thanksgiving dinner. He wanted to spend some time with his best friend, Bob, and I hadn't seen Jessica in forever so I was okay with it. I wasn't really feeling like company though because I was still worried about Melissa. I called Summer every day with the hope, maybe even the expectation, that she would have news about her. She didn't. I was losing hope. *How does someone just disappear from your life?*

"Hannah...Hannah...Hello, are you there?" Jessica asked.

"Oh, I'm sorry, I was just thinking..."

"About what?"

"My friend, Mel. I haven't heard from her in like a month and I'm worried about her, err, more like what her parents have done to her."

"What do you mean?" I told Jessica about Melissa's sexuality and how repressive her parents were. I told her about Halloween. I reiterated why I was so scared. Jessica and I weren't really that close. We were only friends by association. We didn't seem to have much in common other than the fact that our dad's grew up together. She was much more introverted than me. Jessica was the kind of person that would ask questions of other people and expect them to answer, but would never be willing to share anything about herself. I didn't really care though. I was an open book with her and told her everything that she wanted to know. Jessica and I sat on my bed and waited for the turkey to be finished as I continued plodding through her interrogation. I was supposed to be a good host and entertain Jessica while our parents caught up.

"But, you're not gay...Are you?" Jessica inquired.

"No, I'm not gay." *At least I don't think so...*

"Do you have a boyfriend?"

"I had a boyfriend."

"What's his name?"

"Joe."

"What happened?"

"A lot. But in order to save time, he was just an asshole. I mean, he is an asshole."

"Is he cute?"

"Yeah, I guess so."

"Did he break up with you or did you break up with him?"

"I broke up with him."

"Why? Are you trying to be alone?" *What the heck?*

"No, look, Jessica, he cheated on me all right!"

"Ohhh, sorry, I guess I hit a nerve."

"No, it's fine, it's whatever, you know. We were just not a good fit."

"Who is a good fit then? What's on your list?"

"My list? What do you mean?"

"You know, your list: At least six feet tall, with six pack abs, and a six inch..." Jessica was a year ahead of me and already in high school so she was more corrupt than me, at least in her head. No one would ever know it just by looking at her. She had long brown hair and a nice complexion, but her conservative choice of clothing camouflaged her inner-thoughts well.

"Six inch what, Jessica?" I said and then laughed.

"You know, his banana." We both laughed.

"Seriously, have you even seen a banana in real life?"

"Maybe..." *I don't think you have.*

"Come on, Jessica, dish!" Jessica didn't say anything though. "Jessica, do YOU have a boyfriend?"

"Maybe..." *You are so frustrating.*

"Fine, you don't have to tell me, but it is kind of bunk that I tell you everything and you tell me nothing...don't you think?"

"You really tell me everything?"

"Yeah, I think so." *Actually, probably not.* Jessica gave me a confounded look like she didn't believe me. Before I could convince her otherwise, my dad knocked on my door and then let himself in.

"The turkey is finished, cooked to perfection by the master chef and is ready for consumption," my dad sang. *What a dork.*

"You're referring to mom, right?" I said and tilted my head sideways.

"Funny," my dad replied. "Come on." Jessica and I got up from my bed and followed my dad out to the table. Jessica's mom and dad were already seated next to each other. My mom was fixing something at the counter and my brother was playing his Gameboy on the couch. Jessica and I sat down next to each other. I leaned in to whisper in Jessica's ear.

"Where did you get that 'six feet, six-inch thing' from?"

"I think it was from my mom's Vogue, you know, the magazine," Jessica whispered back. I smiled.

"Aren't you a little too young for that particular publication?" I giggled under my breath.

"Nope," Jessica said. We both laughed and my dad looked at us funny before turning his attention to my brother.

"Michael, turn that thing off and come to the table," my dad insisted. My brother put his Gameboy down on the couch and then sat next to me. My dad towered over everyone as he cut slices off of the turkey. He stacked the perfectly sliced pieces on a serving platter in the center of the table. "Before we eat, I want each of us to say what we're thankful for." *Every year...* Jessica and I looked at each other and rolled our eyes in protest. "I'll start." *What else is new?* "I'm thankful for my beautiful family, my motorcycle, and my truck." My dad and Jessica's dad laughed." *Why is that funny?*

"Well, I'm thankful for my beautiful kids," my mom interjected. "...My thoughtful husband, and my job, which allows us to have a pretty good life if I do say so myself..." My mom earned a lot more money than my dad and I could tell that this was always a point of contention among my parents even though they never said so outright. My dad always seemed flustered when the topic of money came up. My mom knew what she was doing.

"Moving on...Michael, what are you thankful for?" My dad asked.

"I'm thankful for the Green Bay Packers, Brett Favre, Nintendo, my Gameboy..." My brother trailed off. "Oh yeah, I almost forgot candy and ice cream. And pizza. I think that's it." *What is he NOT thankful for; that would have been a better question.*

"Hannah, your turn..." my dad demanded. I looked around the table. I looked at all twelve eyes looking back at me. I felt overwhelmed with anxiety. *I'm not thankful for anything...*

"Dad, I really don't want to do this...Not this year." Everyone was silent.

"What do you mean you don't want to do this!?" My dad barked. "This isn't a difficult question, Hannah." *But it is though. Mel. Her parents are awful. I wonder what she's thankful for.*

"I'm thankful for..." *At least I don't have Mel's parents.* "I'm thankful that I have parents that actually care about me."

"You see; that's nice, thank you sweetie," my mom said.

"...Unlike Mel's parents who kidnapped her away from her friends because they couldn't handle the truth. Stupid homophobes," I snapped.

"Hannah, that just wasn't necessary, let's keep things positive, shall we?" My dad protested. "You don't even know the whole story..."

"And you do?" I said sharply and stood up.

"Well, no, but, Hannah, sit back down," my dad instructed.

"You're making a scene," my mom added. Jessica pulled on my arm very slightly as if to encourage my compliance. I pulled my arm away from her and started walking towards my bedroom.

"I'm not hungry," I said as I made my way down the hall.

"Hannah!" My mom shouted.

"No, let her go," my dad said. "We can't force her to eat."

"More for me," my brother said. As I made my way past the bathroom and to my bedroom door, I felt a tap on my back. I turned around and saw Jessica.

"WHAT!?"

"If you're not going to eat then neither am I."

"You don't have to do that. Go eat." I looked back toward the dining room. "You're being rude to your parents."

"Oh, as if, Hannah!" *Oh yeah, duh. I didn't think about that one before it came out of my mouth.*

"Fine, come on." I opened my door and let Jessica in. I sat on the edge of my bed and Jessica sat right next to me.

"What is going on with you?"

"I don't know. I'm just not myself lately."

"No, I can see that."

"I just...Life just sucks. It's not fair."

"...Is this about your friend?"

"Yeah. I have to find out what happened to her. I have to find out where she moved, or more like, where her parents forced her to move. I need to know that she's okay...If she's okay."

"I'll bet she's fine."

"I hope so...Jessica?"

"Yeah."

"I have to find her...This is all my fault. Everything..."

"How is this your fault?"

"I was supposed to be there for her. I was supposed to be there when she came out to her parents."

"Do you really think that would have made a difference?"

"I don't know...I don't know. And now I'm never going to know. It's too late. I could have made a difference and I didn't do anything." I started crying and Jessica put her arm around me.

"Listen, Hannah, I don't think...I think you're taking this too personal. It's not your fault."

"This is personal. I promised that I would be there for her and I failed. I can't think of anything more personal than that."

"I'm here for you. If you need my help with anything..."

"Thanks, Jessica." I wiped the tears from my face and felt a renewed sense of optimism. *I'm going to find her.*

I sat in silence waiting for my dad to pick me up from school. It was three days before Christmas vacation, and I still hadn't heard anything about Melissa. Summer and I called everyone we knew and everyone claimed they didn't know anything. We came to the conclusion that they did know something, but they didn't want to tell us. *This is not a coincidence. Someone knows something!* We became suspicious of everyone. *Why would everyone lie though?* I was starting to question my own sanity when I saw Ryan walking up to me. *Oh God, what does he want?* "What do you want, Ryan?"

"Can I sit down?"

"No."

"Why not?"

"I'm saving it for Summer."

"No, you're not, Summer didn't even come to school today." *Shit, he got me there.* Ryan sat down on the bench next to me and handed me a folded paper.

"What's this?"

"Open it."

"Okay..." I unfolded the paper and read it to myself. *Hannah, I'm really sorry. I messed up. I messed up really bad. I want you back. I know I screwed up. Jade just isn't doing it for me. Yeah, so, we should get back together. You're still single and now so am I. Will you be my girlfriend again? Circle one: Yes. No.* I laughed. "Hold on a second..." I opened my backpack and pulled out a black sharpie. Below 'Yes' and 'No,' I wrote: HELL NO! and circled it. I crumpled up the paper and handed it back to Ryan. "There you go..."

"He's not gonna like this, Hannah."

"I don't care. I will never, ever, ever be Joe's girlfriend again. If he were the last guy on earth, I would join a convent. Understand? Go away, Ryan."

"Why do you have to be such a bitch about it? You could have just said no, but damn," Ryan said and then walked away.

"Bye, Ryan!" I said sarcastically. *I will never date another guy like Joe.*

On Christmas Eve, my dad drove us to Visalia to spend some time with my grandparents. I liked my grandparents on my mom's side much better, but they lived in Ukraine. I hadn't seen them in years. The trek to Grandma and Grandpa O'Conner's house was becoming another family tradition that I really wasn't too interested in. My dad was like that though. We always had to do the family things even if we didn't want to. It was all right most years, but I was feeling different that year. It was Melissa. I couldn't focus on anything else. I couldn't even consider having any fun if I knew that Melissa was suffering. I stood and stared at my grandparent's Christmas tree while getting lost in the blinking lights.

"Hannah, sweetheart, what's wrong?" My grandma asked, which woke me from my daze.

"Oh...It's nothing Grandma."

"Are you looking forward to opening your presents this year?"

"No, Grandma, I'm really not..."

"Oh?"

"It's just that...The only thing I want for Christmas is to know that my friend Mel is okay."

"What happened to your friend?"

"Her parents...She moved, and I don't know where...I'm worried about her." My grandma reached her arm around me and gave me a hug. She didn't say anything.

"Aren't you going to tell me that I have nothing to worry about, you know, like everyone else?"

"Oh dear, I would never tell you how to feel."

"Thanks, Grandma." My grandma squeezed my arm and then started walking away to the kitchen. "Grandma, can I use your phone?"

"Sure, sweetie, who do you want to call?"

"Jessica. You remember Jessica, right?"

"Yes, yes, of course…You can take it in my room if you want."

"Thanks, Grandma." I walked over to the phone, picked up the handset and went to my grandma's room. I heard boisterous laughing coming from the kitchen. *I'm glad everyone's having a good time. Really. I am. I just wish that I could be happy.* My grandma's room smelled strange. It was a smell that was difficult to describe. It wasn't pleasant. *Jessica…I should probably call Jessica, but I don't want to. Summer. Yeah, maybe Summer has heard something.* I dialed Summer's number and she picked up after one ring.

"Hello?"

"Summer?"

"Hannah!?"

"Yeah, it's me. I called to see…"

"…Hannah, I've been trying to call you." Summer interjected. "Where are you?"

"I'm at my grandparent's house in Visalia."

"Visalia?"

"Yeah, it's near Fresno…Doesn't matter. Have you heard from Mel?"

"That's why I've been calling you. She sent me a letter." *Oh my God.*

"What did she say? Is she okay?" I demanded.

"I don't know. I haven't opened it…"

"Why?"

"I don't know…I'm afraid. I kind of thought that maybe we could open it together."

"Yeah. Yeah, that's a good idea. It's good, right?"

"Yeah…"

"It must mean she's okay." I was starting to feel the enormous weight of the unknown leave my tortured mind. I was hopeful. I was happy.

"So, when do you want to read it?" *Right now…*

"We won't be back in Santa Maria until sometime tonight." *That seems so far away.*

"Maybe you should just open it and read it to me. No, never mind, I want to read it myself. Damn, I have to spend Christmas with my family."

"Same."

"How about the day after? I'll have my dad drop me off at your house."

"Okay, yeah, sounds good."

"I'll be over as soon as I can, Summer, please wait for me."

"I will. I'll see you Sunday."

"Okay, bye Summer, Merry Christmas!"

"Merry Christmas, Hannah!" Summer hung up the phone and I walked out to the kitchen to be with my family. I ate some of my grandma's overdone chocolate chip cookies and drank some tepid hot cocoa. I smiled.

"Feeling better?" My grandma asked.

"Yeah. I think everything's going to be okay."

Chapter Ten

Dark winter

I woke up Christmas morning to the smell of burnt coffee and the sound of my brother ripping apart his Christmas presents. *So, this year is no different from last year and the year before that. I don't know why I expected something different to happen this Christmas. I'm pretty sure there was a time when I was excited about Christmas. I just don't remember when.* I sat up on the edge of my bed and stretched my arms out. I let out a robust yawn and then went to the bathroom. When I walked into the living room my dad chuckled.

"Sleeping beauty awakes."

"Yeah, right, dad. I look terrible."

"At least you can admit it," my brother said and laughed.

"Be quiet, Michael," I said. "What did Santa bring you for Christmas this year?" My brother finally realized that Santa was actually my mom and dad last year. He woke up in the middle of the night and caught my parents wrapping some presents. He figured it out on his own after that, but I never wasted the opportunity to tease him.

"Shut up, Hannah, I know he's not real." I laughed.

"Are you sure, Michael? I think I heard footsteps on the roof last night."

"No, you didn't!" my brother pleaded.

"Didn't I? What did I hear then, Michael?"

"...I don't know...MOM!"

"Leave him alone, Hannah," my mom insisted. "Why don't you open one of your presents?"

"Okay, sure, why not?" I looked down under the tree and found a really small package with my name on it. Of course, it also read 'from Santa.' *At this point, who are they trying to fool...themselves?* I tore open the package and it was a bottle of 'Sun Moon Stars.' It was a perfume that I really liked after smelling it at Macy's during a shopping trip with my mom. *It's kind of crazy that she remembered.* "Thanks, mom."

"Don't thank me dear, thank Santa." *Oh God.*

"Seriously?"

"Yes."

"Thanks, Santa," I said and smiled while looking at my brother. He looked back at me as confused as ever. I could see the cogs turning in his head and then stop. He didn't know what to believe and that made me smile even more. I looked over at my dad. He was holding a cup of coffee. *I don't know how he drinks that stuff.* "Hey dad, you have the day off tomorrow, right?"

"That's right." My dad smiled and then seemed to sigh. *He works so hard. I wish he could take more time off.*

"I was wondering, if you're not busy, if you could, maybe, drive me over to my friend's house tomorrow."

"Sure," my dad said. *Without even thinking about it...cool.*

"Wait a second," my mom said. *Oh great...* She put a plate down in the kitchen and walked out to the living room. "Which friend are you talking about?"

"...Summer," I said.

"I really don't want you hanging out with Summer."

"Why not? It's not like it's a party. I want to go over there during the day." *Duh!*

"Well, maybe if you told me what happened at the party, I would trust you."

"So, you don't trust me now?"

"Can we please not do this today? Of all days, not today. It's Christmas. Can we have one day where we're not arguing about something?" My dad growled.

"I don't want her over there, Patrick!" My mom pleaded.

"What's the big deal? Isn't that your boss's kid?" *Yeah, dad, tell her!*

"Yes, but she's hiding something."

"Hannah or her friend?"

"Both!" My mom said. I didn't say anything because I was hiding something. I learned about self-incrimination and the fifth amendment from my dad. He would always use the phrase, 'I'm taking the fifth,' especially when talking to my mom. *I'm taking the fifth, but I'm not going to say I'm taking the fifth because that would obviously make me look guilty. I wonder if dad knows that when he's using it on mom...* My dad walked over to my mom and whispered something in her ear. My mom laughed. *What's so funny?* "Okay...you can go to Summer's house, but I'm going to pick you up at four, after I get off work."

"Thanks, mom," I said. *What did he say to her?*

"You're welcome...Now open your presents so we can put the movie on!" The movie that we had been watching on Christmas day for the past two years was 'Home Alone,' and was on its way to becoming a family tradition. The next gift I opened was a small, red astrology book. The third was another astrology book. This book was huge though and it looked like it was used. It was titled: 'Linda Goodman's Sun Signs,' and it was from my mom. *Not Santa. Heh...* "I hope you like it. I've had that book for a long time and now it's yours."

"Thanks, mom, are you sure though?"

"Of course, it was just collecting dust in the garage." I finished opening my gifts and expressing my gratitude to everyone, even Michael, who got me the Smashing Pumpkin's Siamese Dream CD, which I knew was actually from my dad. My mom poured the eggnog for everyone, not forgetting to add the requisite alcohol for herself and my dad, and we sat down to watch 'Home Alone' for the third time.

"Thanks dad." I opened the door on my dad's truck and stepped out onto Summer's sprawling driveway. "Hey, dad, what did you whisper to mom yesterday, you know, to let me..."

"I just reminded her what it was like being your age," my dad interjected and then smiled.

"Did mom get into a lot of trouble when she was my age?" My dad laughed.

"You'll have to ask her about that yourself." *The answer must be yes.*

"I will. Bye dad." I shut the door and looked at my dad smiling and shaking his head as he drove around the driveway. *It's probably bad. She'll never tell me.* I walked over to Summer's front door and rang the doorbell. *I can't wait to read that letter.* Summer opened the door almost immediately and pulled me inside of her house. "Good to see you too, Summer, can I have my arm back?"

"Come on," Summer said and then pulled me upstairs and into her room. "Look." Summer grabbed the letter off of her dresser and pointed at the front of the envelope. "Look, read it!" *Sacramento?*

"They moved to Sacramento? How far is that from here?"

"Far. Like, really far."

"Well, at least we have her address now."

"Yeah, but how are we gonna get there?"

"We could take the bus," I reasoned.

"Ehhh, you mean like Greyhound? Don't homeless people sleep on that? So gross."

"Do you have a better idea?"

"Yeah, we could fly?"

"Isn't that expensive? I don't have any money."

"I'll borrow it from my parents."

"And they're going to just let you get on a plane by yourself?"

"I won't be by myself. I'm going to be with you."

"You know what I mean, and I know exactly what my parents will say. It's going to start and end with no."

"We'll figure that out later. Let's open the letter."

"Okay." I was anxious to read the letter, but I was also afraid. Summer carefully slid her fingernail into the envelope and pulled out a single sheet of lined paper folded over twice. Summer unfolded the paper and held it out in front of us and I took a deep breath.

Dear Summer,

By the time you get this letter, I'll be dead. I'm going to steal my parent's car while they're sleeping and take this letter to the mail box. Then I'm going to get on the freeway and then cross the median. I'm going to go as fast as I can. I'm not going to wear my seatbelt. I'm going to crash into the first car I see. I think that will do it. The pills didn't work. I'm too afraid of blood to cut myself up. My parents don't have a gun. This is the ONLY way! I'm not changing my mind!

They tried to lock me in my room! For fucks sake, they moved us to Sacramento! Bumb Fuck Sacramento! They said it would be good for me...That we had to start over. That I couldn't be gay. They want to send me to conversion therapy. That's obviously not going to happen now. IS IT MOM!? All they had to do was accept me for being who I am. Not good enough for them. They HAVE to change me. They keep the only phone in their room...All I can do is write this letter. They keep the keys to the car in the kitchen though...They would never expect me to take their car! But I'm going to.

All they ever talk about is God this and God that. THERE IS NO FUCKING GOD! And even if there was a God. No, never mind. My parents think that I'm wrong. Me being alive is wrong. It's not the RIGHT way. Fuck that! I'm trapped like a rat in a cage in this FUCKING world. Well, this rat is going to make her escape. No one is ever going to accept me. My parents will be sorry though. They'll be sorry WHEN I'm FUCKING GONE.

Oh my God, Summer. I'm so sorry! I didn't mean to...I love you. I'm sorry. I wasn't thinking about you. I mean I am, because I'm writing this letter to you, but...I don't think I can be happy. I'm stuck. I need to escape. I need to go. Oh. Tell Hannah that I'll always love her too. She was my first love. I know she's not gay, but I can't, I couldn't hide my feelings.

I'm going to go now. Don't be sad. Be happy. I'm happy now.

Mel.

Summer and I turned to face one another. I just stared into her eyes and she did the same. We didn't say anything for a few seconds. Finally, I said, "this can't be real, right?"

"I don't know, Hannah. This is a lot...To take, you know...And maybe we should tell my parents."

"You don't think..." My heart sank and I struggled to find the words. "...That...She...You know, actually did it. It's just a cry for help, right? Summer?"

"I would have...Thought, but she did try to kill herself before. I don't know, Hannah. We need to tell someone."

"Yeah, we do. How long does it take for a letter to go from Sacramento to Santa Maria?"

"...I don't know, Hannah. Let's take the letter to my mom. She'll know what to do."

"Okay, I don't have a better idea, so..." Summer and I walked downstairs to find her mom in the living room sipping on a glass of what looked like red wine. *It's not even noon! How is she going to help us? I don't know about this.* Summer handed the letter to her mom.

"Mom, we need your help. Mel needs your help," Summer said.

"Mel, but I thought..."

"Just read the letter...Please. We didn't know what to do." Summer's mom stared at Summer for a few seconds before looking at me. She took a deep breath and set her wine glass down on the coffee table in front of her. Summer and I stood in silence as her mom read the letter.

"Okay, girls, we need to call the police," Summer's mom slurred. *The police!? Are you sure you should be the one to make that call?* Summer's mom gingerly got up from the couch and walked over to the kitchen. She picked up the phone. "Wait a minute. Summer, did Mel write the return address on the envelope?"

"Yeah, she wrote it from Sacramento."

"Sacramento, huh? Okay," Summer's mom said and then turned on the phone. She dialed 0 for the operator and then waited. "Hi, yes, can you please connect me to the Sacramento police department? Yes, thank you." She waited again. "Oh shit, Summer, what's Mel's last name?"

"Garcia, mom, come on!"

"...Hi, my name is Autumn Braithwaite and I'm here with my daughter and her friend. Yes...Yes...I'm in Santa Maria. Yes. I'm calling because my daughter received a letter from her friend, Mel...Melissa Garcia. It was a suicide note...No. No, it's not specific. She wrote that she was going to steal her parent's car and then drive it into oncoming traffic...I don't know...They did...Okay. Can you give me their number? You can't...Okay. Can you call me if you hear anything? Yes, I understand, yes...Goodbye." Summer's mom turned the phone off and then set it down on the counter.

"Well, what happened?" Summer asked. I didn't say anything, but I was ready to hang on her every word.

"Mel's parents reported her missing last week." *Missing? What does that mean? Is she okay?* "She did steal their car, but no one by her description has been in an accident."

"What does that mean?" I said in frustration.

"It means that she's missing," Summer's mom said.

"But, how can someone just go missing after stealing a car? Can't they, I don't know, track the car?"

"I guess they are, but they haven't found anything."

"Well, thanks for calling, mom," Summer said.

"I had to...Look, girls, she's probably fine. It sounds like she just ran away from home. She'll go back home eventually. She'll have to when she runs out of money or gets hungry." *Wow, that is very comforting, thank you...* "When I was her age, I ran away. I came back though. It's just something that some people go through." *Did she even read the letter? This is so not the same thing!* "Everything will be fine," Summer's mom said and then walked back to the couch and started drinking her wine again." *That's just great.*

"Come on, Hannah, let's go back to my room," Summer said and I followed her upstairs. I sat on the edge of her bed. I picked up the envelope that was lying right next to me. I stared at the Sacramento address intensely and Summer sat down beside me.

"We have to go to her house," I insisted.

"Hannah, I know you're not going to want to hear this, but I think we need to let this go..."

"What do you mean! How can we let this go!?" I scowled.

"Because, Hannah, we're thirteen! What are we actually going to do?"

"...I don't know."

"Exactly. We can just hope for the best. Mel's fine...Just like my mom said."

"I have a really bad feeling."

"There's nothing we can do."

"Maybe I'll steal my parent's car and go find her..."

"You're talking crazy, Hannah."

"Am I?"

"Yes, you are."

"Mel may be the only one that's not crazy. Maybe everyone's crazy but her. Maybe you're crazy. Me too. Mel actually did something. What are we doing?"

"I don't know what to say, Hannah...Do you want to come to my New Years Eve party?" *You can't be serious...*

"My mom would never let me, because, you know, Halloween..."

"It doesn't hurt to ask." *You don't know my mom.*

"Are you going to invite Joe?" Summer laughed.

"No, you don't have to worry about that."

"Ryan?"

"Nope. I'm thinking about making it a girls only type of thing..." *I can only imagine...* I laughed.

"Feeling better?"

"I want to feel better."

"Come to the party."

"I told you, there is no way my mom is going to let me."

"Well, you're invited anyway, so there!" *I don't think we should be celebrating anything...Especially the new year, without Mel.* I let Summer have the last word on the party. I reached over to her dresser where she had put the letter. I started reading it again. I wanted to see if there was some clue I was missing. "Nope, let me take that." Summer took the letter from me and put it inside the top drawer. "We are going to have some fun."

"I don't really feel like..."

"I have some board games. We could watch TV. You like MTV, right? They have some really cool music videos." *I guess I do have some time...* "What time is your mom picking you up again?"

"Like, around four."

"Okay, come on!" Summer grabbed my hand and led me downstairs. We got some Doritos and Dr. Pepper from the kitchen and then vegged out on the couch and began watching the endless spectacle of music videos. Summer's mom had vacated the living room and was nowhere to be seen. It was just Summer and I eating junk food, watching TV, and making small talk for hours. At a little after four O' clock, my mom picked me up from Summer's house.

"Mom," I said very quietly as we drove home. "Mel sent Summer a letter..."

"A letter?"

"Her parents moved them to Sacramento."

"Did they? So, how's she doing?"

"I don't know...It was a suicide letter."

"...I'm sorry, Hannah. Sometimes..."

"Summer's mom called the police in Sacramento."

"Autumn called the police?" My mom asked sarcastically.

"Yeah, and they're calling Mel a runaway, but they don't think she killed herself."

"Well, that's good."

"MOM! You act like you don't even care. She needs help!"

"It's not that, Hannah. I have my own family to worry about...Your dad..."

"Dad what?"

"I don't really want to talk about it yet. Not until we're sure..."

"Sure about what? What's going on?"

"I shouldn't have said anything."

"But you did...MOM!"

"That's enough, Hannah, we'll talk about it when there's something to talk about." *That's wonderful. Mel needs my help and now my parents are keeping secrets from me.*

"Hannah, your dad and I are going out tonight for New Years. We need you to babysit your brother..." *Hmmm, I could steal the truck and drive to Sacramento. I would have to take Michael. I would feel bad if I left him behind.* "...Hannah, did you hear me?" My mom asked.

"Yeah, I can watch Michael." *It's not like I have anything else going on. Wait! Summer's party...Nah, I won't even bother...It doesn't matter. I'm going to Sacramento! I can do this!*

"Your dad and I haven't been on a date in...A very long time. In fact, I can't seem to remember the last time..."

"I get it, mom, I already said yes."

"Right. You're a good girl, Hannah."

My parents left for their date night around five. They took my mom's car just like I expected, leaving the truck behind. I had never driven any car before let alone my dad's old truck, but I had confidence that I could. *I can do this. I have to do this. They told me that they'd be home at one. Maybe I should leave them a note.* I went into the garage and navigated around boxes and bins filled with old stuff. *Why do they keep all of this stuff? I need to find a map...* I checked my dad's tools and then a shelf next to his motorcycle. *He never even rides that thing...* I found a book called 'The Atlas of California.' I opened the book. It had detailed maps of every area of California. I turned to the section on the Sacramento valley. *This is perfect.* I started plotting my route.

"Hannah, what are you doing in here?" My brother asked, startling me.

"Michael, don't sneak up on me like that!"

"What are you doing?"

"Okay, Michael, I'm going to tell you something, but only be-cause I have to take you with me..."

"...What...What are you talking about?"

"Michael, you remember Mel?"

"Yeah."

"She's in trouble and needs my help. It's my fault that she's in trouble so it has to be me that helps her. You understand what I'm saying?"

"No, not really."

"...Okay, let me make this really simple. I'm going to take dad's truck to Sacramento to find Mel and you're coming with me." My brother laughed. "I'm not kidding, Michael..."

❦❦❦❦❦ ❦❦❦❦❦

"Dad, how do you do that?"

"Do what?" My dad asked and chuckled.

"Drive like that? It looks complicated."

"Hannah, sweetie, you're only twelve years old and you're al-ready trying to learn how to drive?"

"Yeah..."

"...Okay, but I can't let you actually drive. Your mom would kill me."

"Ahhh, come on, dad, I can do it!" I pleaded and my dad laughed.

"I'm sure you can, but it's still against the law."

"The law?"

"Yes, the law...And your mom..."

"...I promise I won't, I don't know, get into an accident."

"And I promise you that as soon as you can legally drive, you will, and I'll teach you."

"When can I legally drive?"

"Fifteen and a half."

"Why the half?"

"...You know, I'm not exactly sure..."

"The law is stupid," I reasoned and my dad laughed again.

"Yeah, for some things, I agree."

"...So, how are you going to teach me how to drive if I can't actually drive?"

"When you're old enough..."

"No, I mean, like now."

"You can be quite persistent, can't you?"

"Yes, I can." My dad smiled and looked over at me.

"...I can't believe...Anyway...Watch everything that I do and I'll tell you what I'm doing as I do it. That way when you are old enough, you'll be ahead of the game."

"Ahead of the game?"

"It's an expression. It means that you'll have a head start on everyone else your age."

"Oh, yeah."

"This is a manual transmission. It means that you have to change the gears yourself. It's more work, but it's more fun too." My dad pointed to his left foot. "That's the clutch pedal. It disengages the transmission from the engine so you don't grind the gears. That's bad. You don't want to do that." We came up to a stop sign and my dad turned off the truck. "This is the hard part." He turned the truck back on. "Starting from a stop. Clutch in. First is up and to the left. Slowly release the clutch, give it some gas, and we're a go. Clutch in. Shift to second...Clutch in. Shift to third...Clutch in. Shift to fourth..."

"Cool. How do you back up?"

"When the truck is totally stopped; not moving at all, you clutch in and pull the shifter all the way to the left and then pull down. Clutch out slowly and you're off."

"Seems easy enough."

"I thought you said it was complicated?"

"It was until you explained it. Thanks, dad...Hey, dad..."

"Yeah."

"I've never seen mom drive your truck." He laughed.

"I tried to teach her once. It was before you were born. It didn't go well."

"What happened?"

"I'll let her tell you that story..."

❧❧❧❧❧ ❧❧❧❧❧

"You're not old enough to drive. You don't have a driver's license. You don't have any money for gas," My brother asserted. *Money...Right!* My parents kept cash for emergencies in an old shoebox in their closet. *It's an emergency...*

"Michael, you're a lot smarter than I give you credit for."

"Ummm, thanks, I guess. Wait, what are you doing?" I walked past my brother and went to my parent's closet. I found the old NIKE shoe box buried in the corner under some folded clothes. "What are you doing in mom's closet?"

"I need money for gas, like you said." I opened the shoebox. There were hundreds of dollars of cash in the box. "How much do you think we'll need?"

"You shouldn't be doing this."

"Look, Michael, I'm responsible for you so I have to take you with me. I don't have a choice so you don't have a choice, okay?" I took one-hundred dollars out of the box. "That should be enough." I put the box back where it was and then walked out to the kitchen. "Michael, go put whatever you want to take in your backpack." My brother went to his room and I picked up a pen from the counter and tore off a piece of paper from my mom's stationery.

Dear mom and dad,

Don't be mad and don't be worried. I took the truck to Sacramento to find Mel. She needs my help. I took Michael with me. Oh, I also took one-hundred dollars for gas. We'll be fine. We'll be home tomorrow.

Love,

Hannah.

That's good. I think. I put the pen down and left the note on the counter. I went to my room and put on a hoodie. I patted the front pocket of my jeans to make sure the money was still there. I looked around my room. *Do I need anything? Nah, we won't be gone very long.* "Michael! Are you ready?"

"Yeah, but..."

"We'll be back tomorrow, Michael, it'll be fine."

"Okay..." *I think I'm forgetting something. Right! The maps.* I walked back into my parents closet where I had left the California Atlas.

"Here, Michael, take the book; put it in your backpack."

"Okay."

"All right. The keys are in the kitchen drawer." I walked to the kitchen and got the keys. "Are you ready?"

"No..."

"Okay. Let's go." My brother and I walked outside and I closed and locked the door behind us. I took a deep breath. *I'm going to do this. I have to do this.* I walked out to the driveway and opened the passenger door of the truck and let Michael in. I walked around the back of the truck and felt terrible anxiety. *What am I doing? This is so stupid. Shut up! I have to do this.* I opened the door and then sat down in front of the steering wheel. I closed the door. I looked over at my brother.

"Do you know what you're doing?" My brother asked.

"I think so. Push the clutch down, turn the key, put the stick thing in reverse, slowly let the clutch out while adding gas..." I visualized every ride I had with my dad. *I can do this.* I pushed the clutch to the floor with my left foot and pressed hard into the brake with my right foot. I put the key into the ignition and turned it. The truck roared to life. I smiled. "See, Michael." *Okay...Reverse is back.* I reached down and pulled the stick back and it made a loud grinding sound.

"That doesn't happen when dad does it..." *Thanks, Michael, I know.*

"Let's try that again." I pulled on the stick with more force and it made the grinding sound but then stopped. "I think I got it." *Okay. Slowly release the clutch and add gas.* I let off of the clutch very slowly and the truck died. *Damn it. I probably need to give it more gas.* I turned the key again and the truck started. *Okay, more gas this time.* I pushed my right foot into the gas pedal and then slowly released the clutch. Nothing happened, but it didn't die either. I continued releasing the clutch. The truck violently lurched forward and died. *Why? Why can't I do this? God damn it!* I started crying, but was interrupted by my brother. "Hannah, can I have the keys? I want to go back inside." I handed my brother the keys to the house. He got out of the truck, but I stayed inside and continued crying. *What am I going to do now? Mel still needs my help, but I can't do anything!* I eventually went back into the house. My brother was already playing video games in his room like nothing had happened. I walked over to the cabinet above the refrigerator. I pulled down a bottle of vodka. *Who cares? It doesn't matter anymore.* I opened the bottle and started drinking. It burned my throat and tasted terrible, but that didn't stop me from taking another drink. I looked over at the counter and grabbed the note I had written to my parents. I crumpled it up and threw it in the trash under the sink. With the vodka bottle in hand, I went to my parents closet and returned the money. I went back to the living room and turned on the TV. There was a countdown to the new year in some other country on the news. *What the hell is everyone so happy about?* I took another drink of vodka and sank into the couch. After about an hour of intermittent, random drinking, I began to feel very sleepy. I took another drink and stood up. *I should put this back before...* I heard a knock on the door. *Oh shit!* I ran over to the front door almost tripping over my own feet. *That would have been bad.* I looked through the peep hole in the door. *Joe! What the hell is Joe doing here? Oh my God! What do I do?* Joe knocked again. *Maybe he'll go away if...*

"Hannah! I know you're home. Open the door." *Shit! Shut up, Joe. Damn.* "Hannah!" I opened the door.

"Joe, what the hell are you doing here?" I slurred.

"I see you started the party without me..."

"What party?"

"Are you going to let me in. It's cold out here." *Good.*

"If you don't let me in, I'll just stay out here all night." *Yeah, you would wouldn't you. Fuck...*

"All right, fine." I let Joe inside and he immediately gestured for the bottle. "Fine." *I don't care.* Joe took a couple of drinks from the bottle and then handed it back to me. I drank again.

"How long have you been drinking?" *Not long enough, apparently.*

"Not very long."

"So, what's wrong? This isn't like you..." *No, it's not. What am I doing?*

"It's Mel...Long story."

"Oh."

"How did you know my parents weren't home?"

"I didn't." *Asshole.*

"How did you know that I was home?"

"I didn't, but I was hoping that you were so we could talk."

"We don't have anything to talk about."

"I want you back."

"Hey, you can't have people over!" My brother said as he opened the refrigerator.

"Michael, go back to your video game!"

"It's not fair. You can have people over but I can't. It's not fair," my brother mumbled, grabbed a soda, and then went back to his room.

"Can we go talk in your room?" I started to feel even sleepier and I had a hard time keeping my eyes open.

"No, Joe...You should go. I'm really tired. I think I'm going to go to bed." Joe put his hand on my back and guided me down the hallway to my room. He shut the door behind us. He took the bottle of vodka from me and put it on my nightstand. He pulled my hoodie off over my head and then went to unbutton my pants. *I don't care anymore...*

"We should be together," Joe said. I shut my eyes. Joe kissed me. I didn't stop him. "You are so hot..." My head started spinning. I felt good and then I didn't feel anything at all.

Somebody get that damn phone. Oh my God. My head is killing me. Worst headache of my life. The phone continued to ring. I rubbed my eyes which made the sharp, stabbing pain in my head unbearable. *I have to answer that damn phone.* I went to open my door when I felt something wet dripping down my leg. *Oh no...Joe...Shit. Where's Joe? Where did he go? Gross.* I pulled a blanket off of my bed and wiped my leg clean. I put on a fresh pair of underwear and some sweatpants. I opened the door and walked past my brother's room.

How can Michael sleep through the phone ringing? I answered the phone and the incessant ringing stopped.

"Hannah?"

"Yeah, Summer, is that you?"

"Yeah." *Oh my God, I don't feel good at all...* "I know it's late and you're probably not coming over, but..."

"Hold on, shit..." I felt all of my bad decisions boiling in my stomach, fighting for a way out. It was the worst nausea that I had ever experienced. I ran to the bathroom with the phone still in my hand and dove into the toilet. I violently threw up to the point that I woke my brother up.

"Hey, are you okay?" My brother asked.

"No, Michael, go back to bed!" I screamed.

"Okay, sorry for asking," he said and went back to his room.

"Michael...Shit." *Oh shit, Summer. I never hung up the phone.* I flushed the toilet, washed my hands, and wiped my face on the hand towel. I picked up the phone off of the floor and put it to my ear. I looked at myself in the mirror. *Who are you?* "Summer..."

"Yeah..."

"Summer..."

"Are you okay, Hannah?" I went back to my room and shut my door.

"No, Summer, I messed up, really bad."

"What happened?"

"I think...Joe and I..."

"Joe!? What happened, Hannah?"

"Well, where do I start? Okay. I tried to take my dad's truck to go find Mel..."

"What!?"

"But it wouldn't move...So I cried. I didn't know what to do so I drank a lot of vodka.

"Uh oh..."

"And yes, I realize the irony."

"I wasn't going to say anything..."

"Joe showed up. I answered the door. I know I shouldn't have but..."

"Did you and Joe, you know..."

"I think so..."

"You think so?"

"Yeah. I was really tired and he started kissing me and..."

"And..."

"I don't remember, but I woke up with his, you know, stuff dripping down my leg so, yeah, there's that..."

"HANNAH! You were raped! Joe raped you!"

"I don't think so...I mean, you can't rape the willing, right? I didn't say no..."

"You passed out. That's automatically rape!" *It is?*

"I lost my virginity to Joe..."

"I'm sorry, Hannah..."

"And I don't even remember it..."

"You were raped, Hannah!"

"Okay, I get it, Summer, sheesh."

"You need to call the police or something..."

"I'm not going to call the police. I'm not hurt or anything...He didn't hurt me."

"You might be pregnant. How are you going to explain that to your parents?" *Shit. Oh shit...*

"You can't get pregnant from doing it once," I reasoned.

"Yes, you can...That's what they said in health class." *They did? Shit. What did I do?* "Hannah, you have to tell someone."

"I don't want to tell anyone. I just want to pretend like it didn't happen..."

"What if he rapes someone else? You have to say something...You have to stop him from doing it again...If you don't say something then I will..."

"...No, you won't, Summer...I'll never forgive you if you do."

"I can't just let this go, Hannah."

"Summer, please, forget about it. It didn't even happen to you!"

"That really hurts...I'm your friend. I'm just trying to help."

"You can help me by forgetting about this."

"What would Mel do, Hannah? What would Mel have you do?"

"That's low, Summer, even for you?"

"Even for me?"

"I have to go," I said. I looked at the clock. *It's almost midnight.* "My parents are going to get home in an hour. I have to clean everything up."

"Hannah..."

"Don't say anything! Promise me."

"I promise. I won't say anything..."

"...Thank you...Bye, Summer."

"Bye, Hannah...Happy New Year..."

"You too." I hung up the phone. *Yeah, real happy New Year. This is all my fault...Shit.* I went to my room and grabbed the bottle of vodka and put it back in the cabinet. *Maybe...Yeah, they won't even notice...I hope.* I cleaned the toilet, which I had absolutely destroyed. *Michael...* I slowly opened my brother's door and saw that he was fast asleep. "Michael. Michael...Michael, wake up."

"What?"

"Hey, I'm sorry I yelled at you earlier..."

"Okay..."

"It's not your fault. It's my fault."

"Okay."

"Michael, I need you to keep everything that happened tonight a secret. You can't tell mom or dad anything."

"Anything...But what if they ask about..."

"Michael, you can't...Say...Anything! Okay? Do you want me to be sent away to a convent?"

"What's a convent?"

"It's a place far away where you won't get to see me ever again."

"...No, I don't want you to go to a convent."

"Then you have to promise not to say anything."

"Okay, I promise." My brother yawned and then put his head back down on his pillow.

"Okay, good. Go back to sleep."

"Goodnight, Hannah."

"Night..." I shut my brother's door and stood in the hallway. *The note...*I went to the living room and turned off the TV. I got the note out of the trash, put it in my pocket, and turned out the lights. *If they ever knew...* I walked to my room and shut the door. I got into bed and started crying. *I think Mel had the right idea...*

Chapter Eleven

Test for life

I was feeling very anxious when school started back a week later. I felt like I didn't belong there. I was having constant nagging memories of the fourth grade replaying on a loop in my head. *Sunday bloody Sunday...* All of the feelings of embarrassment and the humiliation I went through were still coursing through me. *Mel. I can't even imagine what's she's going through...Went through...Shit!* My nerves calmed as I realized how trivial my problems were in comparison to Melissa's. *I don't have any problems.* I was sitting in math class and was quickly brought back to reality when I looked over at Joe. He was smiling at me. *He has absolutely no shame.* I hadn't talked to him since that night. He didn't call me. I was also late to class, thanks to my mom, so he didn't get a chance to bother me before school. *Maybe he was ashamed. Nah, I doubt it. I don't think he has that feeling.* I looked away from him and tried to recall what happened. *Was it rape? I don't feel like I was raped. But, how am I supposed to know what rape feels like? If I weren't drunk and I said no, would he have done it anyway? Hmmm. Maybe. Probably. I don't know. What difference does it make though? Oh my God...What if I'm pregnant? Mom and dad will kill me. Literally. I need to get a pregnancy test. But how? Hmmm.* Joe leaned over to me and whispered,

"Hey, you wanna meet in the bathroom at lunch?"

"FUCK YOU, JOE!" I snapped and stared at him as though he were Jimmy and needed to be choked out of existence.

"That's enough! Hannah, go to the office," Mr. Gomez said. Mr. Gomez was the strictest teacher at Fesler and everyone knew not to interrupt his class. I wasn't everyone though. I didn't move. I continued staring at Joe like his life was about to end. None of our classmates had the courage to say anything. There was absolute silence until Mr. Gomez started walking towards us and his giant cowboy boots clacked against the linoleum floor and echoed around the room. *Shit. Get up! Go to the office...Nah.* I didn't move. I was committed to my defiance. Mr. Gomez stopped right in front of my desk.

"Did you hear what I said?" Mr. Gomez asked. *Yes...* "Hannah O'Connor!" Mr. Gomez cracked the ruler that he was holding across my desk. "Now, Hannah, go NOW!"

"Fine," I said and pulled my backpack off of the floor. I walked out of the classroom, but I didn't go to the office. I went out to the basketball courts and sat on a bench. *I miss her. It's not the same without her. I don't wanna be here...* I waited on the bench until the bell rang and then started walking to my next class. On my way, Summer found me in the crowd.

"Hannah! Hey, I didn't see you this morning."

"I was late."

"You were late to Gomez's class?"

"Yeah, but he just looked at me funny. He kicked me out after I yelled at Joe."

"Oh my God, that's right! Doesn't he sit right next to you?"

"Yeah. You're never gonna guess what that asshole said to me."

"Something stupid?"

"Worse than stupid. He asked me if I wanted to go to the bathroom at lunch."

"That guy is the definition of sleaze."

"I know." *I should have known better. I did. I guess I can only blame myself.*

"Hannah, I know you don't want to talk about, you know, but I've heard rumors that he's done that to other girls."

"You're right. I don't even want to think about it."

"But don't you think he deserves to be, I don't know, in prison or something."

"Yeah...But nothing's going to happen to him. It's just my word against his. And I was drinking. Not like that's legal. Then it's a whole thing. I'll end up in more trouble than him."

"We can't let him get away..."

"...I'm sorry, Summer," I interjected. "I just want to forget about it."

"Have you thought about what I said, about, maybe, being pregnant?"

"Yeah..."

"What are you going to do?"

"I guess I'm going to have to get a pregnancy test."

"Do you want me to go with you?"

"Yeah...and thanks, Summer...for not saying anything."

"Sure."

"Have you heard from Mel?"

"No...Hannah, I think Mel, whether she did or didn't, you know, made her choice...and maybe, if she didn't, doesn't want to be found."

"Yeah. Maybe she is happier now."

"That's what I'm thinking."

"Summer, you always say the right thing. Thanks, I feel better."

"That's what friends are for, right?"

"Right."

"I gotta get to class. I wouldn't want to be late." Summer smiled.

"Yeah. Me too. Talk to you later." Summer gave me a hug and whispered in my ear,

"You should get your class changed. You don't wanna see Joe every day, do you?"

"No. You're right. It wouldn't hurt to ask." Summer let me go and then waved at me.

"Bye, Hannah."

"Bye." I watched Summer walk away from me and then made my way to Mr. Gomez's classroom. *I wonder if I can get into Summer's math class. Her teacher can't be worse than Gomez.* I walked into Mr. Gomez's class and then went over to his desk. He was sitting down and doing something on his computer. "Mr. Gomez," I said softly.

"Hannah, what are you doing here?"

"I just wanted to apologize for what happened in class. Joe has been harassing me and I guess I just lost my temper."

"Harassing you?"

"Yeah, I wanted to ask, if maybe, you could move me to another math class. I just think that..."

"...You'd have to talk to your counselor about that. The best I can do is move your seat to the other side of the room."

"Ummm, okay."

"I'll do that right now. All right, you're gonna be in the fourth row in the back. You should still talk to your counselor though."

"Right, I will, thanks...Ummm, can I have a pass to my next class...I wouldn't want to be late again."

"...Yeah. Here's a pass." Mr. Gomez handed me one of his personalized hall passes. "Now hurry up."

"Okay, thanks." I turned around and walked down the center aisle of the classroom. All of Mr. Gomez's second period students stared at me like I had something written on my forehead. *What's their problem?*

At lunch, I walked to the middle of the school and waited for Summer. Crowds of people walked by me with the same look on their face from earlier in Mr. Gomez's class. *Seriously, is there something on my face?* I pulled my compact out of my backpack and looked at my face carefully. *No, there's nothing wrong...*

"Hannah!" Summer yelled. I turned around to her practically running towards me.

"Summer," I said taking a step back. "What's up?"

"It's Joe, Hannah, he's telling everyone about that night."

"Wait, he's telling people that he..."

"...No! That's the thing. He's saying that you begged him for it. He's referring to you as 'his slut.' He's also bragging about taking your virginity." I laughed.

"I don't even remember it. I don't think it counts."

"Hannah! He thinks he owns you!"

"Ha! Is that what he said?"

"Well, I heard some people talking about it." *Really? Not this again. I need to find him.*

"Well, let's go find him."

"Okay, but are you sure you want to do that? I mean, he did rape you."

"Yes, I'm sure. I think I know where he is."

"Where?"

"The boys locker room." Summer and I walked over to the locker room where Joe was standing in a circle with Ryan and two of their friends. "Joe, what is wrong with you," I said.

"Oh, hey, Onion, you want to hit up the bathroom after all," Joe said and laughed. He started playfully pushing his friends as they laughed with him."

"No, that's so gross. Are you telling people about the other night?"

"Maybe..."

"Are you telling them the truth?"

"What do you mean, the truth?"

"You know, like the fact that I wasn't...Awake."

"What are you talking about? You loved it." *I figured as much...*

"I couldn't have loved it because I was unconscious, Joe!

"You weren't...Unconscious." Joe swallowed hard like he was finally realizing the seriousness of the situation.

"You fucking raped her, asshole!" Summer said and then pointed her finger into Joe's chest. *Oh no! Summer...* Joe's friends let out a chorus of noises as if it were feeding time at the zoo.

"Fuck you, dyke! You wanna act like a man, I'm going to treat you like a man! Joe leaned back in a way that I knew that he was going to hit Summer. I stepped in front of her. Joe saw me at the last second and pulled back, but still made contact with the side of my head. It didn't hurt, but the look on Joe's face made me want to smile. I didn't smile though. He looked mortified and I took the opportunity to sell it like he did hurt me. I held the side of my head and conjured some tears. Summer hugged me close to her. Joe and his friends stood still and quiet. Mr. Collins, one of the teachers on lunch duty that day, ran over to us. Mr. Collins was an English teacher but he was also the head football coach.

"Joe, did I just see you hit that girl? Please tell me that you didn't hit a girl," Mr. Collins pleaded.

"Coach...I wasn't trying to hit Hannah, I was trying to hit...Shit..."

"He was going to hit me, but Hannah jumped in front of me and stopped him," Summer said. "She's my hero." Summer hugged me tighter and I continued to act distressed.

"What the fuck!?" Joe said while squinting his eyes.

"All right, Joe, that's enough, let's go," Mr. Collins said.

"Go where?" Joe asked.

"Don't play dumb," Mr. Collins said and led Joe by the shoulder toward the office. I was expecting Ryan to say something stupid, but he didn't. Ryan and his friends simply walked away.

I still hadn't gotten a pregnancy test as Valentine's Day approached. I was spending my days at school trying not to focus on the inevitable possibility that I may be pregnant. My grades started to improve because I spent most of my time on my school work. My parents were impressed with how 'mature' I had become. On the outside, I showed a compliant school-girl who was diligently planning her future. On the inside, I was an anxious, depressed mess of a person; an almost laughable cliché of any teen girl ever portrayed in the media. I had no intention of letting that girl out. Summer and I had become very close. I knew that she had feelings for me and she knew that I would be nothing more than a friend to her. We both pretended otherwise. I didn't want to lead her on, but at the same time, she was all that I had. Joe got suspended for 'assaulting' me that day, but only for three days. When he came back, he didn't even attempt to talk to me. I wasn't sure why he suddenly lost interest in me, but I was sure that it had something to do with Summer always being by my side. I had never seen Joe rattled like he was when Summer called him a rapist. 'Onion' simply ceased to exist, which I could not have been happier about.

Valentine's day was on a Monday that year and everyone at school seemed to be with someone, except for me. I was alone. There were flowers, balloons, candy, and stuffed animals everywhere and in every classroom. I met Summer at lunch like I did every day, but something was different that day. Summer walked up to me with one of her hands behind her back.

"What's going on, Summer? What's with your..." Before I finished my question, Summer brought her arm around revealing a single white rose with a pink tip."

"It's beautiful, Summer, thank you."

"I was thinking since I didn't get you anything for your birthday..."

"It's okay, you didn't have to...Fourteen isn't exactly a milestone."

"I know, but I wanted to..."

"Well, thanks, it's really pretty." I brought the rose to my nose and breathed it in. "It smells really good too."

"Hannah...I was wondering...Can I kiss you?" *What am I going to do now?* I paused for a second. *Don't wait too long. Say something.*

"Yeah, okay," I said. *It's not a big deal.* Summer walked up to me and I closed my eyes. She pressed her lips very softly against mine and wrapped her hands around my waist. It felt good, but it also felt wrong. I also didn't want to hurt the feelings of the only person I had in my life. The kiss didn't last long though because of some raucous laughter near us. Summer and I stopped kissing and turned to the source. It was Joe, Jade, Ryan, and a few of their friends.

"Gayeeee! Ryan quipped and laughed like a starving hyena.

"So what, Ryan," I said, "you're a stupid jerk."

"Ohhh, stupid jerk, you really got me there." Ryan turned to Joe who was holding Jade's hand. *She's still with him? I feel sorry for her.* "Joe, check out the carpet munchers." *Carpet munchers? Oh wait, I get it...* Ryan laughed again, but he was the only one. Joe didn't say anything. He looked at me solemnly and then started walking away. His friends followed him and Ryan eventually got the hint. "What's wrong with you guys? Hey, wait for me."

"That's funny," Summer said after Ryan was out of earshot.

"What's funny?"

"I don't think I've ever seen Joe not say something, you know?"

"I think he's afraid of you."

"Good!" Summer and I laughed. *Shit. Pregnancy test.*

"Summer?"

"Yeah."

"I've been putting this off because, I mean, I don't feel like I'm pregnant, not that I have a clue...And I got my period after my birthday, but I just want to make sure."

"Yeah, of course, so, you wanna get a test?"

"Yeah, but I don't have any money and if I asked my parents then they would be super suspicious and want to know what it was for. I just don't want..."

"...I'll give you the money."

"You will?"

"I'd do anything for you." *Yeah. I know.* "How much do you think it costs?"

"I don't know, like ten bucks?"

"That's okay, I have forty right now."

"Wow," I said and smiled. "Somebody's rich..."

"My dad gives me an allowance. I don't even ask for it and it's not like I need it." *That must be really nice.* Summer swung her backpack off of her shoulder and unzipped the front pocket. She pulled out two twenty-dollar bills and handed them to me."

"Summer!" I laughed, "This looks like a drug deal." Summer laughed.

"No, it doesn't, you're silly. Hey, you wanna go get it right now?"

"Well, yeah, but..."

"We've ditched before, remember?" *Yes...I remember.* "We didn't get caught then and we won't..."

"I think we just got lucky last time."

"It's not luck. The teachers say they take attendance, but I'm not sure they do. I think we proved that they don't."

"Hmmm, maybe you're right. Maybe they only take attendance first period and then just figure that you're here or you're not."

"Yeah, yeah. Exactly."

"Okay, same plan as last time then?"

"I don't even think we have to pretend this time."

"No basketball shenanigans?" Summer and I both laughed.

"For sure, no."

"Okay, so what's the closest store?"

"Drugstore...Walgreens? I don't think we could walk to the Walgreens. That's pretty far."

"Hmmm. What about Vons? I think they have pregnancy tests and it's right across the street."

"That's right. So, let's go." Summer and I slowly walked to the basketball courts and to the back fence. We checked to see if anyone was watching. There wasn't any supervision on the basketball courts. We shrugged our shoulders and hopped over the fence.

"Do they just assume that we're not going to ditch?"

"I guess. It's funny though."

"I wonder what would happen if they found out?"

"Probably build a higher fence," Summer said and we laughed as we made our way to Chapel Street. We crossed over Chapel Street onto Concepcion Avenue.

"Oh, no," I said as I read the street sign.

"What's wrong?"

"Concepcion Avenue...That can't be good..."

"What do you mean?"

"I have to cross 'conception' to buy a pregnancy test."

"Hannah, you're being silly again. This street has always been here."

"Yeah...I guess you're right. It seems a little spooky though. Like, it's foreshadowing my test results!"

"And here I thought that I was dramatic!"

"I think we're both equally dramatic. Aquarius and Libra. What are you gonna do?"

"Right...The astrology thing..."

"I have it on good authority that astrology is the honest to goodness truth."

"Whose authority?"

"Mine..." I smiled and Summer laughed. "I have books to prove it."

"Okay, well, you'll have to lend me one of those sometime."

"I will. You'll see and you won't doubt me ever again!"

"We will see about that...Hey let's cross right here." Summer grabbed my hand and we crossed Concepcion Avenue to get to the back side of Vons. We walked through the alleyways past the dumpsters and then made it around to the front of the store. We went straight to the 'feminine hygiene' section and looked for a pregnancy test. *Oh my God, there are like a million different ones.*

"So, what am I supposed to get?"

"I heard Clearblue Easy is good."

"Okay...So which one?"

"Well, let's see..." Summer picked up a box. "...You can get this one for nine bucks or that one..." Summer pointed to another box. "You get two tests for Fourteen bucks. You're fourteen now...Maybe it's a sign." Summer giggled.

"Nice one, but I definitely don't need two tests!" I took the box with a single test from Summer."

"All right, let's go."

"Wait, we have forty bucks, you wanna get a sandwich or something?"

"Sure." As we walked down the aisle, a box that read: 'VCF' caught my attention. "Oh, yeah, I remember my mom telling me about this stuff. I guess it like kills sperm."

"That's awesome, maybe we should get a box for Joe and Ryan." Summer and I both laughed a little too loud for the required decorum in a supermarket. A lot of old people looked at us funny, but we were unaffected and casually walked to the deli counter. We both ordered a turkey sandwich and a large Pepsi and then went to the check out in the front of the store. We put the sandwiches, sodas, and the pregnancy test on the conveyer belt. *Two sandwiches. Two sodas. One pregnancy test. Totally normal combination...* The cashier looked at us just like the old people had earlier. *What's her problem? Oh, wait...It's probably because we look like we're supposed to be in school...Which we are. Makes sense.*

"That'll be $24.64," The cashier said. I handed her the forty dollars and she handed me back the change. Summer and I picked up our food and drinks and I smashed the pregnancy test under my sandwich. "Have a nice day."

"You too," I said. Once outside, I handed Summer her change, which she shoved into her front pocket. "Summer, can you hold my food?"

"Of course." I put the pregnancy test in my backpack and then Summer gave me my food. We slowly started walking back to school, mirroring one another with our sandwiches in our right hands and our sodas in our left hands. In between eating and drinking we made small talk about trivial things like the weather and how the random people around us dressed. When we got back to the fence behind Fesler, Summer became much more profound. "Hannah, what if you're pregnant?"

"Well...I don't know. I haven't really thought about it."

"Hannah, you're fourteen! You would get an abortion, right?"

"Summer, I don't know if I could do that. I don't think I could kill my own baby...Even if it were Joe's."

"But...You're fourteen!"

"It's not the baby's fault that I'm fourteen." *Oh my God, what am I even saying? What baby?* I took the last bite of my sandwich and washed it down with some Pepsi. "Summer, I really don't think I'm pregnant, so it doesn't matter."

"Then why?"

"I just wanted to be sure. Peace of mind, you know?"

"Okay, so, what's that word...Hypothetically. Hypothetically, if you were pregnant, you would want to keep the baby?"

"I don't know. I think so, yeah."

"Wow, Hannah, how would you take care of it? You think Joe's gonna drop out of school and get a job and then the three of you are going to live happily ever after!?" I could hear the agitation in Summer's voice. *She seems to be taking this personally.*

"You said hypothetically, right?"

"Right..."

"Well, hypothetically, I would keep the baby and then figure it out."

"But..."

"...I know," I interjected. "Because it's hypothetical, it's easy to say that. If I were actually pregnant, I'd have a lot to think about. By the way, are you going to finish your sandwich?" I smiled hoping to ease the tension between us.

"Huh...Oh, yeah, no, I'm full." Summer wrapped the remainder of her sandwich up and put it in her backpack. "Hannah, do you plan on going to college?"

"Probably. I don't know. I guess so. I haven't thought about it...Summer, we're not even in high school yet...Are you going to college?"

"Yeah. I'm not sure where though...My parents want me to go to Berkeley..."

"That's cool..."

"Yeah. You know, if you were to have a baby...You know, hypothetically, it would be really hard, if not impossible, to go to college." *She's still on this, huh?*

"Summer?" I smiled. "Do you want me to pee on the stick right now?" Summer blushed.

"...No. But if you want to, I won't stop you." *Seriously?*

"I was joking, Summer, I'm going to take it at home like a normal person."

"Oh, yeah, I know..."

"You have to relax though. You're younger than me and I think you're about to have a heart-attack."

"I'm not about to have a heart-attack."

"You are too..."

"No, I'm not."

"Are too..." Summer and I laughed.

"Okay, but can you promise me one thing?"

"Sure."

"Call me tonight as soon as you know."

"I'll call you tonight, Summer."

"Thanks, because..."

"Summer, relax, please," I said and gently put my hand on her shoulder.

"I know. I'm just worried..." *I need to change the subject...*

"I had a really good time with you today...thanks for coming with me."

"Me too. Hannah, I know you're not gay." *Ahhh crap, can we go back to talking about my hypothetical baby?* "But...Maybe you could be bisexual, you know, because, well..."

"Summer, I honestly don't even know what to say..."

"You don't have to say anything...Just think about it okay?" *Think about what?* Before I had the chance to think of a response, I heard the voice of our principal on the intercom.

"Hannah, O'Connor, please come to the office...Hannah O'Connor to the front office."

"Oh shit," I said. "Busted."

"What are you going to do?"

"I think I should go."

"Okay...I'm gonna stay here." Summer hugged me. "Don't forget to call me." *I will if I can. Shit...*

"Yeah, first thing. Bye, Summer."

"Bye." Summer crouched down under the tree and I hopped over the fence. I made my way to the front office where Mr. Vincent was waiting.

"Hannah! Where were you? Your teacher said you weren't in class." I looked down at my Pepsi, which I still had not finished.

"Okay, look, Mr. Vincent, I'm not going to lie. I went to Vons to get lunch."

"Unbelievable! Do you think this is high school? College!? Hannah, this is not an open campus, you can't just come and go as you please. We're responsible...You know what? We'll deal with that later, you're here now and you're safe." *Sounds serious. I wonder what's going on...* "Please come into my office."

"Okay, but this is obviously not about me ditching school, so what is it?"

"That's right, but, please, have a seat." I sat down in one of the chairs facing Mr. Vincent's desk. He shut the door and then sat down at his desk. "Hannah, a serious accusation has been made. I need you to answer a question and I need you to tell me the truth." *This doesn't sound good at all. Accusation? By whom? About what?*

"Okay, Mr. Vincent." He took a deep breath and shuffled around some papers on his desk. *Are you okay?*

"...Did Joe Anderson rape you?" My heart sank and my eyes widened. *He knows? How does he know? Summer was the only one...No...Summer...No, wait. It couldn't be Summer. She was with me...But who else? I can't tell him the truth.* "Hannah, it's okay, you're not in trouble, but if Joe raped you then you have to tell me. *No, I don't. I have to say something though...* "Hannah, Coach Collins reported that Joe hit you last month...Joe said it was an accident...Hannah, was it an accident?"

"Yeah, it was an accident."

"...Okay. I know it's hard to hear, but I have to ask you again...Did Joe rape you?" *What am I going to say? If I say yes, what's going to happen? Was it even rape? I don't know. Summer thinks so...Maybe she's right. What if I say no and then I turn out to be pregnant? I'm not pregnant though...I think. Oh my God!* "Hannah!" Mr. Vincent raised his voice. *He's losing his patience...I have to say something.* I could feel the pressure building inside me as Mr. Vincent's eyes flickered as if he were possessed.

"I'm sorry...I was just surprised by the question. Joe didn't rape me," I said quickly. Mr. Vincent took another audible, deep breath. *I don't think he believes me.* "Hannah, is that the truth?" *No. Maybe. No...* "Joe didn't rape you?"

"No, Joe, didn't rape me."

"Hannah, are you sure?" *What's that supposed to mean?*

"We dated for a while, but he didn't rape me."

"You were boyfriend/girlfriend?"

"Yeah...But I broke up with him."

"Why did you break up with him?"

"Do I have to say?"

"Yes. Tell me the truth, Hannah." *Jade...*

"I broke up with him because he cheated on me."

"Cheated on you? With whom?"

"Really, Mr. Vincent?"

"It's important." *I guess it doesn't matter.*

"Jade...Ummm, I don't remember her last name...She's a seventh grader."

"I see." Mr. Vincent grabbed some papers off of his desk and stacked them into a collated pile. *Is that it then?* "Okay, Hannah, I think I understand what's going on here..." *You do?* "...You're free to go back to class...And make sure you actually make it there, Hannah!"

"You're not going to call my parents about ditching, are you? I won't do it again, I promise."

"We already called your parents." *Oh shit.* "We were only able to leave a message though. You're lucky, we were about to call the police." *Lucky huh? Yeah right. Wait...*

"Wait, who made the accusation?"

"That's confidential, Hannah, now please, go to class." I shook my head in disbelief but began walking to my last class. *How am I going to explain this? Not good. Not good at all. It couldn't have been Summer...*

My dad picked me up from school and as I walked up to his truck, I knew that I was in trouble. I could see the look on his face from a mile away. It wasn't actually a mile, but I could feel the anger radiating from his face. I opened the door and didn't have a chance to say anything.

"You're grounded!" My dad said. *I figured.* "Get in the truck."

"I was going to..." *What did he think I was going to do?*

"Don't get a smart mouth with me!" *Sheesh! I guess I shouldn't say anything at all. Smart mouth? Dude.* I sat down, put on my seatbelt, and my dad started driving. "Do you have any idea what you put me through?" *No, I really don't.*

"No."

"The school calls and leaves a message that you're missing. I'm thinking, 'how is that even possible, where is she?' I was asleep. The next message was that you ditched and went to lunch at Vons. What the hell is going on, Hannah?"

"Summer and I..."

"The girl that's gay?"

"Yes, dad, Summer's gay, and she's my friend so..." My dad took a deep breath and then exhaled abruptly. "...We wanted to get sandwiches at Vons...So we went."

"You can't just..."

"I know, dad."

"But you did it anyway."

"Yeah." *I didn't have a choice.*

"Who paid for them? Did you steal them?"

"Summer paid for them. Her parent's..."

"...I don't care, Hannah. You can't just do whatever you want because you feel like it. There are rules." *Yes, thank you, I know.* "I talked to your mom before I picked you up. You're grounded until further notice."

"What does that mean?"

"It means we don't know how long it's going to be. It breaks my heart. We have to be able to trust you and you're making that very hard to do right now."

"I'm sorry. I don't know what to say."

"Whose idea was it to ditch school?"

"Mine."

"I don't believe you. We didn't raise you that way." *What are you talking about? What way?* "I don't think you should hang out with that girl anymore."

"DAD, that's not fair! It wasn't her; it was me; I swear."

"She's a bad influence on you." *You're a bad influence on me.*

"You don't even know her."

"I know enough to know that I don't want my daughter to be around her." *Fuck you, dad!* "You may not like it, but that's the way it is. It's for the best." *Right...And this has nothing to do with her being gay...*

"You wouldn't even care if she weren't gay."

"This has nothing to do with that." *I don't believe you.*

"Can I at least call her to tell her I'm grounded?"

"You can ask your mom. My vote is no." *I know. Maybe mom will be more sensible...*

"I will."

"Good luck," my dad replied. I didn't respond. I looked out of the passenger side window and waited in silence for the remainder of the ride home.

I waited for my dad to go to work before I went to the bathroom to take the pregnancy test. As soon as he left, I pulled the test out of my backpack and read the instructions. *Well, it seems simple enough. Plus, I'm pregnant. Minus, I'm not pregnant.* I went to the bathroom and peed on the stick. *What am I going to do if I am...I'm sure I'll have a convent reserved for me in no time. Ugh.* I turned the test upside down so I couldn't see the results. I waited five minutes. *Do I really want to have Joe's baby? Fuck. No. I don't know what I would do if...*I slowly turned the test over. *Minus. That's negative right? How long did I have to wait again?* I looked at the instructions again. *Okay...So, that is not a plus. I'm not pregnant. Dude, I already knew that. Why was I stressing so hard?* I put the test back in the box and put my head against the door to listen for my brother. I didn't hear anything so I opened the door and went to my room. *What am I going to do with this thing? I guess I could throw it away at school.* I put the box in my backpack. *I can't risk...Oh my God...My life would be over.* I Sat on my bed and started my math homework. My mom wasn't home from work yet. I put my pencil down. *I should call Summer.* I opened my bedroom door and walked down the hallway past my brother's room. *Oh shit! Where's Michael? How did I not notice? I didn't even ask. What is wrong with me?* I went to the kitchen and picked up the phone. I dialed Summer's number. No one answered. *I guess she isn't home yet.* I put the phone down and went back to my room. About twenty minutes later my mom got home.

"Hannah!" My mom shrieked. *Oh great.*

"I'm in my room," I said. My mom rumbled down the hallway and stopped at my door.

"Hannah, why? What? What were you thinking!?"

"I guess I wasn't thinking."

"You're grounded." *I know.*

"Dad told me."

"No friends. No phone. No TV. Nothing! You go to school, do your homework, and that's it."

"For how long?"

"...How about until high school?"

"What!? I'm grounded for..." I tried to do the math in my head, but I wasn't sure whether she meant May or August. I didn't want to ask for fear that she would choose the latter. "Can I at least call Summer to tell her I'm grounded."

"No!"

"But I told her that I would call her."

"That's too bad."

"That's not fair!"

"Hannah..."

"I mean seriously, you act like you never ditched school."

"That's not the point."

"Isn't it?"

"No! We're talking about you here."

"You're a hypocrite!"

"Maybe, but I'm responsible for you and you can't..."

"...Whatever, mom, I have to do my homework."

"Hannah, I have to tell you...your father and I..."

"Can you close my door, please? I need to focus on my homework." *Yeah right.* My mom shook her head and didn't say anything. She closed my door and I heard her walk down the hallway. *Good, go away. I guess Summer will have to wait for the good news. I guess it's good news. What's wrong with me? She'll be happy about it; I think. That's kind of weird though. Maybe it's not. I don't know...*

My mom dropped me off at school the next day. I walked to the basketball courts to find Summer as soon as I got on campus. As soon as Summer saw me, she ran up to me and gave me a hug.

"Hannah, what happened? You didn't call me last night."

"I did, but no one answered. I don't think you were home yet."

"Yeah, so what happened?"

"I got grounded.

"Why?"

"Mr. Vincent called my house because I wasn't in class."

"I don't get it."

"Someone told him that Joe raped me." I stared at Summer as if I expected her to explain herself even though I knew it couldn't have been her."

"...It wasn't me. I didn't say anything."

"I know, Summer, but someone did. Who else knew?"

"No one. I can't think of anyone."

"Something's going on. I just don't know..."

"I promise you...I didn't say anything...To anyone...Shit, Hannah, did you take the pregnancy test?"

"Yeah."

"And?"

"I'm not pregnant."

"Thank God! I mean, that's a good thing, right?"

"Yeah...I'm too young to have a baby...Right?"

"Right."

"Summer...My parents want to ground me forever. At least it seems like it."

"I'm sorry, Hannah."

"It's okay, it's not your fault."

"I know, but you don't deserve that."

"They won't let me use the phone."

"That's okay."

"No, it's not."

"I know, but what I meant was that we still have school."

"Yeah, you're right, they can't stop me from coming to school. Not that they would want to. They completely lost it after ditching one day. Seriously."

"So, how long are you grounded?"

"My mom said until high school."

"What!? That's ridiculous."

"I know. I don't believe her though. She was just mad."

"I hope so...I may want to see you outside of school every now and then."

"Yeah, me too, Summer. You know that you're my only friend."

"That's not true."

"It is though...And it's enough for me..."

"Me too, Hannah, me too."

A week before Spring Break, I was sitting on my bed doing my homework as diligently as ever since I was grounded, and I heard a knock on my door. My dad opened the door and walked in.

"Hannah, we're having a family meeting." *A family meeting? Did someone die?*

"Okay..."

"Can you come out to the living room?" *Do I have a choice?*

"Yeah, what's going on?"

"We'll tell you. Just come out to the living room."

"Okay." *I guess. Maybe they're going to let me be...not grounded.* I followed my dad out to the living room and sat down on the couch next to my brother. I looked at him inquisitively. "What's going on?"

"I don't know," my brother said. "I was playing videogames..."

"Hannah...Michael," my dad said with trepidation in his voice. *Yeah, someone died...* "...I know that Santa Maria is, well, all you know, really, but sometimes...In life..." *Santa Maria?*

"What your dad is trying to say is..." *What's going on?* "...We're moving to Visalia," my mom said. *Visalia? Jessica? Summer...*

"I think the move is going to be good for all of us," my dad added. *Is this all because of me?* "My job wants me to transfer and your mom is going to work at the hospital there."

"How long have you been planning this?" I asked.

"...We knew about it during the holidays," my mom said. *What the hell!?* "But we didn't want to say anything until we were sure. Now, we're sure," my mom said.

"It's a fresh start for all of us," my dad said. *It is because of me...* "What do you think, Michael?"

"I think it's cool," my brother said. *He doesn't have any friends. Of course, it doesn't matter to him.*

"Hannah, I know this is hard, but it's for the best," my dad added. *That's what you guys keep saying, but how do you actually know what's best?* "We're going to wait until you two finish the school year and then we're moving. We already bought a new house. We got a really good price too." *Who cares?*

"I don't get it," I said. "Why are we moving anyway? This is stupid. It's not because I ditched school, is it?"

"No, Hannah, it's not," my mom said.

"Yes, it is...You just hate Summer," I replied.

"Summer?" My dad said and laughed. "This has nothing...Listen, my job wants me in Visalia so that's where we're going. It's that simple."

"So, you want me to forget about my only friend and just move away...Like she never existed?"

"Don't be so dramatic," my dad said. "There is a thing called the phone." *Oh, that's just great.*

"So, I'm not grounded anymore?" I asked and looked at my dad and then at my mom.

"When we move to Visalia, you won't be grounded anymore," my mom said.

"That's just great. I don't even have any friends in Visalia."

"You have Jessica, she's your friend, right?" *Jessica, yeah, I don't know. I don't really...*

"I guess," I said halfheartedly.

"There you go!" my dad said. "It's going to be good, trust me. This move will be good for all of us."

"It's easy for you to say," I said. "You already have your best friend there. This is good for you..."

"Hannah, you can either see this move as a positive or a negative, but it would behoove you to see this as a positive. It hasn't been easy for you here..." My mom reasoned. *Yeah, I know. Thanks.* "You have the opportunity to put all of this behind you." *Hmmm.*

"We want you two to start packing and throwing stuff away that you don't need anymore. We're not moving for a month, but it's good to get a head start. We're moving the day after school ends," my dad said.

"So that's it, huh? You make this decision to change our lives forever and we are just supposed to accept it and move on?"

"Yes!" My dad barked. "Like I said, my job..."

"I heard you the first time...It doesn't make it right." I got up from the couch and walked down the hallway towards my room.

"Hannah! Get back here," my dad shouted.

"Let her go. She'll be fine," my mom said. I shut my bedroom door behind me and leaned my head against the wall. I started crying. *A fresh start...Summer...Mel...What happened with Mel? She started over...I think...It was her decision though. Joe...At least I won't have to see Joe's stupid face anymore...That's a good thing...Maybe It won't be so bad...*

Part Two

Chapter Twelve

Visalia Times-Delta

I eventually made my mind up over the last month of school that I was going to make the best of the situation that I found myself in. I didn't have a choice about moving. Complaining about it wasn't going to make a difference, so I didn't. I went to class every day. I did my work. I got straight A's. I told Summer about my family moving to Visalia. She was sad. She cried when I told her, but I promised her that I would call her every day. I was actually relieved to a certain extent because I wouldn't have to pretend to be interested in a possible relationship with her. After our graduation, I walked up to Summer and gave her a hug. I wanted to talk to her before my parents and brother made their way down to the field.

"I'm going to miss you, Summer," I said as I let her go.

"I'm going to miss you more, Hannah." I saw the tears begin to fill her eyes.

"Don't cry, Summer, we'll be friends forever. I'm never going to forget you."

"I know. It's just so sad. What am I going to do without you next year?"

"You're going to find someone that deserves you. You're awesome, Summer...I mean, you know, if I weren't, you know, then I'd..."

"Yeah, I know. I just wish things were different."

"And when I get my license, I'll come visit you..."

"Promise?"

"Yeah. I'll be sixteen before either one of us even realizes it."

"That's true...Promise me something else, Hannah..."

"Yeah..."

"Find a boy that...I don't know, that isn't anything like Joe."

"I will, trust me."

"I'm sorry that I have to go to the same school as his rapey ass. I hate him so much..."

"I know...but, I don't know, I'm not, you know, totally innocent here. I didn't have to open the door that night."

"No, Hannah, don't even think that. You didn't do anything wrong. Joe's an asshole rapist and you didn't deserve that."

"I know, Summer, thanks...Oh shit, my parents are coming...Shit, we're leaving tomorrow morning. We're already packed. I'll call you as soon as I get to Visalia."

"Okay, Hannah. I love you."

"I love you too, Summer." I hugged Summer and then she walked into the crowd away from my family.

"Where's your friend running off to?" My dad inquired.

"She knows you don't like her. Way to go on that, dad."

"That's not true." *Whatever, dad.*

"Congratulations!" My mom said. "This is a big milestone."

"Thanks, mom, but I honestly think this is kind of dumb. It's just eighth grade. Who even cares? It's not high school."

"Okay, okay, but it's nice that they do something for you," my mom said. "We didn't have a graduation from junior high back..."

"...And that's the way it should be," I interjected. "I don't get why they make a big deal out of this. It's not a big deal."

"It's not a big deal," my brother agreed. "Can we go home now?"

"Michael!" My mom scolded.

"What?" My brother asked.

"This is your sister's day," my mom responded.

"I don't even care," I insisted.

"Fine, let's go home. We have to get ready. Tomorrow's the big day," my dad said and smiled. *Yes, tomorrow is the day...I'm okay with that. I think I'm ready to move on. I think it's time...*

Everything was already packed into the U-Haul truck that my dad rented. My brother and I stood at the end of the driveway and stared back at the only house that we'd ever known. *This is sad. I'm not going to cry though... It's okay...*

"Let's go," my dad said. "It's a new chapter in the lives of the O'Connor's..."

"...Dad, you're such a dork," I said and laughed. My brother joined in my sentiment.

"Yeah, dad, get a grip," my brother said.

"Get a grip? What does that mean?" My dad asked and we laughed harder. "Seriously..."

"Serious, dad...let's go," I said. My mom shook her head and put her hand on my dad's shoulder as if to console him. We piled into the truck. I was the last one in and shut the door against my arm. I couldn't move and I barely managed to fasten my seatbelt. I snapped it in place and my brother started whining.

"It's too tight...I can't move," my brother whimpered.

"Michael, it's only three hours, relax," my mom said. My dad put the truck in gear and pulled away from our house.

"Dad, what are you going to do about your truck and mom's car?" I inquired.

"We're getting them tomorrow. Your grandpa is going to drive us back. Everything's taken care of, Hannah..." My dad said assuredly. I spent the majority of the drive to Visalia staring out the window at the bleak, desolate landscape that seemed to go on forever. After an hour of driving, I turned to my dad.

"Dad," I said, "I know that you grew up in Visalia and there's Grandma and Grandpa, but, well, what's so great about it? I mean, well, why?" My dad laughed.

"Well, nothing really. It's okay. It's a nice town. Good people. But, it's the economics, Hannah." *Economics, huh?* "My job wanted me out here and so that's it," my dad argued.

"It just seems like there's nothing out here..." My dad and mom laughed.

"Just wait until we get there. It's a good-sized city. It's a lot hotter than Santa Maria but you'll get used to it." *I will? I guess. I don't mind the heat.* "We still have to enroll you at...I think, because of where our new house is...That you'll be at Mt. Whitney. I'm not sure though. I want you to go to Redwood. You'll get to go to school with Jessica!" *Ummm, okay, that's a good thing, right?*

"Redwood...That's where you graduated?" I asked.

"Yep, it's a good school, but I don't think you'll be able to go there, I don't know. Who knows. Maybe." *Okay...* "Mt. Whitney's good too. They're Redwood's rival though" *Okay.* I listened to my dad's nostalgic story about his playing days with Redwood and how he met my mom. I had heard the story maybe a thousand times and my dad was insistent that I hear one more time. I wasn't interested though so I tuned him out and continued staring out the passenger side window. *Wow. I don't think I ever noticed how little there was out here. It's all a variation of brown. Dirt. Nothing. There's some cows! What are they eating? Dirt? I laughed.*

"Hey," I said. "What are those weird looking things out there?" *How did I not notice those before? Super weird. Dude...* My Dad laughed.

"Oil pumps," my dad said. *So, we have dirt, oil, and cows. Awesome.* "There's a lot of oil out here." *Why do I get the feeling that this isn't an upgrade?* I watched the world go by until I saw a sign that read: Hanford. "We're almost there."

"Can we get McDonald's," my brother asked.

"Yeah, Patrick, stop at the McDonald's," my mom said.

"Okay, when we get to Visalia," my dad said. After about twenty minutes, I saw the sign for Visalia. My dad pulled off of the freeway and we went to McDonald's. I got chicken nuggets and ate them as we made our way to our new house. When we pulled in front of our new house, I saw a band playing at the end of the cul-de-sac. *That's so cool.* "Here we are." I got out of the truck and looked down the street. I smiled and waved at the three boys that we're playing in the garage and then helped my brother out of the truck. We all walked to the front door of our new house. *This is weird. This looks just like our old house. I wonder if it's the same inside too...I should go introduce myself...Hmmm, maybe this won't be so bad after all...* I walked inside of the house as was astonished at how similar it was to our old house.

"Dad, did you plan to buy the same house that we had in Santa Maria or was that just a coincidence?" My mom laughed.

"What!? It's not the same..." My dad argued, seemingly annoyed at the idea. He went to the sliding glass door in the back and pulled the blinds aside. "Look, the back yards different."

"It's okay, dad, I believe you," I said and laughed.

"Leave your dad alone," my mom said.

"So, Michael, do you want your old room?" My brother and I laughed.

"Yeah, I guess so..." We walked into the first room down the hallway. "Yeah, it's the same."

"I'm going to check mine." I walked to the end of the hallway to check my room. *Do they build these houses on an assembly line? I wonder...Like that Ford documentary I saw in History class.* I walked back down the hallway and found my parents in the garage where my dad was talking about fixing up his motorcycle. I wasn't very interested in that conversation so I went back to the living room and stared out the window. I saw one of the boys from down the street walking by. He had dirty blond hair and was wearing a grey cardigan sweater and torn blue jeans. *He kind of reminds me of Kurt Cobain...* I kept looking out the window and another one of the boys slowly rode his bike by the U-Haul truck. This one had long black hair and was much skinnier than the first one. *Huh? I guess practice is over...What are my parents still talking about?* "Mom! Dad! Are we going to move our stuff today or, yeah..." My mom and dad came out of the garage smiling. *What?*

"Yeah, I'll open the truck," my dad said. We walked outside to the U-Haul truck. My dad went to the back of the truck and opened the door, which made a thunderous roar as it settled at the top. All of our stuff was packed in pretty tight. *This is going to take days to unpack.* Out of the corner of my eye, I saw the third boy riding his bike around the truck.

"Hey," he said.

"Hey," I replied. My dad was digging through some boxes in the back of the truck, but stopped when he heard the boy's voice.

"I'm Chris. I live down the street." Chris pointed to the open garage where I saw the boys earlier. *He is really cute. Like really cute...He sort of reminds me of...Joe...Uh oh...* I had flashbacks of Summer's face as she implored that I never date another guy like Joe. "So, you're moving in...Do you need any help?" I didn't say anything. My dad came out of the back of the truck and walked down the ramp.

"No, we don't need any help, thank you for asking..." My dad said.

"Chris, dad, his name is Chris."

"Well, Chris, thanks, but I think we've got it."

"Okay," Chris said and began riding his bike again. "Let me know if you do. You know where I live." I looked at my dad who was scowling at Chris as he rode away. *That's not good. Chris is cute. He seems nice. Hmmm...* I watched Chris ride home and then smiled.

"Hannah...Hello, Hannah!" I turned back to my dad. "Grab these boxes first. It's the kitchen stuff."

"Okay, okay..." I grabbed the first box of stuff that my dad handed to me and took it to the kitchen. "Michael!" I yelled. "Go help dad bring the stuff inside." My brother was already playing on his Nintendo, which he apparently didn't pack in the truck. *Michael is so lazy. Sheesh. Chris is so cute. He has a really nice smile...He seems so nice. He didn't have to ask to help...Hannah!* I heard Summer's voice in my head. *Hannah! Didn't you think the same thing about Joe? Yeah, I think I did...I don't know...* "Mom, when are we going to have the phone hooked up?"

"I think it's going to be a few days...Why, who do you need to call?" My mom inquired.

"...Ummm, *Not Summer. They hate her...* "I was thinking about calling Jessica." *Yeah, perfect, they love Jessica.* "So, you know, she can catch me up on all things Visalia."

"Okay. I'll let you know when it's connected. Now stop day-dreaming and go help your dad."

"All right." I went back outside and grabbed another box. We spent the remainder of the afternoon unloading the truck, filling our rooms, and putting things back together. I hadn't even started putting my bed back together when I was accosted by my parents.

"Hannah, we need you to watch your brother. We're going to take the U-Haul back and then your uncle is going to help us get the cars," my mom said.

"Okay."

"We're going to order a pizza before we go...Hannah, you are not allowed to leave this house...or Michael," my dad added.

"And don't answer the door," my mom said. *Okay. I get it...*

"We won't be back until after midnight..." My dad said. "I have to be able to trust you...I can trust you, right?"

"Yes, you can trust me. It's not like I know anyone yet anyway. What am I going to do?" *Please don't answer that...*

"That's a good point," my mom said. "But if you do leave this house, you'll be grounded until...Until you're forty!" *Forty, mom, seriously?*

"Mom, I won't leave, I promise."

"Okay, we have to leave right after we eat," my mom said. *Oh my God. I wasn't even thinking. If I can be grounded until I'm forty, which, I guess is kind of funny, even though it's not actually funny, then that means that I'm not grounded now...* My dad ordered a pizza from Domino's because they said that they would have it to us in twenty minutes or less. Much to my amazement, they did. My parents said we didn't have time to wait for good pizza. The pizza really wasn't bad though and just like my mom said, they left as soon as we finished eating. I locked the door behind them, my brother immediately started playing video games, and I started putting my bed back together.

A week later, after we rebuilt our life in our new house, we finally got phone service.

"Mom, can I call Jessica?" I asked. *Maybe I should call her...*

"We just got service and you already need to be on the phone!?" My mom quickly snapped.

"Well, yeah. I need to, you know, make plans...I'm not grounded anymore, right?"

"I guess it's okay, but make it fast, I want to call your grandma later."

"Okay, yeah, I can be fast." I grabbed the phone off of the kitchen counter and walked to my room. I shut the door and dialed Summer's number. The phone rang multiple times before Summer picked up. "Summer?"

"Hannah? Hey! I thought you said you were going to call me every day?"

"Yeah, sorry, the phone company is really slow here...and oh my God is it hot! I miss Santa Maria...I miss you."

"Ahhh, I miss you too, Hannah...Hey, I have to tell you something..."

"...What is that my dear?"

"My dear...That's cute...Sorry, yeah, I got distracted...So...Oh yeah, Joe's in jail!"

"What!? Joe's in jail?"

"Yeah, you're never gonna guess..." *I hope this doesn't have anything to do with me.*

"I'm afraid to ask..."

"It's Jade..."

"Jade?"

"Jade, or her family I guess, brought charges against him."

"Wait, for what?"

"Oh, I thought I set that up right...Rape, Hannah, rape!"

"Shit. Well, karma, I guess."

"Karma!? Hannah, you have to tell them what happened...That he raped you too." *No, Summer, I don't...*

"Summer, I just want to forget that even happened."

"But...He..."

"Summer, you promised me..."

"I know and I haven't said anything."

"Thank you. It sounds like Joe's going to get what he deserves anyway. I just want to leave the past in the past."

"Okay, but If you did say something, I'm sure he would get more time...Like life in prison."

"I'm not really a vengeful person, Summer."

"Yeah...But it makes me smile to think of Joe getting raped in prison for the rest of his life." *Wow, Summer, Sheesh...*

"That's kind of harsh."

"I don't think it is..." Summer and I both laughed. *I shouldn't laugh. That's not funny.*

"Speaking of Joe, I met this guy named Chris. He lives on my street. He's really cute..."

"Hannah, what do you mean?"

"He kind of reminds me of Joe..."

"Hannah!"

"He's really cute and he seems nice. Summer, he offered to help us move stuff into our new house!"

"Hannah! No Joes! Even Joes named Chris." I laughed.

"I should at least give him a chance..."

"No, you shouldn't. You're better than those guys!"

"Thanks, Summer."

"No problem...Hey I gotta go. My mom wants me to go shopping with her...As if I'm into that kind of stuff."

"Yeah...Okay." I gave Summer my number. "Call me when you get the chance or I'll call you."

"Okay, bye." I said goodbye to Summer and I walked toward my bedroom door. *Oh, shit, I should call Jessica...* I dialed Jessica's number and her mom answered. "Oh, hi, is Jessica there?"

"Yes, may I ask who's calling?"

"It's Hannah."

"Hi Hannah, yes, I think she's been expecting your call." *Great.* "Hold on a minute."

"Hannah?" Jessica said.

"Hi Jessica."

"So, are you guys moved in?"

"Yeah, there's still boxes and stuff to unpack, but pretty much, yeah."

"Cool, so you wanna hang out this summer?" *I don't know, maybe. I've got nothing else to do...*

"Yeah, we could do something..."

"I have to go to the mall next week if you want to go...My mom can take us."

"Yeah, sure, sounds fun. Here's my new number...Give me a call when you want to go."

"Okay, I'll call you."

"Okay. I gotta go though..."

"You just called me..."

"Sorry, my mom wants to call my grandma. I have to get off the phone."

"Oh, okay, bye Hannah."

"Bye." I hung up the phone, walked down the hall, and handed the phone to my mom. "I gave Jessica our new number."

"Oh, okay. Hey, can you take Michael outside? He's been playing his game all morning."

"Yeah, sure...Michael!" I yelled. I walked to his room. "Michael, mom wants you to get off of your game and go outside."

"Fine," my brother said and put his game down. We walked outside and I immediately looked down the street. Chris's garage door was open and the three boys were standing around seemingly getting ready to play. *Oh, cool, we should go listen to them...*

"Michael, do you want to go watch that band play?"

"Yeah, I guess so..." My brother and I started walking down to the end of the cul-de-sac. There seemed to be some sort of commotion going on. It looked like some of the neighbors were arguing with the boys in the band. *Hmmm, I wonder what's going on...* The boy with blond hair started walking towards us. I smiled at him, but he angrily looked straight ahead. *Wow, what's his problem?* We got to the end of Chris's driveway and the boy with long black hair approached us. He was taller than Chris or the boy with blond hair. He was wearing a plain white t-shirt that accentuated his thin frame and oversized baggy jeans. He wasn't cute like Chris but there was something about him that I liked. *He's definitely not Joe.* I waved at him and smiled. He walked right up to me with his bass guitar hanging off of his shoulder.

"Hi, I'm Hannah...this is my brother, Michael," I said.

"I knew that was your brother. I saw you guys moving in last week. I'm Will, nice to meet you, Hannah." He pointed back to Chris. "That's Chris, this is his house." *Yeah, we've met.* "And that was Rob." Will pointed down the street. *Rob, huh?* "He has an anger problem, but he'll get over it." *Anger problem?*

"Cool. How long have you guys had a band?"

"We've been playing together for like, what, two years, Chris?"

"Yeah, I think it's been almost two years," Chris said.

"You guys are really good," I said. *Stupid...* "What's your band name?" *I haven't really even heard them play...*

"...Ummm, we don't have a band name. We've never played an actual show. How did we not think about having a band name?" Will asked.

"You should come up with a name. I could help if you wanted," I said.

"Yeah, we should talk to Rob about it," Will said. *Is Rob the boss?*

"Yeah, for sure," Chris said. "And playing a show. We're good enough to play a show...Aren't we?"

"I think you guys sounded great," I said. *What am I saying?*

"Yeah, you're really good," my brother said without thinking. *Thanks, Michael!*

"Cool, thanks!" Will said. *Wait...No one's even questioning us. Hmmm.* A police car pulled up behind us and two cops got out of the car. One of the cops started looking around Chris's garage.

"We got a noise complaint. You kids in a band?"

"Yeah, but we're done playing for today," Will insisted.

"Hannah...Michael...Get over here!" I heard my mom yell from our yard. *Great.*

"That's my mom, I gotta go. See ya later," I said.

"All right, bye Hannah," Will said.

"See ya," Chris added. I turned around and started walking back to my house. My brother followed closely. The cops went back to their car.

"Okay guys, just keep it down," One of the cops said before leaving. My brother looked over at me with a funny look on his face.

"Why are you walking like that?" He asked.

"Walking like what?" I inquired.

"Like this..." My brother said and put his hands on his hips, accentuating each step he took. He started laughing.

"Shut up, Michael! I'm not walking like that." *Am I? Nah...*

"Yes, you are...Weirdo."

"I'm walking normal, Michael...That's how I walk." My brother laughed again. We approached my mom who was standing with her arms crossed as was usually the case when we were about to get yelled at.

"What were the police doing here?" My mom asked.

"I guess they were too loud and someone called them. Nothing happened though," I said. Michael didn't say anything and took the opportunity to run back inside the house to undoubtedly play video games.

"I don't want you just hanging out down there, okay, Hannah?"

"What? We weren't even doing anything. We were just going to listen to them play."

"I don't want you just hanging out..." *What are you talking about?*

"Well, there's nothing else to do out here..."

"I'll have your dad put up the basketball hoop this weekend." *Great, thanks...*

"All right." My mom and I started walking back toward the house. My mom grabbed my shoulder and stopped.

"Hannah, I'm starting my new job on Monday...And your dad needs his sleep, which you know..." *Yeah, I know...* "...We need you to stay out of trouble...And keep Michael out of trouble..." My mom's eyes momentarily glanced down the street.

"And you think they're trouble?"

"Yes, I do...Loud music, the police...Probably drugs..."

"MOM! Seriously, aren't you being a little judgmental?"

"It's my job." *What is that supposed to mean?*

"You're a nurse."

"You know what I mean...You are something else, Hannah! Come on, let's go inside."

My dad did as my mom asked him and pulled the basketball hoop out of the garage over the weekend. I didn't use it after he put it up though, in protest against my mom. After I finished my breakfast Monday morning, I put on my sports bra, some sweats, and my shoes. I grabbed a basketball and went outside. After a few minutes, I saw Will riding by on his bike. "Hey, Will, do you want to play?" I grabbed the ball off of the ground and saw that one of my shoes was untied. I kneeled down to tie my shoe and then quickly turned around. "Well, are you afraid to get beat by a girl?" Will stared at me without saying anything. "Take a picture, dude, it lasts longer." I said and smiled.

"Oh, sorry, I was just thinking...I need to go see about Chris. He got grounded on Saturday. I guess we were playing too loud. The cops...His parents were not happy," Will said.

"Oh yeah, my parents weren't happy about it either. They didn't want us hanging out down there. Play a game with me, to twenty-one."

"Well, since you put it that way." Will put his bike down next to the curb. He was wearing a big black White Zombie t-shirt and oversized blue jeans. He did not look ready to play basketball or any sport for that matter. *I wonder if he can even play...* "Do you have a thing for my hair?" Will asked and started pulling his hair back. *Maybe he can play...*

"Yeah, hold on." I ran inside of my house and got a scrunchy from my bathroom and ran right back out to Will. "Here's a scrunchy, it's got some of my hair in it."

"Hannah, with the quickness," he said.

"That's right, you wanna race?" *Super corney, Hannah!*

"Nah, maybe another time, thanks for the hair thing."

"It's a scrunchy."

"That's a weird word." I smiled and picked up the basketball.

"Okay, we're playing to twenty-one. Two points for lay-ups and three points for jump shots. And no dunking. My dad hasn't put the sand in it yet."

"No problem."

"Your ball."

"Ladies first," Will said and smiled.

"Your funeral," I replied. I took the ball and started dribbling toward him. He had his hands out to guard me so I couldn't go by him for an easy lay-up. I stopped and turned around. I started backing into him to close in on the basket. He put his hand on my lower back which stopped my progress. I quickly turned and shot a lay-up into the backboard. It was good.

"Nice shot," he said.

"Thanks. Let's play losers. Your ball." Will took the ball and didn't dribble past where he already was. He took a jump shot and it was an air ball. *Ahhh, that is so sad...* I grabbed the ball and quickly shot another lay-up. It was good.

"Four to zero," I said with elation.

"I'm a little out of practice," he said. *You don't say?*

"Me too, I haven't played for months!" I said with authority. I took the ball and started dribbling toward him picking up speed. I stopped, pulled up, and took a distant jump shot. Will fell backwards and lost his balance because of his pants. His hands hit the ground while I heard the sound of a perfect shot. *Swoosh.* "Are you okay?" I kneeled down next to him and took hold of his hands. He was bleeding a little, but seemed okay. He looked into my eyes and I looked into his. *Hmmm...*

"What color are your eyes?" He asked.

"Brown with green speckles," I answered. "And your eyes are light blue, almost hazel, but more blue than green. Much prettier than mine..." *I'm a little jealous.*

"That's not true, you have beautiful eyes."

"Thanks," I said. "So, are you hurt? You want to keep playing?"

"I'm fine, of course I want to keep playing. I have to redeem myself."

"All right, cool. seven-zero. let me help you up." I stood up and reached out both of my hands. He grabbed on and pulled himself up. He leaned over and rolled up his pant legs so that they were no longer dragging on the ground. *That's funny.* The score rang off in quick succession. "Ten-zero, twelve-zero, fourteen-zero, seventeen-zero, nineteen-zero, twenty-two and game." *That was embarrassing.* "Good game," I said and put my hand out.

"Good game for you." *Yep.* "You're actually really good at basketball." He shook my hand and then stared at it as if confused.

"Did you expect any less?"

"I guess not," he said with a subtle smile on his face. *Yeah, dude, I kicked your ass. Don't be mean...*

"Better luck next time."

"So, there's going to be a next time?" He looked into my eyes and then let go of my hand.

"Yeah. There has to be. You have to redeem yourself, remember?"

"Yup. So, I have to go talk to Chris." He walked over to the curb and picked up his bike. "I'll see ya later."

"All right, cool," I said and took another shot at the basket. *Perfect game.* I watched Will ride down the street and felt a sadness building inside of me. *Mel...I'm only good at basketball because of you. I hope you're okay...*I held the ball against my hip and slowly walked across my lawn and inside the house.

The next morning, after breakfast, I asked my brother if he wanted to play basketball with me. He wasn't amused.

"You're just going to beat me like you always do," he said.

"Come on, Michael, just one game. I'll be easy on you."

"Promise?"

"Yeah."

"Okay, but just for a little bit. I want to play Nintendo." *Just like every other day...* My brother and I went outside and I looked down the street. I saw Will and Chris standing at the end of the cul-de-sac. *I wonder what they're up to? Maybe they're going to play...*

"Hey, Michael, lets go see what's going on..."

"I thought you wanted to play basketball."

"Later, Michael, they might be playing. You wanna hear a real band play, right?"

"I guess so..."

"Good, let's go." My brother and I walked down to where Chris and Will were standing. *Are they eating cookies?*

"Hey, are you guys gonna play today?" My brother asked.

"Yeah, we're gonna play as soon as our guitar player gets here," Will responded.

"That's so cool...Can we watch you guys play?" I asked.

"Yeah, you're always welcome. Do you want a cookie?" Will said and removed a single cookie from the package.

"Yeah, I'll have a cookie," I said and Will handed it to me.

"Michael?" Will asked.

"Yeah..." We all stood in a circle eating cookies when Will asked me if I wanted another one.

"Are you trying to fatten me up?" I said and smiled.

"Nah, I like you just the way you are." I smiled again. *Not bad, Will.* I heard Chris sigh.

"You like my sister? My brother said while eating. *Thanks, Michael...*

"Shut up, Michael!" I responded.

"I just meant that I don't think you could ever get fat. What are you like 100 pounds soaking wet?" Will inquired. *Do you like that?*

"Yeah, something like that..." I responded and took another cookie. "...But, you're just as skinny as me, dude," I playfully said.

"Oh, burn!" Chris exclaimed.

"I didn't mean anything mean by it," I said. *I don't want to hurt anyone's feelings here...*

"No worries," Will said. "I weigh like 147 pounds..."

"Soaking wet?" Chris sneered.

"Yeah, soaking wet," Will agreed. "I can't gain weight no matter how much I eat." *I like that, Will. Own it.*

"Same," I said and smiled. I put my hand under Will's and took another cookie from the package.

"I'm gonna go tune my drums and wait for Rob," Chris said. A little boy my brother's age ran into the garage.

"Oh, Hannah, Michael, this is Chris's little brother, Mitchell," Will said. *That gives me an idea...*

"Michael, why don't you take Mitchell to play basketball?" I asked.

"Yeah, okay, Mitchell, do you want to play?" My brother asked. "It's set up at the end of our driveway."

"Ummm, sure..." Mitchell and my brother walked down the street.

"Best friends forever," I said as they walked away.

"Yeah, that was easy. Kids...go play. Okay!" Will said and then looked at me up and down. I watched him as he watched me. *Do you like what you see, dude?* "There's Rob. It looks like it's time to practice..."

"Oh, cool, what are you guys practicing for? Are you going to play a show?" I asked.

"Nah, we're just playing for fun right now," Will said indifferently. *Maybe I could help...*

"That's cool. Hey, I have an idea. I'll go ask all of the neighbors if they want to come watch you guys play. Then you'll be playing a show!" I reasoned.

"Sounds good to me," Will responded quickly.

"Okay, cool beans," I said. "I'll go get my brother and his new friend and then we'll go door to door." I walked back to my house to get Mitchell and my brother, passing Rob in the process. He looked at me, but it seemed like he was ignoring my existence. *Seriously, what is that dude's problem?* I got Mitchell and my brother to follow me around to all of the neighbor's houses. After going door to door, I got ten people to watch the show, including a girl named Casey, who lived two doors down from Chris. We walked over to Chris's garage and sat on the grass on the side of his lawn. Mitchell and my brother ran around being obnoxious as the band played. They were playing a song called 'Smells like Teen Spirit,' by Nirvana. They were really good. Rob sounded just like Kurt Cobain. When they finished playing the song we clapped loudly and Rob stepped up to the Microphone.

"Thank you," Rob said. "...About a girl." *About a girl? Is that the name of the song?* They started playing the next song. Will made eye contact with me the entire time. *Wow, that's pretty good. He's not even looking down.* I turned to Casey.

"He's pretty good. He doesn't even have to look while he's playing," I said.

"Who...Will?" Casey said.

"Yeah. Look, he's staring right at me..."

"I think he likes you...But, you're not thinking about..."

"I don't know..." Casey and I laughed. I started nervously pulling strands of grass from the ground. *What is going on with me? What am I doing? Stop killing the grass!* They finished playing the 'About a Girl' song and once again Rob thanked the audience after some applause. The next song Rob announced was 'Dive' and Will started playing it.

"Whoo-hoo!" I yelled while clapping. *I hope I don't mess him up!* I was having a great time and I didn't care that everyone but Casey and I were the last ones watching the show.

"Oh my God, Hannah, I don't think Will has taken his eyes off of you..."

"Yeah, I think you're right." Casey and I laughed and I smiled at Will. They played 'Breed' and when they were finished, Casey and I clapped with ferocity.

"Hey, do you wanna come hang out at my house after..." Casey started to ask.

"...Yeah, sounds fun," I replied quickly and smiled.

"Not bad," Rob said through the microphone.

"Hey, Rob, let's take a break, I gotta take a piss," Chris said.

"Chris is so cute," Casey whispered into my ear. *Does Casey like Chris? Hmmm...*

"Yeah, he is," I agreed. Rob said some other stuff through the microphone that I wasn't paying attention to, but afterwards Will walked over to us. "You sounded great."

"Yeah, you guys were great," Casey said. Rob walked up to us as well.

"Dude, you sound just like Kurt Cobain," I insisted.

"Thanks," Rob said. He looked at Casey. "Hey..."

"Hey, Rob," Casey said. "You guys are awesome."

"Thanks," Rob said and turned around and went back into the garage. "I need to detune my guitar." *What's his damage?*

"What's his problem?" I asked.

"I'll let you know when I figure it out," Will said and we all laughed.

"He doesn't seem very social," I added.

"More like anti-social," Will said. "I don't think he talked to anyone before I came along. It's weird. We're friends, but I still don't get him..."

"Hey, I'm gonna go over to Casey's house for a while, see ya later," I said.

"Okay, see ya later," Will said. "Bye Casey, thanks for coming by."

"Anytime," Casey said. We started walking over to Casey's house and I looked back at Will and smiled. *I really like him...* I turned around and followed Casey into her house. We went into her room and I was amazed by what I saw. There were stuffed animals everywhere. It was like the prize section of a carnival game. *How old is she? Like ten?* Casey sat down on her bed and then made room for me by moving a couple of stuffed bears. "So, Hannah, you like Will, right?"

"I don't know Casey, maybe. I mean, I don't really know him."

"But, when you know, you know, right?" *Yeah...*

"We played basketball yesterday..."

"Oh yeah?" Casey asked and then smiled.

"Yeah, I beat him twenty-two to nothing." Casey laughed.

"It sounds like he let you win...Because he likes you..." *Hey, no! I resent that. I beat him fair and square! Ugh...*

"...I'm pretty good, Casey, I don't think he let me do anything."

"Okay, but he does like you." *I think so...*

"Maybe, I don't know..."

"...And you like him."

"He's different...And I guess I do like that. There's something about him..."

"He is kind of mysterious...With the black hair..."

"Yeah, his hair is cool, but there's something else...I don't know how to explain it. He just seems so cool, like nothing bothers him."

"Yeah, he is pretty cool. I've known him for...It's been a while...Do you think he's going to ask you out?"

"I don't know..."

"...I've had a crush on Chris since forever..." *I figured...* "...But I don't think he even knows I exist. I know he does though because he's lived next door for years...Hannah, what do you think I can do to get his attention." *Ummm, Casey, I don't think..."*

"I don't know, Casey, just be yourself."

"That hasn't worked so far." *Sheesh. How do I say this...*

"Maybe you need to flirt with him...Like, maybe he doesn't know that you're interested in him...Guys can be pretty dumb about this stuff..."

"Yeah...Can you help me? I don't know how to flirt."

"Yeah, it's easy..." I talked to Casey for twenty minutes about how to flirt with a boy to get him to like you. I didn't really know what I was talking about but it seemed to make Casey feel better. Casey's mom came into the room and asked if I wanted to stay for dinner. "No, I can't tonight, but maybe another time?"

"Anytime you want. You just moved down the street, right?"

"Yeah. We're from Santa Maria."

"Oh, it's so beautiful there." *Yeah, it is...*

"What's your name, dear?"

"Her name's Hannah, mom," Casey said.

"Okay, Hannah, nice to meet you."

"Nice to meet you too," I said awkwardly. "I should probably go. My mom's going to be home soon."

"What does your mom do?"

"She's a nurse."

"That's great. I hope I get to meet her soon."

"I'll tell her that you want to meet her."

"Please do."

"Okay, I'll see you later, Casey."

"Okay, bye," Casey said. Casey's mom walked me out to the front of their house.

"Bye," I said and started walking back home. I looked over to my right and saw Will sitting on the curb in front of Chris's house. *I have some time. He looks sad. What's going on?* I sat down right next to him without saying a word.

"Where did you come from?" Will asked. "I didn't see you walk up."

"I snuck up on you. Pretty good, huh?" I insisted.

"Yeah, I guess I'm just not paying attention." He said and looked down at the ground.

"What's wrong?" I quietly asked.

"Nothing. I don't know. Just depressed, I guess."

"Depressed about what?"

"I don't know, life, I guess."

"That sucks, dude, you should be happy." *Here I am giving advice...*

"Thanks, I should consider that." He smiled and I smiled back.

"See, it's that simple. Happiness is a choice. My dad taught me that."

"Hannah, how old are you?"

"Fourteen."

"Wow, I seriously thought you were like seventeen. You seem so much older than fourteen."

"My parents tell me the same thing. I suppose I am mature for my age. Age ain't nothing but a number...I think that's an Aaliyah song..." *Yeah, it is...I heard it on the radio.* "It's true though. How old are you?"

"I'm fifteen. I'll be sixteen in September. Then I'll be able to get my license and be able to stop pedaling my ass around all the time."

"September what?"

"September twenty-eighth." *It all makes sense...*

"I knew it! You're a Libra!" *That's the something...*

"I am a what now?" *My perfect match!*

"...It's your astrological sign. I'm Aquarius. I have a book on astrology. I can show you. It all makes sense!"

"Does it? Sure, Hannah, I'm always down for learning new things..."

"Awesome. I'll bring the book by tomorrow. You guys are gonna practice, right?"

"Yeah, I think so. That's the plan. So, if you're fourteen, you're gonna be... A freshman?"

"Yeah, Mt. Whitney." *I think that's it...*

"I'm gonna be a sophomore at Whitney. We don't pronounce the 'mount' part. Insider tip."

"Thanks, good to know."

"I had a pretty shitty freshman year so I'm hoping that this year will be better."

"It will be. It's in the stars." *I found my Libra boy! I have to call Summer!*

"...Yeah, well, I appreciate your optimism..."

"...It's true. You'll see." I smiled and pressed my hand into his arm.

"Hannah, it's time for dinner!" My dad yelled from our driveway. I got up and brushed the dirt off of my pants.

"I've got to go. See you tomorrow?"

"Yeah, see you tomorrow," Will said and I started walking back to my house. My dad stared at me, waiting impatiently.

"Be happy!" I said as I turned back towards Will. He simply nodded his head and I smiled. I turned back towards my house and walked up to my dad.

"I thought your mother told you that we don't want you hanging out down there..."

"I know, dad, but I was just talking to..."

"...Get inside, Hannah," my dad interjected. *Sheesh. Won't even let me finish my sentence...* I walked inside of my house with my dad following. My mom and my brother were already sitting at the table waiting on me so they could eat.

Chapter Thirteen

Libra boy

A fter my mom left for work, I peeked into my parent's room to make sure that my dad was asleep. I waited a second at their door to listen for my dad's comical snoring. Once I heard it, I knew I was in the clear. *I don't get how he doesn't wake himself up.* I turned around and walked to the kitchen. I picked up the phone and dialed Summer's number. I walked in to the garage to help conceal my conversation from the prying ears of my brother. I let the phone ring twenty times before I gave up and hung up the phone. *Hmmm, I guess no one's home. Who am I going to talk to? I could call Jessica...*I looked down at the phone receiver. *Nah, I'll wait for her to call me.* I put the phone down on the counter. *Wait! Casey! I'll just walk to her house.* I went to my room and got dressed. I looked over at my astrology books. *Which one do I want to give to Will? Hmmm, I'll give him the red one.* I grabbed my little red astrology book off of my desk and took it out to the kitchen counter. *Wait, I have an idea.* I grabbed a red pen off of the counter and turned to the Aquarius woman/Libra male section and circled it. I wrote my number followed by a heart on the page. *If he calls, then I'll know he read the book! I'll leave this right here for quick access.* I opened the front door very slowly and then shut it carefully. I walked down the street and saw Chris and Mitchell outside doing yard work with their dad. They waved and I waved back. It seemed like Chris wanted to talk to me, but as he made his way onto the street his dad grabbed his arm and pointed at the grass. *That's funny.* I smiled and made my way over to Casey's house. I knocked and her mom answered the door almost immediately.

"Oh, is Casey here?" I asked.

"Yes, dear, she's in her room, come in!" Her mom said emphatically. *Very friendly.* I walked inside and she shut the door. "Casey, your friend Hannah's here." Casey came running down the hall smiling.

"Hey, Hannah, what's going on?"

"I just wanted to talk."

"Cool. Mom, we'll be in my room," Casey said and her mom smiled and walked to the living room. We walked to Casey's room and sat on her bed.

"I just had to tell you," I said.

"Tell me what?"

"Will's a Libra!"

"Will's...A Libra?"

"Yeah, I'm so excited! You have no idea how long I've..."

"Ummm," Casey interjected. "Sorry, what's a Libra?" *She really doesn't know.* I looked at her, perplexed. *It would be so much easier if I had the book to explain this...Maybe I should...* "Oh wait, I know!" *You do?* "I had my first Spanish class last year." *Spanish?* I smiled. *Where is she going with this?* "Libra means book, right?" I laughed. *Wait, does Libra mean book?* "What's funny?"

"Why would I say Will's a book?" We both laughed.

"I don't know...Because, maybe, he's smart, like a book."

"No silly, I'm talking about astrology?"

"What's that?" *This could take a while. I could let her borrow my other book...*

"Okay, Casey, crash course...Astrology is about where the planets were aligned when we were born. There are twelve signs. I'm an Aquarius and Will is a Libra...That makes us a perfect match!"

"So, what am I."

"What's your birthday?"

"January thirtieth." *Aquarius!*

"You're an Aquarius too!

"Is that good?"

"Yes. The air signs get along really well together."

"Ummm, the air signs?" I laughed.

"I'll let you borrow my book..."

"...Okay...Hannah, do you think Chris is a Libra."

"No, I don't think so Casey."

"Why don't you think so? How can you tell?" *I'll bet he's a fire sign...like Joe. He's probably a Leo. Ugh.*

"It's just a feeling. Ask him what his birthday is and then you'll know. I'll help you figure it out. Some of the days overlap...Anyway, yeah, ask him."

"I don't know, Hannah, I don't know if I...Can you ask him for me?"

"I really shouldn't do that, Casey."

"Why not?"

"Because he might think I'm interested in him...And I'm not."

"Oh, I get it. That makes sense...But I still want to know...Maybe Will knows Chris's birthday."

"Maybe...You wanna go see if they're practicing yet?"

"Okay, but I don't hear anything..."

"I want to give Will the book before they start practicing, though. Let's go see if they're out there."

"Okay, let me put my shoes on." Casey put on her shoes and we went to the living room to tell her mom that we were going outside. When we got outside, we saw Chris mowing his lawn with his shirt off. "Oh my God, Chris is so hot..."

"Yeah..."

"He plays football you know." *Well, that figures...*

"No, I didn't know that, Casey." Casey smiled as she gawked at Chris sweating in the sun. *I need to get her out of here.* "Casey, look...Mitchell and my brother are playing basketball. Let's go play!"

"Okay, but you're on my team."

"What, no little boys on your team?" Casey and I laughed.

"Nope. Especially not Mitchell. He's so annoying."

"Have you met my brother?" We laughed again and walked down to my house and challenged them to a game. Half-way through the game, the score was eleven to zero and the boys were starting to lose interest in losing. My brother stopped dribbling the ball.

"This isn't fair," my brother said.

"What's not fair, Michael, getting beat by a couple of girls?" I said.

"No!" My brother whined with exasperation.

"Then what's the problem?" Casey added.

"You're bigger than us!" Casey and I laughed.

"Stop crying, Michael, and finish the game," I said.

"I'm not crying!"

"Would Brett Favre quit if he were losing?" *How about that, Michael?*

"...No."

"Okay then, game on, it's still your ball." My brother checked the ball to me, but then stopped short of passing the ball out to Mitchell. *What is he waiting for?* I turned around and saw Rob walking behind us. I smiled at him but once again, he barely acknowledged me, or any one of us. *What is his problem? Sheesh...Will should be coming soon. I can just feel it.* My brother passed the ball to Mitchell. Casey guarded him closely. Mitchell attempted to throw the ball back to my brother but I intercepted it and quickly turned for a perfect jump shot. That's how the rest of the game played out. It was twenty-one to nothing after I made the final lay-up.

"I want a rematch," my brother barked.

"Are you sure, Michael? I mean do you really think you have a chance?"

"...Yes." *I guess he's taking the Brett Favre thing seriously. He's so easy to manipulate...*

"Okay, Michael, your ball." We started playing our second game and once the score was six-zero, I saw Will riding up to us on his bike. "Will! Hold on! Let me grab my astrology book," I yelled. I ran inside of my house and grabbed my perfectly placed little red astrology book and ran back outside to Will. "Look." I opened the book and pointed to the Libra section. "Check this out. These are your positive characteristics and these are your negative characteristics."

"Wow, Hannah, this seems pretty spot on," Will said. Casey stood by and smiled while Mitchell and my brother fought over the ball.

"You can take it home and read it if you want," I said.

"Sure, I'll read it tonight," Will said and put the book inside of his pocket. *He could probably fit me in those pants!* "You going to watch our practice?"

"Yeah, of course!" I said excitedly.

"All right, I'm going to head over there."

"See ya," I said and watched Will ride down the street.

"Hannah...Hannah!" My brother exclaimed.

"What, Michael!?"

"Are we going to finish the game? We can still win, you know." Mitchell shook his head and Casey smiled.

"No, we're going to go watch Will's band play, right Casey?"

"Right...You guys need to practice anyway."

"Yeah, that's a good idea. You and Mitchell should practice...Maybe you'll have a chance against us next time."

"So, you forfeit then?" My brother asked.

"No, Michael, it's not a forfeit," I argued.

"Yes, it is. We want to play and you guys don't." I looked at Mitchell who was giving my brother a funny look. *Right...* "So, you forfeit and we win," my brother responded.

"No, Michael, we already have six points, so, if we were to stop right now, we'd win," I reasoned.

"No, we would!" My brother proclaimed and started chanting "forfeit, forfeit, forfeit." For some reason, Mitchell joined him even though it was obvious to me that he didn't want to continue playing.

"All right, shut up, Michael! Casey, let's finish them off really fast."

"Okay." My brother's chanting stopped and a much more reserved look appeared on his face. *You wanted this, kid.* We continued the game. My brother took the ball out and passed it to Mitchell. Mitchell took a jump shot which was an airball and the rout was on. I heard the band playing, which distracted me. I missed some shots, which prolonged the game, but the boys didn't make any of theirs. "Twenty-two. That's game." Mitchell and my brother pouted. "It's okay, just practice and get better," I offered and handed the ball to my brother. "Casey, let's go."

"All right," Casey agreed and we started to make our way to the end of the cul-de-sac. "You're really good..."

"You too, Casey."

"Hannah, you made all the points..."

"Yeah...but...you're really good at passing." I smiled and Casey laughed. "We make a good team."

"Hey, listen, they're playing 'In Bloom.' I know this song. It's always on the radio."

"Yeah...Hurry up." Casey and I ran down to Chris's driveway just in time to start singing along during the chorus. We sang and laughed and laughed and sang. We couldn't hear each other very well, but we were having fun. After they finished playing 'Smells like Teen Spirit' Casey and I clapped enthusiastically. *This is so cool.*

"Same time tomorrow," Rob said. *I guess they're done.* Rob walked past Casey and I and said, "hey." *Hey, Rob...better than not saying anything.* Will and Chris came out of the garage.

"I'm so tired of this," Will said. *Uh oh, what's wrong?* "Same thing every day. We should be writing our own music."

"We don't know how to write our own music," Chris said.

"You could learn? It can't be that hard, right?" I reasoned.

"Yeah," Casey said.

"That's right! We can do whatever we want to do! *I love that about you.* I know that Rob is the band, but at the same time, I think he's holding us back," Will said.

"You think so?" Chris asked.

"You don't?" Will inquired.

"No, not really. I never thought about it," Chris answered. *I know...My notebook.*

"Hey, I have an idea," I said. "I'll go get a notebook and you guys can start writing some stuff down." I looked at everyone, but I didn't wait for a response. I ran down the street to my house, went to my bedroom, and tore open my backpack, looking for my notebook. *Where is it?* I looked around my room and then checked under my bed. *How did it get there? Oh well.* I grabbed my notebook and a pen and ran back down the street.

"Oh my God, Hannah, you missed out," Casey said.

"What happened?" I asked.

"Rob was planning to kick Chris out of the band. Chris wanted to kick Rob's ass. Will and Chris want to start their own band now and kick Rob out. It's crazy." *I was only gone for a couple of minutes, sheesh.*

"Wow. Here's the notebook. Where do you want to start?" I asked and handed the notebook and pen to Will. "I think you should start with a name." We all sat down under the tree in the middle of Chris's lawn. I sat very close to Will. Chris and Casey sat across from us staring at the notebook.

"What's a good band name?" Will asked. We sat in silence, which was only broken by the occasional chirping bird, and looked around the neighborhood. After a few minutes, without warning, Will said "Anarchy."

"That's a great idea!" I agreed. *Where did that come from?*

"It is?" Chris inquired.

"Yeah, no government," I said.

"I thought it meant chaos, like how the world is crazy," Will said.

"Nope. It means to not have a government. Government means to control the mind. Anarchy means no mind control," I said. *Why is everyone looking at me like that?*

"How do you know all that?" Chris asked.

"My dad told me. He watches a lot of political stuff and I was watching with him one day. He talks to the TV a lot," I said and laughed. *And I remembered...*

"He sounds like a very smart man," Will said. *I know he's going to like you!*

"Yeah, he is. He didn't go to college or anything, but he's really smart..." Will was sketching the word 'Anarchy' onto my notepad when Chris looked over and blurted,

"Dude, what are you doing? That looks like the Metallica logo." *Hmmm. That's kinda true...*

"Yup, it does," I said. *Sorry, Will.*

"Yeah, I can't draw for shit," Will said. "I'm just messing around." Will put the pen down on the notepad and then looked back up. *Ahhh, don't feel bad...* "Hannah, is that your mom?" I turned around and saw my mom walking toward us. *Shit...What's she doing home? What time is it?*

"Yeah, what does she want?" *I know what she wants...Or doesn't want...No hanging out, Hannah!* My mom stopped on the street and crossed her arms. She stared directly at Will. *This is not good.*

"We don't want Hannah just hanging out down here. It's okay if you want to play basketball at our house, but no hanging out and doing nothing. *Does she not see the notepad? Come on, mom...* "Hannah, it's time to come home. We're going to have an early dinner before your dad goes to work. Say bye to your friends." I got up from the ground and Will handed my notebook and pen back to me.

"Bye, guys, see ya later," I said. My mom started walking back to our house and I followed her.

"Bye!" Casey shouted. I turned around and waved at Casey while still walking. I made eye contact with Will and mouthed the words 'read the book' to him. He nodded and I turned around.

"We told you about hanging out, Hannah." *Oh, here we go. What are you going to do? Ground me again. I am so tired of this...*

"I was trying to help them come up with a band name...We were doing something."

"I don't like the look of that guy," my mom asserted.

"What are you talking about?"

"He looks like a punk."

"You're judging him on how he looks! *I think he looks good.* "You don't even know him. He's really smart."

"He looks like a troublemaker."

"He's not a troublemaker!" *You suck!*

"We'll talk about this later, Hannah, I have to get dinner started." I followed my mom into the house and my dad sat up on the living room sofa.

"Hannah, were you hanging out down there again!?" *Oh shit.*

"Yes, but we weren't just hanging out..."

"Hannah, I'm not going to tell you again..." *You always say that.* "Stay in front of the house!"

"Fine!" *No!* I walked to my room and shut the door. I opened my notebook and stared at Will's 'Anarchy' logo. *What am I going to do?* I put the notebook down on my desk and then sat up on the end of my bed. I pushed my pillow behind me against the wall and stared at my door, waiting for my mom to finish dinner.

"Hannah, it's Jessica," my mom said and handed the phone to me.

"Hi, Jessica, what's up?"

"Nothing much. My mom's going to take me to the mall to shop for clothes. Wanna go?"

"Ummm, yeah..." *It'll get me out of this house.* "Let me ask my mom. Mom, can I go to the mall with Jessica? She's going shopping for clothes."

"Yeah, I'll give you some money." *I say Jessica's name and my mom just says yes...Hmmm.* "Do you need a ride?"

"My mom says we can pick you up," Jessica said.

"Jessica said her mom will pick me up."

"Okay, sounds good," my mom said."

"All right, cool," Jessica said. "We'll be there in, like, twenty minutes."

"Okay, see you then," I said.

"Okay, bye," Jessica said and I hung up the phone.

"How much money do you think you'll need?" My mom asked while rummaging through her purse. *Wow, I don't know. What should I say?* I want you to buy clothes for school and nothing slutty. *Give me a break.* "Is one-hundred enough?"

"I guess, so," I said. "I'm not sure." My mom handed five twenty-dollar bills to me.

"If it's not, I can always take you before school starts."

"Okay." I went to my room and changed into my blue jeans and an orange t-shirt. I sat on my bed and waited for Jessica while I opened the bookmarked portion of my good astrology book: 'Aquarius and Libra.' I read the last sentence of the section over and over again. *Your romance contains the missing ingredients to love and happiness...We are perfect for each other. I wonder if he read the book yet...*I turned back through the pages in the Aquarius and Libra section and started re-reading everything. Before I knew it, I heard the doorbell. I put my book down on my bed and walked down the hallway. My mom had already let Jessica inside.

"Hey, Hannah," Jessica said.

"Hey, Jessica," I said. "Why are you wearing a long-sleeved shirt?"

"I don't know, I like it, I guess."

"Isn't it too hot outside for that?"

"There's air conditioning in the mall, Hannah," Jessica snapped.

"It's just a question," I said. *Sheesh.*

"Are you ready to go? My parents are waiting."

"Yeah, I'm ready, let's go." Jessica walked outside and I passed by my mom. *Why is she smiling.* I followed Jessica out to her car and got inside.

"Hi, Hannah, so, what's new?" Jessica's mom asked.

"I'm just getting used to Visalia...You know, how hot it is." I laughed and I could feel the scorn radiating from Jessica beside me.

"You miss Santa Maria?"

"Yeah, a little, but I am warming up to Visalia." I smiled and Jessica looked over at me. She squinted a fake smile at me and then turned around. *I thought it was funny. Some people are so sensitive...* Jessica's mom turned on the radio when it became obvious that Jessica and I weren't interested in making conversation. *Jessica's mom likes country music!? So weird.* When we got to the mall, we walked to the food court. *Everyone in Visalia must be here.*

"Okay, girls, we need to go to Sears. I want you to meet us over there at two."

"Okay, mom," Jessica responded. "We'll meet you at two."

"Have fun," Jessica's mom said and her parents walked away. I looked over at Jessica. She was still pouting.

"Are you still mad at me?"

"...No." *Yeah, you are!*

"Okay, so where do you wanna go first?"

"JC Penney's." *So, you can get a sweater to go over that long-sleeved shirt?* I laughed.

"What are you laughing about? What's wrong with JC Penney's?"

"Nothing." *God...* "I was just thinking Abercrombie and Fitch or Gap or somewhere, maybe, where I wouldn't find my mom shopping. And I want to go to Claire's too."

"There's nothing wrong with JC Penney's."

"I didn't say there was."

"Whatever, Hannah, let's go." *Sheesh, Jessica, relax.* Jessica and I walked to JC Penney's and started browsing through some shirts.

"Maybe you should get some t-shirts," I offered.

"I'll get what I like, Hannah, and you do the same." *Remind me not to come shopping with you again.* So, Hannah, are you looking forward to all the high school boys?" *That was random.* "I remember after I got out of middle school, I was looking forward to the high school boys."

"I'm interested in one high school boy. He's a Libra."

"What!? But you haven't started high school yet."

"I met him...He's friends with my neighbor...They have a band."

"What does he look like?"

"He's tall and skinny and has shoulder-length black hair."

"Really!?"

"Yeah, he's different. I like that about him."

"Doesn't sound like my type at all." *You have a type?*

"That's good, because he's mine."

"Okay, Hannah." We both laughed.

"Hey, Jessica, aren't you getting your license next month?" *Yeah, she's going to be sixteen, right?*

"...No, I don't need to drive."

"Don't you want to, though?"

"Not really." *Hmmm, that's weird, oh well.*

"I just thought it would be cool to have a friend that drove," I reasoned. Jessica didn't respond. *Okay.* Jessica bought some clothes from JC Penney's and then we went to Abercrombie and Fitch where I bought a new pair of jeans for fifty bucks. Jessica couldn't believe that I paid so much for just one pair. *They're nice pants.* We walked out of Abercrombie and Fitch and saw the neon pink glow of Victoria's Secret. "Let's go inside."

"I don't know, Hannah, I don't think they have anything for me."

"Yeah, they do, come on!" I walked into Victoria's Secret and Jessica reluctantly followed me. I walked over to the panties section where the prices were marked: '3 for $10.' *That's a good price.* "A girl always needs underwear."

"Those are kind of slutty." *Don't buy anything slutty!*

"You sound like my mom."

"I'm just saying..."

"And maybe a new bra..." I picked up a beautiful pink bra and turned it over to read the label. "Perfect and it's my size and everything."

"34B?"

"Yeah, what size are you?" I glanced at Jessica's chest. "We look the same."

"Don't tell anyone, but I'm...32A." *Wait, what!? What's going on? I think I was 32A when I was ten...* Jessica got close to me and whispered in my ear. "I stuff my bra."

"Stuff your bra? With what?"

"Tissues."

"Wait, what happens when you're with a guy?"

"...You're not going to make me say it are you?"

"No, I get it, Jessica, but why?"

"You should see the girls at Redwood...Oh never mind, look at you. You're fourteen and you're more...Developed than me."

"That's okay, you'll catch up eventually..."

"Yeah..."

"And in the meantime, keep doing what you're doing. Could have fooled me."

"Thanks, Hannah. It's so embarrassing." *Yeah, I guess...*

"Come on, I'm gonna buy these," I said and walked to the register. After I paid for my underwear, Jessica and I walked towards the front of the store and I saw Chris with his arm around a girl.

"Hey, Hannah."

"Hey...Chris..."

"Oh, this is my girlfriend, Angela."

"This is my friend, Jessica." Everyone said 'hey.' I looked at Angela and watched as she stared me down. *That girl is giving off some bad vibes.* After a few seconds of silence and growing awkwardness, Chris said,

"...Will's at the food court if you want to..."

"Will's here!?"

"Yeah, he was right here, but he got scared and..."

"...Chris, don't be a dick!" Angela scolded.

"What, I'm not..."

"Where did he go?"

"The Chinese Gourmet place, I think," Chris said.

"Okay, I'm going to go find him. Jessica, let's go. Nice to meet you Angela..."

"...Same," Angela said as Jessica and I walked past them and made our way to the food court.

"Chris is cute," Jessica said.

"Yeah, and he has a girlfriend...My friend, Casey likes him...This is going to break her heart."

"Casey?"

"Yeah, she lives down the street from me." Jessica looked at the big clock in the middle of the mall.

"Hannah, we need to go meet my mom, it's almost two!"

"Okay, I just want to say hi to Will. It will only be a minute." *There he is...All alone...So cool.* I walked up behind him and tapped him on his arm. "Hey, Will, your friends told me that you were looking for me...Well, Chris said he saw you and I thought I would say hi."

"Hi," Will responded.

"Hi! Oh, this is my friend, Jessica."

"Nice to meet you, Jessica."

"You too," Jessica said.

"Wow, Hannah, you make friends fast."

"Actually, we've been friends for a long time. Our dads are best friends."

"That's cool. You guys wanna sit down?"

"Yeah." Jessica and I sat down across from Will as he ate from his chicken bowl.

"Jessica goes to Redwood."

"Does she now?"

"How do you like it over at Redwood, Jessica?"

"It's fine, I guess," Jessica replied nervously. Will finished eating and set the bowl in the middle of the table.

"I was going to call you yesterday, but I..."

"...It's okay, call me whenever you want," I said quickly.

"Is there a time that's good for you? I mean, I don't want to call you if you're busy."

"My mom works days and my dad works nights. So maybe call me when my dad's not home." I looked over at Jessica and she smiled at me. *I know, I know...It's two.* "He usually leaves for work around 4:30. What'd ya think of the book?"

"I thought it was very interesting," Will said and smiled.

"Did you read the whole thing?"

"Most of it. I read the Aquarius section really closely." *That is so cool...He's actually interested!*

"Oh my God, Hannah, you're getting him into that stuff?" Jessica asked skeptically.

"Yeah, he asked for it."

"Seems pretty accurate from what I've read..."

"I don't believe any of it," Jessica retorted. I leaned into Will and whispered,

"She doesn't want to believe it."

"Hey, I heard that!" Jessica exclaimed.

"I said it loud!" I replied with a smile. "She's a Cancer."

"Ahh, I see." Will and I laughed. *He's my soulmate!*

"Whatever," Jessica said.

"Did you need the book back?"

"No, you can keep it; I have a better one at home."

"Thanks. I'll be sure to finish it..."

"Anyway," Jessica interjected, "we should go find my parents."

"Yeah, it's been a while since we saw them, and they're our ride, so..." I reasoned. Jessica and I sat up. Will got up after us.

"I should go find Chris; his mom is my ride." Will said and looked around. "I can't wait to get my license and I can come and go as I please."

"September twenty-eighth!" I said excitedly.

"That's right, I'm getting that thing as soon as I can."

"Jessica turns sixteen next month, but she doesn't want to drive."

"Really! Why not!?" Will inquired.

"I don't want to, all right!" Jessica pleaded. I moved in very close to Will and whispered,

"She's scared."

"Shut up, Hannah! We need to go right now," Jessica said. Jessica grabbed my hand and started pulling me away. I looked back at Will. He waved at me and smiled. I waved back and said,

"Call me." Will nodded and Jessica yanked on my arm even harder. "Jessica, relax, we're not that late."

"Hannah, my mom said two...And now it's past two. I'm not trying to get into trouble."

"Yeah, yeah, Jessica, like your parents would ever get you in trouble. You can't do any wrong. You know they'll just blame us being late on me."

"But it is your fault!" *Story of my life.*

I hadn't seen Will in a week. I played basketball as much as I could. I would look up and down the street. Every day. I stood in the middle of the street in front of my house. It was too quiet. I didn't hear the band practicing. *Are they even still together? They did say they were going to kick Rob out...He's really good though. They shouldn't do that...I should go see what Casey's doing.* I walked down to Casey's house and knocked on her door. There was no answer. *I feel so alone. I don't want to be alone.* I envisioned my first day of high school going just like my first day of middle school. *Mel...I miss her.* I was afraid that there wouldn't be a Melissa at Mt. Whitney to save me. I stood on Casey's porch like a lost child at an amusement park. *Where's Will? Why hasn't he called? Maybe he didn't read the book...Maybe he didn't get to that section. I should have put my number in the front! Maybe he doesn't like me...I'm so stupid...I have to find out what's going on.* I stepped off of Casey's porch and stared at the tree in the middle of Chris's yard. *I have to check...*I walked over to Chris's house and knocked on his door. *He's probably not home.* I turned around and started to walk away. I stopped quickly when I heard the door open.

"Hannah?" I turned around. *Shit! He is home. Now what? Say something...*

"Oh, hi, Chris, I didn't think anyone was home."

"I'm home." *Yes, I can see that...*

"Have you seen Will?"

"Nope." *Shit...*

"Do you have his number?" *Of course you do....So dumb!*

"I do, but it's not going to do you any good." *What is he talking about?*

"Can I have his number?"

"No."

"Why not!"

"It's not my place to give it out." *Such bullshit.*

"Come on, Chris, I need to talk to him!"

"Like I said, it won't do you any good."

"Are you going to keep up the subterfuge or are you going to tell me what you're talking about?"

"The what!?"

"Never mind," I said, defeated. Chris smiled.

"...He's on vacation." *Vacation? Why didn't he tell me?*

"Where did he go?"

"Ummm, it's something like...I don't remember..." *Why are you lying to me about it? Ugh!*

"Yes, you do, Chris!"

"No, I really don't remember."

"When is he coming back?"

"I don't know that either."

"He didn't tell you when he was coming back?" *Something isn't right.*

"He told me he didn't know when he was coming back."

"That doesn't make any sense. You guys are friends. You have a band, right?"

"Yeah...He does this every summer though. It's not a big deal. He'll be back when he's back. Why do you care so much anyway?" *Just tell him...*

"...I, ummm..."

"If he really cared what you thought, he would have told you he was leaving." *Oh my God...* I felt like crying. My heart shattered, but I didn't want to give Chris the satisfaction of seeing how much he hurt me. *Maybe he's right, though...*

"Look, Hannah...I was thinking...Will's skinny and weak, you could do so much better. We should hook up." *Oh Fuck!*

"What!?"

"You're like, really hot, and so am I, so..." *Oh my God, he is Joe! Summer was right!*

"I know you have a girlfriend; I met her the other day, remember?" Chris looked at me like he had been caught in a lie and had no memory of the mall at all. *What is wrong with you?* Chris didn't say anything. He shrugged his shoulders and smiled.

"Seriously!?" I asked.

"Hey, I had to try..." *Oh my God.*

"Bye, Chris." I turned around and walked away.

"Your loss," Chris said and I heard his door shut. *What an asshole!*

I spent the following three weeks playing basketball, reading my astrology book, and hanging out with Casey. I talked to her about Will and she talked to me about Chris. I didn't have the heart to tell her what happened between us, or that Chris had a girlfriend. I talked to Jessica a couple of times and called Summer a few times too. I was hoping to get her advice about Will; about what I should do. I trusted her opinion, but I was never able to get ahold of her. I came to the conclusion that she was on vacation with her family, like Will. The only thing that I could do was wait and then wait some more. I was on a stubborn crusade to find out if everything I believed was true. I refused to believe that I was wasting my time when my heart told me to be patient. It was the day before the fourth of July. I met Casey outside of her house that morning to talk about the fourth of July block party that was happening on our street.

"I don't know, Casey, I want to stay positive, but..."

"He has to come back sometime, right!? School starts soon."

"Yeah, this summer has gone by really fast...I just wanted to spend some time with him..."

"He'll be back before you know it! You guys will be together and everything will be fine."

"Thanks, Casey, I don't think my heart can take much more of this waiting."

"Well, we've got fireworks and stuff tomorrow. That'll be fun! Chris will be out here..." *Oh, Casey, I wish I could say something...* "And I bet that Will's here too."

"Casey, I don't really want to get my..."

"I know he was here last fourth of July." *Wait, really!?*

"You're sure?"

"Yeah."

"Well, why didn't you say so sooner, silly!" I smiled.

"...I don't know..." Casey and I laughed.

"Hey, you wanna go kick the boys butt in basketball again?"

"Yeah, sounds like fun. Maybe I'll make a shot this time..."

"Keep shooting...One is bound to go in eventually." Casey smiled and we walked over to the basketball court. Mitchell and my brother were playing a game of HORSE. "Are you ready to play us again, Michael?" My brother looked at Mitchell and Mitchell shrugged his shoulders in a way that reminded me of Chris. *Ugh...*

"Yeah, game on!" My brother said emphatically. The game went exactly as the first. It was another rout. At nineteen to zero, Will pulled up on his bike and watched the end of the game. I acknowledged him but I didn't overreact. I was excited to see him, but I was also cautious. Casey passed me the ball and I took an easy jump shot.

"That's game," I said as I passed the ball back to my brother. "Practice up, Michael." I walked over to Will and Casey followed me. Will was leaning over his handlebars and had a slight smile on his face. "Hey, stranger, where have you been?" I inquired while undoing my ponytail.

"I thought Chris told you. I was on vacation in Camarillo."

"I didn't know you were in Camarillo. Where's that?"

"It's pretty close to Ventura."

"So, what did you do there?"

"We spent most of our time at Magic Mountain."

"That's cool. Who are we?" *Your family...*

"My old best friend, Brad." *Huh?*

"Your old best friend, huh, so who's your new best friend?"

"Good question. I guess it has to be Rob or Chris. Yeah, I'll go with Chris." *I wonder if I should tell him...*

"I have a question for you, Hannah..." *It's about time. Just ask.*

"Do you?" Will started to ask. Casey looked at me and smiled.

"Shoot," I said.

"...Isn't it too hot to be playing basketball?" Casey and I looked at each other, disappointed. *Seriously, dude, do I have to strip off my clothes, or what!?* "Did I say something wrong?" Will pointed at his own chest. *Yes. You didn't say anything. So indecisive. Do you like me or not? Sheesh...*

"No...I'm going to go take a shower," I said and walked inside of my house. *I think I need to take this up a level. I think he needs some motivation.* I walked into my room, shut the door, and took off all of my clothes. I looked at myself in the mirror. *How is this not good enough? Shit...Okay. I know he's different...But, he's still a guy...Okay.* I looked around my room and walked over to my dresser. I opened the bottom drawer and stared at my orange bikini. *Yup, this is it. This will do it.* I put the bikini on and walked out to my garage. I turned on the sprinklers and walked outside. Mitchell and my brother were already running through the sprinklers and making a lot of noise. *Damn, they're loud.* I got a little wet and then walked over to Casey, who was walking up the street. She stopped at the basketball hoop to stay clear of the water.

"Hannah," Casey said. "I thought you were going to take a shower." I smiled.

"Well, I kind of am."

"...I wish I had your body...Then maybe..."

"I want to give Will something to think about. You know, some motivation."

"Well, yeah, I think that'll do it." Casey and I laughed. "He went to Chris's though."

"He'll be back."

"...Hannah..."

"Yeah..."

"I kind of got mad at Will for not asking you out." I laughed.

"What did he say?"

"He said he was going to ask you out."

"When!?"

"He didn't say..." *Figures...*

"Hmmm, well, I'm going to play in the sprinklers...Until Will comes back down here. Go put on your swimsuit."

"I'm good. I don't need a swimsuit," Casey reasoned.

"Okay," I said and ran into the middle of the yard. Casey ran in after me. The four of us ran around the lawn trying to avoid the sprinklers as they spun around. The planned futility made for a lot of fun. After a few minutes of rambunctious play, I was soaking, dripping wet. Will walked up with a grin on his face. *Like what you see?* I ran over to the front of the house and grabbed the hose. I turned the water on and walked over to him. He stopped short of my lawn and I pointed the hose at him.

"Don't do it!" Will pleaded. "Don't even think about it."

"Don't even think about what?" I switch the nozzle to 'Jet' and soaked Will from his head down to his Chukka boots. He didn't move. He didn't try to run away. He just took the soaking as if he knew he deserved it. *Impressive.* I pointed the hose down and release the trigger. "It's so hot today. Luckily, I have this to cool you off." I walked back to the front of my house and turned the water off.

"Thank you," Will said. "I was getting hot, I needed that." I smiled as I watched him stare at my body. He shook his arms in an attempt to dry himself off, but never broke eye contact with me.

"My eyes are up here," I said. *I don't mind at all though...*

"...Yeah, but give me a break; your body, you're beautiful." *You're so sweet!* Casey stopped moving around the sprinklers followed by Mitchell and my brother.

"Thanks," I said and dropped the hose. Casey ran down the street which seemed to inspire Mitchell and my brother to do the same. It was just Will and I staring into each other's eyes. I went in to hug him and just as I was about to feel his embrace, I saw my front door open. I stopped at looked at my dad standing in the walkway. He had a horrified look on his face, the likes of which I had never seen before. *That can't be good.*

"Hannah!" My dad yelled. "Get inside NOW!" *Oh no.* I looked at Will. He seemed mortified. "NOW!"

"Sorry, I've got to..." I attempted to say.

"NOW!" My dad found a higher, louder octave. I walked past my dad and then he turned around and slammed the door behind us. "What do you think you're doing?" *I know exactly what I'm doing...* I didn't respond. "Hannah!? HANNAH!"

"It was hot, and I thought that I..."

"And dressed like that?" *You bought it for me, duh!*

"I'm wearing the swimsuit that you guys bought for me..."

"You're not swimming!" *Thank you, I think I know.*

"But I was getting wet..." My dad seemed to get more upset. "What!? It's hot."

"Hannah...Fine...I don't want you hanging out with that guy."

"What guy?" I responded facetiously.

"That guy outside with the black hair! Hannah, don't play games with me..." *I'm sorry, dad, but that's not going to happen.*

"Dad, he's my soulmate."

"He's your...Soulmate? That's so stupid, Hannah, you don't know anything about him." *I know all that I need to know.*

"He's my Libra boy...Remember?" My dad shook his head. "I told you about..."

"It doesn't matter! Stay away from him!" *Not going to happen.* My brother opened the door and walked inside. He looked at me and then at my dad. He didn't say anything and went straight to his room. "We'll talk about this later. Go put some clothes on." *Whatever.* I walked down the hallway to my room and closed the door. *He can't stop us from being together. I won't let him.*

Later that night, after my dad left for work, I heard the phone ring. My brother picked it up and then walked over and handed it to me. I covered the handset.

"Who is it, Michael?"

"Will." *He did read the book!*

"Okay...Hey, don't tell mom."

"Okay..." My brother seemed confused and then walked away. I started to take the phone to my room.

"Hello?"

"Hey, Hannah, It's Will."

"Yeah, my brother told me. I've been waiting for you to call." *Like forever!*

"Who is it?" My mom came out of nowhere and asked.

"It's Jessica, Mom." *It could be...*

"Lying to your mom, Hannah?"

"Yeah, trust me...Mom, I'm gonna take this in my room...Hey, sorry about that..."

"...Nothing to be sorry about. Your dad was pissed today. Are you okay?"

"Yeah, silly, my dad has a bad temper, but he doesn't beat me." I laughed.

"That's good, I was a little worried about you."

"He was mad that I was outside in my bikini. Duh, it's the middle of the summer, Dad. What does he expect? They bought it for me."

"Maybe it has to do with the fact that a skinny, grungy, punk rock kid with long hair is hanging around his daughter." I laughed again. *Yeah, that could be it...*

"Maybe...I don't care what he thinks though."

"That's good, because well, Shit, why is this so hard? I really like you, and..." *Just do it!*

"I really like you too!" *That should make it easy...*

"So, I was wondering if you would want to go out with me..." *Ha. I'm gonna fuck with him a little...*

"...Ummm, well, I'm not sure if...Shit. Yes! Ha-ha, I had you going there, didn't I?"

"Yeah, ya did...Funny girl." *I have my moments.*

"You deserve it, dude. I've been waiting for like a month for you to ask me out."

"You could have asked me out..." *He must be kidding...*

"...That's not the way it works, dude." *Seriously. As if...* "What are you doing tomorrow? It's the fourth."

"Chris's parents are having a thing so I'll be down there. Barbeque and fireworks."

"Cool, my parents are having Jessica and her family over and we're going to do the same thing."

"Jessica, huh? Oh, good times...We should call in the fun police to keep her in check." I laughed. *That's a good one!*

"She's not that bad...She's just shy. Besides, she's good cover so I can see you tomorrow, Billy." *Yeah, that sounds right...*

"Billy? Seriously?" *Yeah.*

"Yep, seriously. What? You don't like it?"

"Ummm, it's okay, I guess, I just haven't heard that since I was little when my mom called me that."

"Ha-ha, nice, I like it. So, are you guys going to play tomorrow?"

"I don't think so, not unless Rob shows up. He's not answering our calls."

"Okay, well, I should probably go before my mom gets suspicious. I'll see you tomorrow, Billy." Will laughed.

"Okay, Hannah, see you tomorrow...Bye."

"Bye." I smiled and hung up the phone and set it down on my desk. I sat up on my bed and grabbed my astrology book. *Billy...My Libra boy.*

Chapter Fourteen

Jealousy

"Hannah, I'm sorry I yelled at you yesterday. I know you're at the age where you're going to want to..." *Yes, dad, what am I going to want to do exactly?* "...When you're going to be interested in boys..." *If you only knew...I'm glad you don't.*

"I'm not interested in boys, dad, just one boy."

"You're just so young." *No, I'm not.* "How old is he?"

"Fifteen."

"He looks older than that."

"He's going to be sixteen in September."

"When in September?"

"The twenty-eighth! I told you, he's a Libra."

"That's like a year and a half older than you, Hannah." *Who cares?*

"And? What difference does that make?"

"I don't like it...When he starts driving...You're too young." *Nope.*

"I like him, dad, and he likes me. Nothing else matters."

"Everything else matters, Hannah, which is what I'm talking about. You're too young to possibly understand all of the implications of a relationship...And teenaged boys, and their intentions." *Like what, dad...Sex? Drugs? Alcohol? Pregnancy? He must seriously think that I'm five!* I didn't respond to him. *There's nothing I can say...* "I just want to have a nice Fourth of July with my family, is that too much to ask?"

"Well, no, but..."

"But nothing. Please, just do as you're told...I didn't mean it that way..." *Yeah, you did.* "Please, just do what your mother and I ask you to do." I heard the beginning of 'Smells like Teen Spirit,' ring through the neighborhood and into my kitchen where my dad and I were standing. My dad grimaced as if in pain. *Okay. I'll try to play your game.*

"Dad, can I go watch the band play?" My dad started to shake his head. "Dad, I just want to watch them play. I'll come right back home when they're done playing."

"...Fine. Come right back home afterwards. Hannah, when I hear that music stop, I better see your face." *Shit.*

"Okay, dad, I promise."

"All right, get out of here. Don't forget what I said..."

"I got it dad, sheesh." I walked outside and saw Mitchell and my brother running around in the street and saw Casey walking toward me. I met her halfway.

"I was just coming to get you," Casey said.

"I was just coming to get you!" I responded and we both laughed. "It looks, I mean, it sounds like the band's still together."

"Did Will call you?"

"Yep, Casey, he asked me out last night!"

"I'm so excited for you!"

"I know...I'm so happy...My parents hate him, but I don't care what they think."

"But they don't even know him..."

"Thank you, Casey. See, you get it."

"I do...I completely understand," Casey said pompously. I laughed. *It's too bad...*

"Casey, it's too bad that we won't be going to the same school next year."

"Yeah, one more year of middle school."

"It sucks...What am I going to do without you?"

"We live on the same street..." Casey and I both laughed.

"Yeah...So, let's go watch the band!"

"Okay, lead the way," Casey said and we started walking to the end of the cul-de-sac. Mitchell and my brother were quick to follow behind us while they played tag. *These boys are so immature.* When we got to the end of the driveway, I locked eyes with Will as he concentrated on playing his bass guitar. *Billy...So cool.* They played through five songs ending on one that I didn't know the name of. Rob set down his guitar and stepped in front of the microphone.

"Let's take a break and then practice 'Heart Shaped Box,'" Rob said.

"Nah, I think we're done, Rob," Will said while putting down his bass. *That sounded kind of...Ominous, Billy.*

"Yeah, Rob, we're done," Chris said. "I have to quit the band." Casey and I gasped and walked into the garage. Mitchell and my brother started pushing each other and ran around Chris's yard. I walked up to Will and gave him a hug.

"Hey, Billy," I said. I pulled him close to me and squeezed my chest into his. He moved his hands down my waist stopping just above my butt. *You can keep going...*

"Hey, Hannah, you smell great," Will said as he stepped away from me and locked his eyes onto mine.

"It's Sun, Moon, Stars."

"That's a perfume, right?"

"Yeah, what else could it be?" I reasoned.

"I just thought you naturally smelled like flowers."

"Ahh, that's so sweet, Billy!" I hugged him again.

"Billy? What is happening right now?" Rob Inquired.

"So, you finally asked her out?" Chris said. "It's about damn time."

"You can say that again," I said as I rubbed my hand against his arm. Casey smiled. *And fuck you, Chris. Sorry Casey.*

"Maybe we can double date sometime," Chris said. *That's going to be a fuck no.*

"Great. Everyone has a girlfriend but me," Rob said. Casey glanced at me with concern. *I'm sorry, Casey.*

"Wait, you like girls?" Chris asked?

"What! Yeah," Rob responded. *Poor Rob. I kind of feel sorry for him.* He looked at Chris with disdain. *It's okay, Rob, I hate Chris too.* "So, you're quitting the band, huh?"

"Yeah, I have to move in two weeks. We have to get all of this stuff moved out of here."

"Okay, that's fine. I'll call my dad to pick up the equipment." I put my hands over Will's right ear and whispered,

"Did you know about this?" He looked at me and nodded. Rob packed up his guitar and turned back to Chris.

"Can I use your phone?" Rob asked and walked toward Chris.

"Yeah, you know where it is," Chris responded. Rob walked in to Chris's kitchen and Chris followed. Will put his arm around me and rested his hand on my hip. Casey looked at us and smiled, but I could see it slowly fade. *It's okay, Casey, we'll find you someone...*

"I'm happy for you guys," Casey said. "You look so cute together."

"Thanks, Casey," I said.

"Yeah, thanks, Casey," Will agreed.

"Like Chris said, it's about time," Casey added. *Like Chris said...Ugh.* Will looked into my eyes and then over to Casey.

"Thanks, Casey...I wonder if I'll ever hear the end of it..." Will said. *Not a chance.*

"Nope. I'll be here to remind you," I said and pulled Will close to me and put my hand in his cavernous back pocket. Casey laughed.

"Are you still gonna have a band with Rob?" Casey asked.

"Well, actually, Chris and I plan to start our own band, but Rob doesn't know that yet, so keep it to yourself," Will asserted.

"Oh, okay, wow," Casey said.

"Rob's still my friend, but musically, I think we're going in two different directions. I've been thinking about this for a while." Rob and Chris came back into the garage and Rob unplugged all of his equipment.

"Are you going to help or are you just going to stand there?" Rob barked.

"Yeah, I'll help," Will said.

"I don't use any of that stuff, but yeah, I'll help," Chris added.

"Hannah, do you wanna come over to my house for a while?" Casey asked while walking out of the garage. *That's the same look that she gave me before...*

"...Yeah, okay, Billy, I'll see you later." I gave Will a hug and touched his fingertips as I walked away.

"See you later," Will said as Casey and I walked toward her house.

"Hannah, what's going on with Chris?"

"I was going to tell you..."

"He has a girlfriend?"

"Yeah." *Think of something...* "I don't think it's serious though."

"It isn't...How do you know?"

"I met her at the mall."

"Is she pretty?" *She's pretty, I guess. I don't know...*

"She's all right...She's not very nice though."

"She's not?"

"She yelled at him. It was kind of embarrassing...Wait..." *Shit, my dad!* "Hey, come with me to my house really fast. I need to ask him if I can go over to your house...My parents are being really weird."

"Yeah, okay." Casey and I turned up the street and walked to my house. I opened the door and smiled at my dad who was sitting in his recliner watching baseball on TV.

"You wanted to see my beautiful face...So here I am."

"You're welcome," my dad responded. *Wait, what?*

"I'm welcome?"

"For your face," my dad said and laughed. Casey joined him.

"Casey!"

"What? It was funny..." *You're not allowed to take my dad's side.*

"Ha ha," I said. "Dad, this is Casey, from down the street."

"Hi, Casey, from down the street," my dad facetiously said.

"Can I go to her house for a while?"

"...Sure, yeah, but remember, your mom gets home at four and Bob and his family are coming at around five." *Jessica...*

"Okay, I'll be back before then. Bye dad," I said.

"Bye," my dad responded and continued watching his baseball game. I walked outside with Casey and shut the door.

"So, yeah, I guess you're going to meet my friend, Jessica, tonight."

"Jessica?"

"Yeah, she goes to Redwood. We've been friends forever. Our parents are friends so..."

"...Can we talk about Chris..."

"Yeah..." Casey and I walked down to her house and went straight to her bedroom.

"I can't believe you didn't tell me Chris had a girlfriend." *I can.*

"Casey...I know I should have told you, but you're so positive, and I love that about you...So I didn't want to make you sad, I guess."

"I'm not mad at you. I just can't believe he has a girlfriend..." *Yeah, but if it were anyone, it would be that girl...* "I mean, I can because he's hot, but I don't want to believe it."

"Casey, you heard what he said, right?"

"What do you mean?"

"He's moving."

"That's okay." *It is?* "I still want to be with him." *How do I get her to...Who am I kidding?*

"Well, if that's what you want..."

"Hannah! I helped you with Will..." *Chris is not a good guy...I'm not going to change her mind, though.*

"...I appreciate that, Casey, I really do." Casey dropped her head and pouted. *Ugh.* "I'll have Will talk to him..." *Damn it. I really don't want to do that.* Casey perked back up.

"You will!?"

"Yeah, they're best friends."

"Thanks, Hannah." Casey and I continued talking for about an hour in her room. At a certain point I became weary of Casey gushing over Chris. "Casey, let's go back over there and see what they're doing."

"Oh, okay, do I look all right?" *You look fine, Casey.*

"Yeah, you look really cute."

"Do you think I should put on some makeup?"

"No, you don't need any makeup."

"Are you sure? Does his girlfriend wear makeup?" *Yeah, like a clown at a kid's birthday party.* I smiled.

"Yeah, and way too much, Casey."

"I just want to look older...Maybe that's what Chris likes..."

"Casey, guys don't like all that makeup."

"They don't?"

"No, Casey, they really don't."

"Hannah, have you had a boyfriend before?" *Oh no...*

"...Yeah, I have...But I don't want to talk about it..."

"Oh, okay..."

"It just wasn't good...He wasn't good."

"Okay, before we go, do you think I should change clothes?" I looked at Casey's t-shirt and jeans.

"No, why? You look fine."

"Fine as in good or fine as in okay?" *Casey...*

"If Chris doesn't like you for you, then he doesn't deserve you!" I said aggressively.

"...You're right...Okay, let's go." Casey and I started walking over to Chris's house and looked down the street. We saw a row of orange cones at the beginning of the cul-de-sac. "They're shutting down the street?"

"It's probably for the fireworks." When we got to Chris's house, we noticed that his garage was closed so I knocked on his door. Chris answered and then looked back toward his living room.

"Hey. It's Hannah and Casey," Chris said and then turned back around to face us. "You wanna come in and hang out?"

"Yeah," I said. Casey and I walked into the living room. I sat right next to Will on the couch. Casey and Chris sat across from each other in chairs on either side of the room. I put my hand on his thigh and moved it up and down. *Hi, Billy!*

"What are you guys doing?" I asked.

"Just watching MTV, eating some cookies," Will replied.

"That's cool. We just found out that they're going to shut down the entire street for fireworks tonight. It's gonna be like a block party," I said.

"Nice. I'll be there. Well, I'm already here and I'm not going anywhere...Hmmm, here or there?"

"You're so cute, Billy," I said while squeezing his leg.

"Why do you call him Billy?" Chris inquired. *I don't like you.*

"Because I want to, got a problem, dude!? I said with authority. Chris put his hands in the air. *So stupid.*

"No, no problem, just wondering," Chris said. Casey smiled at Chris and he looked away from her and toward me. "Hey, I'm gonna call Angela again. No one answered the last time I tried. I need to tell her I'm moving."

"Yeah, good luck with that," Will said.

"When I tell her I'm going to Golden West, she's so gonna break up with me...Again. I should just break up with her first."

"You don't know that," Will said. "I mean, it's probably going to happen, but you've been together so long. It's just sad."

"Yeah, I'm gonna go get this over with," Chris said as he grabbed the phone and walked down the hallway to his bedroom.

"Hey, Will," Casey said. *What are you doing, Casey?* "Do you think Chris and I...If he breaks up with his girlfriend? I looked at Will attentively. *What is he going to say?*

"I don't know, Casey, maybe," Will responded.

"Could you, maybe, talk to him later for me?" Casey pleaded.

"Casey, you heard that he's going to Golden West, right? That's on the other side of town," Will said.

"That's okay. Will you talk to him?" I stared at Will, patiently waiting for an answer. *I'm torn. I do want Casey to be happy...*

"...Come on, Billy, don't you owe her a favor?" I argued. *This is wrong but I guess it's just not that simple.*

"Sure, Casey, I'll talk to him, but only if they break up. I'm friends with Angela too and I wouldn't do that to her," Will said. *What the fuck! They're friends?*

"I understand, thanks," Casey said. My mood changed immediately and I moved my hand from Will's leg to behind my head.

"How long have you been friends with this Angela girl?" I inquired.

"A long time. Longer than they have been together."

"Really. Just friends?" *Why am I getting mad?*

"Yes, just friends. You'll meet her soon enough, at school." *We've already met and I don't like her.*

"I think I already met her that time at the mall, but she didn't say anything to me. What's her sign?"

"I have no idea, Hannah; I don't know what her birthday is." Will put his arm around me and looked into my eyes. "You have nothing to worry about, trust me." I smiled. *I believe you.*

"I do trust you; I just don't trust her." *Especially because of Chris.*

"Like I said, no worries. I don't even hang out with her." *Really? Hmmm...* Chris came back into the room and put the phone down on the table.

"Yeah, we broke up," Chris said.

"That sucks," Will replied. "Did she..."

"...I broke up with her" Chris interjected. "I told her that I'm going to a different school and that we should break up. She wasn't even mad..." Casey sat up in her seat and stared at Will. *Gwen!*

"Oh my God!" I shouted. "I love this song." No doubt's 'Just a Girl' came on MTV and I started singing along.

"Holy crap! You can sing!?" Will asked.

"Yeah, I got it from my dad. He's a triple threat."

"What's a triple threat?" Will inquired.

"It means someone can sing, dance, and act."

"That's cool. You've got a really good voice; better than Gwen."

"Thanks, Billy, but it's Gwen. I'm not better than Gwen." *No one's better than Gwen!*

"What do you guys think? Better than Gwen?" Will asked and looked at Casey and then Chris. Chris nodded and Casey said,

"I agree with Will. Hannah, you are better than Gwen." *But I'm not...*

"Thanks for the backup, Casey!" Will squeezed my arm. "See, Hannah, we have a consensus." *That doesn't make it true.*

"Thanks, guys, I appreciate it, but I don't think I'm that great," I said. Chris's parents came through the door and walked into the living room.

"Chris, come help unload the groceries! Oh, wow, we've got a full house," Chris's mom said. "Will, you can help too; you're staying over, right?"

"Yes, ma'am." Will said and stood up. *Ma'am... That's funny.* I laughed and looked at Casey.

"Hey, Billy, we're gonna go get ready," I said.

"Okay, ready for what?" Will inquired.

"The block party, silly." I gave Will a hug and Casey stood right beside me as I let him go. "See you, later," I said.

"Remember..." Casey said and we made our way back to Casey's house.

"Hey, I have to go home and wait for Jessica," I said.

"Okay...Do you think that Will is gonna talk to Chris..."

"Yeah..." *I hope not.* "I'll see you later, Casey."

"Okay, bye, Hannah."

"Bye." I waved to Casey and then walked back to my house. My mom's car was in the driveway. *I guess she got home from work early. Wait, what time is it?* I went inside my house and my mom was in the kitchen preparing some food. My dad was still watching baseball. *Really?* My mom turned around.

"Hannah, where have you been?"

"At Casey's house."

"Casey?"

"You know, Casey Green. She lives down the street. She's always over here playing basketball with me..."

"Oh, okay..." *As long as I'm not with him, right mom?*

"I'm gonna go take a shower," I said.

"Don't take long, you don't want to keep Jessica waiting." *What!? Oh, of course not! We can't keep Jessica waiting... Why don't you just adopt her already?*

"I won't," I said and went to take a shower. I changed my clothes and then sat down on the couch across from my dad. He glanced at me for a second before turning his attention back to the game.

"Are you excited about the fireworks?" My dad inquired while keeping his eyes fixed on the TV. *Are you!?*

"Yeah, it sounds fun...Hey, when Jessica gets here can I take her to go meet Casey?"

"I don't see why not. Ask your mom, though." *Sheesh.* I got up and walked to the kitchen.

"Mom..."

"I heard what you said..."

"And?"

"You can take Jessica to meet your friend but you need to come back here if you want to hang out."

"But what if her mom wants her to stay down there?"

"That's too bad then. You have Jessica..." *Awesome.* I sat back down on the couch and pretended to watch baseball with my dad.

"Who's playing?" *I don't care...*

"The Dodgers are playing the Giants. We're up three-two and it's the top of the eighth." *Why did I even ask?* I stared at the screen waiting for the time to pass by. I watched my brother come and go in and out of the house with Mitchell by his side every step of the way. *He gets to do whatever he wants. I'm so much older than him and they let him do whatever he wants! It's not fair!* When the game ended my dad got up from the recliner and coincidentally, Jessica and her family had just pulled up in front of our house. My dad opened the door and everyone exchanged our normal pleasantries. Bob and my dad got the barbeque stuff from the garage and set everything up on the front lawn. The whole neighborhood was starting to come alive. It seemed like my family was the last on the block to do so. Everyone had their food and fireworks ready to go. We were two steps behind. I looked down the street and saw Chris's garage open. I saw Will, Chris, and Rob all standing at the end of the cul-de-sac. It looked like they were already eating. My mom was still inside of the house talking with Jessica's mom. I walked up to my dad who was in the middle of a heated conversation with Bob. *Are they arguing about baseball? Weird...*

"Dad," I said, "I don't mean to interrupt, but can I take Jessica to meet Casey?" My dad gave me a confused look. "Mom already said it's okay."

"Oh, okay, yeah." Bob and my dad went on debating which team was better, the Giants or the Dodgers. *Like it even matters...* Jessica and I walked down the sidewalk.

"Who's Casey?"

"She's my friend..." *Ugh.* "It doesn't matter."

"I thought you wanted me to meet her, though. That's what you told your dad."

"They're being really stupid about me seeing Billy...Will...And I..."

"...Need me as an alibi..." Jessica smiled as if she was happy that she had leverage on me.

"Yeah, kinda..."

"It's okay, I'd do the same thing." *Wait, you would?*

"Well, I'd like to say that I'm not surprised, but I am totally surprised."

"I have my rebellious side, Hannah. You don't even know."

"I guess not...Anyway, let's go talk to Billy."

"Billy...Is that like a nickname or a pet name you gave him?" I laughed.

"Maybe both..." Jessica and I walked to the end of the cul-de-sac where the boys were eating. I went right up to Will and gave him a hug. He set his plate down on the ground and I grabbed His hand as soon as he stood back up.

"Hey, babe, did you miss me?" I inquired.

"Of course, I missed you," Will replied. I squeezed his hand tighter and looked over at Jessica.

"This is Jessica."

"Yeah, I remember, from the mall," Chris said. *I wasn't really talking to you...* Rob didn't say anything and kept eating his hotdog.

"Hi," Jessica said.

"Do you guys want some food?" Will asked.

"I'm good, Jessica?" I responded.

"No, I ate earlier." Jessica replied. *No, you didn't, Jessica...Maybe I was wrong about her.* The sun gradually went down and people started setting off fireworks in the middle of the street. Mitchell and my brother were in front of our house, Will and I looked to the left and saw Casey running up to us.

"Hey, guys, this is so cool," Casey said. "Hi, Chris."

"Ummm, hi, Casey," Chris said as he walked away. *I hope she sees that he doesn't care.* The sun went down below the horizon and everyone seemed to set off their fireworks in unison. We all stood around Chris's lawn looking down the street. Will and I held hands and I gently rested my head on his shoulder. *This is perfect.* Past the light of the fireworks, I saw my mom come outside and look down the street. *Shit.* She saw us standing at the end of the Cul-De-Sac.

She said something to my dad while he went to the middle of the street to set up a firework for my brother. My mom then walked down the street toward us.

"Shit, Hannah, your mom's coming," Will said and pulled his hand away from mine. I reached back for his hand and held on tight with both of my hands. *I want her to know...*

"I don't care if she knows about us. What's she going to do?" *Nothing. There's nothing she can do!* My mom got closer and closer to us and then stopped short of Chris's lawn. She gestured for me to come to her. "Come on, mom, leave me alone!" I pleaded.

"Would you rather that your dad come over here?" *Shit.* I let go of Will's hand and gave him a hug. *I guess you win.*

"Fine, whatever." I walked past my mom and Jessica followed behind. My mom caught up to me and I scowled at her. "You can't keep us apart, you know!"

"Is that right? Why don't we ask your dad about that?" *Ugh! You make me so mad!*

"Why do you always have to bring him into it?"

"Because, Hannah, you're obviously not going to listen to me." *I'm not going to listen to him either!* My mom walked over to my dad, who was still in the middle of the street and Jessica and I sat on the curb in front of my house. I stared down the street to the end of the cul-de-sac and tried to make eye contact with Will. *What is he doing? What's going on over there?* Casey ran up to me and sat down on the curb and then covertly handed me a folded piece of paper.

"It's Will's number...I think he wants you to call him," Casey said and I smiled. *Casey... Yes, wow...*

"...Thanks, Casey, I owe you another one..."

"Do you think that Will talked to Chris?" *Ugh. Well, I can't be mad now.*

"I'll ask him tomorrow, Casey, but I'm sure he did."

"Because, well, Chris didn't seem to..."

"I'll find out what's going on, Casey, I promise."

"Okay, thanks, Hannah."

"Oh, yeah, duh." I looked over at Jessica. "Jessica, this is Casey. Casey this is Jessica."

"Hi Casey," Jessica said.

"Hi!" Casey responded. "How long have you guys been friends?" Jessica laughed.

"Forever...Long enough to know this isn't the first time that Hannah has been in trouble...Or the last." Casey and Jessica laughed. *Hey! Yeah...* The light and sound from the fireworks crackling and booming was almost overwhelming. I looked at Will's number and then pushed it deep into my front pocket. I looked back down the street and smiled into the darkness hoping that Will could still see me.

I woke up to my parents arguing about what they were going to do about Will and what they were going to do about me. I sat up in my bed. *Do they think I can't hear them? Do they even care? Ugh!*

"Patrick, you need to keep her inside of this house!"

"Stacy, I think we need to be rational about this...We can't just lock her in the house all day. She starts high school next month for Christ's sake!"

"Would you rather she ends up pregnant in a ditch somewhere." *Uh oh. Shit...*

"Don't be so dramatic! I think you're overreacting."

"I'm overreacting!?"

"We raised a good girl..." *Ahhh, thanks, dad.* "It's not like she's going to go around and have sex with the neighborhood trash." *On second thought, that's just fucked up. Fuck both of them...*

"And what if it's not her choice?"

"What do you mean by that?

"Rape, Patrick, I'm talking about rape..." *Oh shit! This just got way too real.* "I can't even tell you how many times girls Hannah's age are brought to the hospital..." *Mom...Seriously?*

"Stacy, this is Visalia, I don't think..."

"...You don't know, Patrick, because I don't talk about it. I don't want to talk about it."

"She's fourteen, Stacy."

"I know how old she is, Patrick, and I also know how old she looks!" *How old is that?*

"...What do you want me to do? Seriously, Stacy, we both work all the time..."

"Just keep her away from that boy with the dirty black hair." *It's not dirty! Ugh!* "I don't like him. I don't like his face. I don't like the way he looks at Hannah." *Wow...How do you really feel? This is almost funny.* "Let's start with that..."

"Fine...I'm too tired to argue about it anymore."

"I swear, I thought this move would be good for her. I thought maybe, just maybe, we could leave this drama in Santa Maria...I have to go to work."

"Have a good day," my dad said.

"Keep her home!" My mom screeched and slammed the door behind her. I could hear my dad grumbling down the hallway. *Oh shit!* I quickly pulled my blankets over my head and pretended like I was still asleep. I heard my door open. My dad stood in my doorway for a few seconds, sighed, and then shut my door. *Shit.* I heard the front door open. "I forgot my purse," my mom said and then shut the door again. I got up and looked out of my bedroom window and saw Will riding his bike. *Oh shit! She's gonna see him! Yeah, she saw him...* I got back in bed. I was afraid that my dad was going to come back in my room and find me awake. *He might want to talk...I'm going to take a pass on that.* I pulled my blankets over me and tried to force myself back to sleep. After about thirty minutes, I stopped trying to sleep. I wasn't tired and it was getting hot. I opened my bedroom door and went to the bathroom. I heard my dad in the garage. *He's probably messing with his motorcycle.* I made myself some Eggo waffles and then took a shower. After I was finished, I checked the garage because I didn't hear anything, and my dad wasn't there. *That's weird.* I checked my parent's room and he was in bed, fast asleep. *Perfect.* I quietly walked back to my room and grabbed my worn jeans off of the floor and pulled Will's number out of the front pocket. I walked down the hallway and stopped outside of my brother's room. *I don't hear anything. I guess Michael can sleep through anything.* I grabbed the phone off of the counter and went to the garage to call Will. I dialed his number and the phone rang twice before he picked up.

"Hello?" Will answered.

"Is Will there?" I asked.

"It's me...Hannah?" *I know, silly.*

"Yeah, it's me, Billy. I saw you ride by my house this morning."

"Your mom mad dogged me something fierce."

"She doesn't want me anywhere near you."

"I figured that much after last night."

"You don't even want to know what my dad said...I don't care what they say though. I wish that they would just chill. They can't control the guys I go out with." *Stupid; Shouldn't have said that...*

"Especially when school starts, what are they even thinking?"

"I really like you and I don't care how long it takes for my parents to understand that. Why can't they just be happy for me?"

"I guess they're just worried about you."

"I can take care of myself..." *Yeah, I'm just gonna tell him "*...Hey, I need to tell you something..." *Bye Chris. Sorry, Casey...* "Chris asked me out when you were gone on vacation."

"What!?"

"I just thought you should know. I don't want to cause any problems." *Well...*

"I don't believe it! That traitor!"

"I turned him down and told him that I liked you."

"Did he try anything?" *Ha!*

"No, I would have kicked his ass," I said and laughed. "He just made fun of you and basically said I was stupid."

"What'd he say?"

"It doesn't matter."

"It does matter. I want to know. We've been friends for years and to find out he went behind my back. He knew that I liked you."

"He said you were skinny and weak and that I could do better, like him. I told him that he was stupid and that was it."

"He was still with Angela then too. What the hell?" *Yep. Joe's long-lost brother...*

"That's the way guys are..."

"That's not the way I am. I would never cheat on anyone."

"That's why I like you, you're different."

"I feel the same way about you."

"No matter what, I'd always pick you over Chris; I just hope that he doesn't come between us."

"That's not going to happen. I guess it's a good thing that he's moving." *Yes, it is.*

"Are you going to stop being friends with him?"

"I don't know."

"Maybe it's best if you guys aren't friends." *Not maybe, it is...*

"I don't know. I don't know what to think right now...I need to see you."

"My dad's asleep right now, but if he woke up and I wasn't here he'd probably lock me up for good."

"Yeah, we're going to have to figure this out..." *I could sneak out...*

"If you want, I can try to sneak out tonight after my dad goes to work and my mom goes to bed."

"Do you think you'll get away with it? That sounds risky as hell."

"It's not as risky as my dad being here. He wakes up a lot. My mom sleeps like a baby."

"Well, in that case, I'm down. What time?"

"Meet me outside of my house at midnight."

"You know there's a ten O'clock curfew, right?" *Come on, dude, really?*

"No, I didn't know that. If you don't want to..."

"No, I do, I really want to see you."

"Okay, it's settled then. Midnight. What are you going to do about Chris?"

"I guess I should call him. We we're going to practice today, but I don't really feel like doing that anymore."

"Are you going to tell him that I told you?"

"I would like to hear him admit to it..."

"What if he lies about it?" *Which he will...*

"I don't know...I guess I won't even bring it up. He's moving in two weeks. Why should I care, right?" *Right!*

"Exactly. I like that, Billy, be the bigger person. But, hey...I should get off the phone before my dad wakes up and takes it from me."

"All right, babe, I'll see you tonight."

"Babe? I like it. Okay, sweetie, don't be late. Bye!"

"Bye," Will said and I hung up the phone. *How cute...Babe...* I walked into the kitchen and put the phone back on the receiver. *Hmmm. I should probably keep a low profile today...I'll just stay in the house. They'll be a lot less suspicious if I don't do anything...* I went to my room and sat on my bed. I opened my astrology book and turned to the section on Cancer. *I think I'm going to need Jessica...We may not get along very well, but let's see what makes her tick...* I Started reading about the Cancer personality traits in depth. *Introspective. Overly-emotional. Not impulsive...She is literally the exact opposite of me. Nothing's ever easy...* I continued reading and lost track of time. My dad knocked on my door and came into my room. I looked up and smiled.

"Oh, hi, dad."

"Hi, Hannah, what are you up to?"

"I'm just reading."

"You're not playing basketball today?"

"No, I thought I would just hang out inside the house today..." *Wait...Is my being less suspicious actually more suspicious?*

"...Okay, well, I'm going to make a sandwich for lunch. Do you want me to make you one?"

"No, dad, I'm not hungry, thanks though..."

"Hannah, are you feeling okay?" *Uh oh...*

"Yeah, dad, I'm fine..." *Think...* "It was just a long day yesterday and I wanna chill."

"Okay...I'll leave you to your 'chilling' then," my dad said and laughed while closing my door. *I think I'm good...* I read throughout the afternoon and was only interrupted once when I heard another knock on my door.

"Come in," I said. *That's weird. They usually just let themselves in...Oh, Casey.*

"Hi, Hannah, your dad let me in. You don't mind, do you?"

"No, it's fine Casey, what's up?" *Let me guess, Chris?*

"...Well, you weren't outside and I was just wondering if you were okay." *Oh, wow, maybe this is suspicious.*

"This morning..." I whispered. "...My parents got in a big fight about Will and me...mostly me, and I'm trying, I guess, to not give them something to argue about."

"I'm sorry, Hannah, that's not cool, but I'm glad you're okay."

"Thanks, yeah, I'm okay."

"...Did you call Will?" *And, here we go...*

"Yeah, I called him this morning."

"Did he mention anything about Chris?"

"...No, Casey, he didn't. I'm sorry..." *Not about you, at least.*

"Are you sure?" *Yeah...*

"Yeah, Casey, my memory's not that bad," I said and laughed.

"What I mean is...Maybe Chris doesn't like me and Will doesn't want to tell you...Or you don't want to tell me...If you know anything...I can take it."

"I know you can Casey. We're a lot alike. I would tell you if I knew anything. I just don't know."

"...Okay. So, what should I do?" *Forget about him.*

"Maybe you should just go talk to him..." *Don't listen to me!*

"Can you ask Will one more time...Please, Hannah, just one more time and I won't bother you about it again."

"Sure, Casey, I'll talk to him," I said and Casey lunged at me and gave me a hug.

"Thank you so much, Hannah!"

"I don't want you to get your hopes up too high though...I don't know what's going on with their band and Chris is moving. There's just a lot going on."

"I know...I understand...You wanna go outside and play basketball...Maybe we could get Chris to..." *Nope!*

"Maybe another time, Casey, I kind of just want to relax today."

"...Oh, okay, tomorrow then?"

"Yeah, Casey, tomorrow..." *I hope I'm not this pushy...*

"Okay, I'll come by tomorrow. See ya, Hannah."

"Bye," I said and Casey let herself out of my room. *That girl is persistent...Hmmm, right, yeah...So am I...*

I was watching the early evening news with my dad when my mom got home from work. She put her purse down on the counter and looked right at me.

"Hey, what did you do today?" My mom asked. *I planned my escape.*

"Nothing. I did a lot of reading. I hung out with dad..."

"Is that right?" *Uh oh...I know that tone.*

"Yeah, she didn't leave the house," my dad said.

"Really?" My mom said and stared at my dad.

"What!?" My dad pleaded. "She wanted to stay in today."

"It's true," I said. "I wanted to catch up on my reading...And I did."

"...Okay. I was going to make chicken for dinner..."

"Chicken sounds good," I said and my dad agreed. My mom made dinner. When she was finished, I went outside for the first time that day and got my brother, who was still running around with Mitchell, to have him come inside to eat. My parents didn't mention anything about the fourth or Will. When I finished eating, I stood up and said, "I think I need to take a shower."

"You took a shower this morning," my dad said. *Ugh!*

"Dad, I'm on my period, and I'm feeling, kind of, not clean..." *Heh.* My mom laughed.

"Yeah, I didn't need to know that," my dad said.

"No one did!" My brother added. "Thanks, Hannah, I was still eating!" *Ha! It worked.*

"Hannah, go take your shower," my mom insisted. *Perfect. I have to get ready.*

At midnight, I listened for any movement at my bedroom door. I didn't hear anything so I slowly walked over to my window and cautiously lifted it up. I stopped and listened again. *I wonder if they know there's no screen on my window...* I lifted my right leg over and then straddled the windowsill. I listened again. I brought my left leg over and then lowered the window an inch from being closed. *I hope this thing doesn't close. I would be so screwed...* I tip-toed my way to the side gate and unlatched it. I slowly opened the gate and then gingerly pushed it closed. I stopped again and listened. I walked around my mom's car and saw Will waiting for me. *Right on time!* I walked up to him and gave him a hug. I moved my hand down his arm to hold his hand.

"Hey, babe, we should probably go somewhere," I whispered.

"I didn't know you were a ninja," Will said and smiled.

"It's not the first time I've snuck out. Let's walk down to that school," I said while pointing down the street.

"Mountain View. Yeah, I went to that school in sixth grade. There's a park over there too." Will and I held hands and walked down the street until we reached the intersection. We waited for all of the cars to pass and then ran all the way to the school. We checked the gates and they were locked.

"What are we going to do?" I asked.

"We're gonna have to jump the fence? I'll go first and help you over." *Dude...*

"I think I can jump a fence without help."

"It'll make me feel better..." Will said and then jumped up on the fence. Before he was on the other side, I grabbed onto the fence and pulled myself over.

"See, I'm not just a girl..." I said and smiled.

"But you do look like Gwen Stefani."

"Yeah, sort of, a little bit." *I do love her.* We started walking toward the concrete benches.

"Nope, more like a lotta bit. It's a good thing." *I know...But...*

"Okay, I can do that too..." I stopped walking and dropped Will's hand. I looked him up and down and then walked around him.

"What are you doing?"

"Trent Reznor, the 'Nine Inch Nails,' guy. You look exactly like Trent Reznor." *It's the hair.*

"Oh yeah...I guess that's not too bad."

"I was messing with you. I thought you looked like Trent Reznor the first time I saw you playing bass in Chris's garage.

"We should probably talk about Chris."

"Talk about what? I told you what happened. It's not a big deal." Will and I sat down next to each other on one of the concrete benches.

"I called him and asked him about it. He didn't deny it. It wasn't good. I said some things..."

"I thought you were going to let it go." *I'm glad you didn't.*

"Why did you turn him down? I guess what I'm saying is why me over him?" *That's easy.*

"...Honestly...He reminds me of my ex-boyfriend, Joe...He was a jock too; good looking, athletic, you know, like an Abercrombie and Fitch model. He also treated me like shit. When he broke up with me, I told myself that I would never date another jock."

"So, I'm the anti-jock..." *No, Billy, don't take it that way.*

"You're different, in a good way. That's what I like about you." I held Will's hand tight. "And, you're a Libra, which makes us perfect for each other."

"It's just that everyone keeps telling me that you're too good for me." *Oh no, who?*

"That's not true. I think you're too good for me."

"I can't believe you're my boyfriend. You're so sweet and such a nice person, it's hard to believe that you would go out with me. I'm only saying this because I've never really felt the same way with a guy like I feel with you. So many guys treat me like shit, it kind of was a shock that you didn't. I think it's because you're almost sixteen and more mature."

"I knew that you liked me, but I didn't know why."

"Now you do. I was afraid you didn't like me. I didn't think you were ever going to ask me out."

"Well, I was a little intimidated by you. You're super-beautiful, smart, nice..." *Ahhh...*

"That's so funny, I was intimidated by you, but you make me feel so comfortable." I got off of the bench while still holding Will's hand. "Let's go on the swings."

"All right." We walked over to the swings, sat down, and started swinging. I reached over to Will and put my hand on top of his.

"I feel so safe with you."

"That's a good thing, because you never know what could be out here at night, Will said and laughed. "It's okay, though, I'll protect you."

"Maybe I'll protect you." I responded and stopped swinging. I got up and sat in Will's lap sideways. Will laughed.

"That doesn't look comfortable." I put my arm around his neck and I started swinging. I rested my head against his chest.

"It's perfect," I said and then began to feel very sleepy. I slowly drifted off to sleep and when I woke up, I was on the ground. *Huh? What happened?* "Hey, babe, what time is it?"

"It's almost two-thirty."

"We should go back. My dad gets off at four."

"All right, give me a minute. My legs are asleep."

"Ahh, poor baby," I said and started rubbing his legs. "Better?"

"Yeah, much better. You ready to go back?"

"Yeah, let's go." I got up from the ground and brushed myself off. I put my hand out and Will grabbed on. I pulled him up and he stumbled forward until he was able to grab onto the frame of the swing. *He weighs more than he looks...* "You okay?" I laughed and continued brushing the dirt off of my pants.

"Of course," he said while walking over to me. "What are you talking about? Hey, you missed a spot," he said and brushed the dirt off my jeans. *You so just wanted to...*

"Was there really dirt on my butt or did you just want an excuse to touch it."

"Yes..." He said and smiled.

"Smooth." We went back to the front of the school and jumped the fence again. Will wrapped his arm around my waist and I put my hand in his back pocket. "I have to check for dirt," I said while smiling.

"Really, what'd you find?"

"Nothing, actually..." *Ha. Just kidding.*

"Ha-ha," he said. I smiled.

"Let's go," I said and we started walking back. "Do you think you're going to work things out with Chris?"

"I don't know. I don't think so. Why?"

"I know that your band matters to you and you've been friends for a long time so I figured that you would want to fix things." Will laughed. *That was funny?*

"Well, I did tell him to fuck off so that might be a problem." *Nice.*

"I know you're not the type of person to hold grudges."

"I'll think about it, Hannah, but I don't think it matters. I think I'm gonna start hanging out with Rob more."

"Rob, really? I thought you didn't like him."

"He is really hard to get along with, but at least I can trust him."

"What's his birthday?"

"You mean for the astrology thing? I think it's like May tenth or something."

"Yeah, that would make him a Taurus; stubborn and bull-headed, but also loyal, so that sounds exactly right."

"The thing is that I want to play guitar so I'm going to have to talk to him. I also want us to write our own songs and come up with a band name. You know, to be legit."

"'2 Legit 2 quit,' Hammer time!" I said and smiled.

"You're so cute," he said while squeezing my waist. We crossed the intersection fast this time because there was no traffic.

"No, you're so cute," I responded. I grabbed Will's butt and smiled. "So, you're going to give him an ultimatum then?"

"Ultimatum?" *Ugh.*

"Yeah, like, if he listens to you then you'll stay in the band with him and if he doesn't then you'll start your own."

"That's exactly right. It also reminds me: Would you sing for my band? I mean, you have a great voice." *Ahhh. Thanks!*

"...I would love to sing for your band, even though I don't think I'm very good, but my parents hardly ever let me out of the house now."

"Yeah...That sucks."

"I'm so happy that school starts in a couple of weeks, Billy, we'll be able to see each other every day. No parents breathing down my neck."

"Yeah, just the teachers."

"They don't care."

"Yeah, probably not, at least most of them." We got to my house and then stopped behind my mom's car. Will hugged me close and then let me go. "You want to see a movie this weekend?" He whispered.

"Yeah, what do you wanna see?"

"Doesn't matter, we can decide when we get there." *Jessica...*

"I'll have to bring Jessica."

"I'll bring Rob. Call me tomorrow, we'll figure it out."

"Okay, I'll call Jessica in the morning." *Morning...Like now. I'm so sleepy.* I looked into Will's eyes. *Are you going to kiss me or what?* He moved his hands up to my face and pushed my hair back behind my head. *Yeah, he's going to kiss me.* I closed my eyes and I felt his breath on my face. He pressed his lips into mine. *This is nice, so soft.* He backed away from me and smiled. I pulled him back into me and pushed my tongue past his lips. I pinned him against my body and held onto his back. *This is more like it...But it's getting late...*I let go of him and then pulled away. "I should probably go inside, Billy; you don't want me getting caught, do you?" I grabbed his hand and led him over to the fence. I carefully opened the gate and then turned back towards him. I quickly kissed him again while resting my hand on the gate. "I'll call you tomorrow."

"What time?" Will whispered.

"Noon...Bye, Billy."

"Bye, Hannah." I quietly latched the gate and slowly walked to my window. It was still just as I had left it so I carefully opened it and finessed my way inside my room. I stopped and listened for any noise. *I don't hear anything.* I kicked off my shoes, lay down in bed and pulled the blankets over me. *That was fun.*

Chapter Fifteen

Soulmates

I got out of bed at around eleven and realized that I was wearing my clothes from the night before. *Shit. I must have been tired. I didn't even put on my pajamas! Shit...Oh well.* I opened my bedroom door and looked into my parent's bedroom. My dad was fast asleep. I walked past my brother's room and he wasn't there. *He's probably with Mitchell. It's kind of sad. He's about to lose his best friend...Do I have time to take a shower? Yeah. Okay...Take a shower, call Jessica, call Billy...Hope my dad doesn't wake up.* I went to my room to get a change of clothes and took a shower. When I got out of the shower, I went to my room to check the time. *Shit. Only ten minutes!* I walked out to the kitchen to get the phone and my dad was standing there holding the refrigerator door open trying to decide what to eat. *Shit!*

"Hi dad," I said.

"Getting a late start today?" My dad asked. *Shit...He doesn't know, does he? Be cool...*

"...Yeah, just like you, it seems..." My dad chuckled.

"Yeah...Don't try to grow up too fast, Hannah...There's a reason they call it work."

"Okay, dad, ummm, do you think I could call Jessica? I was supposed to call her yesterday, but..."

"Yeah, of course, go call your friend."

"Okay, thanks." I picked the phone up off of the receiver, went to my room, and shut the door. *Shit. Five minutes.* I dialed Jessica's number and her mom picked up the phone.

"Hello?"

"Hi, is Jessica there?"

"Yes, she is, may I ask who's calling please?"

"It's Hannah."

"Hi, Hannah!?

"Hi." *Ugh.*

"Hold on, I'll get her."

"Thanks." *Why does this have to be such a thing? I don't have time for this...*

"...Hello?" Jessica asked indifferently.

"Hey, do you want to see a movie on Saturday with Will and his friend?"

"What movie?"

"I don't know..." *It doesn't matter.*

"Why do you want to see a movie if you don't know what you want to see?" *Classic Jessica...*

"It's just an excuse to see Billy."

"I see...What friend?" *Ahhh damn...*

"Rob...You remember from..."

"...Yeah...I don't think so, Hannah." *Jessica!*

"Jessica, please, just do me this one favor!"

"I don't know..."

"Jessica, I need your help! My parents won't let me go otherwise."

"...Fine, but you'll owe me." *Yeah, I know.*

"Okay...Can your mom take us?"

"I'll ask."

"Okay, but hurry up, I have to call Billy in two minutes."

"You have to..." *Yeah...*

"That's what I told him, so, yeah."

"...Hold on." I waited for one minute." *Come on, Jessica!* "Okay, she'll take us." *Perfect!* "What time do you want us to pick you up?"

"Like around ten, maybe?"

"Okay."

"I've got to call Billy, Jessica, I'll see you tomorrow."

"...All right, bye."

"Bye." I hung up the phone and dialed Will's number. He answered after one ring and I knew it was him.

"Hey, babe, what's up?"

"Not much, I guess you didn't get caught last night..."

"They've never caught me sneaking out. I don't think the thought has ever crossed their minds."

"...That's good, I don't think my mom cares."

"If I got caught, that would be the end of my life."

"That would be a damn shame. There is a lack of beautiful girls in the world."

"Smooth, Billy. I called Jessica earlier..." *Like five seconds ago earlier...* "...And she said she would go to the movies on Saturday. Did you call Rob?"

"Actually, I went over to his house and told him how it was."

"How'd it go?"

"I thought it went pretty good. He said he wanted to see a movie and that his mom would drive us, but that was before..."

"Before you told him off..."

"Yeah, well, I'll call him later to check."

"Guess what, Billy?"

"What?"

"No, I said guess."

"Ummm, okay...The Chargers are going to win the Superbowl this year." *What? No!*

"No, silly, I miss you..."

"I miss you too."

"And it's obvious to anyone paying attention that the Packers are going to win the Superbowl..."

"Nope, not gonna happen."

"You should talk to my brother about it...So, what are you wearing?"

"Is that a trick question? I'm wearing clothes."

"What type of clothes?"

"A t-shirt and jeans, why?"

"That sounds sexy...I'm just lying here in my bra and panties thinking about you."

"What color are they?"

"It's a white bra and white panties with purple flowers. I got them at Victoria's Secret."

"...Now that sounds sexy."

"So, what do you want to do to me?" I heard my dad walking down the hall. "Shit, my dad's awake, I gotta go. I'll try to call you later. Bye, Billy." I hung up the phone. *Awake? Stupid...I know he's awake...Oh well, it doesn't matter...* I opened my door and my dad was walking out of his room. *I hope he didn't hear anything.*

"Dad..."

"Yes, Hannah..."

"Jessica wants to go to the movies Saturday...Her mom will take us..."

"Okay..."

"So, can I go?"

"Ask your mom." *Great, thanks dad.* My dad started walking to the living room. *I should go talk to Casey...*

"Hey, Dad...Can I go to Casey's?"

"Are you sure you're not just telling me Casey and going to..."

"Dad! Look!" I walked over to the front door and opened it. I then led my dad outside. I pointed down the street. "Look," I said again. "They're not even down there. I'm going to go to Casey's house." My dad looked at me suspiciously. *Shit...*

"Fine, you can go to Casey's house, but be back before your mom gets home."

"Thanks, dad, I will." I started walking down to Casey's house. *I wonder...* I turned around and saw my dad staring at me. I waved and smiled at him and then turned around and kept walking to Casey's house. *I still have to be careful...* I knocked on Casey's door and her mom answered.

"Hi, Hannah," she said. "Casey's in her room."

"Okay, thanks," I said and started walking down the hallway.

"Actually, Hannah..." *Huh?*

"Yeah..."

"We're going to Disneyland this weekend..." *Okay, thanks for telling me...* "...And we could use a house sitter. We just need someone to feed our dogs, Bear and Sadie...They're super lovable golden retrievers and they hardly ever bark! You want to meet them?"

"Ummm, sure..." Casey's mom and I walked into the back yard and the dogs immediately jumped up on me. *Oh my God!*

"See, Hannah, they already love you." *Great.* "And we would need you to water the plants out here too..."

"...So, just this weekend?"

"Yes. We're leaving Saturday morning and coming back Monday." *Hmmm, that gives me an idea...Billy...*

"Yeah, I can watch your house this weekend."

"Thank you, Hannah, I'll give you the key Saturday morning." *This is going to be perfect.* "Can you be here at eight?" *That's pretty early...*

"Yeah, I'll be here at eight."

"And we'll pay you, of course."

"That's okay, you don't have to do that...I'm happy to help."

"You're such a responsible young lady!" *Ha!*

"Thanks! I should go talk to Casey..."

"Yeah, she's in her room..." *You already told me.* "I think she's watching TV."

"Okay, thanks." I went to Casey's room and knocked on her door. She opened the door and jumped on me like one of her dogs and gave me a hug. "Nice to see you too..."

"Hannah, so, yeah, what's up?" Casey calmed down and sat on her bed. I sat next to her.

"What are you watching?"

"MTV."

"Cool, cool...It's so cool that you have a TV in your room."

"Yeah, I got it for Christmas..." *Pretty expensive gift...Ugh. This is gonna get awkward.*

"So, your mom told me that you're going to Disneyland this weekend."

"Yeah, it should be fun, but I don't know..."

"What's wrong?" *I already know...*

"It would be better if a certain someone was going with me..." *This is so sad. I need to say something...*

"Casey, I didn't want to say anything...but Chris isn't interested in you..."

"Oh...Okay, well..."

"It's okay Casey, we'll find you someone..."

"What else did he say?" *Who? Oh shit...Right, Will...*

"He said that Chris..." *Shit...I don't know...He didn't tell me anything...I didn't ask him.*

"It's okay, Hannah, I can take it." *...Angela!*

"...He said that Chris wanted to work things out with Angela."

"Oh..."

"There's nothing you could have done..." *I'm going to Hell...*

"Yeah..."

"Hey, I didn't tell you...Your mom wants me to housesit for you guys this weekend."

"That's cool..."

"...Hey, I'm gonna go play basketball if you want to join me."

"I don't really feel like playing..." *What did I do?*

"Okay, if you change your mind, I'll be in front of my house."

"Okay..."

"All right, Casey, see you later..."

"Bye..."

"Casey...There's someone out there for you and I won't stop until I find him."

"Thanks, Hannah." I turned around and walked down the hallway and out of Casey's house. *It's better this way. Chris is terrible...*

The next morning, my brother was being more of a pest than usual because Mitchell wasn't home.

"Michael, why don't you play your videogame?"

"I don't want to play videogames!" *Who are you?* He ran around in a circle in the living room. *He's crazy. The boy has totally lost his mind.*

"Stop it, Michael, you wanna wake dad?" I asked and then the phone rang. He stopped and then ran straight for the phone and answered it.

"Hello," my brother said. "Yeah, hold on." *Who is it?*

"Hey, babe," Will said, "I hope this isn't a bad time."

"No, we're good; my dad's still asleep, but my brother is bugging so I can't talk long, what's up?"

"Well, I just wanted to call to say I miss you." *Ahhh. I miss you too, Billy...*

"Ahhh, you're so sweet...Michael, leave me alone, sorry..."

"It's okay. I also called because Rob is down for Saturday."

"That's good, I'll tell Jessica."

"Rob wants to know if she thinks it's a date." I laughed and heard Rob in the background.

"Oh, is he there? That's funny. I didn't exactly put it that way to her...But, she's a Cancer and he's a Taurus...It's a good match."

"Perfect, I'll tell him not to worry about it."

"Okay, I should call Jessica," I whispered. "You know, to make this call legit." Will laughed.

"Of course..." He responded. "Talk to you later, babe."

"Bye, Billy," I said and hung up the phone. "Michael, stop being such a pest!"

"I'm bored, I'm bored, I'm bored!"

"You're gonna wake dad up!"

"I'm bored."

"Listen, Michael, I'm sorry that your friend is moving, but you have to get over it already!"

"I don't want to!"

"Michael, go outside and play basketball."

"I said I don't want to!" *Ugh...*

"Michael, I need you to be quiet. I have to call Jessica."

"No!"

"Oh, whatever..." I dialed Jessica's number and she picked up. "Hey, Jessica, are we still on for Saturday?"

"Yeah. Ten, right?"

"Yeah...I was thinking we could hang out at the mall for a while and then get lunch before the movie..."

"All right, what movie are we going to see?"

"We'll decide when we're there. It doesn't matter to me. You can choose."

"All right, cool...Hannah, that Rob guy, he doesn't think this is like a double date, does he?" I laughed. *That is so funny. Rob asked the same thing!* "...Well does he!?" Jessica demanded.

"I don't think so, Jessica..." *It could work though...*

"Okay, good, because he is not my type!"

"Who is your type?"

"I don't know, maybe if it was someone like Chris..." *Oh fuck no!*

"That's not going to happen..."

"I didn't say Chris, Hannah, I said someone like Chris!" *Oh please, give me a break.*

"Whatever you say, Jessica..."

"...So, yeah, I'll see you Saturday morning then."

"Yep, bye, Jessica," I said and she abruptly hung up the phone. *She's funny. Hmmm, I guess Michael decided to play videogames after all.* Later that night, after dinner, and after my dad left for work, my mom announced that she was going to take a shower. *Now's my chance to call Billy...* As soon as I heard the water come on, I grabbed the phone and dialed his number. An unfamiliar voice answered the phone. *Oh shit, did I dial the right number?*

"Hi, is Billy...I mean, Is Will there?"

"Yeah, hold on."

"Hello?"

"Hey, Billy, who was that?"

"My brother..." *He has a brother?*

"That's cool, I didn't know you had a brother. How old is he?"

"Old..." *I'm sensing some tension there...*

"...Anyway, about Saturday, we're going to meet up for lunch at one at the mall entrance and then decide what movie we're going to see after that..."

"Okay, sounds like a plan." *He's so cool...*

"All right, Billy, I need to go before my mom gets out of the shower.

"Okay, babe, thanks for calling..."

"Have sweet dreams...About me," I said.

"I dream about you every night, babe," Will responded. *Ahhh, how sweet!*

"Keep those dreams PG-13, mister," I said and laughed.

"I definitely can't promise you that," Will said and we both laughed.

"Okay, goodnight, Billy."

"Goodnight." I hung up the phone and placed it back on the counter. *He really is my soulmate...*

I set my alarm for seven-thirty Saturday morning, which gave me enough time for my mom to go to work and for me to be at

Casey's house at eight. I had no intention of telling my parents that I was housesitting for Casey's family. I was sure that their suspicion would compel them to not allow me to do it. I waited for my mom to pull out of the driveway and then checked that my dad and my brother were both asleep. I walked down to Casey's house and saw Casey's family packing their car.

"Oh, Hi Hannah!" Casey's mom said. "Let me get you the spare key...We fed the dogs this morning, but if you could water the plants that would be great...You'll need to feed the dogs tonight, tomorrow morning, tomorrow night, and then once again Monday morning." *How much are you paying me for this?* "You can water the plants in the back the same time that you feed the dogs to save some time...Oh, yeah, the dog food is in the garage." Casey's mom opened a drawer in the kitchen and then handed me the spare key. She then walked me into the garage and pointed at the dog food. "They get two scoops each in their bowls morning and night." *Great.* "Let me see...Anything else...Make sure that you lock everything up when you leave...You never know..."

"All right, no problem."

"Thanks again, you're a life saver..." *Hmmm. Am I? I didn't do a great job with Mel...* "We really didn't want to have to take the dogs to the kennel."

"I've got this. You guys have a good time."

"Thanks, Hannah, you're a blessing...We're ready to go."

"Okay, I need to say bye to Casey..." We walked to the front of the house where Casey and her dad were waiting in their car. Casey's mom got in the car and Casey rolled down her window.

"Hi, Hannah..."

"Casey...Try to have fun this weekend...Remember what I told you...It'll all work out."

"Okay, thanks, Hannah, see you Monday."

"See ya Monday, Casey!" Casey's mom and dad waved to me and then drove away. *Okay...Water the plants...* I watered the plants in the back yard and played with the dogs for a few minutes before locking up Casey's house and heading back home. I took a really long shower, shampooed my hair, shaved my legs, and got dressed. I had to wait about thirty minutes for Jessica to show up. Jessica got out of her mom's car and started walking up my driveway but I met her halfway.

"Hey, Hannah."

"Hey, Jessica..." *She's looking kind of sexy, like she thinks she's going on a date. Ha!*

"Have you thought about what movie you want to see?"

"Nope."

"All right, let's go..." Jessica's mom drove to the mall and dropped us off.

"Okay, girls, when the movie's over, call me."

"Okay, mom, thanks," Jessica said and we got out of the car and walked into the mall. "We've got a couple of hours...What do you want to do?"

"Let's go hang out at the music store...I think it's called Sam Goody. I want to check out 'Hole's' new album."

"Hole? That's a stupid name for a band," Jessica insisted.

"What!? No, it's not," I argued. "Courtney Love is awesome."

"Who's Courtney Love?" *Really, Jessica!*

"Kurt Cobain...His wife..."

"Sorry, I don't know..."

"It's a good thing we have the time..." Jessica and I went to Sam Goody and I showed her all the music that I liked. We listened to music and walked around the store until it was time to meet Will and Rob in the front of the mall. We walked to the entrance and waited. After a few minutes we saw them walking toward us. I hugged and kissed Will as he approached.

"Hey, Billy, I missed you so much."

"I missed you too."

"I like your hair, Rob," Jessica said. *Hmmm...*

"Thanks," Rob replied.

"Oh, shit, Jessica speaks!" Will said and I laughed.

"Yes, but only when she wants to," Jessica replied.

"So, Hannah, Rob wants to thank you for naming our band," Will said.

"Yeah, it's a cool name; Anarchy," Rob said. *Billy... That was all you...*

"Cool, you guys are going to use it? That's awesome!" I asserted.

"We'll be sure to give you credit when we release our album." Will said, smiled, and held my hand.

"It's not that easy to just release an album," Rob argued.

"I'm sure you're right," Will said. "I'm hungry; you guys wanna get some food?"

"Yeah," I said. "What do you wanna get?"

"Subway sounds good to me," Will answered. "I'm thinking about a meatball sub."

"Okay, let's go," I said.

"Sure," Rob added. Will ordered a meat ball sub, a bag of lays potato chips, and a soda. Rob ordered a roast beef combo and Jessica and I didn't order anything.

"I'll share with my Billy," I said.

"Jessica, did you want me to get you something?" Rob asked. *Nice, Rob!*

"No, I already ate," Jessica replied.

"No, she didn't," I whispered in Will's ear.

"Hannah! I heard that," Jessica exclaimed. I laughed.

"...Just get something," I said.

"Yeah, I've got it," Rob said.

"No, it's okay, I'm not hungry," Jessica insisted. We found some seats close to the restaurant and sat down. Will started eating his meatball sub and I opened the bag of chips and started snacking. Rob started eating his sandwich and Jessica sat with her arms folded across the table.

"What movie are we gonna watch?" Jessica asked.

"Batman," Rob quickly answered.

"I don't want to watch Batman, why don't we see something funny..." Jessica replied.

"The only thing I want to see is Batman," Rob insisted. Will and I looked at each other and smiled.

"What do you guys want to see?" Jessica asked as she looked at me and then at Will. I looked at Will and smiled. I looked back at Jessica.

"It doesn't matter to us," Will said. "Anything is fine."

"Hannah!" Jessica said.

"It's up to you two," I insisted. *It doesn't matter...*

"...How about 'Nine Months?' That looks good," Jessica said to Rob.

"Nah, isn't that a stupid chick flick," Rob said. "Will, back me up here..."

"I really don't care, man, we're down for whatever," he said.

"Rob, let's make a deal. We'll watch 'Nine Months' today and next time you can choose," Jessica reasoned. *What is she doing? Interesting...*

"Fine, have it your way," Rob said. "We'll watch the chick flick." Will and I smiled. We finished our food and went to the theater to check the show times. 'Nine Months' was playing at two so we bought our tickets and were able to walk right into the theater and wait for the movie to start. We walked to the very back row and took our seats.

"I'm gonna go get some popcorn," Rob said.

"I'll come with you," Jessica added. "You guys want something?" I handed Jessica five dollars.

"Yeah, get me some milk duds."

"I'm good, thanks," Will said. Rob and Jessica got up and walked back to the snack bar. "What do ya think?"

"About Rob and Jessica?" *I'm not even sure anymore...*

"Yeah, do you think she likes him?"

"Maybe...Jessica's kinda weird. Sometimes I have no idea what she's thinking. But she is the perfect alibi to see you, Billy." I put my hand on his leg and leaned in over the seating console and kissed him. "My parents trust Jessica more than they trust me...I've got a surprise for you, Billy."

"Really? I love surprises..."

"Casey's family went to Disneyland this weekend...Guess who is house sitting for them?"

"You?"

"That's right, Billy, you know what that means right?"

"Not really, I don't even know what house sitting is..."

"...It's no big deal. I just have to feed their dogs and water their plants." I leaned in closer to him and whispered in his ear. "The good part is I have the key to their house..." I moved back and looked into his eyes.

"...Oh, okay, I get it, you want me to sneak out again."

"Yup, tonight."

"But won't your dad be home?"

"Yeah, but Jessica's spending the night. He never bothers me when Jessica's over. It's perfect."

"Okay, I guess I could get Rob to spend the night too."

"Someone's got to keep Jessica busy while, well, you know..." The movie previews started playing and the trailer for 'Clueless' came on. "Oh my God, Billy, I want to see that so bad."

"Okay, I'm down." Rob and Jessica came back with the popcorn and candy. Jessica handed me the Milk Duds.

"Jessica, we have to see this movie." I pointed towards the screen.

"Oh, yeah, 'Clueless,' that looks good," Jessica replied. Will put his arm around me and rested his hand on my leg. The theater went dark and the movie started.

"Hey, babe, you want some candy?" I asked.

"Sure," Will replied. I took one of the Milk Duds out of the package and put it in his mouth. He ate one more and then I tried for a third... *Remember the cookies?* "Okay, babe, I'm good," he said. I put the box of candy in the cup holder and leaned in to kiss him. After about ten minutes of making out, Jessica growled.

"Hey! You guys are loud, stop it! We're trying to watch the movie!" Will and I turned and looked at her. Will whispered in my ear,

"I can see why your parents like her." I laughed.

"Shut up!" Jessica reiterated. *Relax, Jessica.* I put my hand in Will's lap and then rested my head against his shoulder.

We finished the movie and the credits rolled. "Hey, babe, the movie's over," Will said.

"...Oh, okay, what happened?"

"You fell asleep..."

"...No, with the movie..."

"They got married."

"I knew it! Where are Rob and Jessica?"

"Probably waiting on us," Will said as he held my hand. We walked into the lobby and saw Jessica standing in line at the payphone and Rob standing alone by the arcade. Will walked over to Rob and I went to stand in line with Jessica.

"What do you think about Rob?" I asked.

"He seems nice, I guess," Jessica responded.

"So..." *What are you going to do?*

"So, nothing...I don't like him like that. I like him as a friend."

"Are you sure?"

"Yes, Hannah, I think I know..." *Okay, sorry I asked...* Jessica called her mom and then we walked over to Will and Rob.

"Hey babe, what's up?" Will asked.

"Jessica called her mom to pick us up. We need to wait outside for her."

"...And you guys need to stay in here until we leave. I don't want my mom to see us with you," Jessica added. *Jessica! Come on...*

"Okay, we have to go, Billy," I said, and then whispered in his ear, "see you tonight, same time..." I quickly hugged and kissed him. "Bye, Rob..." Jessica quickly pulled me away by my arm.

"Bye," Rob said. Once we were outside, I turned to Jessica and said,

"Jessica, ask your mom to spend the night at my house..."

"...What's going on, Hannah?"

"I'll tell you once you're spending the night."

"What are you up to?"

"You have to trust me..."

"...Why would I do that?"

"Because, we're like best friends now..." *Hmmm... Yeah... Ugh...*

"...Really? I'm your best friend?" *Maybe...*

"Yeah..."

"Okay, I'll spend the night, but you're going to tell me what's up..."

"Yeah, I promise." We spent fifteen minutes talking about how much we liked 'Nine Months,' while we waited for Jessica's mom to pick us up. She asked her mom if she could stay the night at my house and she agreed. We stopped at Jessica's house to pick up her stuff and then we got dropped off at my house. When Jessica's mom drove away, Jessica immediately stared at me.

"So...What's going on?"

"I'm housesitting for Casey's family this weekend..."

"Okay..."

"So, we're gonna sneak out tonight and hang out with Will...And Rob."

"Hannah!"

"Don't worry. It's not like that..." *Shit...* "We're just going to hang out...Like a little party."

"...A little party?"

"Yeah, it'll be fun."

"I don't know, Hannah, we could get in a lot of trouble."

"No one's even going to know..."

"You're a troublemaker, Hannah."

"I am not a troublemaker."

"Yeah, you are." *Okay, maybe...*

"Fine, but at least I'm not boring."

"Are you saying that I'm boring?"

"Yeah. Jessica, how many parties have you been to? Real parties...Not birthday parties that you have to go to..."

"Okay, well...That's not fair."

"Exactly what I thought! The answer is zero, isn't it?"

"Hannah..."

"Come on, Jessica, live a little bit."

"...Fine, but we better not get caught."

"We won't. Don't worry." Jessica gave me a concerned look and I smiled at her.

"Come on, let's go inside." Jessica and I went inside of my house. My mom was cooking spaghetti and my dad was relaxing in his recliner.

"Hi, girls, did you have fun at the movies?" My mom asked.

"Yeah, we saw 'Nine Months.' It was pretty good," I said.

"Oh, that movie with Hugh Jackman? I love him," my mom swooned.

"I heard that," my dad said." We all laughed.

"Is it okay if Jessica spends the night?"

"Yes, of course, she's always welcome." *Yes, she is, isn't she?*

"Thanks Ms. O'Connor," Jessica said.

"Dinner's almost ready, are you hungry?" My mom inquired.

"Yeah, I'm starving," Jessica said. *I wonder why? You never eat!*

"Have a seat at the table," my mom instructed. Jessica and I sat down and waited for dinner. We ate my mom's spaghetti and then went to my room.

"Okay, Jessica," I said. "I have to go over to Casey's house to feed their dogs. We can check things out before tonight..."

"Dogs? I don't like dogs." *God, Jessica!*

"They're golden retrievers!"

"And!?"

"They're harmless. They don't even bark."

"I don't know..." *This is getting old...*

"You don't even have to see them...But you have to come with me..."

"Fine," Jessica said. "They're not in the house?"

"No, they're in the back yard."

"Okay...As long as they stay there." *Wow. Something's not right with you...*

"...They will, relax."

"Okay..."

"Come on, let's go," I said and Jessica and I walked into my living room. "Mom, can we go to Casey's house really fast?"

"Yeah, I suppose...Wait a minute! Are you trying to go see that boy?"

"What boy?"

"Don't play dumb with me, Hannah!"

"Mom, there's no one down there. I don't even think they're a band anymore..." My mom looked over at my dad.

"Yeah, I haven't heard anything for a while," my dad said.

"...Okay, go ahead, but be home before it gets dark."

"We'll be right back." Jessica and I went outside and started walking down to Casey's house.

"I think your mom is on to you..." Jessica reasoned.

"...No, she's not. I'm always one step ahead of her," I insisted.

"You really think so?"

"Jessica, they don't know that I'm housesitting! They don't know I have the key!"

"Wow, Hannah...I don't know what to say." We got to Casey's house and I pulled the key out of my front pocket and opened the door. "This just feels wrong..."

"No, it feels right. It's not like we're going to, I don't know, break anything...Stay here, I'm going to get the dog food." I went to the garage and wrestled the bag of dog food off the ground and dragged it outside. The dogs jumped around me anxiously. I put two scoops of food into each bowl and took the bag back to the garage. *That thing is heavy! What the heck?* I looked to my left and saw a refrigerator. *They have a refrigerator in their garage?* I opened it and it was stock full of beer. *Nice...* "Jessica, get in here!"

"What's wrong?" Jessica asked.

"Nothing's wrong. Check out all of this beer!"

"Really, Hannah!?"

"Yeah, I said it's a party, right?"

"And you don't think they're going to know they're missing beer?"

"There must be over a hundred beers in here...So, no, I don't think they'll even notice a few are missing."

"Wow, Hannah, who even are you?" Jessica inquired and I laughed.

"It's not funny, Hannah!"

"It is a little bit...You need to relax. It'll be fine." Jessica and I went back to my house and watched TV with my mom and brother until around ten when mom abruptly turned it off.

"All right, lights out everyone." Jessica and I went to my room and my mom brought in a pillow and sleeping bag.

"Mom, Jessica can sleep in my bed."

"Oh, okay, I'll just leave these here then." My mom put the pillow and sleeping bag on the floor next to my desk.

"Goodnight, girls," my mom said.

"Goodnight," I said and she shut the door behind her.

"You want to share a bed?" Jessica asked.

"Yeah, what's the big deal?"

"I don't know..."

"Okay," I whispered. "We're going to head over to Casey's house at eleven. That'll give us time for my mom and brother to be asleep and time before Will and Rob show up."

"How are we going to get out of here without your mom noticing?"

"Easy, we're going out the window."

"...Hannah, have you done this before?"

"Maybe...Yeah, I have."

"And you got away with it?"

"We're talking right now, aren't we?"

"That's a good point..."

"You worry too much. You need to relax."

"...Yeah, okay." Jessica and I read some magazines while we waited for eleven O' clock to roll around. As soon as it was time, I took off my pants.

"Hannah," Jessica whispered. "What are you doing?"

"Changing..."

"Into what?"

"These." I slipped on my cut-off jean shorts with fabric hanging from the fringes.

"Is that really necessary?" Jessica asked.

"Nope," I said and quietly laughed.

"Whatever, Hannah...God..."

"Come on," I said. "Wait, be quiet."

"Hannah, I'm not saying anything..."

"Shush!" I listened carefully for any movement in my house. "Okay, we're good." I opened my window and negotiated myself outside. Jessica followed me and we made our way down to Casey's house. I opened the door and we walked inside. "Now we wait," I said and I looked at Jessica.

"This is a bad idea," she said.

"This is a great idea," I responded.

At fifteen minutes until midnight, I heard Will and Rob on Casey's porch.

"Jessica," I whispered. "They're here."

"Well, are you going to let them in or not?"

"Yeah, it probably isn't the best idea to just leave them out there, but we could eavesdrop..."

"Hannah!"

"I'm kidding, relax. I can't hear anything anyway..." I opened the door and Will and Rob jumped up in a fright. Jessica and I smiled.

"...Scared the crap out of me," Will said.

"Yeah, you got me too," Rob added.

"I didn't know you were already going to be here..." Will said.

"Surprise!" I said and smiled. "Get in here before someone sees you." Will and Rob walked in and I closed the door behind them. I gave Will a big hug and then let him go. "Do you guys want a beer?"

"Well, yeah, but do you think it's a good idea to drink their beer?" Will asked.

"They're fully stocked," I said. "They even have another refrigerator in the garage filled up. They'll never know." I got two beers out of the refrigerator and handed them to Will and Rob. "The bottle opener is on the table." Jessica was sitting at the table working on a beer she opened before. I got another beer for myself and started drinking it and walked over to the stereo and turned on the music.

"What're you playing?" Will asked.

"Veruca Salt. They're my favorite." I started singing along with a song called 'Seether.' I sang through the entire song while everyone watched me. After the song ended, I grabbed Will by his arm. "Come on, Billy." I pulled Will into Casey's parents' bedroom and then shut the door behind us. Will looked back like he was concerned about Jessica and Rob. "They'll be fine."

"This is nice, Hannah, but aren't you worried that your parents are gonna find out?"

"Nope, and I don't care. I just want to be here with my Billy." I fell back on the bed. "It's a water bed, lay down next to me," I said and Will cuddled up next to me.

"Hannah, this bed is awful."

"I like it. Here, take off your shoes and put your feet up. It's like you're floating." Will took his shoes off and then I got on top of him. I kissed him and he grabbed me by my waist. He moved his hands up to my bra. I slowly got off of him and he looked deep into my eyes. *Yes, Billy, it's okay...*

"Have you ever done this before?" He asked. *Oh no...*

"What do you mean?" *I know what he means...*

"I guess...What I'm asking you is, are you a virgin?" *No...Yes? I don't know...Yeah, don't say no...The answer is definitely yes...*

"...Yeah, I'm a virgin,"

"So, you've never had sex before?" *...I'm going to Hell...*

"...No, I've done other stuff, but not sex." *Shit! What do I say now?* "I almost did last year with Joe, but it didn't happen..." *That wasn't it, Hannah...Oh my God! Why can't you just tell him the truth?*

"What happened?" My heart raced. *Think of something...*

"I was at my friends Halloween party last year and we were playing 'seven minutes in heaven.' Joe and I were in the closet making out and he started taking my clothes off. I didn't really want to do it, but..." *Great...*

"But what?" *But this is what happened to Mel...Shit...*

"...I would have. Joe's friend opened the door and we were both in our underwear. Joe was pissed. Everyone was laughing at us. I was so embarrassed that I grabbed my clothes and ran outside and then home... *What is wrong with me?* I've never told anyone that, Billy." *That was the truth...* I ran my hand through his hair. "I feel so close to you."

"I'm glad you told me. Maybe we should slow things down." *Wait...What? He doesn't want to...*

"No, it's okay, that was a long time ago...I don't want to lose you." *I just thought...*

"You're not going to lose me, no matter what. You're the best thing that's ever happened to me." *Ahhh...Now I feel even worse.*

"You're everything I've ever wanted." I moved in and kissed him but then pulled back. "You asked me, so I'm going to ask you..." Will told me a story about how he lost his virginity to a girl named Rebecca in Camarillo. There was something in the way he told the story though that made it seem like he was lying.

"That was two years ago..." *He was thirteen? I don't know...*

"...Wow, Billy, that's crazy."

"It's more embarrassing than anything else. I actually can't believe I just told you all of that."

"No, I'm glad that you told me. We have to be honest with each other, right?" *I am such a hypocrite...*

"Yeah, I agree."

"So you were just in Camarillo, right?"

"Yeah, that's where I spend my summers." *Hmmm...*

"Did you see Rebecca?"

"Nope, she doesn't live there anymore."

"How do you know that she doesn't live there anymore?"

"Peg, Brad's aunt, told us when we got there. They were family friends and since we had hung out before, I guess she thought we would want to know. I didn't ask. I was thinking about coming back to you."

"But you would have seen her if she did?"

"No, babe, like I said, I was thinking about you the whole time I was there. This was the first summer that I actually wanted to come home early."

"So, you haven't talked to this Rebecca girl for two years?"

"I didn't say that...I saw her last year, but she had a boyfriend so we didn't hang out." *Something's not right...*

"Do you have her number?"

"No, I don't have her number." *Dude, seriously?*

"Really? You have sex with a girl and you don't get her number?"

"There wasn't any need. We were practically neighbors." *What happened to the music?* "Babe, you have nothing to worry about. Rebecca is in the distant past." *I don't know what to believe...*

"Okay, yeah, sorry, I'm trippin...I need to trust you, it's just hard. Joe lied to me all the time. I'm just paranoid."

"I'm not Joe; I'm not anything like that." *I know, Billy...*

"I know...That's why I'm with you," I said and smiled. *Nirvana?* I got on top of Will and then took off my shirt. I leaned over him and we started kissing again. Will moved his hands all over my body and I pulled his shirt off over his head. I kissed his chest and then moved down to his stomach. I kissed his belly button but quickly sat up as the bedroom door swung open and Jessica stormed in.

"What the hell, Jessica?" I asked.

"Sorry, I just can't...Be out there with him. He tried to kiss me. I didn't know what to do. Sorry, I didn't mean to..." I stared at Jessica and then looked at Will.

"Jessica, just go back out there. What's the problem?" I asked.

"He's gross, Hannah. He smells like cigarettes...Sorry, Will..."

"...I guess I should go talk to him," Will said and then put his shirt on. "I'll be right back."

"...Were you guys about to have sex?" Jessica probed. I Sat up on the edge of the bed.

"Maybe...It was getting pretty hot and heavy," I said and smiled.

"Gross, Hannah." *You're older than me?* I heard the music stop and Will came back to the bedroom.

"He's gone," Will said.

"Oh my God, I'm so sorry guys," Jessica responded. I put my shirt on and looked at Will.

"He left because Jessica wouldn't kiss him?" *That's actually kind of sad. I feel bad for him.*

"...I guess so, it's not like I can call him to find out. Jessica, what happened?" Will inquired.

"We were just talking. You know, about school and stuff. Everything was fine. He changed the CD because he didn't like it and then he sat down right next to me on the couch," Jessica said.

"What's wrong with Veruca Salt?" I curiously asked.

"Hannah!" Jessica scolded.

"Sorry, keep going," I said.

"Okay, so, we kept talking and he said how much better the music was. He shut his eyes and came closer to me. I saw his yellow teeth and smelled the smoke and almost threw up in my mouth. I jumped up and ran down the hall. I didn't know what else to do. What was I supposed to do?" *Yeah...*

"Wait, shit, maybe he's still outside," Will said and walked out of the bedroom. Jessica and I followed him. He opened the front door and walked out onto the yard and looked down the street. He came back inside where Jessica and I were waiting for him.

"Yeah, he's long gone. Don't worry about it, Jessica, he'll be fine," Will reasoned.

"I feel bad though," Jessica said. *Me too...*

"...He'll get over it," Will said.

"I didn't mean to hurt his feelings," Jessica said and Will laughed. *That isn't nice...*

"Before tonight, I didn't think that Rob had feelings," Will said. *Hmmm.*

"Well, he obviously does or he wouldn't have left without saying anything," I said. Will sat down on the couch and I sat next to him. I put my hand on his leg and Jessica sat down in the chair across from us.

"I'm sorry guys, I messed up your night," Jessica said.

"It's fine, there'll be other nights," I said.

"Exactly, don't worry about it," Will agreed.

Chapter Sixteen

Coming of age

I went back to Casey's house Monday morning to double check that I had cleaned everything up from Saturday night. I made sure that Casey's parents' bed was made and that there was nothing left in the living room. I fed the dogs and watered the plants before heading back to my house to call Will.

"Hey, babe, what's up? Did you get a hold of Rob?" I asked.

"Nope, I called him yesterday, but his mom said that he doesn't want to talk to anyone...I hope he doesn't kill himself," Will said. *Oh no, not again...*

"What!? Oh my God. You don't think he would actually do that do you?" *Mel...*

"...I don't know, Hannah, I mean, the more I think about it, the more possible I think it is."

"Over one girl? There's someone out there for him..."

"I'm thinking about it like this: Kurt Cobain killed himself and Rob is his biggest fan. Even though it might not make sense to anyone else, it might make sense to him."

"It didn't even seem like he actually liked her."

"You're totally right. I was the one that put the idea in his head, but I was never able to get a good read on him."

"Jessica should have never led him on."

"It's not her fault. Rob's just weird."

"You should go over to his house to see if he's okay."

"Nah, it's Rob, I think I'll just leave him alone for a while."

"You think that's a good idea?" *This is all my fault.*

"Babe, he's not going to kill himself...At least not with his family around." *Great...*

"...Wow, that's comforting."

"Trust me, I'll make sure he's okay. I think he just needs some time."

"Okay...I don't want to be responsible for someone's death." *Again...*

"It wouldn't be on you. It would be on me."

"I would still be at least partially responsible...Right?"

"Nope, it would not be your fault at all. So, I don't think the whole double date thing is gonna work out for us anymore," Will said and then laughed.

"Yeah, for real, we need to be alone."

"What about tonight? I was thinking we could find a spot at Whitendale Park. We could bring a blanket and lay out underneath the stars...Just us and the insects."

"That sounds fun, Billy, do you want me to bring the blanket?"

"Why don't we both bring a blanket?"

"Perfect! I should probably get off the phone. Promise me that you'll call Rob sometime today. *I hope he's okay...*

"...Yeah, I'll call him later, I promise."

"Thanks, babe, remember, you might be the only person he has."

"No worries, I'll see you tonight."

"I'm looking forward to it, bye Billy."

"Bye." Will hung up the phone and I did the same. *Why do I feel so guilty about Rob? I need to call Summer. I hope she's home.* I dialed Summer's number and her mom picked up after the first ring.

"Hi, is Summer there?"

"Yes, she is, may I ask who's calling?"

"It's me, Hannah, Ms. Braithwaite."

"Hannah!? How are you?"

"I'm good..."

"Summer really misses you."

"I miss her too..."

"Okay...I'll go get her."

"Thanks." I waited for a minute and then Summer shrieked into the phone.

"Hannah!" I laughed.

"...Yeah, it's me, Summer."

"Oh my God..."

"I tried calling you a few times, but I guess you weren't home."

"We went to Hawaii..."

"That sounds fun."

"It was fun for my parents. I just felt like I was tagging along."

"It must have been nice, though..."

"You mean the weather? Yeah, the weather was nice." Summer and I both laughed.

"No, I meant it must have been nice to get away."

"I don't know. I like Santa Maria..."

"Me too. It's so hot in Visalia. As soon as I get my license I'm going to go visit."

"I'm going to hold you to that..."

"...Summer...I need some advice..."

"You called the right person then," Summer said.

"I know I did. I miss you, Summer," I responded.

"I miss you too...So, what's up?"

"I have a boyfriend now..."

"How exciting! What's his name?"

"Will, but I call him Billy...He's really sweet and thoughtful..."

"So, the opposite of Joe...Good choice."

"I lied to him...I didn't really tell him about Joe and you know..."

"That's okay, he doesn't need to know that. You did the right thing by not telling him."

"Yeah, but I still feel bad about lying..."

"That's because you're a good person, Hannah, you can't help it."

"Yeah...Summer...I didn't really call to talk about Will..."

"What's wrong, Hannah?"

"It's his friend, Rob...Long story short: Rob got turned down by my friend, Jessica, and now Will thinks Rob could kill himself..."

"...Oh no, Hannah...And you're thinking about Mel..."

"Exactly. I knew you would understand."

"Okay, Hannah, I know that you already know this but I'm going to tell you again anyway...You are not responsible for the choice that Mel made..."

"I know, Summer." *It would be nice if I could believe that...*

"So, this Rob guy...You're not responsible for his decisions either..."

"I just feel bad...Like I could have made a difference somehow."

"I love you, Hannah, but sometimes I think that you worry about other people too much and not enough about yourself..." *Yeah...*

"I know, but I don't know how to not worry."

"Just focus on what's good. It's sounds like your boyfriend is good so focus on that."

"Yeah, he's good...He told me that he lost his virginity when he was thirteen!"

"Really!? How old is he now?"

"He's fifteen. He's going to be sixteen September twenty-eighth...He's a Libra, like you..."

"Ahhh," Summer said and laughed. "I see why you like him."

"I miss you so much, Summer!"

"...So, you think he's a virgin..."

"I don't know, maybe. His story sounds possible, I guess, and I think I even got a little jealous of the girl, Rebecca."

"You're jealous of a girl that may not even exist?" Summer laughed.

"I know...It sounds stupid..."

"It's not stupid, but I think every guy lies about that kind of stuff..."

"What if he's not lying, though?"

"It doesn't matter either way, Hannah." *Hmmm...*

"Yeah, you're right, what am I going to do about it anyway?"

"That's right...Just look forward."

"Thanks, Summer, I always feel better after talking to you."

"Any time..."

"So, what's new with you?"

"Absolutely nothing." Summer laughed. "I'm looking forward to high school...I hope I can find someone..."

"You will, Summer, you're the most awesome person I know!"

"Thanks, Hannah." I saw Casey's car drive by as I was looking out my living room window.

"It's been really cool catching up, Summer, but I have to go."

"...Oh, okay, call me back soon!"

"I will. I'll call you back before school starts."

"Okay, bye, Hannah."

"Bye, Summer," I said and hung up the phone. I walked back down to Casey's house and saw them unloading their car. I reached into my front pocket and pulled out the key and handed it to Casey's mom.

"Thank you, Hannah, so how did things go?" *I fed the dogs and watered the plants...*

"...Good."

"Awesome! I knew we could count on you." *Yeah...* Casey's mom reached into her purse and then handed me forty dollars. *Nice!* "If we ever need someone, we know who to call..."

"Thanks," I said and turned to Casey. "Hi, Casey...So, did you have fun?"

"It was okay...There was a really cool show one night..." Casey's mom walked away from us carrying some of her luggage. "...But I don't know, I was lonely."

"I understand, Casey...You'll find someone...And I told you that I would help..."

"Thanks, Hannah...I just wish that..."

"I know, Casey...One more year..."

"Yeah...One more year..."

At midnight, I took off my bra and panties and put on my jean shorts and an orange halter top. *Fuck it. This will give him something to think about...* I opened the window just like I had done before and walked out to the front of my house. Will was waiting for me in front of my mom's car.

"Hey babe, are you wearing a bra?" Will whispered.

"Why ever do you ask?" I whispered back.

"Because I can see your nipples." Will brushed his hand over my right breast and I smiled.

"I have a surprise. I'm not wearing panties either." *You like that, don't you?*

"Okay...I don't really know what to say," he said and smiled.

"Let's go." Will and I held hands and walked across the street to the school.

"I think, maybe, we should walk around the school to the park, you know, so we don't have to jump the fence."

"I can jump the fence." *Again?*

I know you can, I've seen you do it before, remember, but, I'm thinking, if you tear your shorts or even your shirt, we're going to have a problem." *That's funny!*

"How is that a problem, Billy?"

"I guess it isn't, but it would make me feel better if you didn't have to run around naked out here."

"We were born naked and we'll die naked." I smiled and walked to the fence. Will grabbed a hold of my arm.

"Please, babe, do it for me, it's not that much further."

"Do you think it's a better idea to walk along the street and maybe get caught or go right through the school? And besides, we have these blankets, just in case," I reasoned.

"You're right. And when you're right, you're right, but be careful."

"Okay, dad," I said and laughed.

"Ouch, that's not funny."

"Sure it is...Let's go." I threw my blanket over the fence and then jumped over. Will jumped over the fence too and followed me to a spot underneath a big tree. We put down both of the blankets and then sat on top of them.

"This is so cool," Will said. "Beautiful girl, beautiful night." He put his hand behind my neck and moved closer to me. He looked into my eyes. "You're the most beautiful girl I've ever seen." I smiled. *Ahhh. He's so sweet.*

"That's not true." *Heh!*

"Babe, just say thank you...And it is true." I smiled again.

"Thanks, Billy." I moved in close to him and we kissed. We fell over on the blankets and made out. Will fingered me and then started laughing. He pulled back away from me and smiled. I smiled back at him.

"What's so funny?" I inquired.

"Nothing, it's nothing, I was just thinking of something."

"Shouldn't you be thinking about me?" *You better be...*

"I was, I mean I am, I'll tell you later..." He smiled. "Trust me, it's not a bad thing."

"Okay, do you have a condom?" *I don't really care, but...*

"...Yeah, hold on," Will said and pulled a handful of condoms out of his pocket. I laughed.

"How many do you have? Sheesh, I guess it's going to be a long night."

"I thought that was what you were all about?" He pulled one of the condoms out of its package and then undid his belt. He tried to put the condom on but it was backwards and wouldn't roll down. I laughed again. *Problems?*

"Ummm, did you want some help?"

"I fucking hate condoms...What is the problem with this thing?" I stared at him curiously. *Hmmm...*

"...You know, there's this thing called VCF that my mom told me about. We could get some of that."

"What's VCF?"

"Vaginal Contraceptive Film." *I think that's it...*

"Hey, what are you guys doing?" A voice called out from the darkness. Will and I jumped up from the blanket.

"Who's there?" Will asked and leaned over to pick up the blankets and then stood in front of me. "Get behind me." I stood behind him and held on to his arm. *My hero!*

"Hey, man, no worries, no worries." An old man walked up to us. He looked like he was homeless. "Do you have any change you can spare? I'm really hungry." *Oh, how sad...*

"No, we don't have any money," Will said. The man looked like he was going to cry and then walked away. "That scared the crap out of me."

"I feel bad for him. He just needs help," I said.

"I'm glad he wasn't some kind of serial killer or something."

"In Visalia, really?"

"You never know, shit, what if that guy had a knife?"

"Yeah...Let's walk closer to the park," I said. Will held both of the blankets while I led the way. We went to the far side of the park and put the blankets down again.

"Now, where were we?" Will asked. We continued making out, but after a few minutes we stopped. "Did you hear that?"

"Yeah, it sounded like a car," I said. We looked toward the parking lot and saw a car parked with its engine running and lights on parked sideways. A flood light from the side of the car lit up the grass. A dog barked angrily.

"Shit, it's the cops. I don't think they've seen us yet. We have to make a run for it," Will whispered.

"Okay, but where are we going to run to?"

"We're going to run through the baseball diamonds and get back to the street on the other side. Follow me...Okay, let's go!" We ran as fast as we could. Will turned around to look at the car. The sound of the dog barking escalated. We ran past the first backstop and then hid behind the second backstop on the far side of the field. "Shit, let's just stay down right here."

"They're going to find us if we stay here!" I pleaded.

"No! They're going to find us if we're moving around. We'll be safe. They're not coming over here."

"I don't know..."

"Trust me, it's going to be okay." *I do trust you.* I held on to Will's arm like my life depended on it. Will sat up to look through the bottom of the backstop. The sound of the barking dog faded away. "Thank God, they left."

"Now that scared me," I said. "I would never see the outside of my room if I had to call my parents from the police station."

"For real, I don't think anyone would even pick me up...We should go back."

Yeah, it isn't a good idea to hang around." Will and I got up and walked back towards the school. Will threw the blankets on the other side of the fence and we both jumped over. We dusted ourselves off and then started walking back to my house.

"Let's walk really slow and keep our eyes open for those cops. If we see any car, and I mean any car, we need to find a place to hide."

"Damn, Billy, we're like Bonnie and Clyde out here." *This is so much fun!*

"I don't know who that is."

"The outlaws, Bonnie and Clyde...They were rebels. It's a movie."

"Never heard of it, but we're definitely rebels...I like that."

"I like it too, Billy, it was scary, but it was fun." I secured the blanket around myself and we made our way around the school. Before we got to the intersection, I heard a car behind us and turned around. Red and blue lights flashed. *Shit!* "What are we gonna do?"

"It's too late to run, just follow my lead," Will said, put his arm around me, and held the blanket tightly against my body. The cop got out of his car and walked toward us.

"What are you guys doing out here this late?" The cop asked.

"We were at a party and it got out of hand. Our ride left without us...So we had to walk home," Will reasoned. *Nice, Billy.*

"How old are you?" The cop asked and pointed his flashlight at Will. *How old does he need to be?*

"Seventeen." The cop nodded and then pointed the flashlight at me.

"And you?" *Shit, well...*

"...Sixteen." He pointed his flashlight at the ground.

"And why didn't you just call your parents?"

"We didn't want to bother them. They work early."

"You know there's a curfew, right?"

"Yes, sir, we know, but we had to leave that party."

"Where was this party?"

"Over off of Goshen."

"And you've walked all this way?"

"Yes, sir."

"Where do you live?"

"My girlfriend lives right down the street and I live off of Caldwell."

"Is that right? Well, it doesn't seem like you've been drinking..."

"No, sir, we haven't. That's why we left the party." The cop shined the light into Will's face and then mine.

"Okay, I'm gonna let you go. Go straight home. I don't want to find you back out here in the middle of the night again. If I do, I'm going to take you in and make you call your parents. Am I clear?"

"Yes, sir, thank you." The cop turned off his flashlight and walked back to his car. He turned around and drove the other way and we continued walking to my house.

"Nice work, Billy. I thought we were busted. You were super-smooth." *Like, really...Where did that come from?*

"...Super-smooth huh? I can't believe he bought it."

"Now we can add lying to the cops to our resume." Will laughed.

"That's not the first time I've lied to the cops, babe."

"I guess that's why you're so good at it..."

"I didn't think it was that convincing...He didn't even ask about the blankets. I mean, seriously, I didn't have an answer for that."

"It's a good thing he didn't ask then."

"I really don't think he cared. Arresting a couple of 'kids' would require paperwork that would take away from his donut eating time, and Scotty's is right around the corner," Will said and smiled. I laughed.

"You're funny, Billy."

"Seriously, though, we shouldn't come out here again. We shouldn't push our luck."

"Yeah, but what are we going to do?"

"We'll have to figure something else out. For a small city, we sure do have a lot of cops." We walked up to my house and stopped behind my mom's car.

"Are you going to call me tomorrow?" I whispered.

"Yeah, I'll call you in the morning," Will whispered back to me. Will pulled on my blanket and kissed me. He hugged me and whispered in my ear, "We'll figure it out, don't worry."

"I'm not worried," I said and went to open the gate. *I had so much fun tonight...*

Casey and I were playing basketball in front of my house when Chris and Mitchell walked up to us. Mitchell ran to my front door.

"Mitchell," I said. "You can go inside, Michael's in his room playing videogames like always..." Mitchell let himself inside.

"So, yeah, we're leaving today," Chris said. "Mitchell wanted to say bye to your brother."

"Yeah, Chris, that's fine..." I passively said.

"Where are you moving to?" Casey asked.

"It's over off Ben Maddox and Noble," Chris answered.

"That's kind of far..."

"Yeah, I'm going to Golden West." *Good.*

"Did you work things out with your girlfriend?" Casey inquired. *Oh no, Casey! You just couldn't let it go, could you?* I dribbled the basketball and then took a shot. Chris ignored Casey's question and watched my shot go down. We all watched as the ball bounced under the hoop and then rolled to the curb. "Chris...Did you and Angela get back together?"

"Why do you care, Casey!" Chris barked. *Shit...* "Mind your own damn business!" Casey started crying and ran down the street toward her house.

"Why do you have to be such an asshole, Chris?"

"What!?"

"You know she likes you?"

"Yeah, Will told me, but I don't like her. She looks like she's twelve...Give me a break.

"She's thirteen."

"And that makes a difference...How?" *I don't know...*

"You don't have to be a dick about it..."

"I don't care at all..." *Yeah, you've made that pretty clear...*

"...So, I wanted to ask you a favor..." *Great...*

"Chris, let me save you some time..."

"...No, it's not that...Can you have Will call me?"

"No, I can't have Will call you, Chris!" I said sarcastically.

"Well, shit, you say that I'm an asshole but you're just a straight bitch!"

"Thanks, I'll take that as a compliment."

"You would...You don't make any damn sense."

"You know what, Chris, maybe I'll have Will call you after all...You won't like what he has to say though."

"Let me deal with that...Shit, Hannah, we've been friends forever and I'm not going to let you come between us..." *Too late...*

"You want my help and this is how you're talking to me? You're pretty dumb, Chris."

"I'm not dumb..." I didn't answer him and walked over to the basketball and bent over to pick it up. I turned around and held the ball on my hip. *Fuck you, Chris!* "...Whatever, do whatever you want then."

"I always do," I said and smiled.

"Tell my brother that it's time to go."

"Tell him yourself. You know where the door is."

"Fuck, Hannah! Just tell him!" *Heh...*

"Fine." I walked across my lawn and into my house. Mitchell and my brother were playing Mario in his room and I didn't want to interrupt them, but I also wanted Chris to go away. *I feel bad for my brother. He's going to lose his best friend. I feel bad for Mitchell too...His brother is Chris!* I watched them play their game for a minute and then said, "Mitchell, it's time to go."

"What? Why?" My brother asked.

"His brother said it's time to go, so it's time to go, Michael! Mitchell, your brother's waiting for you outside."

"...Okay, bye Michael," Mitchell said and put the controller on the ground.

"It's not fair," my brother said and stared straight ahead and continued playing his game.

"I'll call you later," Mitchell said and then walked out of my brother's room. I walked him outside and he slowly walked toward Chris. I watched them both walk down the street. I continued to hold the basketball against my hip. *Wait...Chris's house...No one's going to be there...* I watched Chris and Mitchell get into their parent's car and then I watched them as they drove by. Chris gave me a dirty look and then looked away. *Good riddance...* I walked down to Chris's house as soon as they made the turn at the intersection. *I have to see if it's empty...* I walked through the lawn and looked through the living room window. *This doesn't look shady or anything...Okay, I don't see any furniture.* I walked around the house and opened the gate. I went to the back yard and looked through the sliding glass doors. *I don't see anything...I wonder...* I pulled on the sliding glass door. *Shit, it's locked.* I looked through the doors one last time before walking back to the front of the house. *Yeah, I think they're gone.* I looked over at Casey's house and saw Casey walking toward me. *Shit!* Casey waved at me and I smiled.

"Hey, what are you doing?" Casey asked. *It depends. How much did you see?*

"I was just checking to make sure that they were totally moved out of this house."

"Why?" *Shit... Think...*

"...Casey, I was never going to tell you this, but Chris asked me out..."

"Right now! Today!?"

"No, it was a while ago..." Casey didn't say anything and looked down at the ground. "I wanted to make sure that he was gone for good, Casey, he's terrible."

"I don't know what to say, Hannah..."

"You saw how mean he was to you for no reason..."

"...Yeah."

"I'm glad he's gone."

"...Did he ask you out while he was with his girlfriend?"

"I don't know...I think so...Billy thinks so..."

"Oh my God, you told Will?"

"Yeah, of course I told him...Why?"

"...Well..."

"...You don't think I should have told him?"

"I don't know, Hannah..."

"Casey, you're still going to defend Chris even after the way he treated you?"

"I'm not defending him..." *It sure sounds like you are.* "...It's just...They've just been friends for a long time."

"I know, Casey, which is why I had to say something..." *Shit, I think it's almost ten!* "Casey, I have to call Will, can we talk about this later?"

"Yeah, okay..."

"Casey, everything will be all right, trust me," I said and started walking back to my house. I went inside and grabbed the phone and walked into the garage. I dialed Will's number and he picked up after the first ring.

"Hey, Billy, I miss you," I said.

"I miss you too," Will replied.

"It's Friday! Be happy, Babe! Friday..."

"...It's Friday, and I still don't have a job," Will joked and I laughed.

"I didn't know you were looking for a job..." I responded facetiously.

"...No, the movie, you know, 'Friday,' Ice Cube..."

"Yes, babe, I know," I said and laughed again. "I can be funny too...So, are you ready for school?"

"Yeah, my mom gave me money for clothes and I went shopping yesterday at Miller's Outpost with my brother."

"Ahh, how cute, clothes shopping with your brother."

"Yeah, well, I needed a ride, so..."

"Chris and Mitchell came by this morning."

"Did they?"

"Yeah, Mitchell wanted to say bye to Michael. They're gone, Billy, they moved."

"Yeah...We knew they were moving."

"Michael's still sad though. Mitchell was like his best friend...Chris told me to tell you that you should call him."

"Really? I don't see that happening."

"Well, I hope you guys' work things out..." *Actually, no, I don't.* "...Anyway, I have an idea, Billy."

"What's that?"

"We've been talking about finding a place and I think I found one."

"What are you talking about?"

"Chris's back yard."

"Are you serious?"

"Yeah, it's perfect. No one lives there anymore and there's that patio area..."

"I'm listening..."

"I could bring a sleeping bag..."

"All right, I'm down. I just have to be careful not to get caught on the way over there. I'm sure that cop will be cruising around."

"Okay, I'll see you tonight, Billy."

"I can't wait to see you tonight, bye, babe."

"Bye," I said and hung up the phone. I set the phone down on my dad's work bench and walked to the corner of the garage where my dad kept the camping stuff. *When was the last time we went camping? It's been a long time...* I grabbed a sleeping bag and then picked up the phone on my way out of the garage. I set the phone down and then carefully walked by my brother's room. *Okay, he's not paying attention.* I took the sleeping bag to my room and shoved it under my bed. *I'm getting too good at this...*

There was something in the air as midnight approached. *This is weird.* I changed into a pair of jeans and a long-sleeved shirt. *Is it going to rain? It's July. So weird.* I placed the sleeping bag outside and then picked it up after I shut my window, leaving only enough room for my fingertips to get back inside. I walked down to Chris's old house and set up the sleeping bag on the patio in the back. I watched the moonless night sky illuminate with lightning. *So weird...* I heard the thunder roar in the distance. *I hope Billy gets here soon.* I stood outside of the gate in front of the house and waited for Will. After ten minutes, he rode up to the middle of the lawn and set his bike down. I walked up behind him and grabbed his arm.

"Hey babe, what's with this weather?" I asked.

"I don't know; I've never seen anything like it this time of year," he said.

"Ever?"

"Ever, ever."

"Yeah, we never got anything like this in Santa Maria."

"That's where you're from? That's funny..."

"What's funny?"

"I didn't even know where you were from."

"That's true...Where are you from?"

"I was born and raised in San Diego."

"That's awesome! How did you end up in Visalia?"

"Ask my mom."

"Maybe I will. Come on, I have the sleeping bag set up on the patio. The gate was open."

"Cool, hopping fences was getting old." We walked past the gate and Will closed it behind us. "They didn't take their doghouse..."

"Did they have a dog?"

"No, not for a while. Actually, we hung out in there." *What!?*

"How did that work?"

"Very carefully." *You're funny, Billy...Wait, ugh!*

"...It sounds like you miss your friend. Just call him." *Really...*

"We had some good times, but times change." Lightning flashed across the sky. I got inside of the sleeping bag and gestured for Will to join me. Will got in next to me but then immediately got back out. "...Babe, I think we should move this to the grass."

"Okay, but what if it rains?"

"It's never rained in Visalia during the summer..."

"I don't know, Billy, it really seems like it's going to rain."

"If it does, we'll just move back. No big deal..." Will dragged the sleeping bag to the middle of the yard. "This is better," he insisted and got inside of the sleeping bag. "Come on, Hannah; get your cute butt in here." I took off my long-sleeved shirt and then my pants. I put my hand on my hip and posed like a supermodel. Lightning struck again but I didn't move. I felt the electricity in the air. I felt powerful. I felt like I was in control. The thunder immediately brought me back to earth. "Babe, get over here." Will took off his pants and put them next to the sleeping bag. I got inside of the sleeping bag and we locked eyes. "Hannah, I've got something very important to ask you." *I bet it's going to be something silly...*

"What's that?"

"Hannah, what's your favorite color?" Will laughed and I smiled as I fixed my hair. *I knew it...*

"...My favorite color? It's orange, but why...What's yours? I was not expecting that." *Something like that...*

"...Blue...The whole Santa Maria thing has me thinking. I don't really know much about you, which is kind of crazy, don't you think?"

"I don't know...Maybe." *Billy, you really don't want to know...* I smiled again and then kissed him. We became lost in each other's embrace. The lightning and thunder became more intense. Will reached for his pants. "What are you doing?" I asked.

"I got those things you told me about." *Really? Okay...*

"Oh, okay, do you want me to..."

"No, I got it." *I hope so...* Will pulled off my panties. *Oh, damn!* He tore open the sheet of VCF and then slid it inside of me. He moved his fingers around sporadically. *He has no idea what he's doing...*

"Problems?"

"Nope, not anymore, but that's a sticky bastard." He laughed and then went down on me. I grabbed a hold of his head and started moaning. *Nevermind...babe, where'd you learn to do that? Wait...* He moved his hand over my face and put his finger over my lips. "Babe, the neighbors..." *Neighbors?*

"What neighbors?" I asked and put his finger in my mouth." He moved up and started kissing me and then stopped.

"Babe, my tongue is numb!" Will said and I laughed.

"The price you have to pay..."

"Let me give you some of this payment," he said and kissed me again. *I think my tongue is getting numb now too...What's in that stuff?* The rain began to fall just as Will started fucking me. *This isn't too bad...It only hurts a little bit...* The rain fell harder and faster. Will's hair tickled my face and drops of water made it impossible for me to open my eyes. The rain was beginning to soak through the sleeping bag when I felt Will come inside of me. *Ummm, are you okay?* He lay on top of me for a minute without saying a word. I felt his chest rise and fall as he caught his breath. "We should move to the patio," he finally said.

"Yeah, or we could just stay here," I offered. *This is nice...*

"Yeah, no, I'm gonna go get some shelter." Will unzipped the sleeping bag and then grabbed his pants off of the ground. He walked over to the patio and pulled his pants back on. I got up and wrapped the sleeping bag around my naked body. I felt a warmth streaming down my leg which contrasted against the rain. *Kind of gross...* I stepped up on the patio, bent over, and grabbed my clothes off of the ground.

"Nice, my clothes are still dry." I put my clothes back on and then sat down against the sliding glass door with Will. I wrapped the saturated sleeping bag around us.

"That was awesome, Hannah."

"Yeah, it was."

"I was starting to think that was never going to happen. It seemed like the entire world was conspiring against us. We even had to beat this freak show of a storm..." Will put his arm around me. "...At least it's not cold. That would have sucked." *Yeah...* "I love you, Hannah." *You're so sweet.* He kissed me and held my hand. I rested my head on his shoulder. We stared at the doghouse as the rainstorm relented.

"I love you, Billy..." *What am I going to do about this sleeping bag? Hmmm. Ugh... What am I going to do about me? I can't take a shower...I'll wake my mom and brother up! Damn it... Ugh...*

Chapter Seventeen
Mount Whitney

I t was the first day of high school and I was as nervous as I had ever been. My mom dropped me off just after seven. I had to be at school early to pick up my schedule in the gym. There was a line at least a hundred students long at the table. *Awesome...* The line slowly moved forward as I watched everyone walking around. There were people hugging and shaking hands. There were people laughing. Small groups of people clustered throughout the gym. I felt alone. *I don't belong here...Mel...I'll never forget what you told me...I don't think so though...* A group of girls wearing cheerleading outfits walked up to me and smiled. They stopped and one of them said,

"Are you a freshman?"

"Yeah..."

"What's your name?"

"Hannah."

"Hi Hannah, I'm Tiffany. These are my friends Alyson, Kasia, and Morgan."

"Hi," I said and waved. They all waved back and smiled. *They seem really nice...*

"You're really pretty," Tiffany said.

"Thanks..."

"Cheer tryouts are after school if you're interested," Kasia said.

"We could use some new blood," Alyson agreed. *New blood?*

"...I've never thought about Cheerleading," I said. "I play basketball, though..."

"...Oh, really?" Tiffany asked. Her expression changed to that of confusion. She looked at all of her friends and they all seemed to come to the same consensus without saying a word to each other.

"Hannah," Morgan said, "you're too pretty to be playing basketball..." All of the girls agreed. *No, I'm not... What's that even supposed to mean?* I smiled nervously.

"Thanks," I said. "I'll think about it..."

"Awesome! So, we'll see you after school then?" Tiffany asked. *Wait...* "We meet in front of the girl's locker room. See you later, Hannah..." *I don't even know where that is...*

"Bye, Hannah, nice to meet you," Kasia said.

"Bye, Hannah!" Alyson and Morgan rang off in quick succession.

"...Nice to meet you," I said and the girls walked away from me. *I don't want to be a cheerleader...* The line continued to move and after about twenty minutes, I finally made it to the table. The counselor gave me my schedule. Will told me he was going to meet me in the front of the school near the bike racks so I made my way over there. I walked through the crowd and saw Will and Rob talking in front of the band room. *I guess everything's cool...* Will saw me and raised his hand in the air as if I couldn't see him. I walked up to him and gave him a hug.

"Hey, Rob," I said.

"Hey," Rob quickly said and then looked away from me.

"Babe, you're not going to believe this," I said.

"What am I not going to believe?" Will asked and smiled.

"The cheerleaders want me to tryout..."

"That's funny," Will said.

"...Why is that funny, Billy?"

"Because you're an athlete, babe, and cheerleaders aren't athletes." *He totally gets me...* I smiled.

"And they're fake as fuck!" Rob added. *They we're nice...*

"I don't really know them," I said.

"Doesn't matter," Rob said.

"Rob's right, babe, you don't want to be associated with them."

"Yeah...I'm not gonna do it...So, Billy, are you going to take me on a tour, or what?"

"A tour? Oh, yeah, okay. You got your schedule, right? Let me see it..." I pulled my schedule out of my front pocket and handed it to Will. "Oh no, babe, you got Ms. Rose for English..." Will started laughing.

"What's so funny? What's wrong with Ms. Rose?" I asked.

"She's as old as dirt," Will said. "I had her last year and people would smoke weed in her class and blow the smoke in the air. The whole classroom was a hotbox and she didn't even notice or at least, acted like she didn't notice."

"Shit, I didn't get her, I got Ms. Lane," Rob said.

"Ms. Lane is hot..." Will said and then looked at me. "For a teacher..." *Right...*

"I guess I'll take that over the other one," Rob added.

"We're you smoking with them, Billy?" I inquired.

"No, I was afraid to get caught, but it didn't even matter, I guess. I didn't go to class very often though. Maybe something did happen...Maybe she did do something about it. I doubt it though. She's really old, like really old. You'll see...I don't think she knows where she is...I think she has that old person disease...I forget what it's called..." *I'm sure she's not that bad...* "Come on, I'll take you to all of your classes." Will held my hand and we started walking around campus. Rob followed closely behind.

"...Billy, how many days of school did you miss last year?"

"The better question is how many days did he go to class..." Rob said and laughed. "The answer is not many." *Hmmm.*

"Yeah, babe, I told you I had a rough year, but I have a good feeling about this one," Will said.

"Why is that, Billy?"

"I have a reason to come to school now," Will said and squeezed my hand. He leaned in and kissed me. I heard Rob groan. *He's probably still pissed about Jessica. I feel bad for him...* Will took me to all of my classes and then we walked back to the gym because I had first period P.E. "Okay, babe, I'll meet you after class."

"You're really going to walk your girlfriend to all of her classes?" Rob inquired.

"Yeah...Babe, do you want me to walk you to your classes?" *You don't have to...*

"Sure, if you want to..." I responded.

"You're never gonna make it to your classes on time," Rob reasoned.

"So what?"

"Billy, I don't want you to get in trouble."

"I don't care about that...I only care about you..." *That's sweet, but...* The bell rang.

"Whatever, man," Rob said. "I'm going to class. See you at lunch."

"All right. Meet by the band room?" Will asked.

"Yeah," Rob said and walked away. Will kissed me and then hugged me goodbye.

"Bye, Billy."

"See you soon," he said and walked away. *How did I end up with P.E. as my first class? Oh well...*

At lunch, Will was waiting for me as I walked out of Ms. Rose's Class. He gave me a hug as soon as I cleared the rush of people trying to beat the bell.

"Hey, Billy, Ms. Rose isn't that bad. She's actually nice..." Will laughed.

"Give it some time, babe." We walked over to the band room in front of the school and met up with Rob who was staring at something inside.

"What's up, Rob?" Will asked.

"I'm just looking..." Rob responded.

"...To see if anyone can play anything?"

"Yeah..."

"Babe, do you want to get lunch?"

"No, I'm not hungry."

"Hey, so I was thinking..." Will started to say. "...Maybe we could walk to school together..."

"How are we going to do that? You think my parents are going to let me walk to school by myself? *Come on, Billy...*

"It couldn't hurt to ask," Will said. *Yes, it could...*

"Billy, we are talking about my parents, remember?"

"Yeah...I just thought it would be cool if...We could meet at the end of your street..." *Wait a minute!*

"Billy, I think it could work...I have an idea."

"Yes, my dear," Will said and Rob rolled his eyes.

"It's Casey..."

"What about Casey?"

"My parents don't know that Casey's still in middle school..."

"...Okay..."

"My mom leaves for work pretty early...So, I could tell her that I'm going to start walking to school with her."

"You think that'll work?"

"...Yeah, I think so...My parents are letting Michael walk to school because it's so close..." Will and I both smiled.

"I see where this is going..."

"I'll tell them that I'll walk him to school, which will make them feel better, and continue on with Casey."

"Sounds like a plan..."

"...I actually think it might work," I insisted.

"What about your brother? Do you think he'll rat you out?" Will asked.

"Nope, not if I tell him not to...He can keep a secret."

"All right, cool, ask tonight and give me a call if you're good."

"Okay, Billy, I'll try..."

My dad picked me up after school and I smiled at him as I climbed into his truck.

"Hi dad," I said.

"How was your first day of high school?" He asked and then started driving.

"Good...I was wondering, since I'm in high school now..."

"What do you want, Hannah?"

"I was wondering if I could walk with Casey to school and home every day."

"I don't think that's a good idea."

"I could walk Michael to school so he doesn't have to walk alone..." My dad sighed. "And then you wouldn't have to pick me up..." He groaned. "Dad, I'm not a baby! And I'll be with Casey, so...What do you think?"

"...I think you need to ask your mom." *I knew he was gonna say that.*

"Okay, but it would save her time too..."

"Hannah, honestly, I'm too tired to think about this."

"Another reason why..."

"Hannah! Ask your mom!"

"Okay, okay, sheesh..." I didn't say anything else during the ride home. When my dad pulled into the driveway, I jumped out of the truck and went inside. I made myself a peanut butter and jelly sandwich and waited for my mom to get home. I ate my sandwich and then went to my room. I opened my backpack and took out Ms. Rose's homework. *A five-paragraph essay about what I did over the summer...* I laughed. *Yeah, I can't write what actually happened...Who assigns an essay on the first day of school? No wonder they smoked in her class! Wait! Casey! I guess I'm going to Disneyland...* I wrote my fabricated essay until I heard my mom walk through the door. I went down the hall and accosted her immediately.

"Mom," I said. *Hmmm...* "I was talking to dad about letting me walk to and from school with Casey every day..."

"No," my mom answered. "...Casey's a freshman too?"

"...Yeah..."

"...She looks really young." *Oh no...Plan falling apart...*

"Mom, please..." *Think...* "...I know it's hard on you guys to have to take me to school and pick me up...You shouldn't have to do that every day when I have two perfectly good legs..."

"Patrick, what do you think about this?" My mom asked my dad as he was getting ready to leave for work.

"I don't know...She did say she'd walk Michael along the way..."

"Did she?"

"Yeah," I said. "Casey and I will drop him off."

"Well, I really don't like Michael walking alone," my mom said. *Yes, it's working...I think.*

"So, can I?"

"Stacey, she is in high school. We should give her a little bit of freedom," my dad reasoned. *That's right, dad!* I smiled.

"I just don't like the idea of two young girls walking by themselves, even if it is just to school," my mom insisted.

"Dad!" I pleaded.

"Stacey," I think it's okay..." *Yes!* "It's Visalia..."

"Okay...Hannah, we're going to have to trust you...You're going to walk to school and then walk home...That's it, though."

"Okay! Can I call Casey to tell her?"

"Yeah, and tell Michael that he needs to wait for you."

"Okay, yeah." I grabbed the phone from the counter and dialed Will's number and slowly started making my way to my room. *Please be him...I know they're listening...* The phone rang twice and Will picked up the phone. *Thank God!*

"Hi Casey," I said. "My parents said I could walk to school with you."

"Oh, I get it," Will said.

"So, I'll see you tomorrow at seven-thirty then?"

"I'll be there."

"Okay, Casey, bye."

"Bye," Will, said and I hung up the phone. I walked back to the kitchen where my parents were waiting.

"We're good," I said and put the phone on the counter. "I'm gonna tell Michael and then I have homework to finish." My dad laughed.

"You have homework on the first day of school?" *I know, right?*

"It's a five-paragraph essay on what I did this summer...I'm just gonna write about moving here..."

"Sounds fun," my dad said. "I have to go to work. See you later." He kissed my mom goodbye and I went to my brother's room.

"Michael, I'm walking with you to school now."

"Why?"

"Because mom and dad said so..."

"Okay, I guess..."

"Good, it's settled then," I said, walked back to my room, and continued working on my essay.

The next day, I was waiting for Will to walk me to class in the middle of the hallway. *Where is he? He's never been late before...* I stood still in a crowd of moving bodies brushing against me. *Ugh! Maybe I should just go?* In the distance, I saw Will making his way toward me. *It's about time...* He walked up to me and held my hand.

"Hey, babe, sorry, I was talking to my new bass player...Well, maybe my new bass player."

"Who is it?" I asked.

"His name's Aaron, from San Jose."

"Really? I bet Rob will be happy..."

"Babe, is Rob ever happy?" Will and I laughed as we made our way down the hall to my math class. Everyone that we walked by was staring at us. "Billy, why is everyone staring at us?"

"Because, babe, you're the prettiest girl at school and I'm the luckiest guy at school. Mystery solved."

"That can't be true...Except for the last part; you are the luckiest guy at school."

"It's true, babe, I keep telling you." I got to my math class on time and Will kissed me goodbye. "See you at lunch," he said.

After class, I walked out to the stage and saw Rob waiting by himself. "Hey, Rob," I said.

"Hey..." *As talkative as always...* "I think Billy, ummm, Will has some good news for you."

"Really?"

"Yeah..."

"Okay..." *Wow, well, I tried...*

"There he is," I said. Will walked up to me and gave me a hug.

"Hey, babe," he said. "Hey, Rob, guess what?"

"What?" Rob asked.

"I found our bass player."

"That was fast...How'd you manage that?"

"I met him in my English class. His name's Aaron. I told him to meet us over here right now...There he is...The blond dude."

"Seriously? He looks preppy as fuck," Rob said.

"He's cute," I said. Will and Rob looked at me angrily. "What? He's not as cute as you, Billy." *Ooops...*

"Yeah, right, nice save, Hannah..." *Sorry, Billy.* "Anyway, you said yourself how hard it was to find a bass player so let's at least give him a chance."

"You're right, I did say that...Fine," Rob said. Aaron walked over and shook Will's hand.

"Hey man, this is Rob and this is my girlfriend, Hannah."

"Hey," Rob said.

"Hi," I added. Will grabbed my waist and pulled me right next to him.

"So, Aaron, how long have you been playing bass?" Rob asked.

"About a year or so," Aaron said.

"What kind of music do you play?"

"All kinds, mostly rock though."

"Do you like Nirvana?"

"Yeah, who doesn't? I haven't played any of their songs, but I can learn."

"Cool," Rob said. "We should meet up this weekend."

"Okay, yeah, I'm not doing anything," Aaron said. Will let go of me and got some paper out of his backpack. Everyone exchanged numbers and we walked to the front of the school.

"Hey, check that out," Will said. He pointed at someone playing a single drum. "He's awesome, let's go talk to him."

"Okay, but the marching band is not the same thing as a real band," Rob said. We walked up to the boy playing the drum.

"Hey, man, you're really good, how long have you been playing?" Will asked.

"Like two or three years."

"What's your name?"

"Nate. My friends call me Nate Dog. Don't ask me why," Nate said.

"I'm Will, this is Rob, Aaron, and my girlfriend, Hannah." Everyone said, 'hey.'

"Do you have a set?" Rob asked.

"Yeah, I have a 7-piece Pearl with a double bass pedal and Zildjian cymbals."

"I'm impressed," Rob said. "Have you ever been in a band?"

"No, I mostly just play for my church," Nate said.

"Do you want to be?" Will asked

"Yeah, that sounds awesome," Nate responded.

"All right, let me get your number and I'll call you later. We're going to get together this weekend," Will said.

"Cool, you wanna come over to my house?" Nate asked. "It's a pain in the ass to move my drums."

"Yeah, we can do that," Will said. "Write your address down too." Will gave Nate a piece of paper and he wrote down his number and address.

"I have to get back to practicing for the pep rally on Friday," Nate said and picked up his drum sticks.

"Cool, we'll talk to you later," Will said.

"Later," Nate said and then we all walked over to the grass area in front of the school and sat down.

"I told you, man, simple," Will said.

"I have to give you credit, you were right for once," Rob replied.

"For once, try all the time, son!" Will boasted and pulled a hacky sack out of his back pack. "Anyone down for some hacky sack?" Aaron stood up.

"I'll play," Aaron said.

"Me too," I said and stood up.

"Rob?" Will asked.

"Nah, I'm gonna eat my sandwich." We started kicking the hacky sack around until two girls walked up to us. *Hey, you're... It's Angela!*

"Hey, Will, I thought that was you." Will looked over and seemed surprised to see them.

"Hey Angela, hey Vicki, what's going on? Oh, this is Aaron, and you guys know Rob, and this is my girlfriend, Hannah." Rob waved at us and took another bite of his sandwich.

"Girlfriend? Since when?" Vicki asked. *Uh oh...*

"I don't know, Hannah, what has it been, like a month?" *Yeah...*

"Almost," I said, smiled, and reached my hand out to Vicki. "Nice to meet you..." Vicki stared at me and ignored my gesture. I put down my hand and then reached for Will's arm. I hugged him closely and then held his hand tight. *I've got a bad feeling...* Vicki and Angela continued staring at me long beyond awkwardness. There was an uncomfortable silence until Angela said,

"I just wanted to let you know that Chris and I are back together. He still wants to be friends with you." *Oh shit...*

"I know, Angela, I just don't know," Will said.

"What happened between you guys? You were like best friends...Chris won't tell me. Well, he hasn't told me yet..." Angela insisted.

"Just drop it, Angela," Will said.

"Okay, I did my part, see you later," Angela said and turned to Vicki. "Let's go."

"Bye, Will, see you around," Vicki said and smiled. *You Bitch...* Angela and Vicki walked away from us. I looked at Will and his eyes seemed to be focused on Vicki's ass. *What the fuck, Billy!*

"What was that about?" Aaron asked.

"Yeah, for real, what was that about?" I reiterated.

"I've been friends with Angela forever and Vicki, well..." Will started to say.

"...Well, what? Did you see how she looked at me? I'm pretty sure she wants to kill me," I reasoned.

"Yeah, she's had a crush on me forever. She's probably just jealous." *Why didn't you tell me about her?*

"And you never hooked up with her?" I asked and pulled away from him.

"No, never, she was gross. I was never attracted to her." *Really, dude?*

"She doesn't look too bad to me," Aaron said. *I know, right!?*

"Yeah, it's weird, she used to look a lot different," Rob said. "...In a bad way."

"Babe, you don't have to worry about Vicki. I never liked her and that's not going to change," Will argued.

"She obviously likes you though."

"So...She'll get over it and I'll just avoid her."

"I'm not so sure...How long has she liked you?"

"Ummm, yeah, since sixth grade."

"I think I've made my point."

"Babe, you worry too much."

"I actually don't think I worry enough," I said. The bell rang and Will held my hand. He whispered in my ear,

"You're the most beautiful girl in the world." *Right...* He kissed me on the cheek and then turned back to Rob and Aaron. "Meet after school?" Will asked.

"Yeah, I'll be here," Aaron said.

"Yep," Rob said. Will held my hand and walked me to my health class. We stopped at the classroom door and I let go of his hand. I turned away from him and he gently grabbed my arm.

"Are you mad at me?" he asked. *I kind of am... You should have told me about her!*

"...No...I'm not mad," I responded, "I love you."

"I love you too..."

"You should go to class, you're gonna be late," I reasoned.

"That doesn't matter; I want to make sure that we're good."

"We're good, Billy, I'm just worried..."

"Worried about what?"

"Everything...It's fine, I'll be fine." I kissed him. "I should go in..."

"...Okay, I'll see you after class."

"Happy Friday! We made it through the first week," I said and hugged Will. He put his hands around my waist and then grabbed my ass. He backed away from me, smiled, and then kissed me.

"Did you guys want to get a room? I'm going home..." Rob said. We stopped kissing and Will faced Rob.

"All right, Rob, relax, don't get your panties in a ruffle." Will and I laughed. "We're coming." We crossed street and headed home. Will started slapping my ass while we were walking.

"Stop it," I said. I smiled and slapped his hand away.

"What are you going to do about it?" Will asked.

"You guys are stupid," Rob said.

"Stop it," I continued. "I'm going to kick your ass!" I laughed. We stopped at the edge of a random garage and I punched Will in the arm. He raucously laughed at me.

"Is that it?" He asked sarcastically. He pulled me close to him by the front of my jeans and then passionately kissed me. Rob groaned.

"I'm going home, later," Rob said and ran across the street. Will and I smiled at each other and continued making out. Will put his hand down my pants from behind and ran his fingers over my panties. *Really? Two can play at that game...* I moved my hand down the front of his pants and whispered in his ear.

"Breakin the law," I said. The garage door opened and we quickly separated. Someone popped out from underneath the door before it had fully opened. The middle-aged woman looked at us and then we looked at each other.

"Oh...Ummm, sorry, I didn't mean to interrupt..." The woman said. Will and I looked at each other and then laughed. We walked away from the driveway and then waited for traffic before crossing the street.

"I think we scared her more than she scared us," Will said.

"Oh, for sure, that look on her face was priceless," I added.

"I know, right, kind of like the look of walking in on someone in the bathroom." Will and I continued laughing as we got to Rob's house. Will got his bike from Rob's back yard and then rode alongside me as he held my hand. Before we turned down my street, my dad pulled up next to us. *Oh my God! I am in such deep shit...*

"...Hannah, get in the truck! Now!" My dad looked through the window and scowled at Will. "Right now!"

"Dad, I'm almost home, why do I..." I tried to reason.

"...Now, Hannah, get in the truck!" My dad interjected. I looked back at Will and lipped 'sorry' to him. "Do I have to drag you in here!?" I let go of Will's hand and then stepped up into the truck. My dad sped away down the street as I looked in the side-view mirror. I watched as Will slowly faded into the distance. *This isn't happening...* My dad pulled into the driveway and abruptly slammed on the brakes. He looked over at me. There was anger in his eyes but he wasn't showing it. He didn't say anything and then got out of the truck and went inside the house. *Oh shit...My life is over...* I slowly opened the door on the truck and then shut it with similar ease. I walked inside my house and expected my dad to yell at me, but he wasn't in the living room. *He must be in the garage. Shit...* I went to my room, shut the door, and waited for my impending judgement. I worked on my math homework until I heard my mom get home. I put my pencil down and stood against my door. I cupped my hand over my ear. I heard my dad talking to my mom, but I couldn't make out what they were saying. *Well, at least they're not yelling...* I heard my dad's heavy footsteps echoing down the hallway and jumped back and sat on the edge of my bed.

My dad opened the door and walked in. My mom came in and stood right next to him.

"We told you that we didn't want you hanging around that boy," my mom said.

"His name is Will and he's my boyfriend, so..." My dad shook his head.

"You lied to us," my mom said.

"I never said I wasn't going to see him..."

"Yeah, very clever, Hannah, but using your friend, Casey, to sneak around?" My mom added. *Shit...*

"Well..." *Wait...Who told?"* "You wouldn't have let me walk with Will..."

"That's right!" My dad barked.

"You're grounded, Hannah!" My mom said. *Really...What's new?* "You're constantly lying to us...We can't trust you..." My mom said.

"That boy is a bad influence on you," my dad added.

"You don't even know him..."

"I know that you're lying to us about him. That's all I need to know," my dad said. *You always say the same thing!*

"I wouldn't have to lie if..."

"That's enough, Hannah!" My mom cut me off. "I'm going to take you to school and your dad will pick you up every day. And no phone!"

"I'll still see him every day at school! You can't keep us apart!" My dad looked at my mom and she smiled. *What the hell?*

"We'll see about that too..."

"What's that supposed to mean?"

"It means that if your behavior doesn't change then other things will change," my mom said. *Whatever...* My mom walked out of my room and my dad turned around and shut the door behind him.

Two months later, I was still grounded. I saw Will every day at school but it became increasingly difficult for me to call him. My dad started to work during the day at his job, which made it impossible to sneak out at night. My parents were much happier, it seemed, but I was miserable. I felt trapped just like I felt in Santa Maria. The day before Will's birthday, my parents checked the answering machine when they got home. The only message on the machine was: 'Hannah, you're a fucking bitch and I'm going to kick your ass when I see it.' My mom and dad looked at each other like they couldn't believe what they were hearing. My brother's mouth was open wide.

"Michael, go to your room," my mom instructed. My brother walked to his room, mouth still agape, and shut his door.

"Hannah, what the hell is going on now!" My dad yelled.

"Who was that?" My mom asked.

"...I don't know," I answered.

"Hannah!" My parents said at the same time.

"Seriously, I don't know."

"Are you having issues with anyone at school?" My mom asked.

"No..."

"Then how do you explain this?" My dad asked.

"I can't explain it..." *Wait...* "Play it again," I said. My dad hit the play button and then stared at me. *Vicki? Angela? It could be Angela...I don't know...*

"Anything ring a bell?" My dad asked.

"...No, I really don't know..."

"All right, Patrick, just delete the message. It's probably just a prank..."

"If you say so..." My dad replied and erased the message.

"...Hannah, please stay out of trouble," my mom pleaded. *What the hell?*

"I am! I didn't even do anything..." *Seriously...* I started crying, ran to my room, and slammed the door. I sat down at my desk and heard my parents arguing about Redwood. *Redwood...They want me to change schools? Jessica...Oh my God...*

The next day, I woke up late and got in the shower. By the time I got finished, it was after seven. As I was getting dressed my mom came into my room.

"Hannah, you're going to have to wake up earlier, I'm going to be late for work." *Why is that my fault?*

"Then just go...I can walk to school."

"Hannah, don't even start with me this morning!"

"I'm tired of getting to school before everyone else anyway!"

"If we could trust you..."

"Whatever...I don't feel like going to school today..."

"...You're going to school, Hannah! Even if I have to be late, you're going to school!"

"...Fine...I'll be ready in ten minutes."

"Make it five," my mom said and walked back to the kitchen. *I'll make it fifteen!* My mom dropped me off at school and I walked over to the hall in front of the band room. I sat alone and quietly cried until Will walked up to me twenty minutes later.

"Babe, I've got great news!" He said and studied my face. "Are you okay?" *No, Billy, I'm not...*

"...I had a fight with my mom this morning. She doesn't really have the time to take me to school in the morning and I definitely don't want her to, but my dad, well, you know...So, she's blaming me for everything...And last night, someone called my house and left a message for me. A girl said, 'Hannah, you're a fucking bitch and I'm going to kick your ass when I see it.' *I can't forget...*

"Who would do that? Seriously, it doesn't make sense. How would they even have your number?"

"I think it was Vicki or Angela; probably both. The only way they would have my number that I can think of is Chris...Michael, Mitchell, Chris, Angela, Vicki..." *Just like that...*

"Yeah, but why would Chris just give your number to Angela, unless..."

"Chris wasn't happy that I turned him down."

"Do you think that he told Angela about it? Wait, why would he do that? What would he have to gain by telling her that he asked another girl out while they were together and that he got turned down?"

"I don't know but I'm so tired of all this drama," I said. Will sat down and put his arm around me.

"Look, babe, everything is going to be fine." *Oh shit, Billy!* I smiled.

"...Oh my God, I feel so stupid, happy birthday, Billy."

"Thanks. That's what I wanted to talk to you about."

"I just got so caught up in all of this shit...You said you had good news."

"No worries, babe, and yes, I have awesome news. My brother gave me a car!"

"That is so cool, I'm so happy for you." I smiled and then kissed him.

"I'm happy for us! We'll be able to go anywhere we want..."

"As soon as I'm not grounded that is...And I'm always grounded."

"I still need to get my license, so it's not going to be tomorrow or anything." Will leaned into me and whispered, "I miss you."

"Babe, I'm right here," Hannah said.

"No, I mean, we haven't been 'together' since that night..."

"Ahhh, in that case, I miss you too," I smiled. "Since my dad started working days, it's been hard. I really could use some sexual healing, but I don't know how..."

"You don't think you could sneak out Friday night?"

"I don't think I can...If I get caught..."

"You've never got caught before...Right?"

"Yeah, but with my dad home at night, it's different...I wasn't going to say anything because I didn't want you to worry, but my parents are talking about moving me to Redwood if things don't change."

"Wait, they can do that?"

"I don't know. They seem to think so. They think that having Jessica around will be good for me."

"Yeah, we can't let that happen..."

I was on my way to meet Will at lunch when I saw Angela and Vicki walking toward me. *I know it was them...Fuck! Let it go...* I didn't make eye contact with either one of them, but I could tell that they were smiling.

"Whore!" Angela said as they walked by. I quickly turned around.

"What's your problem, Angela?"

"You're my problem? *How?*"

"Did you call my house last night?" I asked.

"...I have no idea what you're talking about," Angela responded and Vicki laughed. *Yeah, it was you...*

"I think you do...Both of you..."

"I wanna know something...How did you trick Will into being with you? Vicki asked. *What the hell?*

"I didn't trick him..."

"Yeah, you did, because he obviously doesn't know you're a slut," Angela added.

"What the fuck are you talking about?"

"Chris told me what happened..." *Chris...What!?*

"What did he tell you?"

"...He told me that you're the reason he broke up with me..." *That doesn't make any sense...* "...You fucked him, didn't you?"

"No, I didn't fuck Chris, Angela!"

"I think you did, you fucking whore!" Angela pushed me and I punched her in the face. I rushed toward her and knocked her to the ground. I got on top of her and she started flailing around and pulling my hair. I punched her again and she dropped one of her hands to protect her face. I punched her a few more times on the side of her head before I felt myself being ripped away from her.

"Stop it! Stop it!" The assistant principal said as he dragged me away. I looked back at Angela who was being helped up by Vicki and one of the teachers. "What is wrong with you?" I looked around and saw the large crowd of people, but didn't see Will anywhere.

"...She got what she deserved," I responded.

"Can I let you go?"

"Yes."

"Are you going to try to run away?"

"No...I didn't do anything wrong," I reasoned.

"Okay...I'm going to follow you to the office."

"Fine..." I walked to the office and looked around.

"Have a seat right in here," The assistant principal said and directed me into a side office. I sat down and looked at the name on the desk. *Gig Stephens...Okay.* Mr. Stephens came back into his office and closed the door. "All right...Hannah O'Connor..." *Yeah...Wait, is that my file? Ugh...*

"What's that?" I asked.

"Hannah...This isn't your first time in the principal's office, is it?"

"...No."

"I am sure that you're aware of our zero-tolerance policy on fighting."

"...Yeah...But she started it, Mr. Stephens. She was talking shit..."

"...It doesn't matter..." *Yes, it does!* "You should have told an adult..." *Right...* "You will be suspended for five days pending an expulsion hearing at which time I may or may not recommend to the board to suspend the expulsion." *What!?* "That depends on you though..."

"What do you mean?"

"Are you sorry for what you did?" *No, not in the least...What does he want to hear though...* "...Yes, I'm sorry...I should have just walked away...But I hope that's somebody's telling her the same thing. She pushed me first..."

"We'll deal with her, but I have to be honest, Hannah, it didn't look like mutual combat..." *Mutual combat?* "It looked like you were battering her." *Oh...*

"So, nothing's going to happen to her?"

"I didn't say that." *I think you did...* "We already called your mom. You need to wait here until she picks you up." *I am so dead...* I waited in Mr. Stephens' office for about an hour. I stared at the wall until my mom came in. Mr. Stephens followed her and shut the door. "Ms. O'Connor, I am suspending Hannah for five days, starting today, for assault and battery on another student. I am going to recommend to the school board that we suspend her expulsion. If she gets in another fight, her expulsion from the district will be enforced. Do you have any questions?"

"No, I don't have any questions, thank you."

"Hannah, do you have any questions?"

"...No."

"All right, we'll see you next week," Mr. Stephens said and walked us outside. My mom didn't say anything to me as we walked to the car, but as soon as the doors closed, she started yelling.

"HANNAH! What is going on with you?

"...A girl called me a slut and pushed me...and I fought back."

"This is Santa Maria all over again...You can't fight everyone that calls you a bad name, Hannah!" *I know that...* My mom drove the car out of the parking lot. "Your dad and I have been talking about moving you to Redwood..." *I know...* "I think it's time."

"You think changing schools is going to solve anything?"

"Yes, I do...We do...At least you'll have Jessica. She'll keep you out of trouble." *Ugh...*

I woke up the next morning to an empty house. My parents had gone to work and my brother had left for school. I was all alone. *I should call Billy...No, he's probably on his way to school. I have to tell him what happened though...What am I going to do today?* I heard a knock on the door which startled me, but I walked over and looked through the peephole. *Billy! Oh my God...* I ran to the bathroom to look at myself in the mirror. *I look terrible. Fuck it...* I ran back to the front door, opened it and smiled.

"Billy, I'm so happy you came, get in here!" I shut the door and hugged Will like I never wanted to let go. I started crying into his shoulder. *Why do things have to be so hard?*

"Babe, your parents are at work, right?"

"Ummm, yeah, I think so. I hope so..."

"I'm sorry, Billy, I shouldn't have hit her. I should have just walked away." I stepped away to look at him. "She started talking shit. She called me a whore and said something about me being with Chris. I'm with you, Billy; I couldn't listen to her bullshit anymore." I cried and Will hugged me.

"I know, I'm not mad at you, I'm just glad you're okay. You are okay, right?"

"Yeah, well, my parents are pissed, but there's nothing new about that...And I got suspended for five days."

"It looks like I'm taking the next five days off..."

"I love you, Billy, you're so sweet." I kissed him and he put his hands around my waist.

"So, I heard you kicked her ass," he smiled and stepped back.

"Yeah, it wasn't my first fight."

"Really, well, I'll keep that in mind for future reference. Don't piss Hannah off..."

"You know it," I smiled and punched him on the arm. "So, what do you want to do?" Will looked around my living room and focused on my coffee table.

"I don't know, how about a game of cards?" He smiled and laughed.

"Are you serious?"

"Nope...Babe, seriously?" Will kissed me and I smiled. I walked down the hallway toward my room and pulled off my t-shirt over my head and dropped it on the floor. I stopped walking and then bent over, slowly pulling off my panties. I turned around and smiled at Will. His eyes were fixed on me. He almost seemed paralyzed. *That's funny...*

"...Are you coming, or what?" I asked and he smiled and walked toward me. I turned around and continued walking into my room. He followed me and I shut the door behind us.

"Babe, I don't have those VCF things with me..."

"It's okay, just pull out, I'm not worried about it..." *I probably should be...But I don't care...*

"...Are you sure?"

"Yep." I started kissing him. He pulled off his shirt and then his shoes. I undid his belt and he kicked his pants off onto the floor. I pushed him onto my bed and got on top of him. I reached back and pulled his dick out of his boxers and pushed it inside of me. *Thanks, Billy, I really needed this...*

Chapter Eighteen

Insurrection

I was working on another one of Ms. Rose's essays when I heard a knock on the door. I put my pencil down and started walking down the hall. My mom opened the door and then immediately looked towards my dad.

"Patrick!" My mom screamed. *What the hell?* My dad walked over to the door.

"I thought we made it clear; we don't want Hannah seeing you," my dad said. I walked up to the door and stood behind my mom and dad.

"Billy..." I solemnly said.

"You shut up, Hannah," my dad said. *Fuck!*

"It's okay, I'm not here to talk to Hannah, I'm here to talk to you." Will stared at my dad. I was shocked. I didn't know what to do. I couldn't talk. I couldn't move. My dad laughed. *Billy!?*

"There's nothing to talk about," my dad said.

"Yes, there is...Why do you hate me so much?" Will asked. *Billy, no...*

"We don't hate you," my mom said. *Yeah, right...*

"What is it, my hair?" Will asked.

"It's not your hair. I had long hair when I was your age," my dad said.

"Then what's the problem?"

"Is that your car?" My dad asked.

"Yeah, why?"

"That's the problem...Hannah's fourteen...And I know she looks like she's seventeen, but she's not. She's too young to date anyone. It's not about you, it's about her." *I'm not too young!*

"What are you going to do, keep her locked up until she's seventeen?" *That's right, Billy, tell him!*

"...Yes," my dad said and I started crying. *That's so fucked up.*

"You can't just lock her up..."

"This conversation's over," my dad said and then shut the door in his face. *Billy...* "Hannah, go to your room."

"I don't want to go to my room! Why do you keep treating me like I'm a little girl?"

"You are a little girl," my dad said.

"No, I'm not..." I started to say but stopped when we heard Will's car as he revved up his engine. *Billy...*

"Patrick, you should call the police," my mom said.

"No, you're not going to call the police," I pleaded. We heard the car race down the street and then we heard his engine rev again and again. *What's he doing?* My dad walked toward the phone and picked it up. "No!" I pulled on my dad's arm in futility and he hit the power button. Will stopped revving his engine and my dad put the phone down. *Oh, thank God...*

"I think he's gone...That kid is out of control," my dad said.

"No, he's not, dad, he's just sticking up for me..."

"You're out of control too. Go to your room!"

"You are so unfair," I said and went to my room. I pretended to close my door, but then left it ajar just enough for me to hear my parents' conversation.

"I already called the school," my mom said. "They won't let her transfer this late in the year." *Yes!*

"I think I should go down there and demand it!" My dad responded. *No...*

"It's their policy..."

"Screw their policy!"

"There's nothing we can do..." *That's right...Leave me alone!* "We just have to hope that she grows up..." *What's that supposed to mean?*

"Are there any private schools around here?" *No way...*

"We don't have the money for that, Patrick." *Good...*

"Shit...Did you see that kid's car?" *So cool...*

"Yeah..." My mom said and started talking a lot quieter to my dad. I couldn't hear what they were saying anymore so I discretely closed my door and sat down at my desk. I smiled and picked up my pencil.

The next day, my mom dropped me off in front of the school and I waited for Will to meet up with me. After a few minutes, I saw him and ran to meet him half-way. I smiled and gave him a hug.

"Hey, babe, you're in a good mood," Will said. "I thought after yesterday you would be mad at me."

"What!? No, that was impressive. I never thought you would actually confront my dad...And neither did he," I said and laughed.

"What happened after I left?"

"They got mad like they always do, but this time it was different. They talked about how they didn't know what they were going to do. I didn't know before, but they called the school to see if they could transfer me to Redwood, and I guess they can't." I hugged him again.

"That's great news."

"I know, right, I was so afraid that they were going to get their way. So, you guys are going to play tomorrow...First show, are you nervous?" We both smiled.

"Not even a little bit. After telling your dad how it is, I think I can do anything. That's a scary man."

"Yup, you don't have to remind me, Billy, I have to live with him."

I started walking out to the stage at lunch to watch Will's band perform. I looked around campus and everything was decorated for Halloween. There was a sea of orange and black everywhere. Everything I saw reminded me of Mel. All of my memories of Halloween involved Mel. It wasn't the candy or the trick-or-treating or my pain-in-the-ass brother. It was Mel. *I miss her.* I gradually made my way to the stage and saw Will standing there silently playing his guitar. *So cool...* He was wearing black jeans the size of the world and a tight white t-shirt. He looked good but his pants were really silly. *Two of me could fit in those pants.* I smiled and laughed to myself. *The next time he goes clothes shopping, I need to go with him...How am I going to do that? Shit...* Aaron was wearing a button-up shirt and cargo pants. *He's cute...A little preppy, but cute.* Rob stood at the front of the stage. He was wearing a grey sweater and torn blue jeans. *He acts like he doesn't care what anyone thinks, but he sure tries hard to emulate Kurt Cobain...* I looked in the back and saw their new drummer, Nate, who was wearing a white A-shirt. He started playing some drum fills to warm up. *He's really good...Much better than Chris...* I looked around at the crowd gathering and saw Vicki and Angela standing together. Angela caught me looking at her and she quickly looked away toward the stage. *That's right, bitch!* The ASB president, Christian, walked on stage and stepped up to the microphone.

"All right, everyone," Christian said. "Are you ready for our very own Anarchy!" Some people in the crowd whistled and yelled 'yeah.' "Okay, guys, a reminder...ASB is pre-selling tickets to the Winter Ball. They're twenty-five bucks per person or forty per couple. *That seems like a lot for a school dance. Doesn't matter though...* "...Get your tickets in ASB before they're gone!" *Right...* "Ladies and gentlemen, Anarchy!" Rob looked at Will and then Will started playing 'Smells like Teen Spirit.' When they were finished playing 'Teen Spirit' everyone clapped and hollered with boisterous enthusiasm. I clapped and smiled at Will. They went on to play a bunch of Nirvana songs.

"Okay, everyone, thanks for being here," Rob said. "This is our last song, 'Negative Creep.'" The crowd erupted into a frenzy and Rob started playing. Halfway through the song, Will walked over to Rob and started singing the chorus along with him. I started head-banging like they do on MTV. *Daddy's little girl...Hmmm, yeah...* The song ended and everyone clapped. "Thanks," Rob said. Rob and Will did the fist-bump thing. *Hmmm, I've never seen them do that before...* Aaron and Nate walked over to the front of the stage. Will jumped down and gave me a hug.

"You were awesome, babe," I said.

"Thanks, we were okay...Yeah, no, we were awesome!" Will smiled. A bunch of people patted Will on the back and shook his hand. They repeated over and over again how great they were, one after another. *Someone's Mr. popular...* Angela and Vicki walked up to Will and I as the crowd of people started to thin out.

"Will, you were amazing up there," Vicki said.

"Yeah, you guys were great," Angela added. I didn't say anything. I stared at Angela and then at Vicki. *Stupid bitches.* They didn't make eye contact with me. *Good, I'm glad they're afraid...* "Well...We gotta go."

"Bye, Will, see you around," Vicki said. *I don't think so...* Angela and Vicki walked away and I stared at Will. *What the hell!?*

"Why did you talk to those fucking bitches?" I asked.

"Babe, they talked to me. What was I supposed to do?"

"They're so lucky I can't get suspended again..." *Shit...I so much wanted to hit her again...*

"...That wasn't so bad...I remember a very specific benefit to you being suspended." Will smiled.

"Yeah, but I can't get in trouble anymore."

"Come on, babe, smile. Don't worry about them. We can't change what happened in the past."

"I want you to stay away from them. I don't trust them." Will took my hand.

"Neither do I. So, to change the subject on you, do you want to go to the Winter Ball? I was thinking since I have a car now, and a license, and a job, that we could go on actual dates..." I smiled and looked down. *That's sweet, Billy...*

"I don't think my parents will let me."

"Yeah, I figured that much, but what about Jessica?"

"What do you mean?"

"Just tell your parents that you're going stag with Jessica. The dances are open to all the high schools."

"I could try...It sounds like it would be fun."

"Yeah, I mean, if you can't, you can't, but if you can I'll buy the tickets." Nate walked up to us.

"Hey, man, are you gonna help move stuff to the van? The bell's going to ring in five minutes," Nate said.

"Yeah, it's all good though, we have late passes. I'll be right there, man," Will responded.

"Okay...Hey, there's gonna be a party tonight that I guess everyone's going to, did you guys want to go?" Nate asked.

"I can't," I said.

"If Hannah can't go then I can't go," Will said.

"Come on, you guys," Nate said. "This stupid school won't let us dress up for Halloween so I thought it would be cool to..."

"If you want to go, you can go," I said.

"I'm not going without you," Will insisted.

"That's sweet but you should go have fun." *Go meet up with Vicki...*

"I'm not going to have any fun if you're not there."

"If you change your mind, let me know," Nate said.

"Look, Nate Dog, you guys can still go..." Will insisted.

"Nah, the party's in Dinuba and you're the only one with a car...Well, a car and a license. It's cool, man, later," Nate said and went back to the stage.

"I think you should go," I said. *Don't say yes...*

"Babe, I'm not going without you and that's the end of it." I smiled and hugged him. *Good boy, Billy.*

"How did I get so lucky?"

"Babe, I'm the lucky one." I pulled Will by his belt and started kissing him.

"Hey, get a room!" Rob yelled from the stage. "Get your ass over here and help!" *Ha...Maybe we should.* The bell rang and Will hugged me.

"I should go help; I'll see you after school."

"Okay, Billy, see you later." Will kissed me and then jumped back up to the stage. I started walking to class. *What am I going to do? I know they won't let me go...*

After dinner that night, I looked at my mom and then my dad. *Yeah, don't even bother...*

"Mom, do you think that I could call Jessica really fast?"

"...Yeah, but make it really fast," my mom answered.

"Okay, I will." I took the phone to my room and dialed Will's number. The phone rang and his mom answered.

"Is Will there?" I asked.

"Yeah, who's calling?"

"It's Hannah."

"Okay, hold on...Will, it's Hannah..."

"Hey, babe, what's up?"

"I can't talk long, but I asked my parents about the dance and they said no.

"Did you mention Jessica?"

"Yeah, they didn't buy it. They know I want to go with you..." *It's true even if it isn't true...*

"...We have to figure something out. I miss you. We can't really do anything at school."

"I miss you too, but what are we gonna do?"

"I'll think of something..."

"Shit! My dad's coming, I gotta go." I hung up the phone and watched my dad walking towards me.

"How's Jessica?" My dad asked.

"Good...She's just busy with school..."

"...I see...That's good..." My dad walked into his room and I stood in my doorway loosely cradling the phone in my hand. *Shit...He doesn't believe me...*

"Hannah, your dad is going to take you to school today, I have to go into work early."

"Okay..."

"It's just for today." *It's fine, mom, who cares?*

"Okay, mom." *At least I won't have to sit there for an hour by myself...* My dad dropped me off at school fifteen minutes before eight and I went to the band room to meet up with Will. *Today, he'll be waiting for me...He better be...* I saw Will and then he saw me. He walked toward me and I could see a sinister smile on his face. *What is he up to?*

"Babe, I have an idea. Let's go to my house."

"You mean right now? Like, ditch school?"

"Yep, I want to be with you...If you know what I mean..." I smiled. *Yes, I know...*

"Yeah, I know what you mean, Billy, but that's the kind of trouble that will get me sent to one of those religious convent things."

"You're not gonna get sent to a convent. It's simple, I'll call the school when we get to my house and pretend to be your dad. No one will know the difference."

"I don't know. Do you really think that will work?"

"I don't just think it will work; I know it will work. I've done it before. Well, Chris and I used to do it all the time. We always called and pretended to be each other's dad." *Chris...Probably not a good idea.*

"But you said that your dad doesn't live with you."

"That's my point exactly; they never questioned it. They never found out. They're stupid and we can take advantage..." *Wow, Billy, I don't know...*

"I don't know..."

"I promise you; no one will ever know..." *Heh...Summer...I remember...It worked then.*

"...Is anyone home at your house?"

"Nah, everyone's at work. Trust me. Let's get out of here..." *Hmmm...*

"Okay, I trust you, let's go." Will held my hand and walked me over to his car. He opened the passenger door for me and let me in. *That's sweet.* I looked around the interior of the car. It was a strange two-tone green color. I looked in the back seat. It was torn up like an animal had been back there. I looked up at the ceiling and saw the headliner fabric hanging down. *Is this thing even safe?* Will got inside and then brushed my hair off of my shoulder.

"It's going to be fine...Buckle up for safety," he said and laughed. I pulled on part of the seatbelt and then looked around for the rest of it. *Where the hell is it?*

"Where's the shoulder belt?" Will laughed again.

"All you get is a lap belt, this is an old car." *Great...*

"Is that safe?"

"Babe, this car is a solid chunk of steel. If we were to get in an accident, the other car would be paying the price. All these new cars are made out of plastic..." I fastened my seatbelt and Will started the car. *It's so loud!* He drove down the street and then put his hand on my thigh. I put my hand over the top of his and smiled.

"You look so cool driving, Billy," I said. "I would be so nervous...I am not looking forward to getting my license."

"Yeah, but as soon as you get your license, your parents won't be able to control you like they do now..." *Yeah...I'm not sure if that's gonna make a difference...*

"...That's true, but I'm just scared, I guess. I'll probably run someone over." Will laughed. "What? That's not funny!"

"Sure, it is; you're not going to run anyone over..." After about ten minutes, Will pulled into an apartment complex.

"You live here, babe?" I asked.

"Yep," he responded and then parked the car.

"It looks kind of shady..." *A lot...*

"...That's because it is." Will laughed. "Don't worry about it though, let's go." Will opened his door and then I got out as well. "Hold up, I have to lock your door from the outside." Will put the key into the door and turned the lock. "Yeah, I need to fix that." We walked upstairs and went inside his apartment. I walked around the living room and looked at the pictures on the wall. I pointed to one in particular.

"Is this you?" I asked. *It couldn't be...*

"Yeah, I think I was like four years old in that picture."

"You were so cute! And you had blond hair!? What happened?"

"I don't really know. It started darkening up when I was like twelve or something like that."

"That's crazy...So, what do you wanna do?"

"Is that even a question?" Will smiled. "Come on." He grabbed my hand and led me back to his room. "What do you wanna listen to?"

"I don't know, maybe something romantic..." Will smiled. "Well, let me go through my CD's here..." He rummaged through a stack of CD's. "I don't have anything 'romantic.' He continued to look. "Guns N Roses it is." He smiled and put the CD into his stereo.

"I was thinking something like Jewel, but sure...Wait, aren't you going to call the school?" *Shit...I'm glad I remembered.*

"Right, yeah, let me get the phone." He walked out to the living room and I heard him open a book. "Let me see here. Mt. Whitney high school...Attendance...Okay, it's right here." I walked out to the living room and stood next to him. "All right, babe, watch me work." I smiled and watched him dial the number.

"Attendance, please," Will said. *I hope this works...* "...Hi, this is Mr. O'Connor, Hannah's father." *Ha...Mr. O'Connor...* Will lowered his voice. "...Yes, Hannah's not feeling well today, and I'm going to keep her home. Please excuse her absence...Thank you, have a great day, bye," Will said and hung up the phone. "And it's that easy, babe." Will smiled. *Not bad.*

"Damn, Billy, that was awesome, I almost believed you myself."

"Thank you, thank you, I try."

"So, you're sure they're not going to call my house, right?"

"I'm sure, we're good...One thing though. We can't do this all the time. They give us like ten days per year to be absent before they start digging around."

"How do you know all this?"

"If you're going to break the rules, you have to know what the rules are..." *Nice, Billy...*

"You are literally the smartest person I know and you're mine," I said and hugged him. "So, we have nine more 'ditch days' then?"

"Well, yeah, I mean, we could falsify medical notes and shit like that...They don't check that stuff either, but to be on the safe side, yeah..." I pulled Will's arm and I led him back into his bedroom. He shut the door and I jumped on his bed. Will went to his stereo and Guns N Roses started playing. I took off my shirt and motioned for him to come to me. He took off his shoes and then his shirt. He got on top of me and kissed me. I started pulling his belt and he slipped his pants off. Will undid the button on my pants and then pulled off my pants and underwear at the same time. *Shit!*

"Damn, Billy, careful," I said and he laughed and then smiled. We got underneath the covers. Will got one of the VCF packets from under his bed and opened it.

"I love you, Hannah," he said. *Ahhh...*

"I Love you too, Billy." We had sex through a number of Guns N Roses songs and then I rested my head on Will's chest and looked up at him.

"Do you think we'll be together forever?"

"Yes, I do, I would never want to be with anyone else..." *Is that really true? I want to believe you...*

"...I feel the same way, but my parents..."

"I'm not worried about them. Like you said, we're perfect for each other."

"Yeah, it almost feels like we were meant to be."

"We are meant to be, which is why I'm going to do whatever I have to do to be with you."

"Hey, babe, I'm kind of hungry. I didn't eat breakfast."

"What would you like, my lady?" Will asked and I laughed.

"I could really go for some pancakes, smothered in butter and maple syrup!"

"You know what, I can totally do that."

"You can cook!?" *No way!*

"Well. I've never made pancakes before but I've seen my mom do it so I think I can. How hard could it be?" *Ha!* I put my hand down Will's boxers and grabbed his flaccid penis.

"Not hard at all," I said and smiled.

"I see what you did there. I see you still have jokes. "Well. Put some clothes on...I'm gonna make some pancakes." We got dressed and then walked to the kitchen. Will got a box of Bisquick out of the cupboard and I watched him read the instructions and then watched as he made a stack of pancakes. *So cool...* "I think this is how my mom makes them." I grabbed a fork from the dish rack and started eating. "Babe, I'm not even done yet."

"These are so good, Billy," I said and poured more syrup onto the stack. Will grabbed a fork and joined me.

"Yeah, not too bad," he said. I stopped eating after I was full and then stared into Will's eyes. *It would be so nice if...*

"...Wow, Billy, a girl could get used to this kind of thing..." *I wish things could be different...*

"...I'm glad you like it." We finished eating and Will rinsed off the dishes. I walked up behind him and grabbed his ass.

"Are you ready for round two?" I asked and kissed his neck. He put the plate down and turned away from the sink.

"I was just going to ask you the same thing..."

"Happy birthday, Hannah," my dad said. "Wake up!"

"Dad...God, it's like..." I looked over at my clock. "It's not even seven! Go away!

"Okay, but think about what you want to do today." *I want you to leave me alone.*

"Fine, dad...But, I'm only fifteen. It's not a big deal."

"It is though...Your mom and I want to talk to you when you get up..." *Great. What now?*

"Okay..."

"I'll leave you alone..." My dad said and then shut my door. *What is he talking about? Now I'm curious...* I got out of bed and then got dressed. I looked at myself in the mirror. *Yeah, I don't look any different....Just another day.* I went out to the kitchen where my mom was making breakfast. My dad was making noise in the garage.

"Good morning," my mom said. *Is it?*

"...What was dad talking about?"

"We've been talking about you..." *Okay, vague much?*

"About..."

"We want to cut you some slack...I know that we've been really hard on you..." *You think...* "And you're getting older and you're going to have to make your own decisions."

"What does that mean?"

"...Your dad and I aren't going to keep you from talking to your boyfriend." *What!?* "You see him at school anyway...If you want to be with him, I'm going to be okay with that."

"You're kidding, right?"

"No, I'm not kidding...Now, your dad isn't happy about it, but we feel that you need to decide for yourself..." *Is this a trick?*

"So, I can call him and you won't stop me?"

"No...It's your choice. If he treats you right and you feel that he's good for you then...There's nothing for me to say."

"And...I can see him?"

"You already see him..." *Yeah, but...What you don't know...*

"Dad's okay with this?" My mom laughed.

"...Not really, but I convinced him that it's for the best." *How did you do that? Something isn't right...* "We've been under a lot of stress with everything going on and we can't keep it up. Hannah, we're asking you to take responsibility for yourself. Do you think you can do that?"

"Yes, of course I can do that..."

"...Real responsibility, Hannah..." *Huh?* "You have to understand that your actions have consequences and you have to make decisions accordingly...You understand?"

"Yes, mom..."

"Every decision you make affects other people. You have to think about that." *I know, mom, I get it...* My mom stepped away from the stove. "We got you a gift."

"Mom, that's okay..."

"Hold on..." She went to the garage and came back with my dad. My dad was holding a wrapped present.

"Happy birthday!" My mom and dad said at the same time as if they had rehearsed.

"Open it," my dad instructed. I ripped the paper off to reveal a phone.

"You got me a phone!" I said and smiled.

"Yep," my mom said. "Your own phone. Go plug it in..." I hugged my mom and then my dad. I ran down the hallway and then plugged my new phone into the wall at the end of my bed. I turned around and saw my parents smiling in my doorway.

"Can I call..." I began to ask, but my mom finished my sentence.

"...Yes, you can call your boyfriend," she said. My dad looked at her funny like he wasn't completely on board, but he didn't say anything. My mom pulled on his arm and then shut my door. *No way this is happening...* I dialed Will's number. *This is so crazy...*

"Hello," Will's mom answered.

"Is Will there?" I asked.

"No, sweetie, he's not." *Ugh! Hmmm...*

"Do you know when he'll be back?"

"No, I don't..."

"Is he at work?"

"I'm not sure...He's either at work or with his band," Will's mom laughed.

"...Okay, can you tell him that Hannah called?"

"Of course, I'll tell him you called."

"Okay, bye."

"Bye." *Shit. Maybe I should call McDonald's...Nah, I should call Summer.* I sat on my bed and dialed Summer's number. *It's Sunday, she has to be home...* The phone rang a few times and Summer answered.

"Hello?"

"Hey, Summer, it's Hannah."

"Oh my God, Hannah! How are you?"

"I'm really good, how are you?"

"I'm good, but I have some pretty shitty news..." *Oh no...*

"Do I even want to know?"

"...I don't think you do, but I think I need to tell you anyway."

"...Okay..."

"Guess who's not going to Jail?" *Joe...Shit...*

"Joe..."

"...It was his word against Jade's..."

"...And they didn't believe her..." *This is my fault...*

"No, they didn't."

"I should have said something...You were right, Summer..."

"...I don't think I was."

"Really!? Why?"

"I don't think it would have made a difference...Joe's family has connections. They got a good lawyer, well, not good, but you know what I mean..."

"It's just not fair."

"Guys like Joe get away with murder..."

"I'm glad I'm with my boyfriend," I said.

"Oh yeah, how is that going?" Summer asked.

"Good. Billy's so sweet...I tried to call him this morning, but he's either at work or playing with his band...At least that's what his mom told me..."

"...Trouble in paradise, Hannah?"

"I don't know...I'm happy that he has a job and a car and a band, but I just feel like he's forgetting about me."

"You think he's cheating on you?"

"No...It just makes me kind of sad that I'm not the most important thing in his life."

"Have you talked to him about how you feel?"

"No...I don't know what to say."

"Well, if you don't tell him...Hannah, you don't expect a boy to figure it out on his own, do you?" I laughed.

"No, I guess not, thanks, Summer, I always feel better when I talk to you."

"Same...Wait. Isn't it your birthday today?"

"Yeah, you remembered!"

"Of course..."

"My parents bought me a phone."

"That's cool."

"The best part is that they said they're going to stop harassing me about being with Billy."

"Really!?"

"Yeah, my mom gave me a lecture about responsibility and something about my actions having consequences...I mean, like duh, mom...But she said it's my choice who I'm with...It's like they suddenly just stopped caring..."

"Hmmm," Summer said, "sounds like reverse psychology."

"What do you mean?" I asked.

"I'm not saying that is what's happening, but maybe they're acting like they don't care because they think that if they don't care then you'll lose interest in your boyfriend."

"You think so?" *That's kind of fucked up...*

"I don't know, but you said yourself it was sudden..."

"...I was kind of suspicious."

"Yeah, my parents do it to me all the time."

"If that's what they're planning, they're going to be very disappointed," I said and laughed.

"They can join my parents in the disappointment," Summer added and we both laughed. "They think they're so smart..."

"But we're smarter!"

"I know, right, they raised us, what do they expect!?" We laughed again. *I need to find Billy...*

"...It was good talking to you, Summer, but I need to call around and find Billy."

"Yeah, you too...Hey, remember what I said about telling him how you feel...Don't hold it in." *He'll think I'm crazy...*

"...Okay, I'll tell him. I'll give you a call later..."

"Yeah, let me know how it goes."

"I will...Bye Summer."

"Bye," Summer said and I hung up the phone.

Chapter Nineteen
Collapse

"Hannah, have you and Will...You know, had sex yet?" Jessica asked. I laughed hysterically. It was the first weekend of the summer and Jessica and I were hanging out at her house. "Why is that so funny?"

"Yeah, Jessica, we've had sex."

"Really...When? Where?" I laughed again.

"Ummm, how do I answer that?"

"Come on, Hannah!"

"...All the time and everywhere."

"Hannah!"

"...What!?" I smiled. "It's true."

"You've had sex with him at your house?"

"Yep..."

"No way!"

"Yes way...And we've had sex outside too..."

"I don't believe you, Hannah, that's crazy." I smiled again.

"I have no reason to lie to you, Jessica."

"...Yeah...Hannah, how do you get a boyfriend?"

"I don't understand the question..."

"What don't you understand?"

"Well, I don't know...You don't really have to do anything to get a boyfriend..."

"Thanks, Hannah, that's very helpful," Jessica said sarcastically.

"I'm serious, Jessica," I said. "All we have to do is show up and look pretty and sometimes we don't even have to do that much."

"That's just not true..."

"It is true..."

"Hannah, can I tell you something..."

"Yeah, we're talking right now." *She's so weird...*

"No, I mean something that you can't tell anyone else."

"Okay...What's the big secret?"

"...I've never had a boyfriend before..."

"That's okay, Jessica."

"No, it's not, Hannah, I'm almost sixteen and I've never had a boyfriend. What is wrong with me?" I laughed. *Where do I start?*

"It's not funny, Hannah!"

"I know, I know..." *But it kind of is...* "Jessica, you're cute and you've got a nice body, so maybe..."

"Hey, are you saying my personality is the problem?" *Yes...*

"I think it would help if you tried to be more, I don't know, pleasant."

"What does that mean!"

"...try to be nicer."

"I am nice!"

"Do you want a boyfriend or not, Jessica?"

"I really do...I've never even been kissed." I stopped and stared at her like I was observing some mythical creature that only existed in fairytales.

"How is that even possible, Jessica?"

"I don't know..." *Oh shit, Rob...* I laughed.

"You should have let Rob kiss you that night."

"That's so gross, Hannah." I continued laughing.

"Beggars can't be choosers..." *Where did I get that...*

"I'm not desperate!" *Ugh...*

"You sound desperate."

"I'm not that desperate!"

"Do you want my help or not?"

"...Yes..." *I wonder if Aaron has a girlfriend. I don't think he does...*

"Will has a friend that I think you would like..."

"Hannah..."

"He's cute, trust me."

"What's his name?"

"Aaron."

"Hmmm, okay...He doesn't smoke, does he?" *I don't know...*

"I don't think so...I'll set something up with Will so you can meet him."

"...Okay, when?"

"I don't know, I'll talk to Will about it. He's at work right now though."

"Does he work a lot?"

"Yeah...To be honest with you, I think he works too much...I miss him...Sometimes I think he's losing interest in me..."

"That would make him pretty stupid..." I smiled. *And sometimes. ..She says the perfect thing...*

"...And he's not stupid...I just think he needs a reminder..."

"...Hannah, what are you planning?"

"I don't know yet..."

"...Okay, so I'm getting my license next week," Jessica said and I smiled.

"I thought you didn't want to get a license..."

"Well...My mom's making me...She says it's time for me to drive myself to school."

"How exciting! She's right, you know, I'm scared to get my license too, but to be able to not have to ask to go somewhere would be awesome."

"Hey, wait, I'm not scared!" *You're something...*

"Jessica..."

"Okay, maybe I'm a little nervous about running someone over..."

"Like I said..."

The following Friday morning, Jessica called me after she got her license and we made plans to go to the mall. She told me that she was going to pick me up at around noon to get some lunch before we went shopping. I took a shower and then as soon as I walked back to my room to get dressed, the phone rang.

"Hello?" I answered.

"Hey babe," Will said. "I just thought I'd call to say I love you before I go to work."

"Ahhh, that's so sweet, what time do you get off?"

"At four, unless they keep me longer..."

"What are you doing tonight?"

"I was gonna hang out with Aaron. He got his license and wants to cruise around in his car."

"That's cool. Jessica got her license too. We're gonna go to the mall if you wanna meet up. Maybe Aaron and Jessica could..."

"Babe, you know how that worked out last time."

"I think it'll be different this time...Aaron's a Taurus, right?"

"Yeah, but so is Rob..." *Ugh...*

"I think that Aaron is more Jessica's type though."

"Why, because he takes showers?" We both laughed.

"Yeah, that's a pretty good reason."

"No argument from me...So, what's up with your parents?"

"They think that I'm going out with you just to experiment sexually," I said. "My mom said, 'you're curious, that's why you keep going back for more.' I thought that was totally unfair of them."

"I don't know, I think they're just looking out for your best interest..." *Whose side are you on, dude?*

"But they're wrong. I love you and I've never been in love before. It's more than just sex."

"The sex is really good though."

"It is, but they don't understand. They would totally kill me if they knew I wanted to spend the rest of my life with you...That I wanted to marry you."

"They'll come around. Look at how much better it's gotten in the past few months..."

"Yeah, you're right. It's just that every time I bring you up, they try to put you down in some fucked up way. My mom asked me to explain in detail why I love you so much. I told her that words cannot and never will explain my love for you."

"Not bad, babe, what'd she say?"

"She said she had to give me credit for such a clever answer. She's acting like things are all right, but my dad on the other hand is still going retarded."

"Hmmm, well, progress is progress. I'll take what I can get." Will laughed. "Hey, I gotta go to work, what time are you guys going to the mall?" *I have an idea...*

"...Around six, I think."

"Oh yeah, which mall?"

"The Visalia Mall."

"Okay, cool, I'll see you later then."

"Okay, I love you."

"I love you too," Will said and hung up the phone. *I have to finish getting ready...*

A few minutes after noon, I heard a knock on the door. *Jessica...* I walked down the hallway and opened the door.

"Hey, Jessica," I said. "Happy birthday."

"Thanks, Hannah...So are you ready to go?"

"Yeah, I just have to tell my brother I'm leaving..." I let Jessica inside and shut the door.

"You're gonna leave him home alone?"

"Yeah, it's all right. He's old enough even though he doesn't act like it sometimes." I walked into my brother's room. He was playing video games and was seemingly oblivious to my presence. "Michael...Michael!"

"What!?" My brother responded with animosity, but didn't stop playing his game.

"Jessica and I are going to the mall."

"...Okay..."

"Are you going to be all right here by yourself?"

"Yes, I'm not a baby."

"Okay, tell mom that we'll be at the mall until...Tell her that we're going to get dinner there..."

"...Fine..." I walked away from my brother's room and smiled at Jessica.

"I'm gonna leave them a note just in case..." I got a pen and paper and wrote that we would be back around seven. "Okay, let's go." Jessica and I walked out to her mom's car and got inside. "Congratulations on getting your license!"

"Thanks, Hannah."

"...By the way, Billy and Aaron are supposed to meet us around six after Billy gets off of work."

"...Thanks, Hannah, now I'm nervous..."

"...Sorry, I thought that's what you wanted."

"...It is, but I just got my license...And now I'm thinking...And I should be focused on driving..."

"Okay, Jessica, relax...I won't say anything else until we get to the mall."

"...Okay...I'm okay." Jessica started the car and drove down the street. *This is so cool!* I kept my promise and didn't say a word to her the entire time so that she could concentrate on driving. We got to the mall around twelve-thirty and Jessica parked about as far away as anyone could. She turned off the car and we got out.

"Do you think you could have parked any further away?" I laughed.

"I don't want anyone hitting my mom's car, okay!?" We hiked across the parking lot in what must have been one-hundred-degree heat.

"It is so hot here," I said.

"You haven't gotten used to it yet?" Jessica asked.

"I don't see how that's even possible...We're melting out here!"

"It is...You don't hear me complaining..." *For once...I'll give you that one...* We walked into the food court and I immediately felt the cool relief of the air conditioning on my face. *How would anyone be able to live here without air conditioning?*

"So, what do you want to eat?" I asked.

"A chicken bowl sounds good...With a diet coke," Jessica responded.

"Okay..." We walked over to the Chinese Gourmet and ordered our food and then sat down at the table closest to the restaurant. Halfway through eating, A boy walked up to our table.

"Hi, I was just walking by and...Your name's Jessica, right?" Jessica smiled.

"Yeah..."

"We had the same English class..."

"...Oh, okay, yeah..." *Who is this guy? He's actually kind of hot...Hmmm.*

"Keith...My name's Keith."

"Hi, Keith," Jessica said coldly.

"So, who's you friend?" Keith looked at me and smiled.

"Hannah," I said.

"Hi Hannah, do you think I could get your number?" He asked. *Hmmm...* Jessica stared at me.

"No," I said... *Heh...* "But you can give me yours..."

"Hannah!" Jessica said and then looked at Keith. "Hannah has a boyfriend..." Keith started writing his number on the back of a napkin.

"What's her boyfriend have to do with me?" Keith asked. He finished writing his number down and then handed it to me. "Call me, beautiful..."

"Okay," I said and Keith walked out of the food court."

"Hannah, what are you doing?"

"I'm going to give Billy something to think about..."

"You're crazy, Hannah..."

"I'm not crazy...It's not like I'm going to hook up with him. I just want to..."

"...You want to make him jealous..."

"...Yeah...Pretty much, and Keith is kind of hot..."

"Hannah, Keith is going to be a senior. He was in my class because he failed the year before..."

"So...It's not like I'm going to do anything..." *Wait...I know what I can do...* "I have an idea and I want you to play along..."

"I don't like the sound of that..."

"Here's the plan...We're going to go get paper and a pen from...Somewhere...And write down a bunch of guys names and fake numbers and then give them to Billy when he gets here with Aaron..."

"Why would you do that to him?"

"I just want to see what he does."

"I don't see the point, Hannah."

"Yes, you do, Jessica, you already said it...To make him jealous."

"And Keith isn't enough?"

"Maybe, maybe not, but I want to make a statement..."

"Where do you get all of these ideas?"

"From my brain, I guess."

"It just doesn't seem right..."

"...Jessica, I feel like Billy is getting too comfortable...Maybe even complacent. I need to remind him that other guys want to be with me..."

"And you think he doesn't know that already? Seriously, Hannah, Keith barely even looked at me." *I know...* "If I know it then Will knows it too..." *Maybe...*

"Jessica, it's going to be harmless fun..."

"If you say so, but I still think it's a bad idea..."

"Just play along...Please!"

"...Fine..." Jessica and I walked around the mall after finishing our lunch to look for paper.

"I don't think we're going to find paper just laying around," I said.

"What are you going to do?" Jessica asked. *I guess I can buy a notebook or something...*

"They might have something at the bookstore." We walked into the bookstore and I immediately went to the stationery section. I found a notebook with a number of different styles of paper. *This is perfect!* "Jessica, this is it...It cost ten bucks, but it'll be worth it."

"...Okay..." I paid for the notebook and we walked out of the store. *Hmmm. Heh! I know...*

"Come on Jessica!" I pulled on her arm and rushed over to the pay phone. I opened the phone book, grabbed the pen that was already there, and started writing down names and numbers on different pages in the notebook. I tried to vary my handwriting as much as I could to avoid suspicion, but I still needed help. "Jessica..." I said and tore out a few pieces of paper. "...Find some names and write the numbers down...And make your handwriting different on each one..."

"What am I, your partner in crime?" Jessica asked.

"...Yeah...But crime? Come on, Jessica, be real."

"Great..." Jessica started helping me and between the two of us we were done in a matter of minutes.

"Okay," I said. "How many do we have?" Jessica counted eight and I counted twelve.

"Twenty..."

"Perfect..."

"You really think he's going to believe this? It seems like a lot..."

"Yeah, I think so..."

"Maybe you should use like seven or eight..."

"Nah, Jessica, I'm going to be really popular today," I said and then laughed. "Now tear off the edges and make them look...I don't know, legit..."

"None of this is legit, Hannah..." I tore the paper as small as I could without obscuring the names or numbers.

"Like this," I said. Jessica started tearing her papers just like I had done. "Okay, let's see what we have here..." I stacked the papers in my palm and looked at the names as I folded them in half and put them in my front pocket. *Matt...Jacob...Josh...Nick...Tyler...Brandon...*

"What are you going to do with the notebook?" Jessica asked.

"I have to trash it...It's evidence..."

"So, you just spent ten bucks to play a trick on your boyfriend?"

"...Yeah..." *When you put it that way...* I walked over to the closest trash bin and threw the notebook and scraps into it. *Maybe, I shouldn't do this...* "...What should we do now?"

"I wanna go to JC Penny's..."

"What else is new?" I said and laughed.

"Hey!"

"It's okay, come on, let's go." Jessica and I went to JC Penney's and she bought some clothes The time went by quickly between window shopping and people watching. At six O' clock, Jessica and I were in Claire's looking at rings when I felt Will hug me from behind. I turned around and smiled.

"Hey, Billy, I've got something for you."

"Babe, I don't have any more fingers for any more rings," Will said and laughed.

"Yes, you do, your thumbs are still free...But that's not it." *I guess I'm doing this...* I pulled out all of the papers in my front pocket. I put them in his hand and smiled. *Don't be mad...* Will opened the papers one at a time. I looked at Aaron and then at Jessica. "Jessica, this is Aaron." Aaron waved at Jessica.

"Hi, nice to meet you Jessica," Aaron said.

"Nice to meet you," Jessica replied. *Yeah, she likes him...*

"...Hannah, what do you want me to do with all of these numbers?"

"I don't know, I thought you'd want them. I'm not going to call any of those guys," I said.

"Then why'd you take their numbers?" *Heh...*

"Oh shit!" Aaron said.

"...I didn't want to be mean..." I insisted. Will walked to the trash bin and threw away the numbers and then walked back to me.

"Sometimes you should be mean," Will argued. *I agree...*

"She told them she had a boyfriend," Jessica said. *Perfect, Jessica!*

"There was like twenty numbers there. I guess they didn't believe her," Will said and looked at me with disappointment in his eyes. *Babe, don't be mad...*

"It's not a big deal. You're here now so they won't bother us anymore," I said.

"Jessica, did you get any numbers?" Will asked. *Oh, shit! Jessica...*

"...Yeah, but I already threw them away," Jessica answered. *Nice, Jessica...* I leaned in and whispered in Will's ear.

"You have no reason to be jealous, I love you." *It worked perfectly!* I held Will's hand. "Hey, guys, let's go get some food."

"Yeah, I could eat," Aaron said. We decided to order a pizza and then sat at a table in the middle of the food court.

"Jessica, where are you from?" Aaron asked. *Heh...*

"I'm from here...I go to Redwood."

"Do you like it there?"

"Yeah, It's all right..."

"You think it's better than Whitney?"

"Definitely!" Jessica asserted.

"She's just saying that because she doesn't know any better," I said and laughed.

"That's not true, Hannah, it is objectively better," Jessica insisted.

"How so?" I asked.

"...It's prettier," Jessica said and everyone laughed except for Will.

"Babe, why aren't you saying anything? I asked. "You're not still thinking about the numbers, are you?" *Maybe it was a bad idea...*

"Look, I get it, you're the hottest girl here, no offense Jessica, and other dudes are gonna hit on you, but you don't have to encourage them," Will said and I let go of his hand.

"What do you mean encourage them?" I asked.

"Uh oh," Jessica said.

"I could be wearing a winter coat and sweat pants and they would still hit on me," I continued.

"That's not what I mean. You shouldn't take their numbers. You should just say, 'thanks, I have a boyfriend,' and move on," Will reasoned.

"Jessica told you; I did, but they insisted," I said. *I'm going to Hell...*

"Yeah, Will, sometimes it's just easier to take the numbers. Some of those guys are super scary," Jessica said. *Jessica really has my back...I'm actually kind of surprised.*

"...Fine, whatever, let's just change the subject," Will said.

"Babe, I don't want you to be mad," I said. *I really don't...*

"Then maybe you should have just thrown the numbers away and not told me at all!" *Hmmm...*

"Are you saying that you don't want me to be honest with you? I don't want to hide anything from you," I said. *Yup, going to Hell...*

"No, I want you to be honest with me...Look, I'm sorry, I overreacted, and I'm making it awkward for everyone."

"Yeah, you are..." Aaron agreed. *Thank you...*

"All right, I'll shut up now, the pizza's coming anyway," Will said as the pizza guy walked up to the table. He put the pizza down and then walked away. Aaron, Jessica, and I grabbed a slice off of the platter and started eating. I looked at Will who was simply staring at the pizza.

"Are you going to get some pizza?" I asked.

"I'm not really hungry," Will answered.

"More for us," Aaron said.

"Babe, what's wrong? You're not still thinking about..."

"No, well yeah, but that's not it."

"Okay, what is it then? Billy, I'm not going to be able to eat anything if you don't tell me. I'm worried about you." *What did I do? Maybe Jessica was right. Shit.*

"...It's Brad; he's coming next week. I don't know if I should go this summer." *Brad...Oh, shit, I forgot about that...*

"You're leaving us, man?" Aaron asked.

"It's a long story, I'll tell you later," Will answered and then held my hand. "I don't want to be apart from you again like last summer...I mean, we weren't even together and I missed you a lot." *Ahhh...Wait a minute though...Hmmm.*

"It's okay, Billy, you should go," I insisted. *I don't want you to go...*

"I don't think it's a good idea..." Will argued.

"I'll be fine, Billy, I've got Jessica to keep me busy," I said. Jessica stopped eating her pizza and stared at me.

"Ummm, yeah, we could go to Wild Water Adventures or something," Jessica said.

"That sounds fun!" I exclaimed.

"I don't even think I can get the time off from work," Will added.

"Then quit," I said. "What's more important, your lifelong friend or Micky D's?"

"Brad, but I still have my car insurance and gas and food."

"Then get a new job when you get back. Babe, I know you don't like working at McDonald's..."

"...I don't know."

"Well, let me know what you're going to do, babe," I insisted.

"Yeah...I'll have to think about it." I continued eating and smiled at Will. *He does not look happy...* After everyone finished eating, Jessica turned to me and said,

"So, you wanna go find a new bikini?"

"Yeah, you guys wanna come with us?"

"No, I need to get home," Will said. "I've got to work early." *You work every day...*

"Why don't we hang out for a while," Aaron insisted. *I know, right?*

"You can come back if you want, I just need a ride back to my car."

"All right, then, let's roll," Aaron said. I walked up to Will and hugged him goodbye.

"Bye, Billy, call me this weekend," I said.

"All right, see you later, see ya Jessica," Will said.

"Bye! Aaron, are you coming back?" Jessica asked.

"...Yeah, I'll come back, where are you gonna be?" Aaron asked.

"I don't know, Hannah...Victoria's Secret?" Jessica asked. *Sure...*

"All right, I'll see you later," Aaron said. Will and I waved goodbye to each other and they turned to walk away.

"Let's go," Will said to Aaron. Jessica and I watched them walk outside of the mall towards the parking garage. Jessica turned to me and smiled.

"You were right, Aaron's cute."

"I told you...Hey, thanks for having my back...You're a good friend..."

"No problem...So, do you think Will is going to ever get over it?"

"Yeah, I'm not worried about it...I think it worked, thanks to you..."

"Anytime...I still can't believe it worked. He didn't question any of it..."

"See Jessica, you're learning..."

"...Learning what?" I laughed.

"...Come on, we have a date with Victoria's Secret, right?"

"Yeah, let's go." Jessica and I hung out in Victoria's secret and waited for Aaron to come back. We were looking through the swimsuits when Aaron approached us from the back.

"Hey," Aaron said. Jessica and I turned around.

"Hey," I said, "is Will mad at me?"

"I don't think he's happy." *Yeah...*

"I'll have to make it up to him..."

"...I should probably get home," Aaron said. "Jessica, I was wondering if I could get your number..." Jessica smiled. *Ahhh. I'm happy for her...*

"Yeah...Ummm, do you have any paper?" Jessica said and we laughed hysterically while Aaron looked at us as if we were deranged.

"I don't get it..."

"...It's nothing, Aaron, it's just been a long day," I said.

"I don't have any paper but..." Aaron started to say. Jessica and I both controlled our laughter long enough for him to finish his thought. "...I have a really good memory. Just tell me and I'll remember..." *Really? That's pretty smooth...* Jessica told Aaron her number and then Aaron repeated it to her. *Nice...* "I'll give you a call tomorrow."

"Okay, cool," Jessica said.

"All right, see ya...See ya Hannah," Aaron said.

"Bye."

"...Drive safe," Jessica added. *Come on, Jessica...*

"I will, see ya," Aaron said, turned around, and walked out of the store.

"Jessica!" I said and she smiled.

"What!?"

"I told you so..."

The next day, Jessica called me in the early afternoon.

"Hannah?" Jessica asked.

"Yeah, it's me, Jessica, what's up? Did Aaron call you?"

"He called me and he asked me out!" *Wow, that was fast...Way to go Aaron...*

"That's awesome, Jessica, I'm so happy for you!" *Why do I feel so sad?*

"...Thanks, Hannah...I know it wouldn't have happened without you."

"Don't mention it..."

"...I'm so happy! I finally have a boyfriend!" I smiled.

"I'm glad I could help..."

"...If you ever need anything, don't hesitate to ask."

"I won't. You know me..." I laughed under my breath.

"Yeah...Okay, I'm gonna call Aaron back...I just wanted to tell you...And thank you."

"Okay...Call me later."

"All right, bye Hannah," Jessica said with jubilance in her voice.

"Bye," I said and hung up the phone. *Why do I feel this way? What is wrong with me?* About an hour later, Will called me.

"Hey, babe," Will said.

"Hey, Billy, so did you decide what you were going to do this summer?" I asked. *Please don't go...*

"...Yeah, I'm going. I got the time off of work." *Shit...*

"...I was kind of hoping that you would decide to stay." *I don't want you to go...*

"...Hannah, you told me I should go!" *I'm crazy...*

"Yeah, but I changed my mind. I would miss you too much. Jessica and Aaron are together now, and I don't know...I don't want to be their third wheel." *I don't want to be alone...*

"It's too late, I already put in for my time off and I'm going to take it." *This is all my fault! Ugh!*

"So you can hook up with other babes in Camarillo?" *That stupid Rebecca girl...*

"...I'm not going to hook up with anyone else. I'm gonna hang out with my friend and that's it. I don't get you. Have I ever given you a reason to not trust me?" *I don't believe you...*

"No, but I'm just worried that you'll find someone better."

"There is no one better!"

"I don't want you to go." *Please don't go...*

"...I'm going," Will said and I started crying.

"I didn't mean what I said about you hooking up with other girls..." My voice cracked. "I guess I just have to deal with the fact that you're going to do whatever you want, whenever you want to, and I can't stop you." *And you can't stop me...Ugh...*

"I told you that it was a bad idea for me to go and yet you insisted..." *I don't know what's wrong with me...*

"I know, I'm sorry...I was wrong."

"It's too late for all that," Will insisted.

"I guess I just need to be happier about life...Life goes on, right?" *Maybe it's just not meant to be...*

"Look, babe, it'll be fine. I'll call you every day and I'll be back before you know it." *I don't know...*

"I know it's only two weeks, but it's going to feel like two years," I reasoned. *Was I wrong about this?*

"It's going to go by so fast that..."

"...Just promise me that your butt will think about me the whole time, well not your butt exactly, your dick...And get me something wherever you go..." *I don't know...*

"You mean like a t-shirt or something?"

"Surprise me."

"Okay, yeah, I can get you something." *Wait...Maybe...*

"...Do you think we could get together before you leave so I could say goodbye to you?"

"Ummm, yeah, you mean like sneak out?"

"Yeah, you could come pick me up at like, midnight."

"Do you think that's a good idea? Isn't your dad gonna be home?"

"I don't care. I have to see you."

"Okay, I'll be there Tuesday night. Brad will be with me though, so..."

"It's okay, I just want to say bye," I whimpered.

Tuesday night, I was feeling as stressed as I had felt since losing Melissa so I got into the cupboard where my dad kept the alcohol. I took out a bottle of vodka and stealthily returned to my room. *I don't even care...* I opened the bottle and drank until I couldn't feel my throat. *Fuck it...* I put on my cut-off shorts and a halter top, grabbed the bottle of vodka, and escaped from my room. I walked away from my house and made my way down the street. I stopped on the corner and then took another drink. After a few minutes, Will and his friend, Brad, walked up to me. I gave Will a hug as soon as he got close enough. *I'm so sorry, Billy...* He pulled back away from me and introduced me to Brad.

"Hannah, Brad, Brad, Hannah..."

"Hi," I said and smiled.

"Hey," Brad said. Will looked at the bottle of vodka in my hand.

"Whose vodka is that?" Will asked.

"My dad's...Hey, can we go somewhere?"

"We can't stay long...We have to leave early," Will said.

"Please, Billy, can we maybe go back to your place?" Will looked at Brad.

"I guess so, I mean, my brother's not home, but my mom is...We'll have to be really quiet."

"Okay, I can be quiet," I whispered.

"All right, let's go, but lose the vodka first...Why are you even drinking?" Will asked.

"I don't know..." I said and set the vodka down in my neighbor's bushes. I went back over to Will and held his hand. We walked towards Will's car with Brad following us.

"Babe, you should sit in the back," Will said and held my hand as he helped me into the back of his car. Brad got in and then Will started his car. *Shit...*

"Damn, Billy, I hope that my parents don't wake up," I said and laughed.

"Babe, how much did you drink?"

"I don't know...A lot..." I said and laughed again. "I'm fine though...Let's go." Will shook his head and then drove us to his apartment. When we got there, Will helped me out of the car and then helped me walk upstairs. *I feel pretty good...* Once inside Brad sat down on the couch and said,

"Is this where I'm sleeping?"

"Yeah, there's pillows and blankets on the chair over there."

"I don't think I'll need blankets, but thanks." I went to Will's room and he followed me. He shut the door behind us and then sat down on his bed next to me.

"Babe, what's wrong? You're drinking and you don't seem to care if your parents catch you..." *Shit...* I didn't say anything. I quickly pulled off my shirt and undid my bra. Will got up and turned off the light and then sat down next to me once again. He moved my hair away from my face and then started kissing me. I closed my eyes and drifted away. After we had sex, I rested my head on his chest and whispered,

"I hope I didn't wake your mom up."

"No, you were really good, with the help of the pillow that is...Are you going to tell me what's going on with you?" *I don't know, Billy...*

"I'm not mad. I just keep thinking about how much I'll miss you. I just feel that you'll have so much fun without me or that you're trying to get away from me. I know you're really looking forward to going away and I'm trying to be cool about it...But, it's hard." Will hugged me tight.

"Babe, it's two weeks...And I'll be thinking about you the whole time..." *I don't know...*

"I know, Billy, I love you, I'm just going to miss you so much. I wish I could be the one going on vacation with you. I think I'm jealous of your friend..."

"We'll go away together soon, I promise."

"You mean when I'm eighteen?"

"Yeah...It seems like a long time from now...I should probably take you home. I need to get some sleep before we leave tomorrow." I got dressed and then Will took me back home. I retrieved my dad's bottle of vodka and then snuck back into my room. I quietly opened my bedroom door and carefully put the bottle back. I went back to my room and closed the door. I looked at myself in my mirror which was only lit by the trace amount of moonlight filtering into my room. *I can't believe he's actually going...Ugh...*

I got out of the shower the next morning and I heard the phone ringing. I wrapped my towel around myself and went to my bedroom to answer it.

"Hannah?"

"Hey, Billy, are you in Camarillo?"

"Yeah, we just got here, and calling you was the first thing on my mind."

"That's so sweet, Billy, but you should really focus on having fun with your friend..." *Heh...* "...Don't you think you're being rude to your friend?"

"I guess so, but you're more important..."

"Don't worry about me, I'll be fine..."

"I don't understand...Last night you..."

"...I know, but I was thinking...And I'm just being selfish."

"What's wrong with that? I love you. We shouldn't be apart."

"I love you too, but it's not fair of me to ask you to put your life on hold for me especially when you've been friends with Brad forever."

"Okay...I guess you're right..."

"I am...Now go have some fun with your friend."

"Okay, babe, I'll try. I'm going to be thinking about you the whole time."

"Me too, but it'll be good. Absence makes the heart grow fonder, right?"

"Huh?"

"Nothing...It's just something my mom used to say."

"Okay, I guess I'll call you later..."

"Yeah, call me later...You don't have to call me every day, though. Try to have some fun." *And so will I...*

"Okay, bye, babe, talk to you soon."

"Bye, Billy, have fun!" I said and then hung up the phone.

The following weekend, Jessica called me and told me that she was going to meet Aaron at the mall and asked if I wanted her to pick me up. I said yes, and as soon as I got off the phone with her, I rummaged through my dirty pants on the floor and eventually found the napkin with Keith's number on it. I dialed his number.

"Hello?"

"Is Keith there?" I asked.

"Yeah, it's me, who's this?"

"It's Hannah, from the mall..."

"Hannah from the mall?" *Shit....So embarrassing...*

"...Remember, you wrote your number on a napkin...You said you had a class with Jessica..."

"Oh yeah...Pretty blond girl...What's up?"

"Will you meet me at the mall right now?"

"...Like right now, right now?"

"Yeah..."

"...Sure, where?"

"Meet me at JC Penny's." *Heh...*

"Okay, I'll see you there."

"Okay, bye."

"Bye," Keith said and I hung up the phone. Jessica picked me up thirty minutes later. On the way to the mall, I turned to Jessica.

"Okay, don't freak out on me..."

"What are you talking about?"

"Keith is meeting me at the mall..."

"Hannah! What are you doing!?"

"...I'm getting back at Billy..."

"He cheated on you!?"

"Probably...There's this girl, I think, in Camarillo, you know, where he went on vacation? Her name's Rebecca..."

"Rebecca?"

"Yeah, and I think he's gonna hook up with her again."

"But how do you know?"

"I don't. I just have a feeling..."

"Hannah, I don't know...This kind of goes beyond trying to make him jealous."

"I know what I'm doing, Jessica...When we get there...He's meeting me in your favorite place..."

"My favorite place?"

"JC Penny's..."

"Oh...Yeah..."

"...I'm going to kiss him..."

"Hannah!"

"And I want Aaron to see it..."

"Hannah! They're best friends!"

"...And then I want you to tell Aaron to not tell Billy, which will make him tell..."

"Are you sure about this?"

"...Yeah, why?"

"...It could go terribly wrong, that's why!"

"Don't worry..." I assured her. Jessica and I got to the mall and I met Keith in JC Penny's like I planned. I walked up to him and kissed him. I didn't give him a chance to talk. Jessica met Aaron in the food court. I told her to make it seem like an accident when she happened upon Keith and I making out. It worked. Aaron and Jessica saw us. Aaron looked horrified. I stared at them for a few seconds and then went back to kissing Keith. After a couple of minutes, I stopped kissing him and got off of his lap. "I have to go, Keith."

"We practically just got here...Where are you going?" *Heh...*

"I told you; I have a boyfriend..."

"What the fuck! So, you're just going to blue-ball me and go run off to your boyfriend?"

"...Sorry," I said and walked away.

"Fucking shit!" Keith said. "Are you going to call me?" I smiled, but didn't say anything. I kept walking and met Jessica at the food court.

"What happened to Aaron?" I asked.

"He left...I don't think he knew what to say...What did Keith say?"

"He wasn't happy..."

"...I hope you know what you're doing, Hannah."

"Me too..."

The next few days went by quickly. The phone rang and my mom picked it up.

"Hello?" My mom asked... "Yes, she is, hold on, is this Will?" My mom looked over at me. "Okay, hold on...Hannah, it's Will, make it fast."

"Hey, Billy, are you back from your vacation?" I asked while walking to my room.

"Yeah, I am...Is there something you wanna tell me!?" *Heh*...

"...So, Aaron told you..."

"Told me what?"

"That I hooked up with another guy while you were gone."

"Keith?"

"Yeah..."

"Who the hell is Keith?" *Don't be mad, Billy*...

"...He's a senior at Redwood. I met him at the mall and Jessica knew him from school."

"Wow, Hannah, you don't even sound like you're sorry. You cheated on me and you don't even care..." *Like you didn't! Hmmm*...

"...I do care. I made a mistake. We just kissed. That's not cheating."

"So, you're not breaking up with me?" *Perfect*...

"...No, I love you; I just made a stupid mistake. I don't even like Keith."

"Then why would you?"

"I just really missed you. I don't know why I did it, but I did, and now it's over."

"Babe, I don't want to lose you...You're the best thing to ever happen to me. I told you that I shouldn't have gone away."

"You're not going to lose me...I thought I was doing the right thing by encouraging you to go away, but I was wrong. I was just lying to myself."

"I knew it. Why didn't you just trust me? I knew you didn't want me to go."

"Yeah, I know, I'm sorry."

"And we need to talk about this kissing thing...That is so cheating..." *Why does this so sound familiar? Shit....Joe*...

"Okay, so we never talked about that before...It won't happen again...So are we good, or are you just gonna be mad at me forever?"

"No, we're good; I couldn't stay mad at you."

"I'll be honest with you from now on....I don't want you to leave me again."

"Thank you, was that so hard?"

"Actually...Yes, yes it was," I said and we both laughed.

"I'll be honest with you too...It pisses me off even thinking about you with another guy. And Keith...I guess if you didn't have sex with him or anything I'll get over it."

"I didn't have sex with Keith."

"All right, I won't mention him again."

"Thank you, Billy, I love you, you're so understanding..." *You won't ever leave me again...*

"...I love you too, Hannah."

Chapter Twenty

Ambivalence

"Hey, Billy," I said. "Do you want to go to the Weezer show this weekend?"

"Yeah, I'm down...Your parents are cool with it?"

"I'm gonna spend the night at Jessica's. I'm not even going to ask them."

"Oh, all right then, I'll see if Aaron wants to go..."

"...He does. Jessica already asked him."

"Am I the last one to know or what?" Will asked and I laughed.

"Babe, he was there when I was talking to Jessica about it..."

"When was this?"

"Last week...I was at Jessica's and Aaron came over to see her."

"Where was I?" *Dude, really?*

"You were at work."

"Yeah...That sounds about right..." *You're always at work...* "When's the show?"

"Sunday night."

"I guess I could get someone to cover for me." *Who cares about your stupid job!*

"Yeah, Billy, get someone to cover for you...It's going to be really fun!"

"Should I get the tickets now?" *Yes...Ugh!*

"Yeah, you should go with Aaron."

"All right, I'll talk to him at lunch...I guess we could go after school. It's at the convention center, right?"

"...I think so..." I smiled and then held Will's hand. "So, are you going to walk me to class or what?"

"Yeah...Have you seen Rob?"

"No, why?" Will and I started walking to my first class.

"I need to cancel practice on Sunday."

"Oh, do you think he would want to go to the show?" Will laughed.

"Babe, Rob hates Weezer."

"Why?"

"Honestly, I think he hates everyone that's not Nirvana...He's just now starting to warm up to the Foo Fighters and they're one-third of Nirvana!"

"That's too bad..."

"...Yeah, well, I'm not trying to change him," Will said and then pointed to an ASB poster on the wall. "That's crazy..."

"What's crazy, babe?" I asked.

"It's almost Halloween...Time goes by so fast..."

"Yeah...It's unreal."

Sunday afternoon, Jessica picked me up from my house and drove us back to her house. We waited an hour for Will and Aaron to show up and then we met them outside. I hugged Will and Jessica hugged Aaron. Will was wearing a Tool t-shirt and his signature baggy black jeans. Aaron was wearing a Metallica t-shirt with much more conservative khaki cargo pants. *That looks strange...* Will smiled and looked at me curiously.

"Babe," Will said. "Can I talk to you alone for a minute?"

"Sure, Billy, what's up?" Will put his hand on my back and led me to the edge of Jessica's garage.

"Are you wearing a bra?" *Heh.*

"No," I said and smiled. "How'd you guess?"

"I can see your nipples..." I looked down and then laughed. "...Everyone else can see them too..." *And...*

"They're just boobs, Billy..." Will looked back at Aaron and Jessica and then faced me.

"I can't see Jessica's tits..." I smiled and caught myself before laughing. "What's funny, babe?" *Jessica doesn't have boobs...Well...* "It's obvious that she's wearing a bra..." *Oh, Billy...*

"Do you want to see Jessica's tits?"

"What! No, that's not what..."

"...Because I'm sure she'll show you if you ask..." *Not even if she were blackout drunk...*

"...I'm not going to ask Jessica to show me her tits," Will whispered. *It would be funny if you did...*

"Ahhh, why not?"

"...Look, Hannah, there's gonna be a lot of people at the show and I really don't want everyone staring at my girlfriend's tits all night..." *He really thinks a bra is going to stop that...*

"Billy, you're so cute..."

"Wait, what!?" I walked past Will and rejoined Aaron and Jessica on the other side of the garage.

"Everything okay over there?" Jessica asked.

"I'll tell you later," I said and smiled. Will walked up to us and shrugged his shoulders at Aaron. *Hmmm...*

"You guys wanna get food before we go?" Aaron asked.

"Yeah," Will said. "We were thinking about getting some Checker burger."

"That sounds good," I said.

"Yeah, sure," Jessica added.

"Now for the million-dollar question..." Will said. *This should be good...* "Whose car are we taking?" *Oh...* "We have Aaron's super-awesome VW Bug with ten-inch subs in the back...Or, we have Jessica's grandma's Buick..." Will and Aaron started laughing and I smiled. Jessica was not amused.

"Hey! It's my mom's car, not my grandma's! It's a really good car!" Jessica pleaded. "Hannah!"

"What do you want me to say," I said. "...Okay..." I gave Will and Aaron a stern look. "...Stop being mean to Jessica."

"We're not being mean. It's just a joke..." Will said. Jessica pouted and Aaron hugged her. *She is so sensitive...*

"It's a great car," Aaron said.

"It is the ultimate utilitarian appliance..." Will said. *Nice, Billy, but...*

"...I vote to take the Buick," I said.

"Me too," Aaron followed.

"Well, I guess that's settled then...Will!" Jessica snapped.

"Fine...I don't care that much..." Will answered back.

"Good," Jessica said. "...But I don't really want to drive..."

"Oh, for fucks sake," Will said. *Yeah...*

"It's going to be really busy down there...And I'm already a really nervous driver..."

"Seriously?" Will asked. "So, what do you want to do, Jessica?"

"...I still want to take the Buick, but, Aaron, do you think you could drive?"

"Yeah, of course," Aaron said.

"All right, let's get out of here, I'm getting hungry," Will said and put his hand around my waist. *Hungry for what, Billy?* Jessica handed the keys to Aaron, Will and I got in the back seat, and we started on our way downtown.

After we ate our burgers at Checker's, Aaron drove us to the convention center. He parked the car and we made our way over to the line of people waiting to get into the show.

"When did they start lining up?" Will asked.

"If I were to guess, I would say sometime around dawn," Aaron answered.

"Yeah...Shit," Will said.

"It's okay," Jessica offered. "It's not often that a good band comes to Visalia..."

"Yeah, that's true," Will agreed. *Wow, they actually agree about something.* Jessica and Aaron led the way to the end of the line and we stood behind them. Will put his arm around me and rested his hand on my hip. Not even a minute later, I heard two snickering voices from behind us.

"Check it out, man, lesbians..." One of them said. *What the hell!?* I turned around and Will followed my lead. We saw two college-aged guys wearing matching Weezer t-shirts. Their smiles quickly turned sour when they saw Will's face.

"Oh, shit! Sorry, man," one of the guys said. "...I thought you were a chick!"

"...No worries," Will said and started to turn back around. *What do you mean no worries!?*

"What's your problem?" I asked.

"Babe, don't make this a thing..." Will reasoned.

"No, Billy, I wanna know what their problem is?" Aaron and Jessica turned around.

"Hannah! What are you doing?" Jessica asked.

"Look, we made a mistake, get over it..." The first guy said.

"Yeah, maybe your boyfriend should get a haircut or something..." His friend added. Will looked at me and then shook his head. *Aren't you going to say something?*

"...He doesn't need a haircut," I said. "Maybe you guys shouldn't be so homophobic." They started laughing.

"I think she's pissed that you said the L word, Henry."

"What? Lesbian?" Henry asked.

"Yeah, lesbian," Henry's friend replied. "She's probably pissed because she is a lesbian..."

"Babe, don't..." Will said. *Seriously!?*

"That makes sense..." Henry asserted and pointed at Will. "She's with this dude with long hair."

"Yeah, that's it, closet lesbian for sure," Henry's friend said. *What the fuck!* I looked at Will. *Say something!*

"Babe, they're just trying to make you mad," Will said. "It's not that big of a deal." *It is too!*

"That's right," Henry's friend said. "Listen to your girlfriend." Will smiled sarcastically and started to turn around again. Henry looked down at my chest.

"Nice tits, by the way..." *Hit him, Billy!* Will looked at my chest and shook his head. *Really!? You're going to let him get away with that?* I slowly turned around and looked at Jessica. Jessica shook her head at me just like Will. *Really!? Am I in the wrong here? Unbelievable...* The line started moving forward after a few minutes. Aaron looked back at Will.

"I think they're letting people in now..." Aaron said. *Good. I can finally get away from these assholes! I can't believe Billy didn't do anything...I guess he's just being smart, but...Still.* We approached the front gate and security divided us up between men and women for the pat down. I could hear Henry and his friend laughing as Jessica and I moved into the other line. *Fuck!* Jessica gave me a concerned look.

"Hannah!" Jessica said. I rolled my eyes and looked away from her. The security woman waved the metal detector around my body and then passed me off to a second woman who patted me down.

"You're good," the woman said. She did the same to Jessica and we rejoined the boys at the door to the convention center. We slowly shuffled through the entrance and gave the event staff our tickets.

"We're in," Will said. "Babe, come here." Will walked me over to the merchandise stand where all of the Weezer shirts were set up. "Pick a shirt..." *Hmmm...*

"...Any shirt..." *Heh...I know...* I pointed at a pretty blue Weezer shirt with the members of the band on the front. It was the same design that Henry and his friend were wearing.

"I want that one," I insisted.

"Are you sure?" Will wavered.

"Yes, it's the nicest one..." I reasoned. *And every time I wear it, you're going to remember...*

"...But don't you think you should get one that has the tour dates on it?" *I don't care...*

"It does have the tour dates on the back," the man at the table said. *Perfect...*

"See, it has the tour dates..."

"...Okay," Will said and handed the man a twenty-dollar bill. The man handed me the shirt and I folded it over my arm.

"Thank you," I said and started to walk away from the table. Will pulled on my arm.

"Babe, aren't you going to put it on?" *I see why you bought me a shirt...*

"...Right now?" I asked.

"Yeah, that's kind of the point of a band t-shirt..." *Right...* "...And if you put it on then you won't lose it." *That's a good point. Damn! Fine, Billy...* I pulled the shirt on over my head and Will smiled.

"It looks great on you."

"It's too big." I looked down at the shirt puddling around the middle of my thighs.

"I think that's the smallest one they have..." *Yeah...* I pulled the shirt up to my waist and then tied it in the back.

"There, I think that'll work," I said and smiled. *At least I have my waistline back.*

"Do you really need to do that?"

"Billy, I have a twenty-two-inch waist and I'm not going to hide it." *Ugh...Seriously!*

"I'm not asking you to hide it...Never mind, forget I said anything about it..." *Good...*

"Let's go find Aaron and Jessica before the show starts...This is going to be so much fun," I said.

"Yeah, let's go inside," Will said and put his hand on my lower back, cupping the knot I had made in my shirt. *Heh...* Will and I walked into the auditorium and watched people gathering at the front of the stage.

"Do you think they're at the stage?" I asked and Will laughed.

"I doubt it...Knowing Jessica, she probably has Aaron at one of those tables in the back, safely away from other humans," Will answered.

"Yeah...Let's go check the tables..." Will and I walked over to the furthest table from the stage and saw Jessica and Aaron holding hands. *Ahhh, how sweet...I remember when I felt that way.*

"Hey, man, you wanna get closer to the stage?" Will asked Aaron.

"Nah, I'm gonna stay here with Jessica," Aaron responded.

"Are you sure?" Will asked. "I don't even think you'll be able to see the band from here."

"We're fine Will, thank you," Jessica added and I smiled at Will.

"She told you," I said. "...Don't worry, I'll go with you, Billy."

"Well, yeah, I expected you to want to be front and center, babe."

"What's that supposed to mean?" *Hmmm...Be careful...*

"...I didn't mean anything by it..." *Right...* "...We're just a lot alike and I figured you would want to be close to the band." *Yeah, okay...Nice save, Billy.* I grabbed Will's hand and pulled him close to me.

"Have fun!" Jessica said and turned her attention back to Aaron. Will and I walked up to the crowd and then slowly wormed our way to within a few feet of the stage. I turned to Will and smiled.

"Aaron and Jessica seem really happy..."

"...Yeah, they do..."

"Remember when we were like that, Billy?"

"...We're still like that, babe..."

"...Yeah, but you know what I mean..."

"...No, I have no idea."

"You know, like, inseparable..." Will squinted his eyes and then put his arm around me.

"Babe, I always want to be with you..." *You don't get it...* I smiled and looked back to the stage. The pop music they were playing faded away and the lights went out. The crowd started screaming. Will and I did the same. The opening act was a band called Superdrag. They weren't very popular, but they did have one song that MTV played a lot called 'Sucked Out,' that I related to. It was also the song that the band started with. I, along with the rest of the crowd, sang along to the chorus. Everyone knew the words. I was having a great time. I looked over at Will and smiled as his hair thrashed around wildly. At the end of 'Sucked Out,' everyone cheered. Superdrag then started playing a song that one had ever heard before and the crowd at the front of the stage thinned out. I wrapped my hands around Will's ear and he stopped moving.

"Do you want to go back to Jessica and Aaron!?" I yelled. Will looked at me and nodded. I grabbed his hand and we worked our way back to the table. Aaron and Jessica were still sitting exactly as they were before Superdrag came out.

"You guys should come out to the stage," I said. "There aren't many people there now." Aaron looked at Jessica. "Come on guys...Before Weezer comes out!"

"I'll go if you come with me," Aaron said.

"Okay," Jessica agreed.

"I see how it is..." Will said and I laughed.

"She's just more persuasive than you, Will..." Jessica added.

"...Yeah, that must be it," Will responded. I pulled on Will's hand and then dragged him back to the stage. Jessica and Aaron followed us. The area in front of the stage was so barren that we were almost able to put our hands on the stage itself. If it weren't for the security gate in front of us, we would have been able to touch the band's feet. We listened to the rest of their set, which was only about twenty minutes, and then waited for Weezer to come out. The crowd started filling back in and pushed us into the gate. I looked behind me and all I could see were a sea of nameless faces. *I don't think we're getting back out of here...* I looked over at Jessica. She didn't look happy. *Sorry, Jessica.* I held Will's hand tight. About ten minutes later, Rivers Cuomo ran out to the microphone.

"I want everyone to give it up for Superdrag!" Rivers said. We all clapped and yelled as loud as we could. "Visalia! Give it up for yourself!" Everyone cheered. "This is the third time we've played here and it won't be the last!" The cheering continued and the rest of the band came out. They started playing their first song, which I had never heard before, but everyone, including Will, seemed to know. It wasn't until their third song, 'Jonas,' that I started getting into it. I knew that song and was able to sing along. After a few more songs, I started getting hot and felt my shirt sticking to my skin. *This was not a good idea...* One song after another, I felt worse and worse. "Thank you, Visalia! This is our last song...It's called Buddy Holly!" *Oh, finally! I know this song...* After they finished playing 'Buddy Holly,' The band started waving and walking off stage. *Thank God...Let's go...* The crowd started shouting 'one more, one more, one more,' over and over again. *Oh, come on...* No one moved. Everyone chanted. Weezer came back on stage and played a song I didn't know. After the song, Rivers stepped back up to the microphone. "Thanks, Visalia, see ya next time." Rivers walked off stage and the crowd cheered and then dispersed.

"Billy," I said. "I need some water."

"Okay...Aaron, you wanna go to Denny's?"

"Yeah, sure...Jessica?"

"It's okay with me..." Jessica said. We walked outside of the convention center and then walked to the car. I held Will's hand as tight as I could.

"Babe, are you okay? You look like you're going to pass out."

"I'm fine..." *I think...*

"All right...Babe, we're going to Denny's. I'll get you some water there."

"Okay," I said and got in the car. Aaron drove us to Denny's. After we were seated, I immediately started drinking the water that was brought to our table. I turned the glass upside down until the ice met my lips.

"Damn," Will said. "I guess you were thirsty."

"Yeah...I feel a little better now."

"That was a pretty good show," Aaron said.

"Yeah, it was, but I think we could have opened for them," Will said. "Superdrag was okay, but I think we're better." *What are you talking about?*

"I think Superdrag was better than Weezer," I insisted.

"...That's blasphemy, babe," Will replied and we all laughed. I started feeling better. Will and Aaron each ordered an appetizer sampler for us to share. We ate fried mozzarella sticks and chicken and talked about the show. Will and Aaron boasted about how they were better musicians than the people we saw. Jessica and I just smiled and agreed with their assertions. When the food was gone, Aaron drove us back to Jessica's house. I got out of the car and Will walked over to hug me.

"That was fun," Jessica said.

"Yeah, it was," I agreed. I kissed Will goodbye and Jessica kissed Aaron. Will and Aaron walked to Aaron's car and then drove away. I looked at Jessica. Her smile was as bright as I had ever seen.

"...Thanks, Hannah," Jessica said. "I really like him."

"You're welcome...I'm happy for you," I said as she opened the door to her house. We walked down the hallway to her room and fell on top of her bed. She wrapped her arms around me as we slowly went to sleep.

"Hey, babe..." Will said. "...It's Valentine's Day tomorrow..." *Yes, Billy, I know...* "...Aaron wants to take Jessica to Rosa's tomorrow night...Do you wanna go?"

"Rosa's?"

"Yeah. Rosa's Italian Ristorante."

"I've never been there."

"I've been there once and it was the best Italian food I've ever had. They have ridiculously good lasagna."

"Sounds good...Sure, I'll stay over at Jessica's."

"Awesome! Aaron already made the reservations..."

"...Wait. What if I would have said no?" *Just assumed I was going to say yes...*

"...I guess I would have had to go with someone else," Will said and laughed." *That's funny!?*

"What!? I can't believe you just said that..."

"Babe, it was a joke...I would never go without you..." I crossed my arms and looked away from him. *Yeah, right...* "I hope you know that..."

"Just like Camarillo, right Billy?" I looked back at him and he rolled his eyes at me and took a deep breath.

"...That was the past," Will said and forced a smile. "I thought we had moved on from..."

"...I'm sorry, I shouldn't have said that...I just worry sometimes..."

"About what, babe?"

"You know...About you finding someone better..." Will took another deep breath and I could see the frustration in his eyes. *What are you going to say?*

"...Hannah, seriously!?" *Heh...* "It's not like I have twenty girls lining up to be with me... *I know you have at least one...*

"...And what's that supposed to mean?"

"...It just means, and I can't figure this out at all, that you still don't know how beautiful you are..." *Ahhh, that's so sweet, Billy!*

"Thanks, Billy," I said and kissed him.

"So, we're good for tomorrow night?"

"Yeah...I need to call Jessica."

"We can talk to Aaron about it at lunch..."

"Okay...I should probably go to class..."

"I'll walk you there..."

"...You really don't have to..."

"Babe, I want to. Besides, it's on the way to my class."

"...All right." *I really don't want you to...*

I waited for Jessica to pick me up from school the next day to spend the night at her house. I stood on the street in the front of the school and watched all of the cars drive by. After twenty minutes, Jessica pulled up to, and hit the curb in front of me. I started laughing and got in the car.

"Sorry I'm late..." Jessica said. "...The traffic around Redwood is a really bad joke."

"It's okay, Jessica, I'm more worried about your mom's car," I said while continuing to laugh.

"...It's fine," Jessica asserted and started driving us to her house. So, what did Will get you for Valentine's Day?"

"A really big card and some chocolates. What did Aaron get you?"

"He sent two-dozen roses to my homeroom class...It was so embarrassing!" ...*Wow, I think I'm jealous...*

"Embarrassing? What do you mean? That's so romantic!"

"...Yeah, it is," Jessica said and smiled. *Yeah, I'm jealous...*

"Do you think that Billy and Aaron talk about this stuff?"

"I'm sure they do, why?" *Hmmm...*

"I don't know, Jessica, it's like Billy doesn't even try anymore..."

"...You should talk to him about it."

"I know..."

"He is taking you to a nice restaurant tonight..."

"Only because Aaron's taking you...I honestly don't think he even likes me anymore..."

"Oh no, Hannah, not this again..."

"What? That's how I feel..."

"Just talk to him...He's not going to know how you feel if you don't tell him."

"I know, Jessica, you're right...It's just hard. I don't know how to explain it."

"Just promise me that you won't do anything crazy like last time..." *Hmmm...*

"I promise," I said and Jessica turned on the radio. *It wasn't crazy though...*

Jessica and I got ready for our Valentine's date with Aaron and Will and then met them at Rosa's around six O' clock. Aaron and Will were leaning against Aaron's car as we pulled into the parking lot. Jessica parked the car in an open spot a few spaces away. We got out and the boys were waiting for us.

"Nice parking job, Jessica," Will said. Jessica looked back at her car.

"Hey! I'm in between the lines!" Jessica pleaded. Will and Aaron laughed.

"Barely," Will said. "I guess the driver's education at Redwood isn't quite at the level of Whitney..."

"What are you even talking about?" Jessica asked.

"Well..." Will said and pointed at Aaron's car. "Look at Aaron's parking job. It's perfect."

"Billy," I said. "His car is half the size of Jessica's..." Will laughed.

"Aaron, you need to teach your girlfriend how to park," Will said and Aaron smiled.

"I will if she wants me to," Aaron responded. Will and Aaron looked at Jessica and waited.

"...Fine, now can we go inside?" Jessica answered.

"Yeah, let's go," Will said. We started walking to the entrance of the restaurant.

"Billy, why do you always have to pick on her?" I whispered. "You know she's sensitive."

"I don't know, it's funny I guess," Will whispered back but Jessica heard him.

"It's not funny, Will!" Jessica exclaimed and Will smiled. We walked inside and we're seated immediately. There were only a few people there.

"I guess we're early," Aaron said.

"More like right on time," Will insisted. The waitress brought out the menus and water and placed them on the table. "I won't be needing a menu; I'll take the lasagna." *Don't be a jerk, Billy!* She took the menu and then looked around the table.

"We're going to need a few minutes," Aaron said and the waitress walked away.

"What are you going to get?" Jessica asked Aaron.

"I think I'm going with the chicken parmesan."

"Okay, I'll get the same," Jessica said and smiled.

"I guess I'll just get spaghetti," I said. The waitress came back after a couple of minutes and we ordered our food and specialty sodas. She brought back our sodas and we all took a sip from the thin, dainty straws they provided. *Pretty good...*

"So, the counselors came into our English class today," Will said.

"Yeah, they talked about how we needed to start planning for college right now..." Aaron added. *Oh no....* I looked around the table as Will, Aaron, and Jessica all laughed. *Oh my God...I'm going to be all alone...*

"Right Now! Mrs. Mortenson is crazy, man....She's like the college feminazi," Will said.

"You guys haven't thought about college?" Jessica asked.

"Nope," Will said.

"What about you, Aaron?"

"Yeah, I'll probably go to San Jose State like my parents." I looked down at my soda and stared at the little red straws. *It's like I'm not even here...*

"I was thinking that I would go to COS first and then transfer once I figure out where I want to go..." Jessica said. Will and Aaron looked at each other and smiled.

"Mrs. Mortenson!" They said at the same time and laughed.

"She made a big deal about not going to COS," Will said.

"Or any community college," Aaron added.

"She said it's like an extension of high school and that people never actually transfer," Will said. *I think I'm invisible...*

"She called it 'the ten-year plan' and that most people end up stuck there for more than that..." Aaron added.

"...That's not going to be me," Jessica insisted. "...Hannah, you haven't said anything...What do you think?" *I don't feel well...*

"...I haven't thought about it," I said. "I think I'm too young to be thinking about that..."

"That's right," Aaron said. "You just turned sixteen, right?"

"...Yeah, last month."

"Are you going to get your license?" Aaron asked. *Oh, yeah, wow...*

"Maybe, but I don't really need a license..." *Shit, maybe I do...*

"Yeah, but it's cool to have one..." Will said.

"My parents aren't like Jessica's parents...They won't let me go anywhere anyway," I argued.

"...Yeah," Will agreed. The waitress brought our food out and set it down on the table. *That was fast...* We started eating our food with only passing comments about its quality. When we were finished, Aaron and Will paid the bill and we walked outside.

"So, my mom is on a date with her boyfriend," Aaron said. "You guys want to come over to my house and chill?" Jessica looked at me as if she were deferring the decision to me.

"Sure, why not," I said.

"Okay, cool, we'll see you over there," Aaron said and walked with Will to his car. Jessica and I got in her car and she quickly turned to me.

"Okay, Hannah, what's wrong? And don't tell me it's nothing because I know that something's wrong...You hardly said anything at dinner..." *Everything...*

"I'm just in my head again..."

"Care to elaborate?"

"...All this talk about college..."

"...Yeah..."

"...I'm going to be alone my senior year...And I just realized that..."

"You're not going to be alone..."

"How am I not going to be alone? You're all a year older than me..." Jessica didn't say anything and started the car. "Exactly..." She started driving and after a couple of minutes said,

"It's so far away, though..."

"It really isn't, Jessica..." I asserted. The silence in the car became awkward so Jessica turned on the radio. I looked out of the passenger side window and watched Visalia go by on our way to Aaron's house. Jessica pulled into his driveway and parked behind his car. We got out and started walking to Aaron's door. I looked back at Will's car, parked on the street. *I should probably get my license...Everyone's driving but me.* Jessica knocked on the door. Aaron opened it and invited us in. We followed Aaron into the kitchen where Will was standing with a beer in his hand.

"Do you guys want something to drink?" Aaron asked.

"Just water for me," Jessica said.

"What do you have?" I asked and walked over to Will. Aaron opened his refrigerator and looked inside.

"...Pepsi, New Castle..." I looked down at Will's beer. "...And I have a couple of Snapple's."

"Oh, cool, I'll have a Snapple," Jessica said.

"I'll take a beer," I said.

"Babe, you're going to love it. New Castle tastes just like Pepsi," Will said.

"That's why I like it," Aaron added and pulled out the drinks.

"I would have one, but I'm driving," Jessica said. *Yes, Jessica, we know...Wait...So is Will.*

"...One beer won't hurt you," Will insisted.

"I know, but I just don't think it's a good idea," Jessica responded. Aaron handed the Snapple to Jessica and then opened my beer. He handed it to me and I took a drink.

"Yeah, this is really good," I said. "It's not exactly Pepsi, but I can see where you get the idea..." Aaron whispered something into Jessica's ear and she smiled. *Hmmm...*

"Make yourself at home," Aaron said and then left the kitchen holding Jessica's hand. Will raised his beer and then smiled at me.

"Remember when we were like that?" I asked.

"We're still like that..." *No, we're not...* "What's going on with you lately?"

"You see how Aaron looks at Jessica?"

"Yeah...I guess."

"...You don't look at me like that anymore..."

"I don't?" Will looked at me seemingly perplexed and drank what was left in his bottle. "If I knew what that look was then I would..."

"...Never mind," I said. *You don't get it...*

"Are you mad at me?"

"...No, I'm not mad...I just miss you..."

"Babe, I don't understand...I'm right here," Will said and walked over to the refrigerator to get another beer. *I don't know how to explain this...Maybe I am crazy...*

"I guess I'm just worried about the future..." I said and drank some beer.

"What do you mean?"

"...You guys were all talking about college..."

"Babe..."

"And it got me thinking..."

"Hannah, babe, if I'm not thinking about that, you definitely shouldn't be..." Will laughed and sat down on the couch.

"I can't help it..." I pleaded and sat down next to him. I looked into his eyes. *I know he loves me, but...* "...I know I worry too much...I'm sorry."

"Babe, it's okay."

"I'm such a buzzkill..."

"No, you're not...My buzz is doing very well, thank you very much." I laughed.

"You're so funny, Billy," I said and kissed him. "You always know what to say to make me feel better..."

"That's my job, is it not?" Will asked and smiled.

"You mean besides Micky D's?"

"Yeah, don't remind me..." Will turned his bottle upside down and drank the rest of his beer.

"Babe, you should probably slow down...You're driving, right?"

"Yeah, but it'll be a while..." *Hmmm...*

"You think Aaron and Jessica are..."

"...Maybe...He's been talking about it...He has condoms..." I laughed.

"You didn't tell him about VCF?"

"No, babe, that's our thing..." *That's kind of sweet...*

"I hope he goes easy on her...She's very sensitive," I said.

"I'm sure he will, but sensitive, Hannah, that's a serious under-statement...She's a lot to take," Will said and we both laughed. "I don't know how he deals with her..."

"It's in the stars, Billy..."

"Yes, you keep telling me...So, do you want to show them how it's done?" *Wait...*

"What are you talking about, Billy?"

"There's a spare bedroom right down the hall," Will said and smiled. "And you can be as loud as you want..." I felt a sense of excitement that had been missing for a long time. *That's the Billy I remember...*

"You think it's okay?"

"Yeah, why not?"

"You don't think Aaron would care?"

"No, why would he? He's preoccupied with Jessica...And his mom is staying with her boyfriend tonight." *Damn, Billy...Wait...*

"You guys didn't plan this, did you?"

"...No, of course not, babe, we're gentleman with excellent stand-ing in the community..." *Yeah, right...*

"You're so funny, Billy!"

"I know, babe...So, what do you think?"

"I think that you should lead the way..."

"Let's go..." Will stood up and reached out for my hand. I grabbed his hand and he helped me up. We walked down the hallway and then stopped at the end. Will looked left and then right. "Oh shit, they're in his mom's room," Will whispered.

"...I don't hear anything," I whispered back.

"Me neither..."

"You wanna go back?" I asked and Will looked straight ahead.

"Nope. That's the spare bedroom right there..."

"Okay, if you're sure..." Will smiled and held my hand.

"I'm sure, trust me..." We walked into the spare bedroom and Will closed the door behind us. He locked the door and then turned around to kiss me. "I love you, Hannah."

"I love you too, Billy..."

"Now let's give them something to think about..." Will and I fell onto the bed and into each other's embrace. *Maybe I was wrong...*

Part Three

Chapter Twenty-One

Twist of fate

Jessica, Aaron, and I waited in the middle of the food court at the mall for Will to show up. It was the beginning of summer vacation and Will had just quit his job at McDonald's. He walked through the door and waved at us. He smiled at me and gave me a hug.

"Hey, babe."

"Hey, Billy," I said and he kissed me.

"I called Brad. He did not take the news well."

"I'm sorry...It's my fault, isn't it?"

"No, I would rather be here with you than with Brad. It's as simple as that."

"Brad's your old friend," Aaron said. "We're your new friends."

"Nah, at this point, you're old too..." Will responded. We all laughed. "Where's everyone else?"

"Rob's dad is supposed to drop him off," Aaron said.

"I still can't believe he doesn't want to get his license," Will added.

"Yeah, that is weird," Aaron said. *I think they're talking about me too...*

"What about Nate and Casey?" Will asked.

"I talked to Casey before we left and her mom is dropping them off," I said. Over spring break, Will and I got Casey and Nate together. I had lost touch with Casey for a while, but that quickly changed when Will had the idea to help Nate get a girlfriend. At the same time, I was able to keep the promise that I had made to her so long before.

"...Okay, cool, let's get some food," Will said. "I want some pizza." *Billy, you always want some pizza...*

"Shouldn't we wait for everyone else to get here?" I asked.

"Yeah, I suppose..." Will said and smiled." We all sat down at a table in the middle of the food court. After twenty minutes, Nate and Casey joined us and Rob followed ten minutes after that.

"Hey, what's up?" Rob asked. "...We have a show in Fresno tomorrow. A real show."

"Oh shit, how'd you pull that off?" Will inquired.

"My dad knows a guy...Anyway, it pays five-hundred bucks! That's one twenty-five apiece!" Rob said.

"Dude, no fucking way," Nate said.

"Yeah, that's like more than my McDonald's check," Will insisted.

"It's legit. We just have to get there, play a couple of hours, and bank the cash," Rob argued.

"Wait, what's this place called?" Will asked.

"It's at Shakey's pizza..."

"...Ummm, I didn't know that a pizza place...Does our Shakey's pizza have bands play?" Will asked.

"Not sure, but my dad knows the owner of the one in Fresno," Rob said. "So, we just need a way to get there...and move our equipment. My dad can take the amps, but Nate's drums aren't going to fit..."

"Well, shit," Nate said. We all stood there in awkward silence.

"...I can borrow my grandpa's van," Aaron finally said. "I mean, I think he'll let me borrow it, he doesn't use it."

"Why didn't you say something earlier?" Rob asked.

"I just thought of it..." Aaron replied.

"What kind of van is it?" Rob asked.

"It's one of those big vans...Bigger than your dad's mini-van," Aaron said.

"It sounds perfect," Will added.

"Yeah, it does...We need to get a practice in today. Let's get to Nate's house..." Rob insisted.

"Okay, but can we eat first?" Will asked.

"Yeah, let's get some food, but we need to make it fast, I wanna put our set list together," Rob said.

"All right," Will said. Everyone went to get the food they wanted and then we all met back at the table in the middle of the food court.

"This is gonna be a great summer, guys," Will said.

"Damn right!" Nate said.

"Less talking, more eating," Rob instructed. Will took a bite of his pizza and then put his hand on my leg.

"Babe, do you think you can come to the show tomorrow?" Will asked.

"I don't know...If I stayed at Jessica's..." I said and looked at Jessica. Everyone stopped eating at that moment and stared at Jessica. "Do you think your parents will let you go?"

"I can ask them, but probably...Yeah, they'll let me go," Jessica said. "We just have to hope that my parents don't tell your parents."

"Yeah, my parents would never let me go if they knew...I wish my parents were cool like everyone else's parents. I always have to lie to them," I said.

"And I can't tell them not to tell your parents...That would make them suspicious," Jessica added.

"That's true, but I want to go see you guys play, so..." I said and intertwined my fingers with Will and then held his hand.

"It's cool, babe...Your parents have been really cool lately. Why would they even ask?" Will reasoned.

"Yeah, Will's right," Jessica said.

"So, we're going to Fresno tomorrow?" I asked.

"Yeah, I just have to ask my parents..." Jessica said.

"...Aaron, ask your grandpa if we can use his van after we finish lunch," Rob interrupted. *I wonder if he's still mad at her...*

"Oh, for sure, but he's cool. He won't care if I want to take the van," Aaron said. We finished eating and then walked out to the parking garage. Will had the biggest car, so Rob, Casey, and Nate rode with us. Jessica rode with Aaron. We headed out of the mall parking lot and drove to Nate's house. As soon as we got there, I went to give Will a hug. *Jessica...*

"Hey, Billy, can I talk to you?"

"Sure, what's up?" I held Will's hand and led him away from everyone else.

"Do you think it's a good idea for Rob to be in a car with Jessica for an hour?"

"I don't know...I guess so. He has to be over it, right?"

"Why not have Rob ride with Aaron and you can come with us?"

"Aaron's my best friend..."

"And I'm your girlfriend, and I think it would be best if..." Jessica walked up and interrupted us.

"So..." Jessica said.

"He wants to ride with Aaron."

"Jessica, just take one for the team. Rob's not gonna bother you," Will insisted.

"Ahhh, fine, but you're gonna owe me. Aaron too..." Jessica said.

"You got it. I'll be sure Aaron makes it up to you."

"Are you sure about this?" I asked while looking at Jessica. "Because you told me that..."

"It's fine. I just hope he doesn't try to talk to me," Jessica responded.

"Okay, if you're sure," I said.

"He knows you're with Aaron; he's not gonna talk to you. He'll probably just look out the window the whole time," Will reasoned.

"Yeah, okay, I'm good, sorry I made a big deal out of this," Jessica said.

"No worries, let's roll out," Will said. We went back over to Aaron, Nate, and Rob.

"Are we ready to go?" Aaron asked.

"Yeah, what's the hold up?" Rob added.

"It's nothing...Just Hannah worried about her parents," Will said.

"Yeah, I don't know what would happen if I got caught..."

"...That's not gonna happen, right Jessica?" Will asked.

"Ummm, yeah, my parents aren't gonna say anything, they're not like Hannah's parents."

"All right, let's go. Aaron, to the band van," Will said. He hugged me and then got inside of Aaron's van. Rob talked to Aaron for a minute and then got into Jessica's car and sat behind her, next to Nate and Casey.

"Just head west on the 198 and then north on the 99..." Rob instructed. "...You know how to get to the 198?"

"Yes, Rob, I know where the freeway is..." Jessica replied sarcastically. *Uh oh...* Jessica started driving. Before Rob had a chance to say something back to Jessica, I turned around and faced him.

"So, Rob, who's your favorite band?" I asked rhetorically. *Focus on me...* Rob looked at me as if I were dumb. *It worked...*

"You know who my favorite band is...Why are you even asking me the question?" Nate and Casey held hands as they stared at me waiting for a response.

"...I know, it's Nirvana, right?"

"Yeah, duh..."

"Okay, but why is Nirvana your favorite band?"

"That's a good question," Nate said.

"It's not just the music," Rob said. "It's Kurt Cobain. I have a lot of respect for him..." *Hmmm. He did commit suicide, though...* "...He was just a normal guy...He didn't want anyone as a fan that was racist, sexist, or homophobic..." *Hmmm, really?* "He basically told them to not buy their records. He didn't care about being famous or making a lot of money. I think he just wanted to make the world a better place..." *What do you believe?*

"So, you feel the same way as Kurt Cobain?" I asked.

"Yeah, I do...I can't stand people that hate other people just for being different," Rob reasoned. *Wow, I had no idea...*

"I feel the same way, Rob...That's really cool."

"...That's why I don't like many other bands. Their lyrics are so misogynistic. I can't even listen to it...Shit like Guns N' Roses." *Oh, damn, Billy...*

"I think Billy likes them..."

"Figures...He would..." *What's that supposed to mean?*

"I like Guns N' Roses," Nate said.

"Really...What's your favorite song?" Rob asked.

"I don't know," Nate said. "I like that paradise city song..."

"That's what I'm talking about," Rob said. "The song is about treating women like sex objects." *Is it really?*

"I just think it's a cool song," Nate reasoned.

"It's not cool to hate women," Rob said. *So, you don't hate Jessica?*

"I know that, but I don't think..." Nate started to say.

"...What about 'Don't Cry?'" Casey asked.

"That's all about telling women how to feel." *I'm impressed.* "It's misogyny...All of those '80s hair bands. They were all about doing drugs and treating women like shit...That's it."

"I never even thought about it," I said. "I think you're right though..."

"I know I'm right..." Rob insisted. Jessica looked over at me and rolled her eyes. She looked in the rearview mirror at Rob. *Uh oh...Jessica, don't...*

"What about Veruca Salt and Luscious Jackson?" Jessica asked. *Is she trying to piss him off?* "They're all women..." *Ugh...* "And they obviously don't hate themselves...So what do you think about them?"

"...They're all right, I guess," Rob responded. *Thank God...* "I do like other bands...I do have respect for them, for them doing what they're doing."

"And what are they doing, Rob?" *You just couldn't leave it alone...*

"They're fighting the patriarchy that tells women that they can't be in rock bands..." *Good answer, Rob...Wow.* Jessica reached down in the center console and pulled out a cassette tape.

"...So, you wouldn't mind if I put this Veruca Salt tape on, right?" *Jessica!*

"...Not at all, put it on," Rob said. *Cool...* I turned around in my seat and watched all of the barren land go by on the side of the freeway. We listened to one Veruca Salt song after another until we got to Fresno.

"What exit do I take?" Jessica asked.

"Take the Fresno Street exit and then turn right...Turn right on Van Ness...Turn left on Kern...And there it is...Okay, pull around to the back alley." Jessica followed all of Rob's instructions and then parked the car. Aaron pulled up right next to us. I got out of the car and walked over to Will.

"How'd it go?" Will whispered in my ear.

"Good, he didn't say anything to Jessica," I whispered back. *Well, nothing bad...* Aaron opened the back of the van and we all grabbed a piece of equipment and took it to the back door. We were greeted by a man who told us he was the owner of the restaurant.

"I'm Tyrone," The man said, "but you can call me Ty." Rob stepped up and said,

"I'm Rob and this is my band, Anarchy."

"Yeah, your dad and I go way back...Anyway, let's get your equipment inside, you're going on at two." Tyrone led us into the back of the restaurant and I set down one of Nate's cymbals. Jessica and Casey put down some cables and we walked inside of the restaurant.

"You don't think they need any more help, do you?" Casey asked.

"They'll be fine, Casey," I insisted.

"Yeah...Okay," Casey said.

"You wanna get some pizza?" Jessica asked.

"Yeah, sure," I said and we went to the front counter. We each ordered a slice of pizza and a Pepsi. I looked outside and saw a line of people waiting to get inside. *Wow, this is pretty crazy...Oh shit, Vicki and Angela? What are they doing here?* Vicki made eye contact with me and then whispered something to Angela. I smiled and then turned back around to the counter. Jessica, Casey, and I got our pizza and sodas and walked over to a booth on the side of the restaurant. I looked out on the stage and saw everyone setting up. Will was playing his guitar silently when they let the line of people inside. Most of them packed into the front of the stage and some of them ordered pizza. *That's a lot of people. We got lucky...* After about ten minutes, Rob stepped up to the microphone.

"Thanks for coming out, we're Anarchy," Rob said. The crowd roared. *Wow...* People started screaming. I heard Vicki yelling Will's name. *Stupid Vicki...* They played through a few Nirvana songs. When they played 'About a Girl,' Will found my eyes and I smiled at him. Before the end of the song, I heard some commotion at the front of the restaurant and looked back. I saw my dad and Jessica's dad coming toward us. *Oh shit, this is bad...* My dad walked up and pointed at me.

"Hannah, let's go!"

"But dad," I yelled. "They're still playing."

"Hannah, now!" I looked at Jessica's dad who was waving Jessica over to him. *Shit...* I got up from the booth. Jessica and Casey followed me. Jessica and I turned around and waved. My dad turned and pointed his finger directly at Will. Just as the song was ending, Will walked up to the microphone.

"I love you, Hannah," he said. I smiled and mouthed the words 'I love you,' back to him. My dad turned around and we all followed him out of the restaurant.

"Hannah, you're coming with me," my dad said.

"And Jessica, I'll ride back with you," Jessica's dad added.

"What about Casey?" I asked.

"Bob, can you take Casey home?" my dad asked.

"Sure, no problem," he replied. *Wait...No...Ugh!*

"...Dad, that doesn't make any sense. Casey lives right down the street from us."

"I know where she lives..." My dad started to say.

"...Then why don't we take her home?"

"...Fine!" my dad barked and started walking down the street. *Thank God. He's not going to yell at me with Casey in the truck...*

"...Bye, Jessica, I'll call you later," I said.

"Okay, bye," Jessica responded and walked with her dad down the alleyway. Casey and I followed my dad down the street to his truck. We got inside and my dad drove us home. No one said anything the entire time. It was surreal how awkward it was sitting next to my dad knowing that he wanted to yell at me and not being able to do it. I didn't want to test the theory that he wouldn't yell at me because Casey was there, so I didn't say anything. Casey stared out the window probably sharing the same concern. After an hour of silence, my dad pulled into our driveway. Casey got out of the truck and I followed her.

"Bye, Hannah," Casey said and ran down the street. *Shit...* I walked to the front door and let myself in. My dad followed me and then shut the door.

"Hannah, have a seat," my dad instructed. *That's not good...* I sat down on the couch and my dad stood over me.

"Dad, I didn't do anything wrong," I pleaded.

"...Hannah, your grandma's in the hospital..." *What!?*

"...What's wrong? Is she going to be okay?"

"She passed out at home...They're running tests...I don't know, Hannah, she's sick..." *Oh my God...*

"I'm sorry, dad..."

"...Hannah, you're sixteen years old..." *Yes, I know that...* "...Why are you still lying to us?" *Lying?*

"I didn't lie about anything."

"...Here's what I think...And you can stop me when I get something wrong...Every time you tell us you're doing something with Jessica, you see that boy..."

"...It's not like that, dad, Jessica is dating his best friend...So, yeah, we all hang out together sometimes..."

"...You're sneaking around...How are we supposed to trust you when you don't tell us anything?"

"I'm not sneaking around..."

"God only knows what you're doing..."

"Dad, I'm not doing anything wrong."

"Are you having sex with him?" *Uh oh....Shit...* I looked down at the carpet. *You don't want me to lie, so I won't say anything...*

"That's what I thought...Go to your room...We'll talk about this when your mom gets home." *That went better than I expected...* I got up from the couch and walked to my room. I shut the door and then sat on my bed. *I hope grandma's okay...What happened? I need to call Billy...* I looked over at my desk and my phone wasn't there. *Shit...* I started crying. I pulled a pillow off of my bed and buried my face in it. I heard the phone ring and looked up. *Huh? Who is it?* I didn't hear anything. The phone rang again. *What's going on? Billy...* I continued crying into my pillow. After a while I heard a loud knock on the door. *Billy...* I put my pillow down and opened my door. I saw my dad staring outside. I started walking down the hallway and I heard Will's voice.

"I want to see Hannah," he said. I walked up behind my dad and stared at Will. I felt helpless as my dad blocked the doorway. "You can't keep her locked up like this!"

"...I can do whatever I want. She's my daughter and she's my responsibility." I started crying again and felt my tears run down my face. I looked down and watched them hit the floor.

"Yeah, you're a real hero," Will said. "Look at what you're doing to her." My dad made a fist and started shaking. *Oh no, dad, don't...*

"STAY AWAY FROM MY DAUGHTERRRRR!" my dad screamed. *Billy...*

"What are you going to do old man? I'm seventeen...What, are you going to hit me?" I cried hysterically. I felt my dad's anger growing more volatile by the moment. *Please, just stop...* "Go ahead, hit me...I'd love to see you locked up." *No, Billy...* My dad didn't say anything. He growled and then slammed the door. He turned around and looked at me. *Oh shit...* He was shaking. His eye was twitching. His chest moved in and out as he took deep breaths. *This is scary...*

"Go to your room!" My dad yelled. I went to my room without saying a word and shut the door. I sat on the floor against my bed.

I continued to cry. I pulled my legs into my chest and rested my forehead on my knees. *Fuck my life...*

When my mom got home from work, she argued with my dad for a few minutes before they both came into my room.

"Hannah, I am very disappointed in you," my mom said. I didn't respond to her. I put my head back down.

"...Hannah, do you know what statutory rape is?" My dad asked. *Rape...* I looked up at him.

"...What!?"

"It means that it's against the law to have sex with that boy..."

"...What? Dad..."

"I mean it will be...When he turns eighteen...September twenty-eighth, right?" *Oh shit...*

"You either end it with him or I'll end him..." *Fuck...*

"You can't do that," I argued.

"Yes, I can...That's the law. You're too young to consent to sex... *What the...*

"I never said I was having sex..."

"You must think we're stupid," my mom said. *I was hoping...*

"I don't think that you're stupid..."

"...We told you that you would have to make your own decisions...That your choices would have consequences..." My mom added. *Yeah, I know...So...*

"I know, mom..."

"It's more obvious than ever that you're going to do whatever you want to do," my dad said. *Yeah...*

"With that out of the way," my mom said. "You have a choice to make." *You want me to break up with Billy...*

"...I can't do that...I love him..." I started crying again.

"I'm not going to tell you how to feel..." My mom insisted.

"He's a bad influence on you..." *No, he's not...* "We want you to graduate high school and go to college. I didn't go to college and my life is harder...Our lives are harder because of it," my dad said.

"Dad, I have good grades...You know I'm doing well in school..."

"...And what happens if you get pregnant?" My dad asked. *Shit...* "All of that would be over..." *I don't know what to say...* Break up with your boyfriend or he's going to jail, it's as simple as that..." *Fuck...*

"You can't do that..." *Can you? Shit...*

"It's your choice," my dad added. *Yeah, right...Fuck!*

"You're sixteen, Hannah, so we're not going to ground you. We think you're too old for that," my mom said. "Your dad's going to give back your phone...We want you to call him..."

"Make the right decision..." My dad instructed. He walked down the hallway into the kitchen and then came back with my phone.

He set it down on my desk and then plugged it into the wall. *Thanks, I guess...*

"Hannah, please, do what's best for you...And what's best for him..." My mom argued. *Fuck you! You don't know what's best for us...* "Come on, Patrick, let's leave her alone..." *Alone...*

"Okay..." My dad said and closed my door behind them. *All of these threats...Why can't they just? Shit...Leave me...Alone...I don't want to be alone...* I wiped the remaining tears from my face and picked up the phone. I dialed Will's number and he picked up after the second ring.

"Hello?"

"Hey, Billy..."

"Hannah! Babe, are you okay?"

"I'm okay. I can't talk long...Meet me tonight?"

"Yeah...Same time?"

"Yeah."

"Okay, I'll be there."

"Okay, see you then...Bye, Billy."

"Bye." Will hung up but I stayed on for a few seconds to make sure that my parents weren't listening in on me. *This feels like a trap...But, I don't hear anything...* I hung up the phone. *I should call Jessica...Shit, I can't talk to her about this...She's just going to tell Aaron. Summer...* I dialed Summer's number and let it ring twenty times. No one answered. *Shit...I am alone.*

I waited until midnight and escaped out my bedroom window. I walked out to the end of my driveway and stood behind my mom's car. Will walked up to me and gave me a hug. He kissed my forehead and then held my hand. *Shit, what am I going to do?* We started walking down the street toward the school.

"Billy, where's your car?" I asked while looking around.

"I parked way down the street...You know, my car's loud..."

"Yeah..." *I can't do it...* We crossed the street and then walked around the fence surrounding the school. We walked into the park and then sat down on the swings. I reached over and held Will's hand.

"Oh, Billy, my dad...Well..." *Billy... Ugh...I can't...* "...I'm glad he hasn't gotten wise to me sneaking out."

"Yeah, I know...What happened, Hannah? Why was he even there?"

"My grandma's in the hospital...She's really sick."

"That sucks, babe, I'm sorry..."

"It's okay...So I don't know what to do...I feel like I'm in prison. FUCK! I just want to scream. Why do they have to be so rejected?"

"I don't know...Things have to get better though. You'll be eighteen soon enough and then they'll have nothing..." *And so will you...Billy...*

"I love you; I will always love you," I said. "That seems so far away..."

"A year and a half..."

"...Do you think we'll be together forever?" .

"We love each other...That's all that matters." *Shit...*

"What if love isn't enough?"

"Then we fight for it."

"I just want to die. My life is shit. I can't handle..."

"Hannah, it's going to be fine. Where's the girl I fell in love with? That doesn't sound like her." I smiled as he touched my neck.

"You always say the right thing, Billy. I should go back...I have a bad feeling."

"Okay, don't worry, babe, we're going to figure this out," Will said and then walked me back to my house. He hugged and kissed me goodbye. "I'll call you tomorrow...Everything's going to be fine." *I wish that were true...*

"Thanks, Billy...I feel a little better now..." I said and then walked back through the gate, through my window, and into my room.

The next morning, I woke up at nine and stared at my alarm clock for a few minutes before getting out of bed. I heard my parents talking in the kitchen. *What are they still doing home?* I opened my door and walked to the kitchen.

"The prodigal daughter has returned," my dad said and laughed. *What are you even talking about?* I rubbed my eyes.

"Aren't you guys supposed to be at work?"

"We're going to see your grandma today," my mom answered. *Oh, yeah...* "Your dad was going to go to the hospital yesterday, but, yeah..." *Ugh! I know, everything's my fault...*

"...Is she going to be okay?"

"They have her on a ventilator, but they think she'll recover," my mom said. *Ventilator?*

"What's wrong with her?"

"She has pneumonia," my mom said.

"What does that mean?"

"It's a lung infection that makes it really hard to breathe."

"Oh...Okay, so, when are we going?"

"After breakfast. Go get dressed and wake Michael up too." *Great...* I got dressed and woke my brother up. We ate our breakfast and my mom drove us to the hospital. My mom parked the car and then walked us to my grandma's room. She had tubes covering her face. I hardly recognized her. I listened to her labored breathing as my mom and dad walked up to her.

"Mom, if grandma can't talk then why are we even here?" My brother asked.

"Because Michael, that's what families do..." *He does have a point...*

"I don't get it," my brother said. "Why don't we just come when she can talk..."

"Shut up, Michael," my dad instructed. "Hannah, go to the gift shop and get your grandma some flowers." My dad handed me twenty bucks. "...And take Michael with you." *Ugh...*

"Fine. Come on, Michael," I said and walked with my brother down the hall. We took the elevator to the first-floor lobby and then went into the gift shop. I grabbed a bouquet of flowers and walked over to the cashier.

"Why do we have to get grandma flowers?" My brother asked.

"Michael, I'm just doing what dad asked me to do."

"I don't get it though...She's not even awake...She won't even know the flowers are there and when she does wake up, they'll probably be dead."

"Michael! You wanna know why we're here and why we have to get flowers?"

"Yes..."

"...Because grandma might not wake up..."

"...What!? That's not true...Hannah!"

"...You wanted to know." *That'll shut him up.* I paid for the flowers and then we walked back to the elevator. I pushed the button for the third floor and the doors closed. When they opened, I looked down the hall and saw Rob standing outside one of the rooms. *What is he doing here?* My brother and I started walking towards my grandma's room. *Maybe he didn't see me...I should just...*

"Hey, look, it's Rob," my brother announced. *Once again, thanks, Michael...* Rob nodded his head.

"Hey, Rob, what are you doing here?" I asked.

"It's my grandpa...He had a heart attack..."

"...I'm sorry to hear that, I said.

"It's okay, he's gonna be all right..."

"That's good..."

"So, what are you doing here?"

"My grandma's sick..."

"That sucks," Rob said.

"Yeah, but she's gonna be okay."

"Hey, you said she could die!" My brother cried. *Ugh...*

"Michael, I said it was possible...I don't think she's going to die...Here, take the flowers to dad. I'll come in a minute." My brother took the flowers and ran down the hallway.

"So...Yeah, I saw your dad at the show yesterday."

"Yeah, I think everyone did..."

"He looked pretty pissed off."

"That's just how he is...We were supposed to be here yesterday. That's why he was mad."

"That makes sense...He really doesn't like Will, does he?" *What!? Ugh...*

"No, he doesn't, but I don't care what he thinks..."

"...Maybe you should," Rob said. "He's walking over here right now." *Shit...*

"Dad, I was about to..."

"...You're in that band with..." My dad said and pointed to Rob.

"...It's Rob, dad."

"What are you doing here, Rob?"

"My grandpa had a heart attack..."

"...Oh...I'm sorry." *That shut him up...*

"No worries, he's gonna be okay...I should go back inside though...My grandpa means a lot to me and I want to be standing next to him when he wakes up."

"Good man," my dad said. "Hannah, let's go."

"Okay, bye Rob."

"Bye," Rob said and walked inside his grandpa's room. I followed my dad down the hallway.

"I like Rob," my dad said. *I'm sorry...What!?* "He seems like a good young man." *Are you kidding me?* "Does he go to school with you?"

"Yeah..."

"How old is he?"

"He's my age...He's gonna be a junior next year."

"That's good..." *Hmmm...* "So, did you break up with your boyfriend last night?" *Here we go...*

"...No, I couldn't do it..."

"Remember what I said..." *How could I forget? Ugh...*

"September twenty-eighth, right?"

"...You're really going to drag this out as long as you can?"

"Maybe..."

"Delaying the inevitable isn't go to do you any good."

"I was thinking, maybe, you would change your mind..."

"That's not going to happen..." My dad took a deep breath. "...You're going to be the death of me, Hannah," he said as we walked into my grandma's room.

Will hadn't called me for two weeks and I didn't call him either. I was avoiding him. I couldn't bring myself to break up with him and at the same time, I didn't want to lead him on knowing what could happen. *I need to call Summer...*

"Hello?"

"Summer?"

"Yeah, it's me...Hannah?"

"Yeah, can you talk?"

"Of course...I tried to call you the other day and it said that your phone had been disconnected." *What!? That's weird...* "Did you change your number?"

"No...I don't think so..." *Shit, maybe they did...Billy would have called me by now...* "Now that I think about it, my parents probably did change it...I don't know...They want me to break up with my boyfriend."

"Yeah, they don't like him, right? Are you going to break up with him?"

"I don't want to, but they said the day he turns eighteen they're going to call the police..."

"For what!?"

"Statutory rape..."

"Shit, Hannah, that's terrible. Do you actually think they would call the police?"

"Yeah, I'm pretty sure my dad can't wait."

"I don't get it though...It's just their word against yours...Just tell them that you're not having sex with him. What are they going to do, check your vagina?" I laughed.

"Yeah, I guess not..."

"I could picture it now...They put you up in those stirrup things, open up your legs, and shine a light..." *Ummm, gross...* "They would look at each other very matter-of-factly and say, 'this girl here does not have a hymen...Guilty! Send her boyfriend to jail!'" I laughed again. "See Hannah, none of that is going to happen."

"You're right, Summer, but what if they don't need proof? What if they just lock him up anyway...I couldn't live with myself if that happened..."

"I don't think it works that way, Hannah, this is America after all...But I'll be honest, I really don't know."

"...I don't know what to do...I love him. I don't want to hurt him. I don't think I could just break up with him, you know, just like that..."

"You could always get him to break up with you..." *What!?* "I'm not saying that you should, but it's an option."

"How would I do that? Why would I want to do that? Wouldn't that be the same thing anyway?" I asked in quick succession. "Summer...It was easy with Joe."

"You mean thou who shall not be named?"

"...Yeah. He was a jerk...It was easy to break up with him...Billy doesn't deserve that."

"Well, whatever you decide to do, I'm sure it will be the right decision."

"Thanks, Summer, I hope so..."

"...Hey, guess what?"

"I don't know, what?"

"I got my license!"

"Awesome! I'm really happy for you...I still haven't gotten mine."

"What are you waiting for, girl?"

"I don't know..."

"When you get your license, you can come visit me!"

"...Yeah, I could, but you can come visit me too..."

"...To Visalia? Isn't it like really hot there?"

"Yeah, it is really hot," I said and Summer laughed.

"We'll see...Hey, give me a call when you figure out your new number."

"Yeah...I need to talk to my parents."

"Okay, I gotta go though...My new girlfriend and I are gonna drive to Pismo Beach."

"That sounds fun..." *I need to get my license...* "What's her name?"

"Bridgette...We've been together for a couple of months."

"That's cool," I said. "You'll have to tell me about her sometime..."

"It would be better if you came down here, you know..."

"Yes, Summer...All right, I'll let you go."

"Okay, talk to you soon, bye."

"Okay, bye."

I waited for my mom to get home from work and then accosted her as soon as she walked through the door.

"Mom?"

"Yes, Hannah..."

"When were you going to tell me that you changed our number?"

"...Actually, we were going to tell you as soon as you broke up with your boyfriend."

"Mom, I told you...I love him."

"Hannah, I'm going to tell you something that my mother told me when I was around your age...If you love someone, let them go; if they come back to you, then you know..." *Okay...*

"...Is that what happened with you and dad?"

"No, this was before your dad came along...Hannah, if it was really meant to be with that boy, then it will be..." *Wait...What?* "...When you're eighteen, it'll be up to you." *Oh...* "But right now, I'm sorry, it's our choice."

"But, mom..."

"...When you're eighteen, if you still want to be with him, there's nothing that we'll be able to do about it...We'll respect your decision..."

"But what if he doesn't want to be with me?"

"Then it wasn't meant to be..." My mom put her hand on my shoulder, looked into my eyes, and then walked to the kitchen. I went back down the hallway to my room. *Hmmm. I don't know...I don't want to be alone. What am I going to do? Hmmm, maybe Summer's right...*

Chapter Twenty-Two

Spiderwebs

It was the first day of school my junior year and I still didn't have a driver's license. I walked to Rob's house that morning and then we walked to school together. We didn't say much to each other on the way. We walked onto campus and then waited by the gym for class to start.

"Hey, I just wanted to tell you that it was really cool hanging out with you this summer," Rob said.

"Yeah, it was cool..." I answered.

"You really helped me get through my grandpa passing away."

"...I'm sorry, again, I know how hard that must have been."

"Yeah, it was, but everyone dies eventually, right?" *Shit...* "How's you grandma doing?"

"Good...She's doing really well..."

"That's good..."

"...Oh, hey, there's Casey! I haven't talked to her since she gave me your number."

"I don't even know how she got my number...Whatever, though."

"Casey!" I yelled. She smiled and walked over to me. I gave her a hug and then looked at her. "Wow, Casey, you look super-cute."

"Thanks, Hannah...Hi Rob."

"Hey," Rob said.

"So, you're finally in high school? How does it feel?" I asked.

"...Okay, but I feel a little lost..." Casey mumbled and I laughed.

"You'll be fine, Casey...If you need anything, just ask."

"Thanks, Hannah, ummm, do you know where Nate is?"

"He's probably in front of the band room...The front of the school," I said and pointed across campus."

"Okay, thanks, I'm gonna go find him."

"See you later," I said.

"Later," Rob replied.

"See ya," Casey said and walked away. A couple of minutes later, I saw Will walking up to us. *Shit...I have to do this...*

"Babe, there you are. What are you guys doing over here?"

"I don't know...We were just talking," I said.

"But we always meet in front of the band room..."

"Yeah, we were just headed over there," Rob added.

"Anyway, what happened this summer, Hannah, did your parents change your number?"

"Yeah, they did, and they kept the phone in their room. I'm sorry I couldn't call you. They kept me on lockdown as usual," I said. *Oh my God, I feel so bad about this...*

"...No worries, it's not your fault. I'm just glad you're here. I thought for sure they made you change schools."

"They were going to, but they always threaten that."

"Well, I'm gonna go to class; later," Rob said.

"Bye, Rob," I said.

"Yeah, later," Will added. Rob walked away and into a crowd of people. "Babe, you wanna get out of here?" Will asked.

"You mean you want to ditch on the first day of school?" I replied. *This is going to be so hard...*

"...Yeah, who cares? I haven't seen you in forever. I think we need some alone time." *I can't...*

"That's sweet, but we can't miss the first day...Maybe some other time..."

"Okay, school it is then...How about Friday?"

"I don't know..."

"Come on, babe, I really need to see you." *Shit...*

"Okay, Friday," I said. "We should get to class...Don't you think?"

"Ummm, yeah, sure, I'll walk you. What do you have first period?"

"Math, but I'm fine, I'll walk myself."

"Since when did you not want me to walk you to class?"

"Since I'm not a kid anymore...I don't need an escort..." *I'm sorry, Billy...Fuck!*

"...Well, shit...So you were a kid last year?"

"NO! I mean...You know what I mean." *Ugh...*

"What is wrong with you today?" *Where do I start...*

"Nothing, I'm going to class." I turned away from Will and started walking to my first class.

"See you at lunch," Will said. I didn't turn around and I didn't say anything. I felt like crying. I didn't want to be mean to him, but I wasn't sure exactly what to do.

When the bell rang for lunch, I walked to the front of the band room and waited for Will. He ran up to me and gave me a hug, but I didn't return his affection. I let my arms hang by my side. "Babe, what's wrong?" Will asked as he stepped away from me. *Just do it, damn it...*

"Nothing, I'm just having a bad day," I responded.

"Did you have another fight with your dad or something?" *Okay...Here we go...God...*

"...That night, the last night we met up this summer, my parents caught me sneaking back in my room...They were there waiting for me."

"Oh...shit."

"Yeah, so, I lost all of my phone privileges and you won't believe this...They took my bedroom door! I have zero privacy..."

"I'm sorry, Hannah, I know it's hard, but we'll get through this. I love you."

"I love you too, but I don't know if it's worth it anymore...And I was thinking...You're going to go off to college next year, and I'm going to be here all alone and..."

"No, you're not," Will said. "You have friends here and I'm probably just going to go to Fresno State...So I can commute. I'm not going anywhere."

"I don't know...Do you really think we'll be together forever?" *Why do I keep doing this?*

"Yes...You said it yourself...We were meant for each other. You said it; we were meant to be together. I believe that..." *Ahhh...Damn, this is so hard...*

"...I don't know what I believe anymore..." *I'm so sorry...*

"...I love you," Will said and held my hand. "Let's get out of here. Let's go back to my house. I'll prove it to you." I looked around campus and then back at Will. *Fuck it...*

"...Yeah, let's go." Will and I walked to his car and then drove to his apartment. When we got there, he parked his car and then pushed me up the stairs and through his front door. He kicked the door shut and I could hear the windows shake. *Damn...* Will didn't say anything, pulled me close, and unbuttoned my jeans. He pulled them off with my underwear at the same time. I started laughing. "What's so funny?" Will asked.

"You forgot my shoes," I said and smiled.

"It seems I did..." Will took off my shoes. "You can keep your socks."

"Oh, thanks," I said. "I was really worried about losing those..." We had sex on his living room couch and then he sat up and stared at me.

"That's funny...I remember when we started with the top and worked our way down," Will said and I looked down at my naked body. "Now we just go straight for the bottom."

"You mean you go straight for the bottom."

"Yeah, straight to the point, I guess."

"I have to tell you something..." *We can't do this anymore...*

"...What's that?"

"I'm tired of sneaking around...I'm tired of my parents' shit. I'm just tired; mentally, emotionally...I'm just tired of it."

"I know...it's going to get better though...Like when you get your license. I feel like we've had this conversation before..."

"...We have, and that's what I'm saying..." I sat up on the couch and then got dressed. "...Nothing seems to change; it's not getting any better."

"...I'm sorry...What can I do?" *Ugh...*

"Nothing...There's nothing that you can do. You should take me back to school."

"Really? No second round?"

"No, I need to go back. I think I can get away with one period, but not two."

"All right, I'll take you back to school." Will drove me back to school and I walked away from him and headed to my last class. *I have to do something...Right...Summer...I'll get him to break up with me...*

The next morning at school, I sat on the bench outside of the band room and conjured some tears. Will walked up to me and asked,

"Hey, babe, what's wrong?"

"I'm in deep shit...My dad..." I sobbed.

"It's okay, I'm right here." Will sat down and put his arm around me. "What happened?" *I have to do this...*

"...Yesterday, my dad came to pick me up after lunch...My grandma died..." *I'm going to Hell...*

"...Oh shit, I'm so sorry Hannah..."

"...I wasn't here. They know everything now...My parents...My dad said he's gonna get a restraining order against you."

"Wait, for what? I didn't do anything."

"He said when you turn eighteen...He's gonna call the police...Something about statutory rape."

"How does he even know that we're having sex?"

"He's not stupid."

"Well, shit. How does he know I'm turning eighteen?"

"That's my fault...I told them a long time ago."

"Why would you do that?"

"I wasn't thinking about it then...I was so happy about the Libra and Aquarius thing...I just let it slip. I'm so sorry, Billy."

"This is not good..."

"I know...I don't know what to do. I'm scared."

"You're scared? Your dad wants to ruin my life with a bullshit rape charge..."

"...Statutory rape, and yeah, I know it's stupid."

"What's the difference?"

"I guess it means I'm too young to consent to sex."

"You're not even that much younger than me...And they can't prove anything." *Summer...*

"I don't think they have to...My dad..."

"...Fuck your dad!"

"Billy, I know, but I'm worried about you."

"I've never been scared of your dad."

"This is serious, Billy!"

"After all we've been through...What does he want from me?"

"...He doesn't want us to be together anymore."

"Well, no shit, what's new?"

"No, if we don't break up, he's going to call the police. I love you, Billy...I don't want to see anything bad happen to you."

"So that's it then?"

"I don't know what to say. I don't want it to be over between us but we can't really be together if you're in jail."

"This is such bullshit..."

"...I guess love isn't enough...The whole world seems to be against us."

"Yeah, it's never been easy."

"I'll always love you, Billy, forever...Maybe; hopefully, we can be happy together one day..." *If it's meant to be...* I heard my mom's voice ringing in my head.

"...Like when you're eighteen?"

"Yeah...I'm sorry things had to suck out, but what else can we do?"

"I don't know, I guess you're right..." Will said and the bell rang. He looked around seemingly dazed and confused.

"...Well, I've got to get to class...I guess I'll see you later," I said and hugged him. *It has to be this way...*

"...Yeah," Will responded and then walked toward the parking lot. *Where is he going? I feel so bad...* I turned around and started walking to class.

"I LOVE YOU, HANNAH!" Will yelled and I turned back around, smiled, and mouthed 'I love you too' to him. I quickly turned my head and continued walking to class. *Shit... This isn't going to be over until something drastic happens...I have to do it...He's never going to let me go if I don't...*

I met up with Rob at lunch in front of the gym, successfully avoiding all of our friends and their probable questions along the way.

"So, yeah, we broke up," I said.

"How'd he take it?" Rob asked.

"Well, I kind of got him to break up with me..."

"How'd you do that?"

"I just told him what my dad said...And he understands...It was kind of a mutual break up."

"I don't think it was mutual, Hannah..." *Shit...Who am I kidding?*

"...I know...This is really hard. We were together for a long time."

"Where is he right now?"

"I think he drove home...I don't know."

"Well, I think you did the right thing..." *Thanks...I guess.*

"Anything's better than jail," I reasoned.

"Yeah, can't argue with that..." *Okay, I need to do this...*

"So...My dad really seems to like you..."

"Does he? That's good, I think..." *Hmmm...*

"It is good...Because that's what I need right now..."

"...Ummm, what are you saying?" Rob tentatively asked. *It's not like he's going to say no...*

"I guess I'm asking you out..."

"Are you serious?"

"...Yeah." *I have to do this...*

"I'm not stupid..." *Uh oh...* "It's not like I'm gonna say no..." *Right, but...* "It's just that, well, you just broke up..."

"Yeah, I know that, Rob..."

"Don't you think he'll be pissed?" *Yes, I do...That's the point.*

"Really? He's probably with Vicki right now..."

"You don't think he was..." *I don't know why I said that. Ugh...*

"No, I don't think he was cheating on me. I know that Vicki wants to be with him...And now she can..." *I can't believe I just said that...*

"I'm no expert here, at all, but isn't it too soon to be, I don't know, moving on?" *Maybe...But...*

"...If you're not interested, I totally understand. He's your friend and you guys have a band...It could mess things up...I get it." I turned around and started walking away.

"Wait..." *Heh*... I stopped and faced him. "Yes...I'll go out with you." *I know*... I smiled and gave Rob a hug. "I don't think we should tell anyone though...At least not for a while."

"Okay...Yeah, that's probably a good idea..."

The next day at lunch, Rob and I went to the church across the street from the school. Rob wanted to avoid everyone. I wanted Will to see us together, but I went along with Rob anyway. I figured that he would see us together eventually and end all hope of us getting back together. Rob and I were facing the church and he reached for my hand.

"You are the most beautiful girl in the world," Rob said.

"Ummm, thanks, Rob."

"I'm going to make sure to tell you every day..." *Great*...

"You don't have to do that..."

"But I want to..." *Ugh*...

"WHAT THE HELL IS GOING ON HERE!?" *Billy?* Rob and I turned around and saw Will, Aaron, and Nate. I had never seen Will that angry before. I dropped Rob's hand and looked down. *I didn't have to wait after all*... "What the fuck, Rob?" Will asked.

"Hey, we wanted to tell you..." Rob said.

"Tell me what, ROB!?"

"Look, it kind of just happened..." Rob reasoned.

"WHAT JUST KIND OF HAPPENED, ROB?" Will screamed.

"We've been talking for a while and..." Before Rob could finish his thought, Will punched him in the face and he tripped over his backpack, falling to the ground. *Wow, Billy, we have more in common than I thought...Shit...Heh*...

"Rob!" I said as I knelt down next to him. "Are you alright?" Rob's nose was bleeding onto his shirt, but he seemed more embarrassed than physically hurt. "We're not even together anymore, what's your problem?"

"What's my problem?" Will asked and looked at me confused. *I'm sorry, Billy*... "...I still love you, Hannah, and Rob...Is...Was...My friend...Bro code, Rob, shit!"

"I love you too...But what did you want me to do, wait an entire year for..." I insisted.

"...Yes, goddamn it, yes, was that too much to ask?" Will interjected and then looked back at Aaron and Nate. They didn't say anything. Will turned around to face me again.

"...Well, I couldn't do that...I didn't want to be alone."

"Didn't want to be alone? And of all people, Rob? You know what, Hannah? You are a slut." *No, Billy, you don't understand...* I didn't say anything and then looked at Rob.

"Hey, man, watch your mouth!" Rob said and stood up.

"Watch my mouth? That's really funny, Rob, considering you were the one calling her a slut when we first got together." *Oh, really...*

"Oh shit!" Aaron said.

"I should have brought some popcorn," Nate whispered to Aaron.

"That's a fucking lie! I never said that...Hannah, I never said that..." Rob insisted and tried to hold my hand, but I quickly pulled away from him.

"Yes, you did! You said they're all sluts...You even said that she was probably cheating on me with Chris!" Will asserted. *Oh, Hell no...*

"What the fuck!" I said and started walking back to school. Rob followed me and I started crying. He walked beside me and tried to keep my pace.

"He's lying, I didn't say any of that...Please, Hannah, I would never..." *Yes, you would...*

"How could you, Rob? This entire time...You were trying to ruin our relationship..."

"...No, I wasn't trying to ruin anything. I told you; he's lying." *Billy doesn't lie...*

"Why would he lie about that?"

"Because, I don't know, he's mad."

"I don't believe you, Rob."

"Please, Hannah..." Rob continued pleading with me as we crossed the street back to school.

I waited in my room after school until my dad got home from work. I walked into the living room and sat down on the couch across from him. He was sitting in his recliner watching the evening news. My mom was in the kitchen making dinner and my brother was in his room playing video games.

"Dad, I wanted to tell you...I did it. I broke up with Will..."

"...Did you?" My dad slowly looked over at me. "How do I know that you're telling me the truth?"

"...I have a new boyfriend..."

"Really?"

"Yeah, it's Rob..."

"...Oh, okay..." My dad looked back at the TV. *That's it!?*

"Seriously!? You don't have a problem with that?"

"Hannah, what do you want me to say?"

"Anything!"

"...Rob seems harmless...I'm not worried about him." *Shit... Yeah, you're right...He is harmless...*

"...So, you don't mind of I see a movie with him this weekend?"

"No, go ahead." *What's going on here? This is way too easy...*

"Okay...I'm going to call him...Can I give him our new number?"

"Yeah..."

"Dad...I don't know our new number..." He laughed.

"Neither do I...Ask your mom." *Okay...* I got up from the couch and went to the kitchen.

"Mom, what's our number?"

"It's in the drawer over there." *This is getting spooky...* I opened the drawer that my mom pointed to and got the number and took it to my room. I dialed Rob's number and his mom picked up.

"Hi, is Rob there?" I asked.

"Yeah, hold on, is this Hannah?" *Hmmm...*

"Yeah..."

"Okay, hold on..." *How did she know it was me?*

"Hello?"

"Hey, Rob..."

"So, you're not mad at me anymore?"

"No...I'm over it...Hey, how'd your mom know it was me?"

"I tell my mom everything..." *Wow, really? Okay...*

"That's cool...So you wanna see a movie this weekend?"

"...Sure, I don't have any money though..." *Ugh...*

"It's okay, I'll borrow some money from my mom..."

"What do you want to see?" Rob asked.

"The Fifth Element..."

"Really? That's cool, I'm down."

"Oh, I need to give you my number, I almost forgot..." I gave Rob my number and he wrote it down. "I should go though, it's almost time for dinner. I'll see you tomorrow morning."

"Okay, see ya."

"Bye," I said and hung up the phone. *This might just work out...*

I stared at my phone for what seemed like an hour. It was Will's birthday and I really wanted to call him. I wanted to wish him a happy eighteenth birthday. I wanted to know how he was doing. I wanted to know if he had a new girlfriend. I wanted to know if he still thought about me. I saw him at school a few times but he never said anything to me. It was almost like I had become invisible. I put the phone down. *He doesn't want to talk to me...I don't blame him...*

A couple of weeks later, I was sitting in my room doing my homework when the phone rang.

"Hello?"

"Hannah?"

"Yeah...Jessica?"

"Hannah, what is going on!?"

"...You heard about Rob..."

"Yeah...Aaron told me everything..."

"I know it probably doesn't make sense..."

"Probably is an understatement, Hannah..." I told Jessica about my dad and the statutory rape situation. I told her about how my dad liked Rob. I told her about the hospital and Rob's grandpa. I told her about my grandma and she stopped me. "Hannah, why did you tell Will your grandma died?"

"He told you..."

"Yeah...What are you doing, Hannah?"

"What'd you tell him?"

"I told him the truth." *Shit...*

"He was pissed...I take it he hasn't asked you about it..."

"No, I haven't talked to him in a long time...So, how is he?"

"Wait! Why did you lie to him?" *Ugh...* "Jessica, I needed a reason...Look, it doesn't matter now...I'm sorry I lied to him, but it's better than him being in jail..."

"I don't think your dad would have called the police."

"I couldn't risk that...How is he doing?"

"...He seems fine...He misses you." *Ahhh...I miss him too...*

"Is he seeing anyone?"

"...Not that I know of..." *Hmmm...Vicki hasn't pounced yet?* "So, about Rob..." *Ugh...* "Are you just using him?" *Kind of...Yeah.*

"It's not like that, Jessica."

"It seems like that..."

"I like Rob...He's really smart and he treats me really well...Actually, I want to say he worships the ground I walk on."

"And that's a good thing?" *Well...*

"I don't know..."

"...How long do you think you're going to be with him?"

"Jessica!"

"What?"

"My dad likes him, which means I can do whatever I want...I don't have to tip-toe around my parents with him."

"...If that's what you want."

"It's just easier this way."

"But, is easier better?" *No, Dammit, Jessica!*

"...There's nothing I can do about it right now!"

"We've been friends for a long time and I know that you're not happy with Rob..."

"Jessica!"

"But it's your choice and if you think it's right then I'll leave you alone about it." *Good...*

"Thank you!"

"Well, hey, I'm about to meet up with Aaron for lunch, you want me to pick you up?"

"No, thanks for asking though, I'll give you a call later."

"Okay, bye Hannah."

"Bye," I said and hung up the phone. *Jessica's probably right...I remember when I was the one giving her advice...*

The week before Halloween, Rob and I decided to walk to the mall. I told him that I wanted to go shopping for a costume, but I really just wanted to get out of my house. As we were walking down the street, Rob turned to me and had a funny look on his face.

"I can't believe those fuckers started a new band without me," Rob said.

"What did you expect them to do?" I asked.

"They've got Nate on vocals...They're playing butt rock now..." I laughed."

"What's butt rock?"

"It's that new metal bullshit."

"New metal huh? What happened to old metal?"

"Grunge killed old metal...The hair bands...And now there's this shit where white guys are rapping over metal guitars...I think they're trying to be like Korn."

"I think I've heard of them..."

"It's fucking trash...I don't ever want to hear you listening to it." *I'm sorry, what!?*

"I'll listen to whatever I want to, Rob."

"...Whatever...Aaron told me that they got a new drummer too...What a waste of talent..."

"Are you still talking about Nate?"

"Yeah, it's ridiculous. He's a really good drummer and he's going to give that up for rapping and growling...So dumb...I bet it was Will's idea..." *Billy...*

"It sounds like you're jealous..."

"Jealous of what?"

"I don't know...Maybe because Aaron and Nate chose Will over you..."

"They can have him...He's an asshole."

"No, he's not."

"Why are you defending him?"

"I'm just telling the truth...I dated a guy that was a real asshole...I know the difference, trust me."

"Shit, how many guys have you been with?" Rob asked.

"...Just two...Billy and Joe..." I was going to ask him how many girls he had been with, but I already knew the answer.

"...And me, right?" *Oh...Ummm. Hmmm...*

"What do you mean?"

"What do you mean, what do I mean?"

"...I thought you meant sex..."

"...Oh, right...So, when are we gonna...You know..." *Ugh...*

"I want to take things slow. I just got out of a relationship, as I'm sure you're aware..." I said facetiously.

"That was like three months ago. How long do you need?"

"I don't know, Rob, I'll let you know..." *Or not...* Rob pulled a pack of cigarettes from his pocket and then started smoking. *That's so gross. Oh well...*

"Do you want one?" Rob asked.

"No, I'm good, I don't smoke," I insisted.

"...Maybe you should..." *What's that supposed to mean?*

"No, thanks, I like having white teeth and fresh breath."

"You are so superficial..." *I am not...That's just wrong!*

"Rob, that has nothing to do with it...It's just basic hygiene! It's not like smoking is healthy for you."

"If it's not smoking, it'll be something else. My grandpa didn't smoke and he died anyway..." *Oh my God...*

"Your grandpa was old, Rob."

"Still...Doesn't matter." *Ugh...*

"It does though...Shouldn't we try to be as healthy as possible while we can?"

"That's what I'm saying...It doesn't matter. We're all going to die regardless..."

"And you, for some reason, would like to hasten that effort?"

"You're not hearing me...IT DOES NOT MATTER!" Rob Yelled. *What the hell!?*

"What is wrong with you?"

"Nothing..." *I don't know why I'm with you...I don't care that my dad likes you...*

"Rob, I think that maybe..." Before I could finish my thought, Rob stopped walking and grabbed my arm.

"Hannah, if you were to ever leave me, I would kill myself..." My heart stopped in my chest and I almost felt like I couldn't breathe. *Not again...I can't let this happen again...Mel...*

"Rob, I'm not going to leave you..."

"...What were you going to say?"

"...I was going to say that we should just change the subject..."

"Oh...Yeah, right...I'm not joking though...I would kill myself. You're all I have now..." *Shit...* I forced myself to smile and Rob grabbed ahold of my hand. He threw his cigarette on the ground and we continued walking to the mall. *What have I gotten myself into?*

At the end of April, Rob and I were alone in his room and I was watching him play his guitar. He stopped strumming and then looked over at me.

"You wanna go to the prom?" Rob asked. *Hmmm...I wonder...*

"...Sure, Rob, why not?"

"Okay, cool..." Rob started playing his guitar again. *Wait...How are we even going to get there?*

"...Ummm, Rob, how are we going to get there? Neither one of us drives..." Rob continued playing.

"...My mom can take us." *Ugh...How embarrassing. We're not kids anymore...*

"...Don't you think we're a little old to have your mom take us to the prom?"

"No...If you don't want to go, then we won't go. It was just a question. Damn...I don't even want to go..."

"...Then why did you ask me?"

"Because I thought that you would want to go." *Hmmm...*

"I do want to go, but I don't want your mom to take us."

"Why not? Who cares?" *Duh...*

"I do, Rob...Is your mom going to take us to dinner too?"

"...I don't know...Maybe. Shit, Hannah, I haven't thought about it." *Yeah, obviously...I wonder if Jessica and Aaron are going?*

"I could call Jessica...Aaron might be taking her..."

"Okay..."

"We might be able to go with them."

"I don't know...I'm cool with Aaron, but Jessica..."

"It's just one night, Rob, get over yourself."

"...Whatever Hannah." *It's always whatever with you!*

"I don't even know if they're going, but it doesn't hurt to ask, right?"

"How do you know if they'll even want us tagging along?"

"I don't know, which is why I need to call to find out."

"Whatever, do what you want...I'm sure you will anyway." *And don't forget it!*

"If they say yes, will you be okay with it?"

"Yeah, sure, I don't care either way..." *Right...*

"Okay, I'll call her when I get home."

"Why don't you call her right now?" *I don't want to...I need to ask her about Billy...*

"...No, it's okay," I responded. "It can wait until later."

"I'll go get the phone. You should call her right now." Rob put his guitar down and walked out to his kitchen and then came back with the phone.

"...Fine, have it your way, Rob, but she probably won't be home right now." He handed me the phone.

"It doesn't hurt to try, right?" *Yeah... You got me there...* I dialed Jessica's number. *Please don't be home...* On the fourth ring, Jessica answered. *Shit...* Rob sat on the edge of his bed and stared at me.

"Hey, Jessica."

"Hannah!"

"I know I haven't called you in a while..."

"It's okay, what's going on?"

"Rob asked me to prom and..."

"...You're still with Rob?" *Oh shit...*

"...Yeah."

"...Wow, I'm kind of surprised..." *Me too...*

"Is she talking shit?" Rob whispered. I shook my head.

"...Anyway, are you going with Aaron?"

"Yeah...Oh my God, Hannah, it was so romantic. He got down on one knee and gave me a rose before asking me..." *Okay...I'm a little jealous...*

"...That's awesome, Jessica...I was wondering...We were wondering if we could maybe go with you guys..."

"...I don't know, Hannah...I'd have to talk to Aaron about it."

"Yeah, I understand..." *Damn it, I want to ask about Billy...*

"...I don't see why not, though."

"Really?"

"Yeah, I'll call him to make sure..."

"Okay, sounds good."

"I'll call you back later tonight."

"Okay, bye."

"Bye." I handed Rob his phone and he went to return it to his kitchen. *Hmmm, I guess Billy isn't going with them...She would have said something...* Rob came back into his room and shut the door behind him.

"So, what'd she say?"

"She said we could probably go with them, but she had to run it by Aaron first. She's going to call me later..."

"Oh, all right..." Rob went back to playing his guitar. *What am I even doing here? Ugh...* Rob started singing the first verse to 'Lithium' while strumming along. *I can see why you like that song so much...*

Later that night, I was in my room organizing my backpack when the phone rang. *Jessica...* I quickly jumped up off of the floor and grabbed the phone.

"Hello?"

"Hey, it's me."

"Jessica! Oh my God, I've been waiting for your call. I was at Rob's house when I called you earlier."

"Really?"

"Yeah, so I couldn't ask you about Billy..."

"Hannah, what's going on? You're still with Rob, which I don't understand at all, and now you're asking about your ex..."

"It's a really long, boring story..."

"Hannah!?"

"Okay...I was going to break up with him, but then he threatened that he was going to kill himself..." Jessica laughed. *That's funny?*

"And you believed him?"

"Yeah..."

"I turned him down and he's still alive." Jessica laughed again. *Hmmm...*

"Yeah, I guess you do have a point, but you should have seen his eyes, Jessica. It was scary. I believed him."

"Yeah, I get the scary part..."

"So, yeah, what's going on with Billy?"

"He's going out with that Vicki girl." *I knew it!*

"Is he taking her to prom?"

"Yeah...I think they're going with Chris and his girlfriend..."

"...Angela?"

"I think that's her name..." *It is...*

"That's what I was going to ask you...If Billy was going with you guys to the prom...And who he was taking..."

"No, I heard they were getting a limo." *What!?*

"Fancy."

"Aaron's taking us in his mom's boyfriend's red Camaro...It's cooler than a limo. It's a convertible..."

"Nice...So did you talk to Aaron about us coming along."

"Yep, he doesn't have a problem with it."

"Oh, cool..."

"...You're still going with Rob?"

"Yeah, I have a plan though..."

"Uh oh, Hannah, do I even want to ask?" I laughed.

"Probably not..."

"Okay, then I won't," Jessica said and we both laughed.

"Trust me, I know what I'm doing," I responded.

"Hannah, can I ask you a personal question..."

"Yeah, of course..."

"Have you and Rob, you know, done it yet?"

"Nope." Jessica laughed.

"I don't know how you do it, Hannah..."

"Do what?"

"...You have a guy that's threatening to kill himself over you and he's not even getting sex..."

"Honestly, I think I'm his first girlfriend. He doesn't know any better..."

"...And why are you with him again?" *I don't know...* "You could get any guy you wanted." *I know, I know...Billy...*

"Thanks, Jessica, but there's only one guy I want..."

"Will..."

"Yeah..."

"He's with someone though...I mean, he seems really happy." *I don't like that...Happy without me?*

"...I'm going to tell him how I feel at prom, Jessica."

"That sounds like a terrible idea...No offense..."

"None taken...I have to tell him before Vicki gets her filthy hooks in him."

"What if you're too late?"

"I don't think I am...I'm going to be the prettiest girl at the prom. Vicki won't stand a chance! Hey, have you bought your dress yet?"

"No...You wanna go shopping together?"

"Yeah, it'll be fun...How about tomorrow?"

"Sounds good."

"All right, cool, I'll pick you up around ten."

"I'll be ready, see you tomorrow."

"Okay, bye Hannah."

"Bye." I hung up the phone and sat on the edge of my bed. I grabbed the astrology book off of my desk and opened it to the Libra section that I had bookmarked. *It has to be perfect...*

Chapter Twenty-Three

Promenade

I stood in front of my bedroom mirror and slowly brushed my hair as I listened to Luscious Jackson on the radio. My mom knocked on my door and then let herself inside.

"You look beautiful, Hannah."

"...Thanks, mom."

"I really like the dress you chose. It's not as revealing as I thought..."

"...Mom, I'm not trying to look like all the other girls..." My mom laughed.

"What are they going to look like?"

"I don't know...Some of those dresses were fit for a prostitute, so yeah..."

"That's very keen of you...You know, I didn't go to my junior prom...Only my senior prom..."

"It's the same thing, mom..."

"I know, but I didn't get the chance to go my junior year..."

"I'm sorry...Can you zip me up?"

"Yeah, turn around," my mom said and then zipped up my dress. I looked over at my alarm clock.

"Hmmm, Rob should be here by now...He was going to walk over here before Jessica..."

"...Her boyfriend's driving you guys, right?"

"Yeah, Aaron."

"Is he a good driver."

"Yes, mom, he's a good driver." *Come on, really?*

"Isn't he Will's friend?" *Ugh...*

"Yeah, I told you that a long time ago..."

"Is he going to be there?"

"At the prom? I don't know, probably..." *He better be there...* "He has a girlfriend, so..."

"Oh, does he? What's her name?" *Oh my God...*

"Vicki...Victoria, whatever..."

"Are you okay with that?" *What kind of stupid question is that!? Of course, I'm not okay...*

"...Jessica told me that he seems happy...So I'm happy for him." *Nope...*

"That's good, Hannah, It's very mature of you." *Right...*

"Well, I am seventeen..."

"Yes, you are...Almost an adult..." *Thank God...* I looked in the mirror and then turned back to my mom.

"How's my make-up look?"

"Perfect..." *Yes, it does...*

"Good, because I spent all afternoon on it," I said and then laughed.

"I guess it was worth it then," my mom agreed. "Come on, let's show your dad." *Okay...* My mom led me down the hallway and my brother jumped out of his room.

"Why is your dress so fluffy?" My brother asked and then grabbed a handful.

"Shut up, Michael! Stop touching it," I said and kept walking out to the living room. "Hi dad."

"Look at my little girl all grown up..." *I guess...*

"What do you think?" I asked and spun around in a circle."

"I think you look beautiful...You're going to be the belle of the ball..." *Belle of the ball...Hmmm, okay...*

"Thanks, dad," I said and then we heard a knock at the door. "That must be Rob." My dad walked over and opened the door.

"Hi Rob," my dad said. "Come on in." Rob walked inside and stared at me. He was wearing a retro light blue tuxedo and was holding my corsage. *Well, it is different...*

"You look beautiful, Hannah," Rob said and wrapped the corsage around my wrist.

"Thanks, Rob..." My mom grabbed the boutonniere off of the counter and handed it to me. I pinned it on Rob's jacket and he smiled. *I wonder what Vicki's wearing? Why do I even care? Ugh...* My mom got her camera and told us that she wanted us to pose for some pictures. Rob wrapped his arm around me and we both stared into the camera. *Awesome...*

"Hannah, smile," my mom instructed. I looked over at Rob who was as happy as I had ever seen him. *Hmmm...* I turned back to the camera and forced a smile. My mom took multiple pictures of us until we heard another knock on the door. *They're here...* My dad opened the door and let Jessica and Aaron inside.

"Oh my God, Hannah, you look amazing," Jessica said.

"Thanks, you too..."

"Nice tux, Rob...It suits you..." Aaron insisted.

"Thanks, man...Was that a pun?"

"...Yeah, sorry, no pun intended...I think that's what people say..."

"No worries, man."

"I want to get a picture of everyone," my mom said. We all stood in front of the door and my mom took the picture.

"Where are you going for dinner?" My dad asked.

"Red Lobster," Aaron answered. "It's good food..."

"...And it doesn't cost a lot," Rob added.

"Makes sense," my dad said. I opened the door and we started walking outside. "That's a really nice car..."

"It's my mom's boyfriend's car," Aaron said. My dad walked up to the car.

"This is the Z-28?" My dad asked.

"Yeah, it's really fast," Aaron responded. *Uh oh...*

"You're not going to drive it fast, right?" My dad continued his inquisition.

"Right, I'm going to drive safe," Aaron answered. "They wouldn't have let me take the car otherwise."

"Good man," my dad said. *Can we go now?* "...Okay, have a nice evening."

"Have fun," my mom added.

"I want you home by midnight," my dad said as Rob and I got in the back seat of the car.

"Okay, dad, midnight," I answered. Aaron started the car and then drove around the end of the cul-de-sac. I stared at Chris's old house, the tree in the front yard, and then at the fence on the side. *Billy...I miss you...* We drove in front of my house and my parents waved at us as we headed to Red Lobster for dinner. Rob rested his hand on top of mine and then stared at me longingly. *Kind of creepy, dude...* I forced a smile and then turned to watch Visalia go by. When we got to Red Lobster, the parking lot was surprisingly empty. Aaron parked the car and we got out.

"Are we early?" I asked.

"No, we're not early," Aaron answered. "I think that people are just going to the fancier restaurants tonight...Will and them are going to The Vintage Press, so..."

"Aaron!" Jessica lamented. "We talked about this..."

"Oh right, sorry..." Aaron responded.

"It's okay, Aaron," I said. "You can talk about him."

"I'd rather not hear his name," Rob added. *Heh...Hmmm...* We walked into the restaurant and were seated immediately. Aaron had made a reservation, but it didn't seem necessary. There were only a few couples there that were obviously going to the prom and a few other random people eating dinner. The waitress brought out water, a bunch of Cheddar Bay Biscuits, and handed us each a menu.

"What are you going to get, Hannah?" Jessica asked. *Billy likes lasagna...But I don't see that...* I turned the pages of the menu and then set it down.

"I'm going to ask them if they can make me a lasagna," I answered.

"Why lasagna?" Rob asked. "This is Red LOBSTER..." Rob insisted. *Heh...I know where we are...*

"Because Billy likes lasagna." Jessica gasped. Rob squinted his eyes at me and Aaron looked at Jessica, lost for words.

"Why does it even matter what he likes!?" Rob insisted.

"...I guess it doesn't," I answered. Rob didn't say anything. He looked back at his menu, visibly shaken.

"Hannah!" Jessica whispered. "Stop it! Be good!" *Heh...* I smiled and looked back down at my menu.

"I'll go with the lobster linguini," I said.

"I'm gonna get the rock lobster and shrimp," Aaron added.

"Rock lobster...Isn't that a song?" I asked.

"Yeah, I think so...B-52's..." Aaron answered.

"Yeah, Billy really likes that song..." I insisted.

"Hannah, fuck!" Rob responded. *Heh, I don't even know if that's true...*

"...I'll take the same thing as Aaron," Jessica said. *I don't even think that she likes lobster, which means that she really likes Aaron...*

"...I'll go with the surf and turf," Rob added.

"You know who else likes surf and turf?" I asked and smiled. Everyone stared at me indignantly. The tension at the table was palpable and could be cut with a knife. "...My dad...My dad likes surf and turf." Jessica and Aaron let out a sigh of relief.

"Yeah...That makes sense...I guess we have a lot in common," Rob reasoned. *Ugh...Yeah...* The waitress came back to the table and took our orders. We all handed her our menus.

"...It's because you're both earth signs," I said to Rob.

"...What?" Rob asked.

"My dad's a Capricorn and you're a Taurus..."

"...So what?"

"It's why you get along with him," I insisted.

"I don't believe that shit," Rob said.

"Well, I do...Look at Jessica and Aaron..."

"Oh no, Hannah, don't bring us into this..." Jessica pleaded.

"...Jessica's a Cancer and Aaron's a Taurus. It just works..." Jessica and Aaron didn't say anything and no one pointed out the obvious problem with my argument because of Rob and Jessica's history. *I wonder what happened...* "...And Billy and I are..."

"...I know..." Rob interjected. "...Perfect for each other."

"We are perfect for each other," I insisted.

"And that's why you're still together, right Hannah?" Rob quipped.

"If it weren't for my parents..."

"Don't start with that shit..."

"It's not shit," I said.

"It is so much shit, Hannah...You didn't want to be alone...You didn't want him to break up with you before you broke up with him," Rob responded. "You were afraid that he was going to go off to college and leave you behind..."

"...That's not the whole story, Rob." Jessica and Aaron stared at me with intensity.

"Then what is the whole story, Hannah?" *Shit...*

"...I think we should change the subject. We're being rude to Jessica and Aaron."

"No, damn it!" Rob exclaimed and slammed his hand down on the table. The few people that were in the restaurant turned around.

"Rob, stop it!" I insisted. "You're gonna get us kicked out..." *Please...Don't stop...*

"...I don't care," Rob responded and looked around the restaurant. *Heh...* "This isn't over...We're going to talk about this later."

"Whatever you say, Rob," I said. Jessica looked at me and mouthed the words, 'stop it.' I didn't say anything else out of respect for Jessica. We all waited in awkward silence until our food came out. We thanked the waitress and then started eating. Jessica and Aaron made passing comments about the food, but Rob and I sat in isolation from one another while we ate. I enjoyed my food and I enjoyed the silence. I looked over at Rob, but he looked straight ahead as he loudly chewed through his steak. *I may have come here with you, but I shouldn't have...Billy...I wonder what you're doing right now...* I focused my attention back on my food and finished everything on my plate. "...Wow, I must have been hungry..."

"Yeah, I've never seen you finish anything," Jessica said and I laughed.

"Coming from the girl that never eats," I answered back.

"Hey...I eat...Sometimes..." I looked at the chaotic mess that Jessica left on her plate.

"...Ummm, so, were you working on an art project there?" I facetiously inquired.

"...I ate some of it..." Jessica reasoned and we both laughed. After everyone finished eating, Aaron and Rob paid the bill. We walked outside to a setting sun. Aaron drove us to the convention center and parked a couple of blocks away.

"This is as close as I can get," Aaron said.

"It's fine, Aaron, we can walk," Jessica said and got out of the car. She moved her seat forward and let me out. Rob followed. Aaron put the convertible top back on and then we started walking to the convention center. Aaron and Jessica walked in front of Rob and I. They were holding hands and whispering into one another's ears. *Ahhh... That used to be Billy and I.* I held my hands closely to my body to make sure that Rob understood my intentions. When we got to the entrance, there was a sign that directed us to take our pictures first. *I don't want to take a picture with Rob...I think my mom has enough to last for the rest of my life anyway...* We walked inside of the convention center and saw a line of people to the right lining up for their pictures.

"There's the line," Jessica said and grabbed Aaron's hand.

"I'll catch up with you," I said. "I have to use the restroom." I walked into the hall and found the restrooms. I checked my makeup and then walked toward the door. Vicki and Angela walked in. *Oh shit...Of course it's them.* We stared at each other for a few seconds and then I continued walking. "Hi Vicki," I said and opened the door.

"What the hell?" Angela said as I walked away. *I need to find him.* I looked around the hall. *Shit, he isn't in here...* I walked into another area of the convention center close to where they were taking pictures. *There he is! But, he's with Chris...Shit...Oh well...* I walked toward them. Chris made eye contact with me and laughed. *What's funny, asshole?* Will turned around and I locked eyes with him and smiled.

"Hey Billy, Hi Chris," I said. "Ummm, Chris, do you think you could give us a minute?"

"A minute for what?"

"To talk; could you leave us alone for a minute?"

"Sure, yeah, Angela would be pissed if..."

"Yeah, she would," Will interjected. Chris turned around and walked away.

"So, what's up, Hannah? I mean, I don't think we have anything to say to one another. And where's Rob, by the way?"

"So, I hear that you and Vicki are a thing..."

"Yeah."

"That's cool."

"Yeah, it is..."

"...I miss you."

"Where's Rob, Hannah?"

"He's around here somewhere. We had a fight. We're always fighting. It's not like how we were, Billy."

"You can call me Will."

"Billy, don't be like that, you're gonna make me cry." *This is my fault...*

"Why did you lie to me about your grandma dying?" It doesn't make any sense. If you didn't want to be with me, you could have just said so."

"Lie? My grandma did die. Why would you say that?" *Fuck...I forgot about that...*

"...Jessica told me that your grandma's alive."

"Jessica? She doesn't know. I didn't even tell her." *I'm going to Hell.*

"Well, I don't know what to believe. Honestly, it doesn't even matter. I have to ask though, Why Rob?"

"He was really nice to me. I was confused and, I don't know, frustrated with my parents."

"I'm sorry; it just doesn't make any sense."

"I guess, I mean, I guess I just couldn't face being alone."

"What are you even talking about, Hannah...Alone?"

"I knew that you would break up with me eventually when you went to college, so..."

"Nope. I don't think so. We went through all kinds of shit to be together and all of the sudden you think I'm just going to leave you?"

"Yes, I always thought about you leaving me. I started talking to Rob about it, and he was so sweet to me...And he's the same age as me...And my parents..."

"...Great, Hannah, that's just great. So why are you standing here talking to me right now?"

"I had to do something...I had to do something to get my parents to leave you alone. I had to convince them that we were really not together anymore..." *And I did...* "...And Rob...And I already told you...I miss you."

"So, all of this was for me? I just don't buy it, Hannah."

"It's true...I never wanted any of this to happen."

"And what about Rob?" *Who cares?*

"...Rob isn't who I thought he was."

"It doesn't matter anymore. I should go find Vicki..." Rob walked up and put his arm around me. *Ugh...*

"What doesn't matter anymore?" Rob asked. "Why are you talking to my girl?" *I'm not your girl...*

"I was just saying hi, Rob, I haven't talked to him in months," I insisted.

"Yeah," Will said. "Not since I punched you in the face." *Heh...*

"Hey, bitch, if you want to go, we can take this outside," Rob said. *That's funny...*

"...Nah, Rob, I'm good. You two have a nice evening," Will said and walked away.

"Fucking right," Rob said and then led me towards the crowd. "Fuck, Hannah, we haven't even got our pictures and you're over here talking to your ex."

"We can get our pictures taken later, Rob, it's not a big deal," I reasoned.

"Whatever," Rob said and we walked over to wait in the exhibition area to be introduced. "I don't want you talking to him anymore..." *What the fuck! You're not my dad!*

"...I'll talk to anyone I want any time I want," I said.

"No, you won't," Rob insisted.

"I don't know how you're going to stop me..."

"...Fuck!" *Heh...That's what I thought...* Rob and I stood in line for a few minutes before they started announcing the couples and letting us into the main hall. I watched Will and Vicki get in line behind us and Rob brutally pulled on my arm.

"That hurt, asshole!"

"I'm not going to tell you again!"

"...Now I can't look at anyone either?"

"Not him..."

"...Okay, Hitler, whatever you say..." *Heh...Or not...* I turned around and smiled at Will. Rob pulled on my arm again. I didn't react though. I looked straight forward and waited for the announcer to call our names. Rob and I walked into the hall and someone took our picture. I didn't smile. My expression was that of indifference. I wasn't happy. I wanted the picture to reflect that point. *That is going to be the worst picture ever taken. Good...* Rob grabbed my hand and led me out to the dance floor. I heard Will and Vicki being announced as we got closer to the speakers. *That just doesn't sound right at all...* They were playing 'Semi-charmed Life,' which was a song that was over played on the radio, but I liked it. I knew that Rob hated it though, so I decided to start dancing just to see what he would do. To my surprise, he started dancing with me.

"HEY!" Rob yelled. The music was loud. I could barely hear him. "WHAT!?"

"ARE WE GONNA, YOU KNOW, DO IT TONIGHT?" *Is he asking what I think he's asking? Is he kidding? Shit, probably not...*

"...NO!"

"WHY NOT?" *Dude, you're pretty dumb...Isn't it obvious?* I turned away from Rob and started dancing with a boy I knew from my History class named Brandon. Rob grabbed my arm once again and I rolled my eyes. "WHAT THE FUCK ARE YOU DOING!?"

"I'M TRYING TO HAVE FUN..." Rob stopped dancing and then stared at me with piercing intensity. He put his hands on my shoulders so that I would stop moving. I looked into his eyes and could see his anger building. "LET ME GO, ROB!" Rob let go of my right shoulder and then smacked the side of my head. He didn't hit me hard, but I was surprised. The people stopped dancing around us and just stared.

"I ALREADY TOLD YOU..." *Fuck you!*

"TOLD ME WHAT!?"

"IF YOU TRY TO LEAVE ME, I'M GOING TO KILL MYSELF!" *Oh fuck... This can't be happening...* Rob grabbed my arms and shook me. I looked down at the floor and watched the lights flicker and flash in a sea of neon confusion. I heard the chorus to 'Semi-charmed Life' echo in my head over and over again. "DID YOU HEAR WHAT I SAID!?" Rob shook me again and then stopped. He pushed his finger into my chest and jabbed at me as he emphasized each word that came out of his mouth. "IF YOU FUCKING LEAVE ME, I'M GOING TO FUCKING KILL MYSELF." *Fuck...* "DO YOU UNDERSTAND WHAT I'M TELLING YOU!" *I can't do this...What am I supposed to say?* "LOOK AT ME WHEN I'M TALKING TO YOU." Rob grabbed my chin and thrust my head upward. Tears welled up in my eyes and then slowly trickled down my cheeks. I looked into Rob's fiery, reptilian eyes and then pulled back away from him.

"...YOU DON'T FUCKING OWN ME...YOU SHOULD KILL YOURSELF!" I exclaimed. I was exasperated. A sense of sadness overcame me. I didn't want anyone to commit suicide and I felt bad that the words left my quivering lips. I could see Rob's eyes soften though, as if he knew that he had been called on his bluff and he had nothing else to use against me. Nevertheless, he regained his confidence and pushed his finger into my chest again.

"I DON'T THINK YOU HEARD ME!" He jabbed his finger at me with more pressure and intensity with each syllable. "I'M NOT FUCKING AROUND, HANNAH!" Without warning, a security officer grabbed Rob's arm, relieving me of his abuse, and pulled him away from me. Rob continued yelling profanities as security dragged him away and out the door. *Oh shit...* The crowd of people moved away from me and Jessica ran up and gave me a hug. She stepped back, wiped the tears from my face, and then rested her hands on my shoulders.

"ARE YOU OKAY?"

"YEAH...I'M OKAY."

"...I GUESS I DODGED A BULLET," Jessica said and smiled.

"YEAH...I'M SO STUPID, JESSICA..."

"NO, YOU"RE NOT STUPID..." Jessica insisted. I looked behind Jessica and saw Vicki push Will and walk away. *Billy...* I smiled at Jessica and then ran over to Will and gave him a hug. I held his hand and led him outside of the convention center. I stopped and then turned around to face him.

"It's so loud in there, I can't even hear myself think."

"Yeah, you and me both, but what's going on Hannah? What happened with Rob?"

"Ummm, yeah, I don't really want to talk about it."

"Well, I do...I'm pretty sure that Vicki is gonna break up with me over this, so, yeah..." Will said and then laughed. *That's funny?*

"What's so funny, Billy?"

"It's just ironic. I was going to break up with her anyway."

"Why were you going to break up with her?"

"It's really simple actually. I don't like her," Will said and I laughed.

"What's her sign, Billy?" Will laughed.

"She just had her birthday, so, Taurus?" *Heh...* "...I guess it's not a good match, right Hannah?"

"Obviously not a good match..." I Smiled. "...Just like Rob..."

"...What happened?" Will asked and I sighed.

"I may have tried to get Rob to break up with me."

"How did you do that?"

"I told him how good our relationship was and how we're perfect for each other..."

"Then why aren't we together? Why did any of this happen?" Will looked visibly frustrated." *I know Billy, I'm so sorry...*

"...He said if I ever broke up with him, he would kill himself. I believed him..."

"Rob's a lot of things, mostly bad, but he wouldn't kill himself. I know him pretty well and the one thing that Rob loves more than Nirvana is himself..." *Thank God...* I laughed and grabbed Will's hands.

"...Billy, I lied to you."

"About what?"

"My grandma didn't die."

"Oh, I fucking knew it!" *I'm so sorry...*

"...Don't be mad, please, I wasn't thinking clearly back then."

"Back then? How long ago do you think this happened?" *Shit...*

"...I know."

"And then you lied about lying...And that was like five minutes ago. What about that? I actually thought that Jessica was lying for a minute, but couldn't figure out a reason for her doing that."

"I know...I'm sorry...I haven't been myself since..." *To be honest...*

"Since when? I mean, It's a good question...Right?" Will asked. *Since Mel left...*

"...I don't know...Sometime between my dad threatening you and Rob...But it's good...Being with Rob was a good thing..." *Ugh...*

"Are you okay, Hannah? You're not making any sense." *Yeah...*

"No, I am...If it weren't for Rob, I wouldn't have realized how much I miss you...How perfect we are together. I already knew that, but I think I needed the reminder..."

"Well, shit, I should stop by his house on the way home and thank him."

"You see, I miss your sarcasm, Billy, you don't get all mad like Rob."

"What about the whole statutory rape thing? Did that even happen? Because you said since your dad threatened me but that could mean anything..." *Shit...*

"...Oh yeah, he made that threat all the time. I just didn't want to worry you. I was worried about it but I didn't say anything...Until I did...It just didn't happen as recently as I..."

"So, it had nothing to do with that night or your grandma?" *Why can't I stop lying? Shit...*

"...No, I was just under a lot of stress and I was, I don't know...I don't know what else to say..." *I need to stop...*

"What now, Hannah?" Will asked as he pulled his hands away from me. "What's the point of all this? Are we just going to get back together and act like none of this happened?" *I don't know...Maybe.* I looked away from him and then at the ground. "I think it's more complicated than that..."

"...I know, Billy, I know...I'm sorry for everything."

"We should get back to the dance..."

"...Billy, you wanna walk me home?"

"Without telling anyone?"

"Do you want to talk to Vicki right now? You said it yourself...Do you think she's going to be happy right now?"

"No, but what about Aaron and Jessica? And Chris...We came in a limo together. That was expensive."

"Oh, fancy!"

"I'm serious right now, leaving without saying anything would not be cool."

"I know, Billy, oh so serious..." I teased and laughed. Aaron and Jessica will be fine and do you really care what Chris thinks?"

"Yeah, we worked things out." *Really? Hmmm...*

"...That's good," I said and then moved close to him. "Come on, Billy, like old times...Walk me home. Who cares what anyone thinks? I think they know anyway..." I stared into his eyes with smoldering intensity, patiently waiting for an answer.

"...All right, fuck it, let's go," Will finally answered. I pulled him closer and whispered in his ear.

"I'm so sorry, Billy, I fucked up."

"I get it...I really do..."

"I don't want you to be mad at me. I just want us to be happy together."

"I'm not mad at you, well, not anymore at least," Will said and laughed. *How is that funny? Hmmm...*

"...What's so funny, babe?"

"I was furious with you a few months ago and now, well, now I just don't care." *Oh no...Billy...* My heart felt like it was leaving my body. *This is all my fault...*

"...What do you mean you don't care?"

"I'm over being mad at you. You made a mistake and I've accepted that..."

"...I don't know...It doesn't seem like you have," I insisted and stopped walking.

"What do you want me to say?" *That you love me...*

"...I don't know. I'm so sorry. I don't deserve your forgiveness, but please...Everything..."

"...Let's just forget about it."

"Okay...So, what do you wanna do?" *Whitendale Park...*

"...Whitendale Park?" *Jinx!*

"Yeah, let's go!" *We are perfect together...* I put my arm around Will's waist and we continued walking around the convention center and down the street. We walked in perfect unison holding hands without saying a word. When we got to Whitendale Park, I stopped and turned to Will.

"What time is it?"

"I don't know..." We walked over to the playground and Will sat down on one of the swings. I sat down on his lap sideways and he started swinging. *This is really nice...* I wrapped my hand around the back of his neck and looked into his eyes.

"Do you still love me?"

"...Yes, I still love you. I don't think that will ever change." *That's all I need to hear...*

"Me too..." I said and swung my legs around and dug my feet into the ground to stop the swing. I stood up, slipped off my shoes, pulled my panties off, and then slipped them into his jacket pocket. *How about that Billy?* My smile was quickly shaken when Will removed my panties from his jacket and put them back in my hand. *Ummm, okay...What is happening right now?*

"...We shouldn't do this tonight," Will insisted. *Huh...* "We should take things slow." *Billy...*

"Are you sure?" I asked. "...I've missed you, Billy..."

"I've missed you too, but we don't have to...Let's just be here together..."

"Okay, if that's what you want..." *I don't understand...*

"It's all I've ever wanted." *Hmmm...* I leaned in and kissed him and then put my panties back on. I sat back down on his lap and rested my head on his chest. He started swinging again and the time slowly went by as I listened to the crickets and passing cars. After some more time had passed, Will gently swept my hair away from my face.

"Hey, I'm gonna walk you home, it's getting late."

"...Okay, Billy, let's go." We started walking around the school and as soon as we stepped onto the street, my shoes reverberated throughout the neighborhood. I stopped and took them off. "These shoes are loud, it's time to go barefoot." We continued walking and then stopped behind my mom's car. I turned to Will and kissed him like my life depended on it. *I love you, Billy...* He pulled away from me after a few seconds and then looked into my eyes.

"I should probably go, it's getting late..."

"...Billy...I'm going to call you tomorrow...Early, like eight."

"Okay...Damn. We've got a lot of damage control to do, Hannah, this is going to be a goddamn mess."

"I know, Billy, but we'll deal with it together."

"Okay, yeah, call me in the morning."

"All right. Billy, I love you. Don't ever forget that."

"I won't...Good night, Hannah." Will kissed me and then walked away into the darkness. I turned around and looked at my front door. I smiled and then laughed. *At least I don't have to go through the window now...* I walked to the door and went to open it but it was locked. *Shit...* I knocked very softly and my dad answered.

"Hannah? We didn't expect you home so early." *Early?* I walked inside and looked at the clock on the wall. *It's not even eleven...Wow.* My dad shut the door and my mom came down the hallway from their bedroom.

"You're home?" my mom asked. "Did you have a good time?" *Hmmm...What should I say?*

"...No, not really..."

"...What happened?" My dad asked. *Just tell the truth...*

"...Rob was pressuring me to have sex..."

"What!?" My dad yelled. *Well...Yeah, kind of...*

"And I told him no...He started pushing me and yelling...I didn't know what to do..."

"Oh my God...Patrick!" My mom pleaded.

"I don't know what to say," my dad said. "I thought he was a good guy..."

"I guess you were wrong," my mom added.

"...Security took him away...I don't know what happened after that..."

"We're just glad you're okay," my dad said. "I'm gonna break that kid's legs."

"You don't have to do that...It's over..."

"Hannah?" My mom asked. "How did you get home?" *Shit...I should probably lie...Fuck it...*

"...Don't be mad...Will brought me home."

"What!?" My dad barked.

"...He left his girlfriend at the dance to do it too...I hope I didn't mess things up between them..." *Yes, I do...* "Dad, he obviously cares about me...I'm glad he was there."

"Patrick..." My mom started to say.

"...I know," My dad said. "...I'm sorry, Hannah, I was wrong...I think a lot of this is my fault..." *Wow...You think?*

"It's okay, dad, you were doing what you thought was right. I don't blame you for that...I'm really tired...I'm gonna go to bed."

"Yeah, get some rest, sweetie, we'll talk about this in the morning...Your dad and I need to talk anyway..." *I think I did it...*

"Okay, goodnight," I said and made my way down the hallway.

"Goodnight," My mom and dad said in unison. I walked into my bedroom and shut the door. I kicked off my shoes and managed to undo the zipper on my dress. I slipped it off and then stared at myself in the mirror. *What am I going to do? I should call Summer tomorrow...Shit, I need to call Jessica too. Maybe I should call Rob...To make it official...If it wasn't obvious to him...Shit, I don't know...I have to call Billy at eight, though...I can tell there's still something wrong...* I got into bed and pulled the covers over my head. I slowly fell asleep with the hope that everything was going to be all right.

Chapter Twenty-Four

Epiphany

I woke up the next day to the incessant sound of the phone
ringing. I turned over in my bed and covered my ears with
my pillow. *Will someone please get the phone...Oh shit, Billy...What time
is it?* I turned back and looked at my alarm clock. *Seven...I have
time...Good, someone got the phone.* Before I had a chance to relax,
my mom practically broke down my door and put the phone in
my face. *What the...*

"Hannah, it's Rob's mom..." *What!?* My mom had a concerned
look on her face that I hadn't seen since Santa Maria. *What is going
on?* I stared at the phone and then at my mom. *Oh no...* I reluctantly
took the phone and sat up on the side of my bed.

"Hello?"

"Hannah?"

"Yeah, what's wrong?" I could hear the fear and anxiety in her
voice just from the simple utterance of my name.

"It's Rob..." She answered. "...He...He took all of my pills..." *Oh
shit...This isn't happening...* "Hannah...What happened last night?
Why would my son try to kill himself?" Rob's mom started sob-
bing. *This is all my fault...I am so sorry...* "Hannah...Why?" Her words
were barely audible.

"...I don't know," I hesitated. *Shit...Yes, I do...* "Is he going to be
okay?"

"...They think so...We're at the hospital right now...He got his stomach pumped...Hannah, I know that he would want you by his side when he wakes up..." *I don't think that's even remotely close to true...But...Shit...* I looked up at my mom.

"I'll have my mom take me right now," I said and my mom nodded.

"Okay, sweetie, we're going to be in the waiting room...We'll talk when you get here..." *Shit...* "Bye."

"Bye," I said and hung up the phone. I looked up at my mom and started crying. "This is all my fault..." My mom sat down beside me and wrapped her arm around my shoulder.

"I understand how you feel, but it's not your fault..." *How is this not my fault?* "Rob made a choice..." *Just like Mel...Mel made a choice...I could have...I should have done something about that too...Fuck my life...*

"I could have been nicer to him..."

"You did the right thing..." *I obviously did not do the right thing...*

"...Mom, can we just go?"

"Yeah...Go ahead and get dressed." My mom walked out of my room and I got dressed. I met her in the kitchen and then I followed her out to the car. We started driving down the street and I felt an extreme sense of sadness. I felt the same dread and darkness I felt when I read Mel's suicide note. I stared out of the window at the lines on the pavement. The yellow and the white became a blur. Tears trickled down my cheeks. "Hannah, are you okay?" *No...I haven't been okay for a long time...*

"...What am I supposed to say to his mom?"

"What do you mean?"

"I can't exactly tell her the truth..."

"The truth is always the best policy."

"...He just tried to kill himself because of me..."

"...Stop right there! It's not because of you..." *Okay, but it is...*

"She doesn't need to hear what actually happened..."

"...I would want to know the truth..."

"...That her son assaulted me and got kicked out of the dance?"

"Yes."

"That's going to lead to even more questions that I don't want to answer...If she even believes me..."

"Why wouldn't she believe you?"

"...Mom, seriously, would you believe something like that about Michael?"

"...I guess I haven't thought this through...I have to check in for work...Do you want me to be there when you talk to her?"

"...No, I have to deal with this on my own."

"You really have grown up so much, Hannah, I'm proud of you." *I'm not sure that's true...*

"I don't know..."

"...It's true. Your dad too...We're both really proud of you." *Great...Now I feel even worse...Summer...That's random...*

"...Mom, this is going to sound weird, well it's not weird, but thinking of it right now is, I guess, kind of weird..."

"What's on your mind?"

"...I think I want to get my license...Maybe after school gets out..."

"Sure, I'll talk to your dad about it."

"...Thanks, mom." We pulled up to the hospital parking lot and then got out of the car. My mom walked towards the main entrance of the hospital and I started walking towards the emergency room.

"If you need anything..."

"Yeah, mom, I know where to find you..."

"All right..." I continued to the entrance of the emergency room. As the automatic doors opened, I saw Rob's parents waiting. *Ugh...I can't believe this is happening...* I walked up to Rob's mom and she immediately reached out for my hand.

"Hannah," she said and awkwardly held my hand. "What happened last night?" *...We got in an argument...And he got kicked out of the dance..."*

"...I'm not exactly sure why..." *Shit...* "...But he got kicked out of the dance...

"...I don't understand," Rob's dad insisted.

"...I need to talk to him," I responded. "I want to find out what happened too..."

"What could he have possibly done to get kicked out?" Rob's dad asked. I didn't answer his question. I didn't want to make the situation worse than it already was. I nervously shrugged my shoulders.

"...Hannah, he's still asleep," Rob's mom added.

"Can I see him?"

"...Yeah," she answered. "I'll walk you to his room." She got up and I followed her down the hallway. We walked inside of the room and I saw Rob propped up in bed with multiple tubes attached to him. *I should have believed him...*

"...Hannah, is there anything you're not telling us?" *Shit...*

"...Yes, but I don't think I should say anything..."

"What do you mean?"

"...I think Rob should tell you...It's not my place..."

"I'm going back to the waiting room...Will you wait with him?"

"Yeah, I'm not going anywhere..."

"...When he wakes up, can you come tell us?"

"Yes, of course," I said. Rob's mom walked out of the room. I watched Rob's chest rise and fall with labored, mechanical precision. *I seriously don't think I can deal with this...I need to call someone...Shit! Billy... This is bad. Hmmm...Shit...I'll call Jessica.* I picked up the phone next to the bed and dialed Jessica's number. *Please answer...* The phone rang multiple times before Jessica picked up. "Jessica!? Oh, thank God!"

"Hannah? What's going on? What happened last night?"

"...I don't even know where to start...Rob tried to kill himself last night..."

"What!? Are you serious?"

"Yeah...I'm at the hospital right now. I'm sitting right next to him."

"Seriously?"

"Yes, Jessica! I'm not making this up! I need you to come down here."

"I don't know, Hannah..."

"Jessica, I need you right now..."

"...Okay, I'll be there in a little bit."

"Okay, but hurry...He's asleep right now, but I don't know..."

"I'll be there as soon as I can."

"Thanks, Jessica."

"Okay, see you soon, bye."

"Bye." I hung up the phone and then stared outside of the room and into the hallway, waiting for someone to save me from myself. I sat in the hospital chair reflecting on all of my decisions that led to that very moment. Every kernel of advice I had heard from my parents rang like a thunderstorm in my head. *Why didn't I just listen? Why does life have to be so complicated? Why is this happening to me? What did I do to deserve this? I'm not happy... When was the last time I was happy? Third grade? No, I've been happy since then...It's so crazy...The ups and downs...It's too much...Mel...I think I understand...* My mind went on repeat for an hour as I tried to make sense out of something that was seemingly nonsensical. My tunnel vision was only broken when Jessica and Aaron walked into the room. I got up from the chair and hugged Jessica. "I'm so glad you came..." I let her go and then looked at Aaron. "...Hi Aaron."

"Hey," Aaron said. "So, what happened last night?" *He didn't tell you?*

"Have you talked to Billy?"

"Yeah, but I just told him that Rob...You know..." Aaron looked over my shoulder at Rob and shook his head. "...And I told him we were on our way here."

"Billy's coming here right now?"

"...Yeah, I think he's gonna pick up Chris on the way." *Shit...Fuck...This isn't good."* My anxiety increased and I felt myself turn pale.

"Are you okay?" Jessica asked.

"...No, I'm not okay..." I sat back down in the chair next to Rob. Jessica and Aaron sat across from me. I looked over at a small table and saw Rob's jacket folded on top of it. I reached into the inside pocket and pulled out Rob's cigarettes. I held them in my hand and then pressed the box against my leg.

"What are you doing?" Jessica asked. "You don't smoke..."

"I know...I don't know what I'm doing..." I responded and then reached back into the pocket to get his lighter. I held both tightly to my leg.

"...Are you going to start?"

"No...I don't know...I don't know what to do, Jessica!" Jessica and Aaron looked at me like I was possessed. They looked at me like I was crazy. *Maybe I am crazy...* "I don't want to be with Rob," I whispered. "I want to get back together with Billy...But it's so complicated now...I feel trapped...Like, I don't know, like I have an obligation to stay with him now...I don't want him to kill himself over me...And it may not make sense...But I can't let it happen...I just can't."

"Rob isn't your responsibility," Jessica insisted and then whispered, "...If he wants to kill himself, then let him do it..." *Fuck, Jessica!* "...It's not like you can stop him..." *I have to...*

"...Wow, Jessica, that's pretty cold, even for you..."

"Yeah, babe, that is kind of harsh..." Aaron said. "...And he might be able to hear you..."

"What!? I'm just saying you have to let people do what they want to do," Jessica reasoned. *Right... This has nothing to do with that night...*

"If I can do something to help someone not commit suicide then that's what I'm going to do," I said and put my hand over Rob's hand and listened to his heartbeat. I turned and stared at Rob's lifeless face and heard fragments of Jessica and Aaron whispering to one another.

"What's up, man, this is crazy," Aaron said. *Billy...*

"Yeah, it's...Something; some twilight zone shit," Will said. I looked back at Will and tried to conjure a smile but couldn't manage it. I pulled my hand away from Rob and got up from the chair. I held tightly to Rob's cigarettes and lighter and walked over to Will.

"Hey, Billy, can we talk outside?"

"I'm not sure that we have much to talk about, Hannah. It seems like everything's pretty clear."

"Please?" I tried to hold Will's hand but he pulled away from me. *This is not what I wanted to happen...Shit...*

"...Fine, Hannah, this isn't the place for this anyway." Will gestured toward the door and I walked out of the room and down the hall to the lobby. I walked past Rob's parents hoping they wouldn't see me.

"Hannah..." Rob's mom said. "Is he awake yet?"

"No..." *Shit...* "I just need some air...I'll be back..."

"Okay..." I continued out through the automatic doors and immediately took out one of Rob's cigarettes and lit it just like I had seen Rob do a hundred times. I took a drag and coughed violently. *What the fuck!? So gross...* I took another drag and tried to recompose myself. Before I had the chance to become acclimated, Will walked through the doors, I exhaled, and then tossed the cigarette on the ground. *All right...Fuck...*

"When did you start smoking?"

"I don't smoke...They're Rob's."

"That's a pretty nasty habit, you know...That shit will age you something fierce...Wrinkles; you'll lose your teeth; I think your hair will fall out...And, yeah, well, you'll stink pretty bad..."

"...I know, I get it, sheesh. Thanks, Dad...I'm just really anxious...I needed something to help calm me down."

"If I remember correctly, smoking does the opposite."

"I don't know...Listen, Billy, I don't want you to get the wrong idea. I still want to be with you." Will looked at me funny like he didn't believe me. "I'm just worried about Rob. I don't want him to kill himself...Shit, this is all my fault."

"Yeah, it is..." Will smiled and laughed. "...That much we agree on."

"It's not funny, Billy, I'm too young to deal with all of this..."

"...That's actually really funny, like ironic, because I feel the same way. I'm too old to deal with this shit."

"What do you mean?"

"I just need this to be over with."

"What are you talking about?"

"Listen, Hannah, I love you, I'll probably always love you. I'll probably be forty years old and still be thinking about you...About what could have been...But I just can't do this with you anymore..." *No...Billy...*

"...Are you saying you don't want to get back together?"

"I don't want to get back together with you, Hannah, I don't trust you...I don't trust you..."

"...I guess I deserve that. I don't even trust me..."

"Well, yeah, see, that's a problem..." Will smiled and I laughed.

"I don't think I'm ever going to find someone as good as you."

"Yeah, I don't think so either," Will said and laughed. "You should go back and check on Rob." *Ugh...*

"I don't want to be with Rob...I can't deal. He's angry and now he's suicidal. He told me he would kill himself...And now..." Chris, Aaron, and Jessica walked through the automatic doors and stood between Will and I.

"Hey, did Rob wake up?" Will inquired.

"Nah, he's still asleep," Chris replied. "I don't know, man, I don't want to be here all day. It's not like he's going anywhere..."

"Yeah, I was gonna get out of here. I think I need to be alone for a while...I feel like going for a drive," Will said. I stared longingly at him as he dangled his keys in his hand. *Take me with you...*

"Can I call you later?" I asked.

"...Yeah, call me later," Will answered. I smiled slightly and looked at Jessica, Aaron, and Chris before walking back into the hospital lobby. I stopped in the middle of the automatic doors and looked back at Will.

"...I, ummm, I'm sorry, I...I'll call you later..." I nervously said and then made my way back to Rob. I sat down in the chair next to him and then stared at the ground. I put his cigarettes and lighter on top of his jacket and then looked back at him. *I don't want to be with you...I don't want you to kill yourself...Fuck!* Jessica and Aaron walked back into the room and sat down. *They came back!?* "You guys came back...?"

"We'll be here as long as you want," Jessica said. "...Right, Aaron?"

"...Yeah, but, if you want us to go..." Aaron started to say.

"...No, I'm glad that you're here...Do you think you can wait with me until he wakes up?" *What am I even going to say to him?*

"...Yeah, of course," Jessica said.

Two hours later, I caught myself before drifting away to sleep. I was still by Rob's side and holding his hand. I was growing wearier and inpatient as time slowly crept along. I looked at Jessica, who was fast asleep resting her head on Aaron's shoulder, and then at Aaron who gave me a subtle, uncomfortable smile. I smiled back at Aaron and turned to Rob. *What am I doing here?* Without any warning, I heard Rob muttering something incoherent.

"Rob!?" I pleaded.

"Is he awake?" Aaron asked.

"I think so..."

"...I told you..." Rob whimpered. "...Hannah, I told you..."

"Told me what, Rob?"

"...I told you...You didn't listen..." Rob said and then his eyes slowly closed and he went back to sleep. *Great...* I turned to Aaron.

"...Well, he was awake..." I said and Jessica woke up.

"He woke up?" Jessica asked.

"Yeah...But he went back to sleep."

"...Hey, Hannah..." Jessica said and looked at Aaron. "...We need to go..."

"Yeah...I know," I answered. "...You wanna give me a ride home?" *I can't stay here all day...* "...I think he'll be okay."

"Okay, yeah," Aaron said. "Let's go..." We all got up from the hospital chairs and walked into the hallway and toward the waiting room. *Shit...I'm going to have to talk to his parents...Ugh...* I walked behind Aaron and Jessica hoping that Rob's parents wouldn't see me. *Maybe they won't even be here...Ugh...Nope, they haven't moved.*

"Just give me a minute," I said to Aaron and Jessica as I walked up to Rob's parents. "Hey..."

"Hey, Hannah," Rob's mom said. "Did he wake up?"

"Yeah, he woke up for a minute and then went back to sleep."

"Did he say anything?"

"...No, well...He did try to say something, but I couldn't understand him..." *Why am I still lying? Ugh...*

"Okay, sweetie, are you going home?"

"...Yeah, I kind of have some stuff I have to do...Call me if anything changes..."

"Of course...Well, I guess we should go check on him," Rob's mom said and got up from her seat. Rob's dad followed and then they started walking down the hall. Jessica, Aaron, and I walked through the automatic doors and out of the hospital. We started walking towards the parking lot and Jessica turned to me.

"You know this isn't your fault, right?" *Shit...*

"Why does everyone keep telling me that?"

"Because it's true..."

"How is this not my fault?"

"It's just not, okay..." *It is...* I didn't answer her. We walked up to Aaron's car and then got inside. There was an awkward silence as Aaron drove us away from the hospital. Aaron pulled up in front of my house about ten minutes later and Jessica let me out of the back seat. "You don't have to try to save him, Hannah..." Jessica hugged me and then let me go. "It's not your burden to carry..."

"Thanks, Jessica," I said and then waved inside of the car. "Bye Aaron." I turned around and started walking to my front door.

"Call me later," Jessica said. "We need to talk." I smiled and waved as they drove away. *I need to call Summer.* I walked inside and then went to my room and shut the door. I picked up the phone and dialed Summer's number.

"Hello?" Summer asked.

"Hey, Summer, it's me...Hannah."

"Oh my God, Hannah! We haven't talked in forever..."

"Yeah, it has been a while...Sorry..."

"...Hannah, are you sitting down?" *Huh?*

"Yeah, I'm sitting on my bed...Why?"

"It's Mel, Hannah..." *Mel!? What's going on?* "...I don't know how to say this so I guess I'm just going to say it. Mel's alive, Hannah, she's alive!" *Oh my God...I don't...I can't...* I started crying into the phone and then moved it away from my ear. "...Hannah, are you okay? I thought you would be happy..." I put the phone back against my ear and wiped the tears from my eyes.

"...I am happy...I just...I can't believe it...What...Why didn't you call me?"

"Girl, I tried to call you, but you never gave me your new number..." *Oh shit...Duh!*

"...I'm so sorry...So much has happened...My boyfriend tried to kill himself..."

"What!?"

"...And it was with pills..."

"...Hannah, oh my God!"

"And I shouldn't be with him, but I don't want him to die...So, shit...I don't know what to do."

"...That's terrible...And with what happened with Mel...I can only imagine how hard it's been on you."

"...But she's okay? I mean, how, what happened?"

"This is crazy...So, she called me like a month ago and I was just as surprised as you. I thought it was a joke...Like someone was pretending to be her or something like that...But no, it was actually her. It was like we were never apart..."

"...What happened? What about the letter?"

"I was going to say...That's the crazy part...She drove her parent's car to San Francisco and has been there ever since."

"No fucking way!"

"Way fucking...Way."

"...And after all this time? She never thought to call us and say, 'hey guys, I actually decided not to kill myself and I'm good.' Seriously, what was she thinking?"

"Don't get me started. I gave her the third degree...She said that she was embarrassed."

"Mel, embarrassed? Are you sure it was her?" Summer laughed.

"Yeah, it was her...She's got a story...But I'll let her tell you when she gets here."

"What do you mean?"

"She's coming to visit this summer...And you're coming to visit this summer too..." *I am...Wait, of course I am...What am I even thinking?*

"...I'll have to get my license."

"Yeah, you do that," Summer said and laughed again.

"I can't believe this is happening...I feel like, and this is going to sound stupid, I've been in a dream for...How many years has it been?"

"A lot..."

"...And it's like I'm just now waking up..."

"That's not stupid at all...I think when we read Mel's letter, we both died inside a little bit..."

"...Yeah...Do you have her number?"

"Yeah, are you gonna call her?"

"I don't know, maybe, I don't know what I would say exactly...I kind of just want her number...To, you know, have it..."

"I understand, I totally get it," Summer said and gave me Mel's number. I wrote it down and then gave Summer my new number. "Well, there we go...You get your license and I'll call you when Mel's coming...Hannah, you will not believe what she's been through...It's just crazy."

"That doesn't sound good, Summer..."

"There's a lot of bad...But she's good now. She sounded really happy."

"Summer, I am so glad I called you...I think this has changed everything..."

"...What do you mean?"

"I have to figure my life out...It's complicated, but I'll tell you about it later..."

"You have to go?"

"Yeah..."

"But we were just getting caught up..."

"...I promise, we will catch up, but I have to make a really important call."

"Okay, I'll let you go, but call me back soon."

"I will, don't worry..."

"...I'm not worried, I have your number now."

"Yes, you do...All right, cool, I'll talk to you soon then..."

"Okay, bye Hannah!"

"Bye Summer," I said and hung up the phone. *Billy...* I dialed Will's number and waited. I listened to one ring after another and started to feel very anxious. *Shit...Where is he?* I hung up the phone after it rang twenty times. *Hmmm...Aaron...No, he wouldn't be home yet...Maybe I should call Mel...* I stared at Mel's number until I had it memorized. *No...I don't know what to say...*

Later that afternoon, I tried calling Will again and no one answered. *Seriously? Okay...* I dialed Aaron's number and he answered immediately.

"Hello?"

"Aaron? Have you heard from Billy?"

"No...He said he was gonna come by later, but I guess he changed his mind."

"He's not answering his phone..."

"...That's weird."

"I know...So, can you, I don't know, go to his house and see if he's there? I'm worried about him."

"...Jessica," Aaron said, "it's Hannah...She wants me to go see if Will's home."

"Oh, Jessica's there...I'm sorry, I didn't mean to bother you guys."

"No, it's cool...We'll head over there right now."

"Can I ask you for one more favor?"

"Sure..."

"If he's home, can you bring him over here? I really need to talk to him..."

"...Yeah, if he wants to..." *Shit...What if he doesn't want to?*

"Okay, but tell him it's really important."

"I'll tell him...Bye."

"...Bye," I said and Aaron hung up the phone. I picked up my astrology book and started rereading the section on Libra and Aquarius that I had bookmarked. *I hope it's not too late...* Around thirty minutes later, I heard a knock on my door. I put my book down on my bed and walked down the hallway and opened the front door. Aaron and Jessica stood on my porch with concerned looks on their faces.

"Hey," Aaron said. "He's not home. His car isn't there."

"Where is he?" I inquired. *Hmmm...Vicki...Ugh...* Aaron shrugged his shoulders and I looked at Jessica.

"What's going on, Hannah?"

"...I think I figured out what's been wrong with me."

"What do you mean?" Jessica asked.

"It's really complicated...But it goes back to Santa Maria...I need to talk to Billy...To tell him why I've been acting so crazy..."

"...He told me he was going to drive up to Three Rivers..." Aaron offered. *Not Vicki? Three Rivers...Why?*

"...Do you think he's still there?"

"...That was a few hours ago...I don't know why he would still be up there..."

"You don't think he's with Vicki, do you?"

"I don't know..."

"Do you know where Vicki lives?" I pleaded and my eyes flitted back and forth between Aaron and Jessica.

"...Nope," Aaron answered.

"Aaron, I'm worried about him...Do you think we can go to Three Rivers and check on him?"

"...Jessica?" Aaron said and turned to Jessica as if he were asking for permission. *Hmmm...Ugh...*

"...Yeah, sure, let's go," Jessica answered. We got into Aaron's car and he drove us out to the freeway. I told them all about Melissa and Summer on the way. I told them about Joe and Ryan. I told them about the Halloween party. I tried to explain my behavior even though I was still in the process of understanding it myself. Aaron and Jessica listened to me, without interruption, for the entire drive. We drove around a lake and then passed a sign that read: Slick Rock Recreation Area. Aaron slowed down and started turning into the parking lot. I immediately saw Will's car at the far end of the lot with his hood raised.

"Well, that explains that," Aaron said.

"...Yeah," I said. "I hope he's okay."

"He's probably fine, but his car...Who knows..." Aaron added.

"Why would he drive that car all the way up here?" Jessica asked. "It isn't exactly new..." *Jessica!*

"It's only three years older than the car you're sitting in right now," Aaron quipped. *Ha!*

"It is?" Jessica responded obliviously. I smiled but didn't say anything. Aaron pulled up next to Will's car. The windows were rolled down, but there wasn't any sign of him. *Where is he!?* Will suddenly sat up in his back seat, which startled all of us.

"Shit!" Aaron exclaimed. We got out of Aaron's car and Will got out of his.

"It's good to see you, man," Will said to Aaron.

"What happened?" Aaron asked.

"It's my battery...Do you have jumper cables?"

"Yeah, I think so." Aaron walked over to the front of his car, opened his hood, and got his jumper cables. He connected them to both cars and Will was able to start his car. Jessica and I stood next to each other while the boys revved their engines. It was almost too loud to think. After a while, Aaron removed the cables and put them back in his car. Will shook Aaron's hand and was seemingly trying to avoid eye contact with me. He acted like I wasn't even there. He didn't acknowledge me at all.

"Thanks, man, I owe you one," Will said. "I can't believe that not a single person came by...Not one..."

"That's crazy, but you can thank Hannah..." Will looked at me with a hint of suspicion.

"Hannah? What are you doing here anyway?"

"I was worried about you...And I really need to talk to you, so..."

"Shouldn't you be with your boyfriend?" *Ugh...*

"...Anyway," Jessica interjected. "We should go back..."

"Yeah, it's getting late," Aaron said.

"All right. I'll be good as long as I don't turn off my car...I need to go buy a new battery..."

"...Can I ride with you, Billy?"

"No..." Will answered with disdain in his voice. *Shit...* "Aaron, can you take her home?"

"...Yeah, I can take her..." Aaron started to say, but I quickly interrupted.

"...Billy, I came all this way to talk to you..."

"And..."

"...And, well, if it weren't for me...Then maybe you'd still be stuck here...Or worse...Like, maybe, you could have been attacked by a bear or a mountain lion or something..." I reasoned. Will smiled and shook his head.

"That's ridiculous, Hannah, do you even know where we are?" *Hmmm, no, not really...*

"...Will, just give her a ride home already!" Jessica scorned. *Shit...Thanks, Jessica!*

"...Oh, fine...Get in," Will said and pointed to his door. I didn't say anything and immediately got inside of Will's car. "I'll call you tomorrow, man, thanks again."

"No problem, later," Aaron said. Jessica got in Aaron's car and they drove away. Will sat down in his car and looked over at me with his ambiguous eyes. I smiled and he faced forward and started driving.

"...Billy, I need to tell you something..."

"...I'm not going anywhere, Hannah..." *Ugh...Yeah...*

"I had a friend in Santa Maria...Her name's Mel..."

"Okay..."

"Just listen...Please, Billy, this is important..."

"I'm listening..."

"Mel liked me, like, you know, that way...She kissed me and I didn't really stop her...I'm not exactly sure, but I think I led her on..."

"So, your friend is a lesbian and you pretended to be a lesbian?"

"...I didn't pretend...I told her that I wasn't, but I don't think she believed me...Or, she didn't want to believe me...So, I got with Joe..."

"Joe? The dude that you almost had sex with?" *I have to tell him*...

"I lied to you about that..."

"...Why am I not surprised?" *Shit*...

"Joe raped me, Billy! I didn't want to tell you the truth because I was ashamed..."

"...Oh, shit, Hannah...You should have told me..."

"I got drunk and passed out...He took advantage and fucked me...I don't even remember it happening..."

"Fuck...That's crazy...The story about the closet then..."

"...That was Mel and Summer..."

"Summer?"

"She's my other friend from Santa Maria...They started dating...I thought everything was good...It seemed that way..."

"Okay, so, Summer is a lesbian?"

"Yes, Billy...Everything seemed okay, but Mel's parents never accepted her sexuality...One night, she stole her parents' car and sent Summer and I a suicide letter telling us how she was going to crash the car into oncoming traffic..."

"Shit, Hannah..."

"It wasn't the first time either...She tried to commit suicide with some of her parents' pills one time..."

"...Shit...Just like..."

"Rob," we said simultaneously. "I blamed myself all these years for what happened to Mel. I thought I was the reason she died. I couldn't live with myself if I let it happen again."

"...Shit..."

"But...I just found out that Mel's alive!"

"She didn't kill herself then?"

"No, I don't know what happened exactly, but I'm going to see her next month to find out."

"That's good..."

"...The point I'm trying to make is that I've been holding on to Mel...Her death...This entire time. She affected everything I did...She affected us...And now that I know she's alive, well, it's like a weight has been lifted from me..."

"Like our backpacks after a long day at school?" I laughed.

"You're so funny, Billy...Yeah, sort of like that..." I looked out the window and watched the rolling hills and orange orchards go by as the sun was descending on the horizon. I undid my seatbelt and moved right next to Will and rested my head on his shoulder. "Billy, we belong together...We're perfect for each other and I know that you know that..." Will wrapped his arm around me and rested his hand on the seat.

"What about your parents? What about Rob?" *Shit...Rob...*

"I'll deal with my parents...And Rob...I don't know, I don't want him to kill himself, but I have to break up with him..."

"I don't know, Hannah..." *I do, Billy, I do...*

"...Whatever happens is going to happen. I'm not responsible for him or anyone else." I kissed Will on his cheek and then nestled my head against his chest. I looked out over the steering wheel and watched the sky grow darker. ... *The weight of my backpack...Heh.*

"Thanks for finding me...You know, I wasn't really in the mood to fight a bear..." Will laughed. *I missed you, Billy...*

Chapter Twenty-Five

Aquarius rising

"Ⅰ f you fucking leave me, I swear to God, I'm going to kill my-self..." Rob barked. "Did you fucking hear what I said...Fuck-ing bitch, answer me!"

"...Then fucking kill yourself, Rob, I don't care anymore."

"Fuck you, Hannah!"

"No, fuck you, Rob, just make sure you get the job done this time!" I exclaimed and then hung up the phone. *Hmmmm, maybe that was a little harsh...I don't care though...He's not going to do anything...*

"Billy, I was wondering if you wanted to go with me to Santa Maria...I want you to meet my friends."

"I don't know, Hannah...When are you going?"

"I'm not sure yet...Sometime next month..."

"...I have to get ready for Fresno State. There's a lot of shit I have to do...It's kind of ridiculous."

"So, you got accepted?" Will laughed. *I don't want you to go...*

"Everyone gets accepted to Fresno State. I applied to San Diego too..." *That's so far...*

"...What happened?"

"...I didn't get in...Something about the program being impacted."

"What does that mean?"

"Everyone and their brother, sister, and family dog wants to go to school in San Diego, because, duh, and I guess they don't have any space."

"I'm sorry, Billy, that's too bad." *Not sorry...*

"It's fine...I'll get back to San Diego eventually..." *Hmmm...*

"I made an appointment to get my license the day after school gets out..."

"Did you?"

"Yeah...Aren't you proud of me?"

"...Ummm, yeah, sure...One year later than you should have but...Yeah, better late than never." *Hey!?*

"So...I can drive us..."

"...I'll have to think about it..." *Ugh...*

"...Billy, what are you doing this weekend?"

"It's senior ditch day Friday. Aaron and I were talking about driving out to Pismo and staying for the weekend."

"That's cool...Can I go?"

"...Nah." *What do you mean, nah? Billy!?*

"...Is Jessica going?"

"Probably..."

"Then why can't I go?"

"Because you're not a senior..." *Seriously!?*

"...Billy, you can't be serious."

"I am though...Sorry...By the way, how's Rob?" *Fuck...Is he ever going to let it go?*

"He's still in the hospital...They're holding him for three days."

"Suicide watch?"

"...Yeah."

"...You're still together then?" *Ugh...*

"...I guess...Technically, but I'm going to break up with him..."

"Yeah, that's what you told me..."

"...You don't think I'm going to do it?"

"I don't know, Hannah, but I do know you..."

"What's that supposed to mean?"

"...You're probably hoping he breaks up with you so you don't have to do it." *Hmmm. Well...Shit...* "He's not going to do it..."

"How do you know?"

"Call it a very educated guess..." *Okay, okay, I know...*

"...You're right, Billy, I'll do it...I swear..." The final bell for the passing period rang.

"...That's the bell...I have to get to auto shop...I have to fix all the things that the freshman broke. Mr. Graff is riding my ass lately."

"...Okay," I said and went to hug him. He turned sideways and gave me a half hug. It was the kind of hug that girls gave to their frenemies. "See you later?" I asked before he turned away from me.

"Yeah..." Will answered quickly and walked away. *Something's wrong...How do I fix this? Can I fix this? Shit...*

A few days later, I was sitting in my room working on my English final when the phone rang. I picked it up after the second ring and it was Rob.

"Hey babe," he said. *What is going on here? He sounds like nothing even happened...*

"Hey Rob...Ummm, how are you doing?"

"I'm fine, why?" *Am I the crazy one here?*

"...Because...You tried to kill yourself!"

"No, I didn't...What are you talking about?"

"Rob...You were in the hospital...You took a bunch of pills..."

"...Yeah, so what? I wasn't trying to kill myself...Don't be stupid." *What am I dealing with? Psycho much...*

"...Rob, I think you need some help..."

"I think you need some help..." *Ugh...Fuck...*

"...Rob, if it wasn't obvious, you know, at prom..."

"...Prom? What happened at prom?" *Ummm, yeah, shit...*

"Listen Rob, I think we should see other people..."

"I don't want to see ANY other people...EVER!" *Fuck...*

"...Well, I do, Rob...I don't want to be with you anymore...It's over!" *Thank God, I said it...* There was an uncomfortable silence which was gradually broken by Rob's heavy breathing. *What the hell?*

"...Rob, did you hear me? It's over..."

"...I'm going to kill you..." *Fuck!* I quickly hung up the phone and then unplugged it from the wall. *Shit...* I opened my door and walked down the hallway towards the kitchen but before I got to the phone, it rang. *Shit, shit, shit...Should I answer it? Fuck!* The phone rang again and again. *Fuck...* My mom and dad looked over at me. I stood in the middle of the kitchen, paralyzed.

"Hannah, are you going to get the phone?" My mom asked.

"...Ummm..." *Shit...* "...Yeah." I slowly picked up the phone and put it against my ear. "Hello?"

"Bitch...You're fucking dead," Rob said and then hung up. *Fuck...* I put the phone down on the handset and then unplugged the line from the back as stealthily as I could.

"Who was it?" My mom asked.

"...Wrong number," I answered and my parents went back to watching TV. *Oh shit...What am I going to do now?* I walked back to my room and shut the door. I sat down at my desk and stared at my half-written essay. *He's just mad...He'll get over it...I hope...He would never...Right? Shit! I'm losing my mind! Keep it together, Hannah, shit...Ugh...*

I think my butt is going numb. I tried to change positions multiple times and finally decided to sit on my hands. *That's better.* I had been sitting on the bleachers for over an hour waiting for graduation to start. I was smashed in between my family and Jessica's family and growing more and more impatient. *Oh my God...Do they have to have all of the high schools together? Hmmm...Billy...Jessica...Aaron. I'm happy for them...I'm sad for me. I'm gonna be all alone...I guess I have Casey...Shit, I haven't talked to her in forever!* I looked out onto the field where all of the chairs were set up. All of the seniors walked into the stadium with well-rehearsed precision. I tried to identify different people I knew but I was too far away. *I'll have one friend, maybe...And Rob trying to kill me...Perfect...* I laughed to myself about the ridiculousness of everything. I hadn't talked to Rob since the night he threatened to kill me. He wasn't at school either. The principals of all the school's introduced themselves and then the really smart kids gave their speeches. Everyone clapped. *Yes...Everyone is going to have a great life and we're all going to change the world...I wonder what Billy is thinking right now...* I smiled. *...Something like 'this is so dumb.'* I heard Will's voice in my head as if he were sitting right next to me. I listened to the counselors call everyone to the stage. We were instructed to wait until all names were called before cheering and clapping. Without fail though, some people couldn't help themselves. *This is gonna take forever...* It started getting dark and the stadium lights came on just as they finished the last of the names. The seniors all stood up and then threw their caps and tassels into the air. *Finally...* Everyone clapped and cheered and then we started making our way down to the field. *I have to find Billy...* I found Jessica and Aaron first.

"Hey, where's Billy?"

"I don't know, but I think I saw him with Vicki," Aaron answered. *Oh, Hell no! Wait, it's okay...It's not a big deal. They both graduated...It's fine.*

"...Where?" Aaron pointed to a swarm of people. *Great, thanks, Aaron...* "I'll be right back."

"Hurry up," Jessica said. "We're gonna take pictures."

"Okay..." I walked past Aaron and Jessica and through the crowd of people until I saw Will talking to Vicki. I walked up to him and hugged him before he had a chance to react. I pulled back away and smiled. "Congratulations!"

"Thanks, Hannah," Will said. Vicki stared at me indignantly but didn't say anything.

"Jessica and Aaron want to take pictures..."

"Oh, all right..." Will said and looked at Vicki. *What!?*

"It's okay, we'll talk later," Vicki insisted. *No, you won't...* Vicki turned around and walked away.

"Come on," I said and reached for Will's hand. I pulled him back to Jessica and Aaron. Jessica's dad was already taking pictures and my mom and dad were standing to the side, smiling. Their smiles quickly faded as they saw Will and I approach. *Oh, shit...Please don't say anything...*

"Congratulations, Will," my dad said decisively. *Wait, what!?* "What are you plans?"

"Fresno State," Will answered.

"What are you going to study?" My dad pressed further.

"I'm not sure yet...I'm gonna do my general education first and then decide..." *Wait...Are they actually having a conversation? What is happening right now?*

"That's good..." My dad added and I smiled. *Why couldn't it be like this all along?*

"...Hey," Aaron said. "My mom is having a graduation party for me if you guys want to come."

"Yeah, I'm down," Will said.

"...Can I go?" I asked. My dad and mom looked at each other and seemed to communicate without saying a word. "...Jessica's gonna be there too, right Jessica?"

"Yeah, I'm gonna ride over with Aaron."

"See, it'll be fine," I insisted.

"...Okay, you can go," my dad said. *Really!?* "Just don't stay out too late..." *This is unbelievable...*

"...I won't."

"Will, can I expect you to get her home safe?"

"Yeah, I'll bring her home," Will said and then looked at Aaron. "By the way, where is your mom anyway?"

"She's around here somewhere," Aaron answered.

"Well, we're going to head home," my dad said. "Not too late..." My mom, dad, and brother started walking across the field. *There is no way that just happened...*

"Oh my God, Billy, I thought he was about to apologize to you..."

"...I know, that was weird..."

"I'm gonna go find my mom," Aaron said.

"Okay, should we just head over to your house then?" Will asked.

"Yeah, man, go ahead. You might as well try to beat the traffic."

"All right, cool, we'll see you over there," Will said. I held his hand tight as we started to make our way across the field. Before following Aaron, Jessica grabbed my arm and said,

"So, are you guys getting back together?" I looked at Will and he looked back at me silenced by indecision. "No answer huh? That's funny because you're both here together..."

"...We're trying to work things out, Jessica..."

"...Yeah, A lot has happened between us...It's going to take some time," Will insisted. *How much time?*

Aaron's mom and her boyfriend walked through the front door holding Roundtable pizzas and soda. "Sweet! Roundtable!" Will proclaimed.

"All right, get it while it's hot," Aaron's mom said and set the pizzas down on the kitchen island. "We'll be in the back yard if you need us." Aaron's mom and boyfriend went outside leaving the four of us in the kitchen. We all got a slice of pizza and a glass of Pepsi and sat down at the table. Aaron picked up a remote and turned on the radio. Abruptly, Nirvana's 'Smells like Teen Spirit' blasted through the living room speakers. I looked at Will and smiled and then everyone started laughing. Aaron turned it down to the point that it became part of the background and not the main attraction.

"Aaron, are you going to Fresno State with Billy?" I inquired and then took a bite of my pizza.

"No, I'm going to San Jose State."

"Why San Jose State?"

"That's where I'm from...My mom and dad both went there..." *I had no idea...*

"And, I know I haven't told you yet, but I'm going with him..." Jessica added.

"Really...Ummm, that's cool..." I stuttered. *I'm going to be so alone...*

"I wanted to tell you sooner...I was just waiting on my approval letter..."

"...It's okay Jessica, you don't have to tell me everything."

"I know...But I'm going to miss you...You're my best friend..." *She still thinks I'm her best friend...Maybe...*

"I'm going to miss you too," I said.

"Have you decided what you're going to do, Will?" Jessica asked. *What does she mean?*

"Yeah, I'm gonna stay in Visalia and commute to Fresno...I'm gonna need a new car..." I smiled.

"Billy, what's wrong with your car?" Will squinted his eyes as if confused by my question.

"Babe," *Babe...* "That car won't last on the freeway every day...It needs a new carburetor, radiator...Tires...Shit...Yeah, it needs a new car." Aaron laughed and they all looked at me like I should have known better.

"What!? I didn't know," I answered softly.

"It's all right," Will said. "I think I have a job lined up at Fresno State as an English tutor..." *What!? You're going to be working there too?* "So, I'll be able to get something better..."

"An English tutor?" I inquired.

"...Yeah, apparently I'm good at English," Will said and laughed, "At least that's what those stupid Golden State Exams showed...I got like the highest score possible on the economics one...I guess I should be an accountant or something like that..." Aaron and Jessica laughed but I couldn't tell why that was funny. "...Nah, that sounds way too boring for me..." *What happened? I missed so much...*

"...Billy, can I talk to you in private for a minute?" I tentatively asked.

"Yeah...Okay...Ummm, I guess we can go out to the front yard..." Will looked at Aaron and then Jessica. "We'll be right back," Will said and made his way for the door. I followed him outside. "What's up?"

"...Billy, it sounds like you have this whole new life, and, I don't know...I guess what I'm trying to ask is...Are you staying in Visalia just for me?" Will gave me a curious look.

"Hannah, I made the decision to stay here before I knew that we might, you know..."

"Really?"

"Yeah, apartments are a lot cheaper here and gas is dirt cheap too...But to be perfectly honest, Vicki is going to live in the dorms...So, yeah, I don't want to be anywhere near that girl..." *Hmmm, yeah, that makes sense...Wait...*

"...But you were talking to her at graduation..."

"She kind of just crept up on me...Kind of like you did, actually..." *She hugged you too...* "...Anyway, we just congratulated each other for graduating...Pretty standard stuff." *Hmmm...*

"And you're sure she doesn't still want to be with you?" Will laughed. "...I'm serious, Billy!"

"...I'm sure that she does want to be with me, which is why I'm not going to live in Fresno." *I don't know...*

"And you're going to be working there? When were you going to tell me?"

"...I have a job offer...I haven't decided if I'm going to take it."

"Oh...Okay..."

"Yeah, I'm still applying for other jobs...That English tutor job doesn't pay very well...We'll see what happens..."

"Are the other jobs in Visalia?"

"Yeah, but I need something that's going to work around my class schedule...It's kind of a pain in the ass."

"...What's your class schedule?"

"I have my classes set up in the mornings, Monday through Thursday."

"Okay, so, there's still time for us, right?"

"...Yeah, of course...And since your dad doesn't seem to want to kill me anymore...What changed his mind?"

"Honestly, I'm not even sure..." *Rob*...

"Oh, Billy, I almost forgot to tell you...Rob threatened to kill me after I broke up with him..." Will smiled and then laughed. "Billy, that's not funny...He sounded serious."

"...He can't even kill himself...How is he supposed to kill someone else? He's just butt-hurt...I wouldn't worry about it..."

"...You know he didn't come to school for the past two weeks, right?"

"Nope..."

"He could be putting together some kind of elaborate plot or something..."

"...Rob's not that smart, babe..." *Maybe you're right*...

"...All right, let's go back inside, we're being rude to our host," I said and Will laughed.

"Ya think?" *Smart-ass*... "After you..." I smiled and turned around towards the door.

I drove to Santa Maria the week after I got my license. Summer insisted that I didn't bring Will with me. She wanted it to be a 'girls only' weekend. I was sad that he couldn't come with me, but he was more understanding than I wanted him to be. He said he was busy anyway because he was still trying to find an apartment. I pulled into Summer's sprawling driveway and then turned off my mom's car. I took a deep breath, opened the door, and then made my way up the walkway. As I approached the front door, my anxiety increased. All of the memories of what happened that Halloween night flashed in my mind. *Mel...Summer...Joe...Ugh! Fuck Joe!* I smiled and the door opened in front of me before I had a chance to ring the doorbell. Melissa and Summer stood at the threshold. I hardly recognized Summer. She had a shaved head, a nose ring, a lip ring, and was wearing a serious pair of Doc Martens combat boots. *Shit*... Melissa was beautiful. Her hair was longer, but she didn't look too different than I remember, other than her breasts. *Wow...What happened there?* She was wearing skin tight white jeans and a low-cut, spaghetti-strapped black shirt. We stared at each other for a few seconds to take in the years that we had lost. Melissa suddenly lunged at me and gave me a hug. I could feel her starting to cry. I looked at Summer as I held onto Melissa. Summer was as stoic as a British guard.

"It's good to see you, Hannah," Summer said.

"It's good to see you too, Summer." Melissa let go of me and wiped the tears from her face. "Mel, why are you crying?"

"...I'm just remembering...Everything..."

"...I missed you, Mel...I'm so glad you're okay..."

"...I missed you so much...But, I'm not sure if I'm really okay, you know?" *No, I really don't...*

"You look beautiful, Mel," I insisted.

"Looks can be deceiving..." Melissa argued. *Hmmm, what's wrong?* "I've had a really bad..."

"...Let's go inside," Summer interjected. We walked inside and Summer shut the door behind us. We went into the kitchen and I saw two glasses of wine and an open bottle on the island. Melissa and I sat down on the bar stools and she faced me. Summer got another glass from the cabinet and poured some wine into it. She handed me the glass. "You're going to need this..." *I'm afraid to ask...* I took a sip of the blood red liquid and forced it down my throat. *Well, it's not terrible...*

"...I couldn't do it, Hannah...I couldn't kill myself..." *Isn't that a good thing?* "I wish I could have though..." *Mel!?*

"Don't say that, Mel..." I pleaded. Summer took a long drink of her wine and looked more solemn than before. It was obvious that she had heard this before and was not looking forward to hearing it again.

"...It's true, Hannah, I don't want to be alive..." *No, Mel...* I felt my eyes fill with tears. I quickly finished my glass of wine.

"Yep..." Summer quipped and refilled my glass.

"...That night...I drove to San Francisco. I didn't know what I was doing...I didn't have a plan...I wasn't thinking about anything...I just wanted to get away...From myself...I wanted to get away from myself...I didn't care how..." Melissa recalled.

❧❧❧❧❧❧ ❧❧❧❧❧❧

When I got to San Francisco, I drove around for a couple of hours and then finally stopped at a Safeway because I was getting hungry. It was around four in the morning and no one was around. I had a few dollars that I found in my parent's car so I parked and started walking towards the store. A man appeared out of the shadows.

"Hey, sweet thing," he said as he quickly approached me. He was tall for an Asian man, and dressed in a really nice suit. His accent was thick but his English was good enough for me to understand him. "My name's Troy, what's yours?"

"...I'm Mel," I said.

"What are you doing out here this late?" Troy inquired.

"I'm from Sacramento..."

"And you decided to go for a drive..."

"I ran away from home..."

"You're out here all alone?"

"Yeah..." Troy smiled.

"...You need a place to stay?"

"Yeah...I can't go home..."

"How old are you, Mel?" I thought about telling him the truth but I decided to lie.

"...Eighteen..." Troy smiled even wider revealing two silver front teeth. He shook his head in disbelief. It was apparent from his expression that he didn't believe me.

"Okay, Mel...You want to stay with me?"

"...Sure, I guess..."

"Is that your car?" Troy pointed behind me.

"It's my parent's car..."

"...You wanna follow me to my house?"

"...I was going to buy a sandwich...Or something..."

"I have food at my house...I'll cook you something..."

"...Okay..."

❧❧❧❧❧❧ ❧❧❧❧❧❧

"Mel, oh my God!" I screeched. "You didn't..."

"I did..."

"You went home with some random dude in the middle of the night? What were you thinking?"

"Hannah...I wasn't thinking...I was already dead...It didn't matter..." *Oh my God...Mel...* I finished my second glass of wine and Summer promptly topped me off. "Anyway, I got in my car and followed Troy to his house. It was really nice and big. I thought that he was rich..."

"Thought?" I inquired.

"...Yeah, I don't even know if the house is his...Or if his name really is Troy...There were a lot of girls there..."

"You don't mean..."

"Yeah...I do...He made me a sandwich...It was turkey, I think..." *Hmmm...* "He gave me a room...I took a shower...I slept in. He took care of me like that for a couple of weeks..."

"...What happened, Mel?" I asked rhetorically. I didn't want to hear the answer and prepared myself by finishing my third glass of wine. Summer opened another bottle and grabbed my glass.

"No thanks, Summer, I'm not feeling very well," I said. Summer seemed to acknowledge me but poured the glass anyway. She set it down in front of me. Melissa took a drink of her wine and then stared helplessly at nothing. Her beautiful brown hair cascaded over her shoulders as she slumped over the island. She looked back up at me and then slowly opened her mouth.

***

"Hey, Mel, I hope you don't mind but I sold your car," Troy asserted.

"...My parent's car?"

"Yeah, it's not like you were using it...And you've got to start pulling your weight around here...This shit ain't cheap..."

"Okay..."

"...I've got some...Let's call them business associates...They're looking for some company and they really like pretty girls..."

***

"Mel, stop it!" I pleaded. "You don't have to say anything else!"

"...I was a prostitute, Hannah..." *Oh my God, Mel...No...*

"Mel, you weren't a prostitute..." I argued. Mel looked away from me for a moment and then met my eyes again with a deeply affected sorrow.

"...I was fucked so many times that I lost count..." *Mel...* "I was their toy...They called me an escort though...Which is just a high-class prostitute. All the girls at that house were like me...Runaways, orphans, drug addicts...Troy took care of us though..."

"Mel, you can't ever go back there..." I insisted.

"...I know Hannah, I can't..."

"...Maybe you could stay with Summer..." Summer looked down at the countertop. *What is going on?* Melissa reached out for my hand.

"...Hannah, I just wanted to see you...One last time..." *What is she talking about?* Melissa's hand was cold and her breathing became erratic.

"Mel, what's wrong? Summer!?"

"It's okay, Hannah...This is what she wants..."

"What are you talking about!" Melissa intermittently opened and closed her eyes. I got off of the stool and then helped Melissa to the floor. She looked up at me and stared at me with her drowsy eyes.

"...I love you, Hannah...It's okay...I was already dead..." I started crying and then looked up at Summer.

"Call 911! Summer, what are you doing? DO SOMETHING!"

"...No, Hannah, it's okay..." Melissa whispered.

"...She made me promise..."

"Promise what!"

"...To let her go..." *No...This can't be...I have to do something...*

"Summer, give me the phone!"

"...No, I can't...I promised..."

"Summer...GIVE ME THE PHONE!" I got up from the floor and stared at her holding the phone close to her chest. "NOW, SUMMER! HAND IT OVER!"

"...No, I can't..." I ran around the kitchen island and chased Summer into the living room. She started to run upstairs but I tackled her from behind and wrestled the phone away from her. I ran back to Melissa while dialing 911.

"911 emergency," the operator said. "What's your emergency."

"My friend, Mel, she..." I got on my knees in front of Melissa. "She's not breathing...I think she took something..."

"...Okay, do you know what she took?" Summer slowly walked into the kitchen.

"Summer, what did she take?"

"...Oxy...A bunch of Oxy..."

"Oxy..."

"...Okay, we've traced the call and an ambulance is in route...Do you know CPR?"

"...No."

"Put one hand over the other and place both of your hands over the center of her chest..."

"Okay, let me put the phone on speaker." I set the phone down on the floor next to Melissa. "Okay..."

"Push down on her chest the way a heart normally beats..." I started pushing on Melissa's chest but nothing seemed to be happening.

"It's not working," I said exhausted. "Summer, you try..." Summer stood over us seemingly paralyzed. "SUMMER!"

"...Okay," Summer said and got on her knees and started pushing on Melissa's chest. I grabbed the phone off of the floor and got back on the line with the operator.

"My friend's doing CPR...It's not working though..."

"Just keep doing it until the paramedics get there, okay?"

"Okay...Summer, keep doing it until they get here..." I walked to the front door and opened it. *Come on, come on!* A couple of minutes later, I heard the siren and then saw the paramedics speed up the driveway. They ran out of the van and I waved them into the house. They opened a kit that had a syringe with a long needle. *Shit...* Summer backed away from Melissa and one of the paramedics injected the needle into her arm. The other paramedic ran outside and came back with a stretcher. They gently moved Melissa in place, strapped her in, and wheeled her to the ambulance. I ran after them.

"Is she going to be okay?"

"I think we made it in time, but we have to get her to the hospital." *Thank God...* The paramedics drove away with their sirens blaring throughout the neighborhood. I walked back inside of the house. The sirens slowly became inaudible. Summer was sitting on the couch and bending over with her head touching her knees. I sat down next to her.

"I'm sorry, Hannah...I don't know what to say..."

"...You don't let people kill themselves...You get them help! She's our friend..." *Oh no...I am such a hypocrite...Ugh...Rob...*

"I know...She just...I don't know..." Summer looked up at me. "She just gave up."

"We can't give up on her! She needs our help...She needs both of us, Summer..."

"I know you're right, Hannah, but..."

"There is no 'but,' Summer, we're responsible for her now...We thought she was dead for years...And now she has a second chance...We have a second chance..."

"...She...She doesn't want to live anymore..."

"I can't accept that...I won't accept that..."

"What are you going to do? It's not as if you can watch her all day...You have your own life, Hannah..." *Shit...Billy...* "...And so do I..." *I can't lose her again...*

"...Let's go, Summer, we have to get to the hospital..."

"Billy, I need you right now..."

"Hannah? I haven't heard from you all week..."

"...Mel tried to kill herself again..."

"...I'm sorry, Hannah..." I heard Will take a deep breath and then forcibly exhale. "...Hannah...I don't want to have to tell you this, because, well, you don't need any more bad news..." *Oh shit...What now?*

"...Go ahead, Billy..."

"...Rob killed himself last night..." *...I can't...*

"...Shit, Billy...What happened?"

"You're not going to believe this but he did it just like Kurt Cobain..." *Kurt Cobain?* "...I still can't believe it..."

"What do you mean?"

"I really don't want to...It's just...Really messed up." I had forgotten how Kurt Cobain killed himself so I pressed Will further.

"...I don't understand..."

"...He blew off his head with his dad's shotgun..." *Oh my God...What did I do?* I became extremely nauseous and felt my heart tighten in my chest.

"...I'm gonna be sick..."

"I felt the same way...Hannah, it was all over the news..." *Shit...*

"...Billy, do you think you can come to Santa Maria...I'm at the hospital..."

"...Yeah, I'll be there as soon as I can."

"Thanks, Billy...I love you..."

"...I love you too."

A few hours later, Will walked into the room and put his hand on my shoulder. I turned around, looked up at him, and smiled.

"...So, this is Mel?" Will asked. "...She's really pretty..."

"Yeah, she is...I can't let her die, Billy..." Will sat down next to me and held my hand.

"...You can't control what other people choose to do..."

"...Billy, it's my fault Rob...I told him to kill himself...I just wanted him to leave me alone...I could have made a difference."

"I don't think that's true...Don't blame yourself...Rob had a lot of demons...I don't think he was ever right in the head."

"I guess...I don't know...Maybe you're right...But I saved Mel...I saved her from herself."

"...It's not your burden to bear...You can't save people that don't want to be saved, Hannah..."

"You sound just like Summer, Billy...And maybe you're both right, but I don't think that Mel is like Rob. I think that Mel wants to be saved. She waited to take the pills until I showed up at Summer's house...It's not a coincidence, Billy, she wants my help..." I reached over and moved Melissa's hair from her face and tucked it behind her ear. "She's worth saving..."

"...Rob's funeral is on Tuesday...Do you think you'll want to go?"

"...No, Billy, I don't think..."

"...He's going to be cremated...Shit...I guess that's obvious..."

"I have to stay with Mel, Billy...I have to..."

"...I understand..." I smiled at Will and squeezed his hand tight.

"Thank you for being here..."

"Of course, I'll always be here for you, or is it 'there for you?' Either way..." I smiled.

"I love you, Billy...You just have a way of making me feel better..."

"...You feel better?"

"A little bit..."

"When do you think you'll be coming home?" There was a softness in Will's voice. *Oh, Billy...I can't leave...*

"...I don't know, Billy...Stay with me until she wakes up?"

"...Yeah...What are you going to do, Hannah?" Will quietly asked. I could hear the concern in his voice. I could feel his fear. *It'll be all right, Billy...I know you'll be fine...* I squeezed his hand again. I moved my other hand and lightly placed it over Melissa's heart.

"...There's so much darkness in the world, Billy...I have to be the light...If I can..."

About the author

    William Michael Stephens was born in San Diego, California. He graduated with a B.A. in English from California State University, Fresno. He is currently teaching high school English in Salinas, California. He has been a teacher for 16 years and has taught grades 6-12 in Tulare, Fresno, Santa Clara, and now, Monterey county. His hobbies include, aside from writing; cars, football, and guitar. William has written poetry and short stories for the majority of his life. Walking into Spiderwebs is his second novel and is the second book in the About a Girl series. He is currently working on the third book in the series.

Also by the author

https://www.amazon.com/dp/B0B52KZ3LG

Severline Press

severlinepress.com

Please visit us online for additional content and be sure to join our email list for updates about current and future projects. Thanks for reading!